Victims f

Nish Amarnath debuted as an author at eighteen with *The Voyage to Excellence*, a critically acclaimed business biography. She has received awards for her short stories from Scholastic and Infosys, among others.

Amarnath was managing editor at Euromoney Institutional Investor and a senior journalist at S&P Global, formerly McGraw Hill Financial, where she was nominated for the Alerian MLP Awards [AMMYS] in 2017. She previously led a public diplomacy mandate for the UK Government on behalf of an affiliate of French multinational, Publicis Groupe.

Her articles have appeared in *The Wall Street Journal*, *The Street*, *International Business Times*, *India Today*, *The Hindu*, *The New Indian Express* and *The Times of India*'s city supplements, among others. She holds post-graduate degrees in media communications and journalism from The London School of Economics and Columbia University, where she was a James W. Robins reporting fellow.

Her enterprise story, 'Citi and its Scuffle with the Watchdogs', originally a Master's thesis for Columbia University reviewed by Sylvia Nasar, author of *A Beautiful Mind*, was published separately as a book in 2014.

A former Londoner, she now lives in New York City.

Victims for Sale

Nish Amarnath

HARPER
BLACK

First published in India in 2018 by HarperBlack
An imprint of HarperCollins *Publishers*
A-75, Sector 57, Noida, Uttar Pradesh 201301, India
www.harpercollins.co.in

2 4 6 8 10 9 7 5 3 1

P-ISBN: 978-93-5277-601-6
E-ISBN: 978-93-5277-602-3

Typeset in 11/13.6 Adobe Garamond Pro at
Manipal Digital Systems, Manipal

Printed and bound at
Thomson Press (India) Ltd

For Swami, an august originator who thrives in chaos:
I can never verbalize enough the beauty of how our journey together has lent more authenticity to my journey towards truth. I can't even begin to make sense of the magnitude of your love and holistic support for my passage through a path to what I believe could be my destiny.

For my mother, Swati whose spirit has been a driving force for my existence:
The indefatigability of your fighting spirit can never inspire me enough. I can never hold a candle to your genius and creativity. I can never thank you enough for all that you have ever done at every level, including your enthusiasm to catalyze the fruition of this book.

For Chinky a.k.a. Nam, my baby sister who is an angel to all who know her:
This book is most likely a culmination of all of my stories that I read to you every night, including scenes from this book – until you fell asleep, listening to them. The more I read to you, the more I was inspired to write – and tell stories that best reflect who I am.

For Ish, a paragon of innocence and integrity:
I am truly blessed for the resilience of our friendship, your unswerving presence as a mirror of my soul, your innocence and integrity, which strengthened the essence of this book, your prodigy and your undying patience with all my histrionics and eccentricities.

And for every aspiring journalist, every enterprising writer and every voracious reader:

To all of you, your love flows into the kernels of my own consciousness.

1

An Unusual Reception

17 September

A mass of charred and mutilated bodies spilled out from the mangled remains of the train behind me. The reverberation of ambulance sirens was omnipresent and there were police everywhere.

The tide of life and laughter that had governed the vivacity of Mumbai was now a mere space in a hellish temporality that would blotch the annals of history in the time to come.

Looking straight at the camera ahead of me, I was reporting the horror of the Mumbai bomb blasts, for the national multilingual broadcaster ABP News, in a dispassionate tone that takes nerves of steel to put up during such a time. Halfway through my newscast, I froze. Saahil. He was on his way back from a meeting, wasn't he? That meant he would have been on the Western Line at this time. Oh, God …

'You okay?' the accompanying cameraperson asked me worriedly.

'Uh, my boyfriend,' I croaked, whipping out my flip phone.

I speed-dialed Saahil. Nothing had happened to him. Had it?

A male voice seemed to be speaking to me. I exhaled in relief. Saahil's voice? Wait – something was wrong here. For starters, the accent was different. Almost at the same time this intelligent realization dawned on me, my fuzzed brain managed to trace the word 'unavailable' somewhere in the message I was listening to.

The next twenty-four hours blurred before me. All I could recall was clinging to what was recognizable of Saahil's lifeless form in a hospital morgue as I panted, sobbed, squirmed in anguish and eventually threw up all over myself. The inhaler I clutched in my hand was the only indication that I would will myself to live, to go on.

I bolted upright in bed, sweating profusely. If I were in my room back in Mumbai, I would probably have caught the glint of a cockroach on the windowsill. Instead, half-parted maroon blinds framed my view of a roseate sky. *I'm in London now*, I remembered, trying to shrug off my dream. No, this wasn't a dream. It had happened for real, back in June. And a flashback of that ordeal was haunting me in my sleep. I dived back under my duvet and wept softly.

The rustle of a dress resonated into my ears from somewhere below me. Then, a pitter-patter of footsteps. The swish of a curtain. Eerie. Hollow. Foreboding.

It was my first morning as a paying guest with the Sawants, a traditional Indian family living in Britain since the mid-nineties. My phone flashed 'Thursday. 4.15 a.m.'

Was one of the Sawants awake already or was I going crazy?

Throwing back the covers, I padded over to my bedroom door, turned the knob and stepped outside gingerly. A shadow emerged from the study downstairs. But the sounds were coming either from the kitchen or sitting room below. I edged down the stairs and crept into the kitchen.

A cup of coffee would help. I navigated my way through the darkness and put the kettle on. The footsteps grew louder. This time, I heard laboured breathing behind me. I turned around.

A dark figure towered over me – a woman in a long Little Bo Peep dress. A pair of bloodshot eyes glowered at me from under a cascade of thick, unruly curls. A wild grimace pinched her lips. I froze. I had never seen her before.

Dawn light glinted along the edge of her knife.

I took a step backwards. The woman drew closer, tilting her head this way and that, as though dissecting me with her gaze. I backed away further, only to slam against the wall. The woman pointed the knife at my chest, its serrated edge grazing my clavicle.

Squeezing my eyes shut, I—

'ASHA!' A male voice rang out. 'Asha! Stop where you are! Stop!'

A tall, wavy-haired man dashed into the kitchen and grabbed the woman's arm. Nirmal Sawant, the couple's twenty-nine-year-old son who had received me from Heathrow last evening, wheeled Asha around. The knife clattered against the floor. Asha started sobbing. The sob turned into a shrill wail.

'Don't worry, sweetie …' Nirmal held her gently in his arms. 'Don't worry … go back to bed. I'll tuck you in. There. There's my baby … my sweet baby. Come on, now. Come on …'

His voice lowered as he led her away to a room by the far end of the kitchen. He switched the kitchen light on as he passed. I stared after them. Then, I picked up the knife and placed it back on the cutlery stand. My hands shook as I tried to busy myself with the coffee.

What the hell has Sri got me into? I wondered.

My brother, Srivats, or Sri as I call him, works in a real estate development company in Pune, a surging metropolis near Mumbai. We had lost Mom to pancreatic cancer when I was eleven. Since then, Sri had always gone the extra mile to look out for me. So, I was surprised when he initially balked at my desire to enroll in a Master's programme in media governance at the London School of Economics. In the years following Ma's demise, it was the first time he opposed my decision – as did my father, or Appa as I called him. Appa's meagre undertakings as a temple priest in the south Indian city of Tanjore left him indisposed to send me abroad for further studies. However, Sri and Appa eventually yielded to my reassurances – on the condition that I stayed with a decent Indian family, rather than a roommate whom they feared could be a bohemian hipster or worse. That had led to the arrangement Sri made with the Sawants after running into them at a hotel in New Delhi when the concierge mixed up his suite with theirs during a business trip two months ago. And now, here I was.

Why hadn't the Sawants introduced me to Asha yesterday, or even mentioned they had a family member who could be … dangerous?

I felt a hand on my shoulder and turned around.

Nirmal's upturned hazel eyes were full of apologies. 'Are you all right?'

I managed a weak smile. 'I'm okay.'

'I'm really sorry, Sandhya.'

I nodded.

'I'm Nimmy outside the house.' He looked pained for a fleeting second. Then he cleared his throat. 'Umm, Asha is my sister. She's … special.'

'Oh!' I exclaimed in surprise.

'She has a weird habit,' Nimmy went on. 'She's been trying to chop off her bangs. Most mornings, it's an obsession with her. She doesn't know the difference between a knife and a pair of scissors. She must've tried to ask you to cut her hair for her.' Nimmy lightly draped an arm around my shoulders. 'Don't worry too much about it. You should get back to bed.'

'I'm a little jetlagged.'

'Fancy some tea?'

'I've already made myself some coffee.' I tapped against the rim of my cup on the countertop.

'All right, I'll get myself a cuppa. Please, make yourself at home.' Nimmy waved towards a couch by the French windows across from us. I sank into it with my coffee. Nimmy joined me with a steaming cup of tea.

'Been up all night?' I inquired, thinking about the light in the study.

Nimmy nodded. 'Working on a presentation for a consumer markets company I'm eyeing a deal with. I lead M&A efforts for European retail at Deutsche Bank. If this engagement comes through it'll be a crown jewel for us.' He grinned wryly.

I sipped my coffee. 'Is Asha developmentally challenged?' I asked gently.

'Sometimes she's like a four-year-old. Other times, eleven or twelve. On average, she has the mind of a seven-year-old. In reality, she's twenty-two.'

'Will she ever be able to lead a normal life?'

'Some of her behaviours overlap with one another. It's hard to say,' Nimmy said. 'Asha is capable of basic self-care, but she has other emotional problems. I'm determined to help her find her feet.'

'Does she attend school?'

'She did try.' Nimmy sighed. 'But it made her paranoid and she couldn't cope.'

'Some kind of fear psychosis?' I asked softly.

'You're quite knowledgeable about such things, huh?' Nirmal commented, impressed.

'I studied it briefly at school. Clinical psychology, psychometrics and …'

Nimmy let out a low whistle. 'At school? Weren't you too young for that kind of stuff?'

I shrugged. 'I guess I grew up faster after my mother's death.'

'Oh …' Nimmy's expression went from one of somberness to one of empathy. He reached for my hand and squeezed it.

'How's Asha doing now?' I asked.

Nimmy sighed. 'Right now, she's attending a workshop in Watford. She helps service books for libraries and she likes it better. She's able to retain her dignity there and learn life skills that'll make her more independent.'

Suddenly, he leaned forward and grabbed my arm. I drew back, startled.

'Please don't discuss Asha's condition with anyone else here,' he pleaded. 'It won't be taken well if you ask anyone in my family about it – even if you do so by mistake.'

I swallowed uneasily. 'Thanks for telling me,' I said at last.

'Our family still maintains the taboo when it comes to touchy issues like sex or abnormality,' Nimmy continued. 'Please don't think I see these as taboo too, but everyone else at home is rather conservative,' he added quickly.

I drained the last few drops of coffee from my cup.

'I heard you're asthmatic,' Nimmy ventured. 'I hope you're coping well with it.'

My brother or father must have informed his parents about my condition.

'If I weren't I wouldn't be in London now,' I pointed out. 'Well, I should let you get back to work or go to bed.'

Nimmy patted my head like I was his little sister. I smiled feebly. Nimmy rose and tossed our cups in the sink before returning to his study.

I headed to the sitting room and flounced onto a leather sofa. Pandy, the family's Shetland sheepdog was sprawled across a rug, snoring softly. I fought back a sob as I thought about the flashback that had seized my sleep. What was I doing in a new land with an odd Indian family? I idly sifted through a stray magazine until Shailaja Sawant trudged down the stairs fifteen minutes later in a yellow nightgown.

She mumbled an indistinct good morning before disappearing into the kitchen. I followed her in. Shailaja poured a thick stream of decoction from a filtered Indian brew into a tiny saucepan. The strong flavour of chicory wafted through the air.

'This will freshen you up.' Shailaja poured me some coffee into a mug with a Tudor rose painted on it. The sense of discomfort in my chest resurfaced as I took a sip. It tasted funny.

~

By about 7.30 a.m., the pulse of a headache began thudding its way up my temples.

'You look like a battered boxer. You should eat now,' Shailaja suggested when she caught my expression. She slid two slices of bread into a toaster for me. I was buttering my toast when another lady waltzed into the kitchen in a lacy white blouse and a pair of grey slacks, which played up her pear-shaped frame. Her shoulder-length ash-brown hair looked stringy and her nose resembled a cloverleaf. Nidhi, Mr Sawant's younger sister. She guzzled some orange juice and joined me at the dining table.

Nidhi told me she had been living with the Sawants ever since she lost her husband to lymphoma ten years ago. A former defense solicitor for the Snaresbrook Crown Court in East London, she now worked as a campaign manager for Southall Black Sisters, lobbying for anti-violence measures for women and helping wrongfully convicted individuals prepare cases for appeal.

Another woman, whom Shailaja introduced to me as Asha's caretaker Jyoti, helped prepare lunch until a baby started bawling from the alcoves of Asha's room near the dining area.

'I have to feed Sunil,' Jyoti mumbled to Shailaja, hustling into Asha's room with a bottle of formula. Shailaja nodded to her and sat across from me with a bowl of fruit.

Jyoti had left her job at a National Health Services clinic after fleeing from her abusive husband two years ago, Shailaja explained once the young woman was out of earshot. Jyoti now preferred live-in work, which would give her and her son, Sunil, a place to stay along with a paycheque. The Sawants were shelling out a pretty penny to keep her here.

Nimmy joined us at the table in a suit and tie. He wolfed down his breakfast and dashed into Asha's room adjacent to the kitchen. He kissed a sleeping Asha goodbye and left for work with Nidhi in the Volkswagen that he had picked me up in from the airport yesterday.

I saw Nimmy and Asha's father, Ashok, just long enough to hear him tell his wife he would skip breakfast and take the train to Central London. Pandy awoke with a lazy yawn and scurried around until Jyoti placed a bowl of food on the kitchen floor by the door.

When Asha awoke, Jyoti got her ready for work and saw her off at the door where the chauffeur, Paul, was waiting to drop her off. Shailaja had changed into an over-sized button-down and a pair of trousers. She hastily shuffled some papers in a tote bag and rattled a list of instructions for Jyoti. I remembered she was a compliance officer at City University.

'Paul will be back as soon as Asha gets off at Watford,' she told me at the door. 'You can do some shopping at TESCO if you like. Paul will take you in the BMW.'

Do the Sawants have two cars, then? Their decision to take me in as a paying guest seemed even stranger in light of their apparent affluence. I was too heavy-headed to mull it over further.

I showered and slept upstairs until about noon, when Jyoti brought me some lunch. I thanked her and ate silently before curling up in bed again. I didn't know how much time elapsed until I woke up to a loud crash from below.

I shot up in alarm and glanced at the digital clock on the bedside table. 6.15 p.m. I stumbled towards the stairway corridor.

Shailaja, Nidhi and Jyoti were gathered near an overturned wooden chair in the dining area outside Asha's room. Nidhi had Sunil at her hip as Jyoti knelt down, attempting to turn a convulsing Asha to her side. It looked as if a demon was trying to shake Asha from within. Pandy stood behind, yowling forlornly. I rushed downstairs. 'Um, do you need any help?'

'There's nothing we can do until she settles down,' Shailaja said.

Eventually, the interval between each jerk lengthened and Asha stabilised. It was probably no more than two minutes, but it felt like eternity.

Shailaja jammed some buttons on her mobile phone.

'Just be with her until Nirmal gets back. He's on his way,' she told me urgently before disappearing into the sitting room.

I knelt down and touched Asha for the first time. She was running a high fever.

'She needs to be in bed,' Jyoti stated decisively.

Nidhi handed Sunil over to me. Then she and Jyoti helped Asha into her room and laid her gently down on the bed.

'You can take Sunil to the crib upstairs. In case he starts crying while Asha's asleep ...' Nidhi told Jyoti.

Returning to the dining area, Jyoti reclaimed Sunil from me and carried him upstairs. Nidhi went into the kitchen to prepare dinner.

'I just spoke to the doc. He suggested a more customised medication scheme to reduce the frequency of those seizures,' Shailaja informed Nidhi, re-emerging from the sitting room.

When Nimmy arrived, Pandy bounced over to him and stood on his hind legs, as if seeking some reassurance. Shailaja pocketed her car keys and emerged at the foyer.

'Is Asha feeling better now?' Nimmy spluttered.

'She'll be fine. Just be around her. I'm leaving to pick up your father. He isn't getting buses from Hillingdon. The quickest cab is a one-hour wait,' his mother said, scurrying out.

Nimmy hastily flung his suit over the banister and scuttled into Asha's room.

'How are you feeling, baby?' he inquired.

'I'm fine, fine,' Asha said, attempting to sit up. She pointed to herself. 'See ... I'm fine.'

I was both surprised and touched to see Asha's efforts to cheer up a man who looked almost broken upon seeing her. Nimmy sat by Asha's bedside and smoothed her curls.

'You'll be all right soon, promise,' he whispered. 'When you get well, I'll take you to Brighton beach. Deal?'

Asha giggled.

'Have a good night's sleep.' Nimmy pinched her nose playfully.

Nidhi streamed in with a bowl of hot lentil soup and a rimmed coaster that held three pills. Jyoti tied a bib around Asha's neck and started to feed her.

'Good night sleep,' Asha echoed, rocking back and forth. 'No, no, no ... no sleep! I told Sunny I'll play with him.'

'Eat your soup now,' Jyoti said firmly. 'You're unwell. You need rest.'

'How you can forget again? Again? I need to give Sunny that milk.' Asha tried to stand up but Jyoti pushed her down gently and continued feeding her. Some of the food splattered from the spoon as Asha wriggled. 'Look … Sunny is calling me.' She began to sound desperate.

Was Asha hallucinating? I turned to Nimmy. 'Who's Sunny?'

Nimmy didn't reply. Instead, he held Asha by her shoulders. 'Don't you remember?' he said. 'You already gave Sunny milk. Sunny is fast asleep now. You mustn't wake him.'

Asha stared at him, wide-eyed.

'Yes,' Nimmy said firmly. 'You gave him Milo, his favorite milk drink. Then you had a fall. You must sleep if you want to get better. Okay? Now, let's tuck you in.' He kissed her forehead. She reluctantly swallowed the last spoonful of her soup.

Jyoti held a glass of water to Asha's mouth and fed her the pills. Nimmy retrieved Asha's favourite teddy bear, Cuddles, and placed it in her arms. Asha was asleep as soon as her head sank into the pillows. 'I have to get Sunil from upstairs,' Jyoti mumbled.

Nimmy signaled for us to leave.

As I headed up to my room, Jyoti was on her way downstairs, holding her son in her arms and cooing tenderly to him. A tight lump formed in my throat as a distant memory swam to the fore: My own Ma placing an icepack on my forehead, coaxing me to drink a glass of warm herbal juice when I was in bed running a high fever. I was only six then. I swallowed hard. Sometimes, I wondered if I would ever get over losing her.

I settled into bed. Goosebumps prickled my arms. The temperature around me seemed to have changed. I smiled through my tears, knowing that my mother was there with me right then, comforting me in spirit. I hugged myself, closed my eyes and paid attention to the first thought that flowed into my mind. There it was: London. A new beginning. Meandering through that flash of insight was Asha's face. The serenity in her eyes haunted me.

19 September

Nimmy squinted at a portable navigation device on the dashboard and punched the postcode as we drove to a classic country pub in the quaint West London market town of Beaconsfield that Saturday. The Charlotte Hale talk show was playing live on the radio.

A woman was describing how a near-fatal crane accident had turned a young man into a musical savant. A string of mellifluous chords and melodies followed on the piano.

'Incredible, huh?' I marveled.

'Ever heard of the acquired Savant syndrome? Serious head injuries can rewire brain circuitries,' Nimmy said. 'It's rare, but it does happen.'

'I'd love to do such programmes one day. On TV or radio,' I said.

'You will,' Nimmy smiled. 'But you'll have to do your time. Charlotte Hale became a raging success with this show. It specialises in interviews with savants, prodigies, writers, poets, musicians and business leaders who have unusual stories to tell. I remember reading that she started out as an unpaid research assistant at a creative learning organization.'

He pulled into the car park. Off to the right, a classic view of the Chiltern hillside welcomed our gaze as we skipped towards the gardens. 'The Royal Standard of England is the country's oldest free house. They've been serving ale for nearly a thousand years,' Nimmy explained, gesturing towards a large round wooden table in the centre of a grassy lawn.

'I don't drink,' I said.

'Don't think pubs are just for getting drunk,' Nimmy chided lightly. 'At least, not this one. The Royal Standard is a place to sample Grandma's cooking at its best. Locally sourced.'

Keen on tasting traditional English cuisine, I nodded eagerly.

Nimmy ordered a smoked haddock and spinach along with ginger and ale. I chose a fruit punch, and fish and chips. Nimmy's friends trickled in as we waited for the food and drinks to arrive. Nimmy sprang to his feet and thumped their backs boisterously.

'Sal, it's great to see you!' he bellowed. 'Looking good, Carl! How've you been, Ricky boy?' Nimmy turned to me. 'Salvador Flores, Carl Wright and Rick Martinez,' he introduced. 'Sal detests being called Salvador. So, Sal and Carl …'

'Hey!' Sal protested, punching Nimmy's arm jovially. 'It's not that I hate being called Salv—'

'Oh, you do. You think it sounds like Labrador!' Carl interjected.

Sal was red haired, wiry and bespectacled.

Carl was a tall and slim lad with a mop of honey-blond hair, parted in the centre, and spiked and gelled to perfection. In a narco-style, silk blend camp shirt and a summer seersucker dress suit, he seemed like a perfunctory investment banker who seemed ready to ditch his job for a life as a cartel kingpin.

But Rick was the most arresting of all. With his sandy brown hair, deep-set grey eyes and classic Roman nose, he exuded an aura of rugged allure that made him look like a wild hawk and a bashful schoolboy all at once.

'Carl and Sal,' Nimmy went on, 'were my classmates at the London Business School. Rick is a business development manager at Trychlen Technologies. He's joining LBS next year.' He turned to his friends. 'Fellas, this is Sandy.'

I smiled. Sandy sounded smart and fun. A byname I had agreed to, upon Nimmy's request.

'A young journalist from Mumbai,' Nimmy went on. 'She's starting her Masters at LSE next month. She's only nineteen.'

A bubble of awed oohs and aahs wafted in the air.

'Nice to meet you.' I shook hands with the three men.

'We'll place our orders. I'm starving,' Sal informed Nimmy. He disappeared around the corner with Carl and Rick.

My fish and chips arrived along with Nimmy's haddock. Grateful that my family hadn't railed at my decision to recalibrate the practice of Brahmin vegetarianism, I dug a fork into the crisp fish.

Nimmy's friends rejoined us at the table a few minutes later.

'Work is a drag. A darned fussy bunch of Muppets have their heads up their arses,' Carl groaned good-naturedly. He wasn't a banker after all, but a manager at a full-service management-consulting firm, EuroFirst.

More food and drink came by. Shepherd's pie, sautéed potatoes, braised lamb shank, steak and kidney pudding, a bottle of wine and casks of local Chiltern Ale. Carl and Rick dug into their fare enthusiastically. Sal filled up his glass and poured me some wine.

'That's fine, thanks,' Nimmy told Sal. 'Dude, that's enough!' he bellowed suddenly as Sal continued filling my glass. 'A half glass will do for her, Sal. The lady isn't used to alcohol!'

'Oops!' Sal muttered. He offered the brimming goblet to Carl and passed me half a glass.

I fingered the stem of my glass gingerly. 'Go on, taste it,' Nimmy told me. 'It won't kill you.'

I bit my lip. Why did Nimmy lose his temper on one hand, when he was persuading me to drink on the other? He sounded so stern that I raised my goblet and took a huge gulp. I broke into a fit of coughs. Nimmy clamped my arm like a vise. 'Not so fast, Sandy. Wine should be sipped slowly. You'll get sloshed if you gulp it down like cocoa.'

I would be attending one of the best universities in the world. And here I was being admonished like a bumbling first-grader in front of strangers for not knowing how to handle my drink.

An unsettling lull hung in the air.

I excused myself and raced towards the bar around the corner. Inside, I found a washroom and leaned against the countertop of a vanity table, panting heavily.

The motivation I had gathered to bring myself to London was the ultimate gift my boyfriend, Saahil, had given me. But his death also made me emotionally vulnerable. And adapting to a new environment was going to be even harder.

As Saahil's face swam into my mind, the objects around me blurred and bled into one another in a halo of blinding white light. I sneezed and coughed. I blinked repeatedly to clear the double vision, but it didn't help. The dazzling white light clouding over the mirror did nothing to assuage my clogging windpipe. I sniffed into my inhaler and closed my eyes.

A sharp knock on the door gouged the silence of the washroom.

'Sandy, are you okay?' Nimmy's voice.

I sank into a sofa in the vanity room.

'Sandy?'

I continued sniffing into my inhaler. The door swung open and Nimmy barged in.

'This is a ladies' room!' I collapsed into another fit of coughs.

Nimmy gasped. 'Whoa! Sandy, you look sick.'

The frown on his face bore an uncanny resemblance to Saahil's expression when he was deep in thought. For a crazed instant, I could swear that Saahil's spirit was somehow reassuring me through Nimmy. The impression on Nimmy's face dissolved into swift mindfulness almost as soon as it had appeared. I shook my head and blinked. Maybe I was hallucinating.

'I'm dialing triple nine,' Nimmy informed.

'No … just a wheezing attack …' I rasped.

'Come on, let's get you home.'

I let Nimmy take my arm and guide me back to our table.

'Sandy isn't too well,' Nimmy told his friends. 'Carl, can you get her an Earl Grey, please?'

Carl rose from his seat and headed towards the bar.

'You lot make such a cute couple,' Sal said.

It took a while for me to realise that Sal was referring to Nimmy and me.

I grimaced. 'I think there's some confusion. I'm not dating Nimmy. I have … I *had* a boyfriend. He died in a terror attack in Mumbai, three months ago.'

I froze. I hadn't really meant to say that.

A snort emerged from Rick. I looked at him, startled. Was he laughing at what I had said? He doubled over and coughed hard. I was probably being paranoid.

A waiter followed Carl back to our table with a pot of tea and a canister of cream.

'Too much smoking,' Rick explained to everyone. He straightened himself and turned to me. 'I'm really sorry to hear that. I hope you feel better.'

'Good God, Sandy. That must be a tough one,' Sal commiserated.

'She needs to get some rest,' Nimmy told everyone once I was done with my tea.

Nimmy squeezed my hand gently as we returned to the car park.

'I'm sorry about what happened with your boyfriend,' he said softly once we were sat in his VW. I gazed at him blankly. His eyes swam in a billow of emotions ranging from raw concern to intense admiration. After a moment of uncertainty, he wrapped his arms around me. A blanket of warmth and comfort stultified the agony of my loneliness for Saahil as I let my head fall against his shoulder. 'And sincere apologies for my behaviour over there,' he whispered.

'It's okay.'

Nimmy turned on the ignition. 'I do have a fine temper,' he admitted. 'Uh, you see, Asha got hammered at a family wedding two years ago. They were passing drinks around. Another nurse, who was around at the time, urged Asha to try some alcohol. Asha got buzzed and her behaviour turned embarrassing. So, the nurse slapped her across her face. After that, Asha went missing. A passing police car spotted her passed out on the road and took her to the Charing Cross police station. We picked her up four hours later. The families of the couple that got married were miffed about it.'

'That sounds awful.'

'You and Asha are nearly the same age,' Nimmy continued. 'I felt protective towards you when Sal poured you a full drink. But I didn't want you to feel caged in any way. So, I urged you to try some. When you took that huge gulp, the longing to protect you took over again. It was no sign of disrespect.'

We pulled into the Sawants' residence on Capthorne Avenue. I didn't want to trivialize that incident from Nimmy's past, but I wondered why it had influenced his behaviour with me so unnervingly.

6 October

'I'm glad to be your personal tutor this year,' Dr Eidoriana began from the dais of a tiered meeting room at the London School of Economics' St Clement's Building. 'One of the key questions we will examine this term is how good governance can encourage media producers to pursue journalism in the public interest. By the end of this year, you'll also need to have a fair idea of what your Master's thesis is going to be about. The WebCT has archived samples of previous theses, which earned a High Merit or Distinction. Reading some of these will help you understand the general …'

The classroom door slammed open. A young man in tight black jeans and a leather bomber jacket sauntered in. He yanked his Ray-Ban sunglasses from the top of his head, tugged his earphones away and shook his longish brown mane, like a wet bulldog fanning itself dry.

What an arrogant prick!

'… the general formats we entertain at LSE,' Dr Eidoriana finished. Then she turned to the latecomer and made him introduce himself to everyone.

'Ritchie Johari.' He pronounced his surname as Jourry in a proud baritone, rolling the 'r' with a Californian drawl. He gave everyone a tiny wave. 'I'm a filmmaker from Los Angeles. Testing the waters in the film space out 'ere.'

'Thank you, Ritchie,' Dr Eidoriana said. 'Now,' she turned back to us. 'You'll each have a library PIN with which you can reserve copies online …'

Before long, the orientation session was over. As we filed out, several students gathered around Dr Eidoriana outside. I patiently waited for the crowd to clear and edged my way forward just as Dr Eidoriana made for the stairs.

'It was a great session, ma'am,' I said once I was within earshot. 'I'm really sorry for holding you up. I'll need just a minute. I'm Sandhya Raman from the Media and Communications Governance programme. I'm on the research track …'

A snort of laughter came from behind me.

I whirled around to see Ritchie 'Arrogant' Johari skulking around. 'Whoa! Can't imagine facing the music of a research-track programme!' He cried, plastering a hand over his mouth.

I turned back to Dr Eidoriana. Her eyes darted towards her wristwatch.

I got nervous. 'I'd like to know when I could meet you to discuss the thesis proposal development process. I was thinking about …'

'Drop me an email,' Dr Eidoriana cut in. She was gone before I could respond. I stared after her, disappointed.

'Hey, girl …' Ritchie called. My jaw dropped when I saw Ritchie raise a brow, lower his eyes and then look back at me to indicate that I was to stand exactly before him.

Is he really calling out to me like that? He didn't seem to think others were worth talking to. What was he possibly going to say to *me*?

An untraceable expression layered his aquamarine eyes as I approached him.

'You *don't* sound that way when you talk to folks here. "*Ma'am*" and all.' He sniggered.

I wondered if I had committed a gaffe of some sort.

His expression softened. 'I'm on a loan, too.'

'Huh?' I spluttered, wondering if he was psychic.

His arrogant expression was back. 'Well, now … you don't look old enough to be here on a scholarship. You must be … twenty-one? Twenty-two?'

'Actually, I'm nineteen,' I shot back, peeved at his insolence.

'I guess I'm the youngest next to you then. I'm twenty-one. Haven't met anyone else who could beat either of us. Many of 'em are old enough to run for office.'

I glanced at the gaggle of students milling around on the corridor ahead of us. A few weather-beaten faces, wrinkled jaw lines or receding hairlines jumped out at me. I hadn't realised it until Ritchie's little dig at them.

'Those who're here on study loans aren't older than twenty-two. They usually lose out to older, so-called experienced students when it comes to scholarships … or so I hear,' Ritchie explained with a smug half-smile. But now, his eyes looked kind. 'So, back to the topic at hand. You don't sound so submissive when you're approaching a faculty member for help. No one here is bothered about how sorry you are or aren't. It's all about unleashing your potential. You're paying through your nose to be here, you need to understand that you're entitled to any information you want. And these folks are around to help you find it because that's part of their job. That's the kind of daredevil attitude that gets noticed out here.' He pointed towards my chest. 'Being Miss Goody-Two-Shoes does nothing to unlock all that potential.'

Wow. Quite a piece of advice from a stranger.

'I guess you're from India,' he said, suddenly.

I nodded curtly.

'Well then, you aren't to blame, really. The Indian educational system has people behaving submissively. Just the way you did.'

'And where are you from?' I asked as we headed downstairs together.

''Ola, I'm a world citizen.' He shrugged out of his jacket as we paused on a corrugated step outside the building. I stared amusedly at a Walt Disney logo on his tight yellow T-shirt. 'When I finished high school, my parents wanted me to take up medicine or engineering. I had no flair for either. Scooted to the States at seventeen to study television and film.'

'Ah, Indian parents then. But you don't look or sound Indian,' I mumbled as we walked towards Houghton Street.

He winked at me. 'Well, Ritchie is my Anglicised name. Comes in handy in the film circuit. Ritchie became my insignia during my stint with Granada when I did the sales campaign for *Ramsay's Kitchen Nightmares* and *Celebrity Fitness Club*, back in LA.'

Oh, he sounded like a big shot. 'What's your real name then?' I pressed.

Ritchie shook his head. 'You'll never be able to pronounce it. No one here has. Ritchie is how everyone knows me, really.'

'Try me,' I pressed. 'I'm used to complicated words. I really won't get it mixed up.'

'All right,' he relented. 'It's Chitraksh Johari.'

I repeated his name slowly. 'Actually, it *is* challenging to pronounce it correctly,' I admitted.

'The name Chitraksh ain't saleable,' Ritchie affirmed. 'Now, there's my number.' He handed me an embossed business card. 'Give me a shout if you need to. Getting adjusted out here can be a pain in the ass.' The card tagged Ritchie as an independent film specialist. It carried an embossed picture of a flamingo on the corner.

'Flamingo Films. Name of my outfit,' Ritchie mentioned, catching my gaze.

The card listed two mobile numbers, a landline number and an address in north London.

'The media careers information fair is happening at Custom House for ExCel, early November,' he added as an afterthought. 'I think the online tickets sold out a long time ago. But you could ride the line out for one if you have the patience for it.

All the media bigwigs, including Bloomberg and the BBC, are parking their asses there. Folks looking for the best they can hire. Good day, young lady!' He shook my hand briskly, doffed an imaginary hat and walked away in the direction of Holborn station. I stared after him. Strange character.

~

15 October

'We haven't hit pay dirt with our proposal for a sponsorship,' Lanong whined as we hustled out of the Peacock Theatre after an afternoon public lecture.

I had been elected as the LSE television network, LooSE TV's executive head. Zubeen, who went by his last name, Lanong, was a post-graduate anthropology student and had been voted LooSE TV's new business director. I had suggested planting LCD television screens across all student halls of residence and many more sites on campus. But our bid for an external corporate sponsorship to translate that idea into a concrete measure didn't seem easy.

'Endurance, Lan. And persistence,' I said. 'We could …'

A jazzy poster on a wall outside the theatre caught my eye. It was an advertisement for student-run publications and TV stations to apply for a grants programme. A multinational conglomerate, EGG, was running it.

'We should apply for it!' I told Lanong, nodding towards the poster.

That night, I studied the grants programme web page and researched the company. EGG, an acronym for Eric Gregersen Group, was a London-based pharmaceutical and consumer goods manufacturer. Its CEO, Lord Melvin Bradshaw, who had earned a peerage five years ago, seemed to be as much a face of his own brand as the company's. Forbes described him as a much-loved philanthropist and one of the world's most trusted business magnates. He credited his success to his adoptive parents, the Gregersens. My fascination with Lord Bradshaw's ascent from an orphaned child to business baron extraordinaire kept me up for a few more hours. An unusual article poked out at me from a web page as I continued surfing. The story, dated 26 December 1980, opened on the archives of *The Herald-Times*. I studied it with interest. Melvin's former foster parents, Logan and Abigail Fanning, had been caught scrimmaging for insurance money after their two-storey residence in Bloomington, Indiana, burned down in a mysterious fire on Christmas Eve.

Wow. As I climbed into bed, I ardently hoped for an opportunity to meet Lord Bradshaw one day. But first, we had to get that grant.

2

The Tip of the Iceberg

4 November

I fastened Sunil's pewter-silver belt buckle over his wool tartan kilt and kissed the toddler on his forehead. 'The spotlight is on you, Sunil!' Nidhi crooned, waving a Canon.

Pandy wagged his tail excitedly. I scooped the dog up in my arms and leaned against Jyoti, who placed Sunil on her lap and pointed towards the camera with a smile. Sunil glanced up curiously at the flashbulb exploding in our faces. Nimmy watched happily.

Asha and her mother stepped out into the conservatory. Asha's coiffed hair and checkered Chisholm skirt made her look like an angel as she surveyed the scene before her in blithe wonder.

Ashok was in his study, discussing his financial affairs with a tax consultant. Why wouldn't he spend time with his family on a lazy Saturday afternoon? He seemed uncomfortable around Asha.

Nidhi beckoned Asha and Shailaja to move towards the sofa lounge for fresh shots.

A faint clang of the doorbell reached my ears.

Nimmy strode towards the door. He returned in a few seconds, his face white. He glanced at me briefly before mumbling to Nidhi. 'There's this g-g-girl asking for you.'

What's with the stuttering?

Nidhi looked mystified. 'I'll see who it is.'

Nimmy and I followed her to the door. Nidhi opened the door a crack. A drift of cold air gushed into the foyer. Pandy scuttled back through the kitchen into Asha's room.

'I can't see anyone here!' Nidhi cried exasperatedly.

'This girl in a purple parka … I wonder where she went,' Nimmy mumbled.

A scream rang out from the conservatory. Jyoti rushed upstairs, cradling her son in her arms.

Nidhi, Nimmy and I nearly toppled over one another as we ran back through the narrow corridor towards the conservatory.

The scene before me seemed so normal. Yet, I instinctively knew it wasn't.

Shailaja was speaking to a young woman in the conservatory. The visitor did wear a purple parka over a pair of baggy jeans, and her wet raven hair hung down her back like a rat-tail. She had a pale, pinched face. Droplets of water fell from the rim of her parka onto the smooth parquet floors. She had probably rung the doorbell for attention and slipped her way through the hedges towards the back of the garden to enter the house from the conservatory. That meant she knew the architecture of the house well. So, she couldn't be a stranger asking for alms or donations.

'*You*?' Shailaja cried. 'Couldn't you have waited at the door?'

'I stooped in to get away from the rain. I've traveled a long distance to get here,' the girl said.

Shailaja's eyes combed over the expanse of the lawn beyond the conservatory and fell on the shade reaching out from the conservatory rooftop towards the marble lawn table and chairs on the small quad before the garden. Her eyes narrowed disbelievingly. 'What do you want?'

'I have to speak to you,' she said to Nidhi.

'Is your boss harassing you again, Rosie?' Nidhi's voice blared out, dripping with sarcasm. 'How dare you barge into my house on a Saturday? You know Renu and Shahana are in the SBS offices today and can attend to you with equal grace in my absence.'

Rosie looked terrified now. 'I-I didn't know they would be in.'

I was puzzled. Why would a Southall Black Sisters solicitor, who campaigned for victims of violence, be insufferably rude to a young woman who seemed to be experiencing some form of harassment?

Rosie fished out a fluffy, medium-sized purple teddy bear from her messenger bag and turned to Shailaja. 'I brought this for your daughter,' she said softly.

From the corner of my eye, I saw Asha's eyes grow as wide as saucers. I couldn't say whether they widened in fear or excitement. Shailaja made no move to receive the present.

A look of resignation glazed Rosie's features. 'I'll drop by the SBS offices then. I'm sorry for disturbing you.'

When I turned back, I spotted Asha peeking out from the curtains partitioning the sitting room and the dining area. Smiling contritely, Rosie placed the bear on a windowsill near the door and stepped out gingerly. My curiousity got the better of me. I stepped out soundlessly in my floaters. A cold blast of rain and sleet hit me hard as I edged towards the gate and poked my head out. The bounce in Rosie's retreating gait was enough to say she was anything but traumatised. She pulled up the hood of her parka and nonchalantly lit a cigarette as she gamboled down the lane. A few strands of chestnut brown hair peeked out from the rim of her hood. She tucked the black rat-tails wig carefully into the front pocket of her parka as she puffed away and picked up her pace.

'Hey, Rosie!' I called out.

The girl began running. I sprinted after her. When I rounded the corner, I saw that the winding pathway forked out into another, shorter road. The other end of that road led back to King's Road, while the road that Rosie had first gone into opened out into the residential lane of Warden Avenue on its other side. Halfway through my chase, I leaned forward, held my sides and gasped for breath. There was no trace of Rosie anywhere.

A posh black sedan swished by from behind me, a few seconds later. It sped towards Warden Avenue, splashing me with cold, dirty rainwater. A mass of chestnut brown curls bobbed over the edge of the driver's seat. I tried to catch the number on the license plate, but all I could make out in the fog were an 'M' and a '9' before the vehicle disappeared down the road. I fished around for my cell phone to tell the Sawants what I had seen. Then I realised I had left my phone behind at home. I stumbled towards Capthorne Avenue, floundering to remember which roads led the way back – a key feature of West Harrow is the convoluted, circular pattern of the streets and lanes across its suburban colonies.

By the time I returned to the Sawants', I looked none the worse than Rosie. Shailaja swung open the door. 'Sandhya … where on earth have you been? We thought you vanished, too!'

Pandy pounced on me and extended his paw, as if he were trying to tell me something.

'Who else vanished?' I asked.

'Asha's gone!' Nidhi moaned.

Ashok stepped out, tax advisor in tow. I could feel his accusing stare. It was as if he somehow held me culpable for turning a perfectly happy afternoon indoors into an uproarious one. But I decided not to jump to conclusions. 'She isn't inside?'

'She's nowhere in the house,' Nimmy said grimly.

My heart raced. Did Asha's disappearance have something to do with Rosie?

I recounted what I had seen to everyone. Embarrassed, the tax consultant beat a hasty retreat.

Ashok frowned at me. 'Why are you getting involved in our personal affairs? As a paying guest, I think you should mind your own business.'

So, I was right about Ashok. I did not respond.

'Can you write down the license plate number?' Shailaja asked me.

'Let's search for her first,' Jyoti mumbled.

Ashok glared at her. It was the first time I saw her interrupting anyone in the house, especially Ashok. I realised how frightened she must be if she were doing that now.

'Let Nidhi search around the garden and beyond … up until Warden Avenue through Lynton Road,' Shailaja suggested. I remembered that the chauffeur was on his day off as she added, 'Nidhi, take the VW with you. And Pandy, too. Nimmy and I will take the BMW towards Lucas Avenue. Asha can't have gone that far. Ashok can stay home and watch the front door. Sandhya, stay home and give Jyoti and Sunil company.'

'I think we missed the street leading to the Rayner's Lane station,' I said. 'I know that route well. I can do that bit.'

Shailaja nodded. 'Let's get moving then.'

The rain was severe and visibility was poor beyond ten yards of my line of sight. I knocked on the doors of several houses on the street leading to the main traffic lane, inquiring if anyone had seen a curly-haired, squint-eyed girl walk by. No one had.

I called Nimmy. 'Found Asha yet?'

'I'd have called you if I did,' Nimmy said dryly. 'Dad's registered a complaint with the police station. They're sending someone up from West Harrow. We checked Lucas Avenue. We're at Sunningdale Avenue near the Eastcote station. No luck here, either. Where are you?'

'Warden Avenue,' I panted.

'Don't go too far out in this weather,' Nimmy warned.

My long wet hair whipped madly across my face as the wind whistled spryly over the din of the downpour. I sighed. 'Okay, I'm coming back now.'

When I flipped my phone shut, the tails of my umbrella got stuck in my hair. I squawked in exasperation. I whirled around to disentangle it. Just then, I spotted a curly-haired woman near a TESCO Express store across the traffic lane on Alexandra Avenue. She had her back to me, but there was no mistaking her gait and that checkered skirt she had worn.

'Asha!' I screamed, blindly darting across the road.

Two men arranging their shopping bags in the boot of a car outside the shopping store turned around and stared. By the time I got to the TESCO parking area, she was gone.

I zipped out of the car park and ran down the barren boulevard that TESCO overlooked, assuming that Asha had gone down there, further into Rayner's Lane. But, to no avail.

I retraced my steps to a deserted bus stop across the store, wondering if she had ventured inside the store. A security guard would be sure to have seen her if she had.

As I turned to cross the street, I lost my balance on the wet, slippery ground. The umbrella flew out of my hands. I tumbled backwards into what felt like a skein of barbed wire. A searing pain shot up my legs. I hadn't noticed the dense thicket of shrubbery lining the picket fence around the garden behind me. As I looked down, I realised to my horror that my waist and legs were entangled in wild undergrowth. One of my arms was caught in the jumble too.

I began to cry when I saw thorns in the bushes all around me. My free hand meandered through the thorns as I attempted to extricate myself as gingerly as I could. But, whenever I wriggled, I sank deeper into the bush.

I looked around, desperately hoping to see someone pass by. But Rayner's Lane looked too deserted for my liking. I squirmed to reach for my mobile phone. Despite the thick layers of my coat, it hurt whenever I moved. I was sobbing by the time I had the phone in my hand. My phone flashed, before I could dial Nimmy. He was calling me himself.

I heard his breathless voice even as I pressed the green button.

'Sandy? We've found Asha! She was at a neighbour's down by Ovesdon Avenue just across our lane.'

'Nimmy … I'm stuck,' I rasped, starting to feel faint.

Thorns jabbed at me everywhere and a huge stalk was cutting across my chest. I think a twig was piercing my back too.

'Sweet Jesus! Where are you?'

'Down the street across Warden. I think it's Rayner's Lane. TESCO is around the corner,' I mumbled. 'I-I've fallen into a bush. Can't get out.'

I wasn't sure if I sounded coherent enough, but I heard Nimmy say, 'I'm coming right over.'

A clean sheet swaddled me as I lay in bed in my room. Another blood-soaked sheet lay strewn in a hamper across the room. I cringed. How badly had I been hurt?

My phone buzzed from the nightstand beside me. I tried to pull myself up, but my body felt too leaden to cooperate. I picked up my phone, lying in bed; its display was mildly scratched.

'Sandhya? I tried calling you many times. How are you?' My father.

We spoke a few times a week, if I could, but our regular Saturday phone calls were a must-have. And this time, I must have passed out or been stuck in that bramble bush when Appa rang me from India at his usual time, before going to bed.

'All good here, Appa,' I managed. 'LSE is a lot of fun. But I'm still getting used to … um, the family I'm staying with here.'

Of course, I wasn't going to tell him about my fall in the bush. He would be worried sick.

'Good. Ensure you have your inhaler with you all the time. Take all asthma your meds regularly,' Appa said.

'I am.'

'Are you registered with a doctor?'

'Yes – with the medical centre at LSE,' I informed. 'I'll take care of myself. Missing you.'

'Goodnight, my sweetie pie.'

The scarlet filters of light streaming in through chinks between the window curtains indicated it must be well past twilight. 'Sleep tight, Appa. It must be past midnight your time.'

After I hung up, the sudden physical distance from home made it more real and intimidating than the carefree independence I had manifested while in Mumbai.

I saw that the soundproof wooden door to my room was tightly shut. I felt lonely and closeted. I tried to reach for the intercom, but the pain was unbearable. As I struggled to gather my bearings, the door swung open and Nimmy walked in.

'Sweetie, you're up! How're you feeling?' he inquired. His brow furrowed in concern as he strode towards me and felt my forehead for signs of a fever.

'You fainted,' he explained. 'You're badly hurt. Just checking in on you.'

'How's Asha?' I asked.

Nimmy sighed. 'She's a little shaken up, but doing fine,' he said. 'She got really scared. She tottered towards the front side porch and wandered away. A family driving down that way saw her lost. Asha couldn't identify herself when they tried to talk to her. So, they did the decent thing and took her to their home on Ovesdon. Nice folks, the Andersons. They were debating on whether they should call the police to help identify her, but a neighbour-friend happened to call on them. She knew where we lived. Her son and I used to play tennis together. I called you as soon as they came down here with Asha. They were still around when I returned with you. They were horrified to see you like this ...' Nimmy visibly shuddered. 'They were appreciative of your courage, San,' he added. 'Now, let me bring you something to eat. What'll you have?'

My stomach revolted at the thought of food. 'I'll pass.'

'You'll get weak. Trust me, a bowl of soup will do you good.'

He was out the door before I could protest. He returned in a few minutes with a bowl of steaming hot soup on a plastic tray.

My mind was whirling. 'Why was Asha scared? Was it anything to do with Rosie?'

Nimmy placed the tray on the nightstand next to me.

'I guess so,' he said, suddenly looking fierce.

'Do you know Rosie from before?' I prompted.

Nimmy didn't seem comfortable answering that question.

'Tell me, Nimmy. I'm concerned about Asha.'

Nimmy looked pained. 'What can *you* possibly do, San?' he whispered hoarsely.

I winced as he slid an arm around my waist, helped me to an upright position and fed me the soup. Then he gingerly reached out for my hand, careful not to disturb the sheets around me.

'Oh, San!' he murmured. 'You're one of the bravest women I've met. You've been here less than two months and you've looked out for my sister just like Mum and I have.'

No mention of his father there.

'I fell for you right at the airport when I first saw you,' he continued. 'Beauty, intelligence, courage and character … it's a rare combination. But you've got all of that. I realised it when you put yourself on the line today. For Asha.'

Nimmy's Adam's apple bobbed up and down as he swallowed with some difficulty. That's when it hit me hard. He was entirely serious about what he was saying. This wasn't about Asha. It was about him and how I made him feel.

'Nimmy.' Surprisingly, my voice rang out loud and clear. 'I just got here. I'm still recovering from Saahil's death.'

'I understand that.' Nimmy said.

Goosebumps rose up my arms as he tipped my chin gently. 'Your success is foremost for me, San. Clinging to the past is an impediment to your future growth. I want you to be able to enjoy and grow through this new chapter in your life. And I would like to be part of that journey.'

He placed the empty soup bowl back on the tray.

I closed my eyes and tried to envision Saahil. This time, his face seemed so far away. In the image that swam across my mind, Saahil was a pure silver shaft of light that brightened or darkened under the sway of high or low emotions. This time, the halo around him brightened. He was granting me a blessing.

Reclining against the headboard, I drew in a sharp breath and regarded Nimmy tentatively. I caught a glimpse of the anguish he must have borne as a child, when his younger sister had had all the care and attention, even at times when he might have needed it. Yet, he had grown to love Asha with all his life. A sliver of empathy diffused my senses. I felt my resolve weaken as Nimmy's eyes searched mine. I forgot the pain that engulfed my body when he held me with a tenderness I had never known before.

Later that night, I leaned back in my bed and examined the teddy that Rosie had left behind. I had discreetly retrieved it from the conservatory. It had a lilac bow tie and a heart-shaped 'I love you' pendant dangling from a periwinkle satin ribbon around its neck. I couldn't find any letter, post-it or sticker on the teddy that could have served as some kind of a warning to scare Asha away. I absently blew the fur around the teddy bear's padded bluebell paws and sat it by my side. Why would Rosie gift a teddy bear to a twenty-two-year-old if she didn't know that Asha had the mind of a child? Did she share a special acquaintance with Nidhi? Why had she worn a wig and feigned distress? Could Asha have been afraid of the bear? She already had many that she played with. That could mean she likely associated this purple teddy with something that scared her. My mind went blank beyond a certain line of thought. Nothing really made sense to me. All I was aware of was an imminent sense of unrest in this house.

My phone buzzed. It was Lanong.

'San, have you checked your email?' Lanong gushed.

'Not since this morning. Should I?'

'We got the grant! They've invited us to a Gala Awards Dinner on Eighth November – next Wednesday.'

I limped over to the desk, flipped open my laptop and clicked on the tab for my LSE account. There it was:

> 'Dear Miss Sandhya Raman,
> Thank you for your application to the EGG Young Journalists Grant Programme.
> Based on the merits of your chosen topic and the originality of your video, we are delighted to inform you that LSE has been selected as a recipient of the £5,000 award.'

'This is a great start, Lan!'

'You sound like you have a cold,' Lanong said. 'Is it the flu?'

I sighed. 'No. I might catch the flu, though … I've been out in the freezing cold all afternoon.' I briefly relayed the events of that afternoon to him. When I was done, all I heard was silence. 'Lan?'

'I'm here,' he assured. 'The whole scene sounds fishy to me, San. You don't have to live as a paying guest with such a strange family. You have a lot to get on with right now and you've spent shitloads of money getting yourself here. Wouldn't you rather enjoy the zing of community life in a student hall than put up with some family drivel that's affecting you, your safety and, possibly, your commitment to LSE?'

It was my turn to remain silent now.

'Why do you say it's affecting me?' I asked finally.

'You're not that hard to figure out,' Lanong said firmly. 'You told me the circumstances under which you moved in. Don't tell me you don't think about why the Sawants never told you they have a mentally challenged daughter before you moved in or inquired if that would be all right with you. Don't tell me you aren't thinking about cracking the mysterious turn of events this afternoon! Look after yourself and get a move on, San.'

'Maybe they took me in because my rent payments would come in handy for Asha's care.'

'When their son holds a senior post at Deutsche Bank? Come on, San. You're being a fool.'

I began to feel squirrely. 'What do you mean?'

'I'd run for the hills if I were you.'

I sighed. If I applied to a student hall, I would be on the waiting list forever. And I wasn't sure I wanted to leave Nimmy, especially after that moment we shared.

'I'm not being judgmental,' Lanong said. 'But I think the Sawants are hiding something from you. Seems that they're keeping you here for some other reason. Ain't worth the trouble, babe.'

A wave of fatigue washed over me. Could what Lanong was suggesting be true?

3

Reaching Out

8 November

'It's a shame Melvin Bradshaw couldn't make it. I was hoping to discuss the possibility of an interview with him,' I whispered to LooSE TV's president Mark Leatherby as the audiences broke into applause at a speech by an Emmy award-winning actor.

'I do like the idea of getting EGG's CEO to talk,' Mark replied. 'We can always chase him down offline. Meanwhile …' He swept an arm to indicate the motley group of journalists, lawyers, business magnates, policy leaders and fellow grant recipients at the black-tie Gala Awards Dinner in the Drawing Room at Claridges. '… have your eyes peeled for other doyens too, you know? You never know who else you could meet!'

It turned out Mark wasn't entirely wrong.

We confabbed with other delegates in the ballroom as we sipped the best varieties of Bordeaux – I decided to give the claret a try and pecked on crispy canapés and hors d'oeuvres. I felt rather frumpy in this bubble of peplums, silks, tuxedos and diamonds swishing and tinkering in glistering gaiety around me. I was discreetly adjusting the upturned frills of my piebald wine-rose blouse when I felt a tap on my shoulder.

'Miss Raman,' a tall man with curly, strawberry-blond hair and horn-rimmed glasses greeted in a Great Lakes accent. 'Aiden McLeod, account director at Pinwheel Interactive. EGG is one of my key clients. My team put this event together.'

We shook hands. 'Nice to meet you, Mr McLeod! Pinwheel is … based in London, right?'

'The PR agency is headquartered in Brussels,' McLeod said. 'I'm the country head in the UK. Quite a video you folks got up there. Futuristic, but something to think about.'

I smiled shyly. 'Thanks.'

We sat at a large, round table at the banquet and helped ourselves to an assortment of salads, fillets and parsley potatoes. 'Do you work closely with Lord Bradshaw?' I asked.

McLeod spread a napkin on his lap. 'It depends. Why do you ask?'

'I'm executive head at the LSE television network … we would love to air an interview with Lord Bradshaw on …'

McLeod was already shaking his head. 'Lord Bradshaw isn't giving interviews to the media at this time, Ms Raman.'

'The network is student programming. It isn't mainstream. We'd like to hear his tips for aspiring business leaders. That's the kind of interview I have in mind,' I said.

McLeod ran a finger down the stem of his champagne flute and eyed me intently. 'I work with Lord Bradshaw mainly for speaker arrangements, public statements, crisis response planning … that sort of thing. And he's pretty hard to get – even for me.'

I averted my gaze, disappointed.

'I could, however, use you for a project I have in mind,' McLeod said suddenly. 'From the video, I gather you have some knowledge of the telecom space, don't you?'

'Yes.'

'A white paper needs finishing,' McLeod said. 'The client is paying a handsome fee but we're a bit short-staffed at the moment. Is that something you can assist with?'

'What is it about?'

McLeod handed me his business card. 'Meet me in my office at three tomorrow.'

I ran into Lanong in the cloakroom at Claridges later that night as I prepared to leave. 'This guy from this PR agency says Lord Bradshaw is incommunicado …' I said.

'That's how it all begins.' Lanong chuckled. 'Let me walk you to the station.'

We strode out. The blustery night seemed to have done little to intrude upon Mayfair's variegated bustle of diners and carousers.

'Have you thought about moving out of Harrow?' Lanong inquired.

I sighed. 'Yes.'

Lanong raised an eyebrow. 'And?'

'I don't think I'm moving out right now,' I replied hesitantly.

Thankfully, I didn't get any more lectures from Lanong.

'That Rosie girl isn't a threat, is she?' He joked instead.

'Guess I'll find out,' I said at length.

Although a complaint had been registered, the police said they couldn't do much since I didn't have the full license plate of the car I had seen Rosie leave in. The next day, I had tried to talk to Nimmy in the privacy of the lawn to find out what Rosie had to do with his family.

'Why do you want to get involved, San?' Nimmy asked exasperatedly.

'I'd like to help Asha.'

In a frenzied moment, Nimmy swiped against a tall glass on the lawn table and let it smash to the grass below. 'We've all been trying to help her, haven't we?' he snarled, leaping up from his chair. 'You suddenly barrel in and play the Samaritan. What's this new stuff about your desire to help her? If *we* haven't been able to do anything, what can *you* possibly do?' He pounded hard on the table with his fists to emphasise the significance of those last five words.

I sat still, shell-shocked. I realised that Nimmy, who seemed to be the genteel sort, possessed a violent streak.

Nimmy stormed into the house.

'I thought you were having a row of some sort in the garden. What was that about?' Nidhi hissed at Nimmy during lunch shortly thereafter.

Shailaja turned to me with a worried look.

Nimmy looked appropriately puzzled. 'I was just showing Sandy a funny scene I once did for a play at school.'

That seemed to convince everyone. It seemed prudent to give it a few more days before I chatted with Nidhi. But I tried to talk to Asha that evening. It was difficult to get an opportunity to be alone with her. Even if the other Sawants weren't around, Jyoti was always in the vicinity, fluffing pillows, checking up on things and generally fussing over Asha like a mother hen. It was the first time I got irritated with Jyoti. She did eventually leave Asha for a few minutes to bathe Pandy upstairs. I pressed a slab of Green Black chocolate into Asha's hands.

'Why did you run away yesterday?' I whispered.

'Run, run, run!' Asha echoed, opening the wrapper gleefully.

'You were scared, weren't you?' I reminded her gently. 'Who is Rosie? Do you know her?'

Some recognition flowed in Asha's eyes.

'Rosie …' Asha repeated deliberately. 'Rosie, Rosie …'

I leaned forward expectantly.

'She bad,' Asha said finally, scrunching up her face, as if ready to cry. 'Bad, bad.'

I smoothed back Asha's curls.

'Some more chocolate,' Asha pleaded.

'Only when you tell me why you ran away.' But I was already passing extra chocolate squares to her. No matter how hard I tried, I couldn't get Asha to say more.

Lanong's voice drew me out of my reverie. 'You're on the Central Line right? I'm on the Jubilee. So, here's where we part ways.'

I hadn't even noticed that we'd passed through the turnstiles in the Bond Street Underground. 'I'll have to change for the Piccadilly at Holborn,' I groaned. 'It's a long ride back.'

Lanong snorted. 'Be careful in Harrow, San.'

~

9 November

I stepped into the swish lobby of Gregersen Tower at a quarter to three on Thursday afternoon. The building was a massive glass and steel structure with a pyramid pinnacle and a curving frontage overlooking St Paul's Cathedral. A sleek online video art installation on the wall ahead flashed intermittently with a stream of images, which I imagined came from state-of-the-art consoles. I stared at the screen image of a young man jumping over the bulwarks of a condominium, his outstretched palms faced forward. On a stretch of azure sky above him were the words, 'If you don't live your life on edge …'

The picture dissolved into the scene of a crowded sports stadium. The words 'there's no space on earth' flashed over the image.

A few minutes later, I sipped tea in a meeting room in the Pinwheel offices on the fifth floor, as anxious as a contender of a bullfight in Spain. McLeod walked in after half an hour, wearing a grey Sharkskin slim-fit and a checkered tea-rose tie that struck a perspicacious balance between the image of a barrister and the wardrobe of a news anchor.

'I'm sorry I'm late. I was held up in a call. Thanks for coming by,' he said.

'Thanks for taking the time to see me. This building is regal!'

'Oh, the Gregersen Tower is owned by EGG, but many bigwigs have leased office space here, including Haymarket and Novartis,' McLeod grinned. 'It originally belonged to an English real estate company. EGG bought the property later.'

McLeod got right down to business. 'There's a CEM Summit in Barcelona next month. My client, Ericsson, is dishing out some announcements there. We're scrambling to put together a white paper on trends in customer experience management solutions. It needs to go for production next week. One of our key researchers has fallen ill and the other one is in a conference in Shanghai. The client is panicking.'

'Well, I have written product reviews and other assorted tech stories for ABP News Online,' I informed. 'I've scripted a bunch of comedy sketches and interviews, too.'

Aiden McLeod rubbed his palms together. 'Very well, then. This is a one-off project. It'll involve some research and information synthesis. That's about it, really. I'll have my account manager email you research materials and a blueprint for the white paper. She's your go-to person for any questions, clarifications and follow-ups.'

I cleared my throat hesitantly. 'How does, um, the compensation work ...?'

McLeod snapped his fingers. 'Oh yes, the fee. For external contractors, we have a separate pay-grade commensurate with experience. For you, it'll work out to about fifteen pounds an hour, I think. Is that acceptable?'

'Yes, of course!'

'Good. Let's see what you can do.' McLeod rose from his seat. We shook hands again before he saw me out.

I wondered why I didn't really like Aiden McLeod all that much. I was indeed grateful for the opportunity but there was something about him that bothered me.

Was it his glibness? *Maybe it's the PR business,* I reflected, deciding that it was not going to be my long-term career destination.

As I stepped out of the elevators in the lobby, I ran into a sandy-haired man who looked distinctly familiar.

'Rick? Rick Martinez?' I exclaimed in surprise.

'Ah, Sandy!' Rick broke into a smile.

'We met at Beaconsfield in September! I'm so glad you remembered me.'

'Of course I do! How are you? Liking it at LSE?'

'It's wonderful,' I said happily. 'I've been commissioned to do a new project for Pinwheel Interactive. I'm just out from a meeting with the country head.'

'That's awesome! You met McLeod?'

My eyes widened. 'D'you know him?'

Rick raked his left hand through his hair. 'Well, I'm just on my way to see him myself. We're collaborating with Pinwheel for an existing client. Pinwheel is doing traditional PR for that campaign and we're handling all their digital outreach.'

'How exciting!' I cried, remembering that he worked for a digital consulting firm, Trychlen.

'Gotta run now!' Rick said. 'Good luck with your project. Send my best to Nimmy. We should all catch up again.'

17 November

The media career carnival Ritchie had told me about weeks ago was as exhaustive as the ExCEL London Centre website promised it would be. I loped into the fair after a three-hour wait for a ticket. Colourful banners of all media bigwigs – from *Bloomberg News* to *The Guardian* – danced before me, from portable stalls swarming with journalism hopefuls and videographers televising the event. The BBC World Service booth was my first port of call. A cheerful, young blonde in a beige linen suit introduced herself as Keisha Douglas and shook my hand at the podium.

'Sandy Raman from the London School of Economics,' I smiled.

'Hey, I'm an LSE alum too!' Keisha chimed in excitedly. 'I graduated two years ago.'

We chatted a bit about LSE.

'I was earlier a crime news reporter for ABP News in Mumbai,' I mentioned, handing her a show reel that ABP had done for me earlier in the year. On its cover was the picture of a globe against a watermarked montage of news stories I had done for the channel. My title card ran across the header. Keisha swiftly scanned the little blurb on the back of my show reel. 'You've covered the Mumbai terror attacks and the travel ban on Indian workers in Bahrain … those migrants were all released, weren't they?'

I nodded. 'About 112 migrant workers, detained in Bahrain for six years were released about two weeks after that story broke out on ABP.'

Keisha's face turned into a broad smile. 'Well, it seems that *I* should be asking *you* for a job!'

I was momentarily taken aback at the unexpected compliment. I began to warm up to her childlike fervour and genuine affability. 'I have a long way to go,' I stated modestly.

'I've started an independent awareness drive for disabled children and teens,' Keisha mentioned, tucking my show reel into a plastic folder on the desk. 'It's called Lionheart. I'm toying with an idea for a more targeted campaign. Would you be interested in leading it with me?'

A novice like me with a BBC TV series producer? I couldn't say more than, 'Wow.'

A brief spell of silence followed before Keisha solemnly inquired, 'Do you have any kind of reporting or campaigning experience in the area of disability rights?'

'Not really. But I've interacted with the mentally disabled. I believe I understand how they think. The niece of a friend, who works for Southall Black Sisters in London, is mentally challenged. I have some ideas that I think will work.'

Keisha smiled and handed me her business card. 'Sounds good, Sandy. Email me.'

Most of the other talent scouts I met were channel editors from ITV, Channel 4, Channel 5 and BBC News. Many were eyeing producers they could commission for documentaries of their choosing. But I wasn't an established producer yet. I paused by a Costa Cafe on my way out. A pair of icy-cold hands roughly grabbed my shoulders from behind. Panic seized me.

A familiar accented voice boomed in my ears. 'Ahh, Sandy … did I freak you out enough?'

I whirled around to see Ritchie grinning from ear to ear.

'Bloody hell!' I exclaimed, exhaling in relief and annoyance as I rubbed my shoulder. 'Have you any idea I fell in a bramble bush just two weeks ago?'

'Oh?'

I briefly told Ritchie what had happened, right up to my belief that one or more members of the Sawant family were in some kind of danger.

Ritchie cast an amused smile. 'So, you're playing detective, eh?'

I laughed.

Ritchie gestured at the menu ahead of us. 'What would you like to have?'

I ordered a hot chocolate and Ritchie got a black coffee with a Cornish pastry.

'That's my lunch,' he grinned sheepishly, when we seated ourselves at a table in the hallway.

'So, you did attend this event after all,' I began. 'Was it useful?'

Ritchie peeled away the edges of paper that stuck to his soggy patty. 'I met a production guy who has a contact in Zurich. Might be a potential client for Flamingo.'

'Fire out!' I exclaimed.

'Good going on the EGG grant,' Ritchie mumbled between munches. 'How's the TV station coming along?'

'Our business manager, Lanong, ordered fifteen LCD screens from Argos last afternoon,' I replied jubilantly.

'Ahh!' Ritchie nodded, impressed. 'Are you replacing the screen at the Quad café? It's lousy.'

'We've identified some high-priority locations. I don't know if the Quad is on that list.'

A faraway look replaced the raptness in Ritchie's eyes. 'Did you read that piece in *The Financial Times* today?' he asked.

'Nope. What's in there?'

'EGG is dishing out money to penniless students like us.' Ritchie fished around in his backpack and slid a copy of the newspaper across the table. It was folded at the page that carried the article Ritchie was referring to.

'Gregersen Foundation Sets up £100Mn Fund for Oxbridge, LSE Students,' the headline read. 'In Europe's biggest private philanthropic push to open up higher education to young international students, EGG's top chief Lord Melvin Bradshaw will seed a scholarship fund with £50 million,' the story began. 'Dubbed the Gregersen International Scholarship, the fund will support its first 100 students from April next year. Lord Bradshaw will release two more tranches of £15 million each. Other donors are being urged to contribute a further £20 million ...'

I glanced up at Ritchie. 'Are you applying?'

Ritchie snorted. 'No time. I'm juggling LSE work *and* two part-time jobs. Building a client base for Flamingo, too. I probably don't need the funds as much as you do.'

'Ever the sparkly entrepreneur,' I grinned. 'Well, I just got some extra cash from a research project I completed for Pinwheel Interactive. In fact, EGG is one of their clients too.'

'That's great, San. Do consider applying though.'

'Why, that was a wonderful surprise, Nimmy. *Fidelio* was magical!' I exclaimed as we walked out of the Royal Festival Hall's famed German opera later that evening.

After a long, tiring day at ExCEL London, I wasn't expecting to do more than chill out with Nimmy over flat whites on Liverpool Street after work. But Nimmy had instructed me to get off at the Bank Underground. From there, we had hopped into a cab to the lavish South Bank complex.

Now, he grinned lopsidedly. 'Leonora made it so much more poignant.'

'The lady who played Florestan's wife?'

Nimmy nodded.

I glanced at him like a starry-eyed high-school girl on her first date. His growing affection for me had urged me to acclimatise to the heady rush of excitement holding sway whenever I was around him. I had long since overlooked his outburst at the lawn garden when we had discussed Asha.

Now, he wore a pair of pale silver chinos and a burgundy panama suit over a matching knitted waistcoat that accentuated the marigold flecks of his eyes. His partial Duchene grin flamed my sensibilities with a fresh yearning.

What was it about Nimmy that drew me to him? Was it his vulnerability? His intelligence? His obscure resemblance to Saahil?

'Given my sparse knowledge of the opera scene, I feel like a dunce,' I gabbled finally.

'You'll catch up soon enough,' Nimmy chuckled. 'Feel like a munch? I know a nice little Turkish bistro in Covent Garden.'

'That sounds exotic!'

We boarded a ferry to the Savoy pier and ambled towards the deck. I let the floodgates of my consciousness open up to a stupefying haze as I leaned forward against the rail and drank in the breathtaking seascape around us – little white boats and clippers being moored on the river, thick tufts of cloud swimming across a bruised sky, the bascules of the Tower Bridge swinging upwards as it glimmered like a tiger's eye in the shadows of an impending nightfall …

A shudder ran down my back as Nimmy twirled a lock of my hair around his finger. I turned to face him. He lifted my chin with a tenderness that made me light-headed. His eyes shimmered with ravenous hunger as he pressed himself against me and gently kissed my lips. I gasped and moaned with longing. 'Good heavens.' I gulped, when we pulled apart.

An announcement for the Savoy Pier rang out from somewhere around us.

A loud sob barreled into my throat. 'What happened to Saahil was too traumatic, too painful. I never imagined I could ever feel this way again after …'

Nimmy placed a finger on my lips. 'Let's just go with the flow, San,' he whispered.

He wrapped his arm around me, murmuring sweet nothings as we joined the line of passengers moving towards the dock.

~

When we got home, I went up to the colonnaded roof-level porch on the third floor hoping to walk off the heaviness from our three-course meal at *Sarastro*. As I strolled down in the terrace, I rang my brother, Sri, on Whatsapp.

Sri, who had been single for all these years, was now going steady with a colleague who had joined his firm recently. Hearing him jabber excitedly about the intense connection he felt with her made me feel happy, but also evoked a jumble of emotions, which alternated between my loneliness for Saahil and my growing attraction to Nimmy.

'You have an early start tomorrow, don't you? It's getting late for you back there,' I told Sri, finally.

'Yes. Love you, Sandhya. Remember to leave the past behind and look ahead to the future. The past is helpful only insofar as it facilitates the future,' Sri said, before we rang off.

I knew he was hinting at my grief over losing Saahil. My father and brother had never openly approved of my relationship with Saahil, but they couldn't have been more supportive after he died. 'You have to go on. It's what Saahil would have wanted for you, too,' Appa had told me as we prepared our joint net worth statements for my UK visa, four months ago, after he mortgaged his home in Tanjore to get a loan sanctioned for me.

I leaned against the terrace wall and stared straight ahead, ruminating over the unexpected course my relationship with Nimmy had taken since Rosie's visit earlier this month. A black limousine glided into view as it neared the bend in the road ahead and halted. Through the window-shield, I saw the silhouette of a couple embracing passionately. The man behind the wheel had his back to me. A fedora hat and the collars of a business suit concealed most of his hair. He leaned towards the woman. She threw her head back and laughed. Then, he pulled her towards him and kissed her. Boy, did they seem happy. Could Nimmy and I be as joyful as them? Or would the concern inherent in Nimmy's affection for Asha spill over into our relationship?

I noticed a car-hanger swinging from the rearview mirror. It appeared to be a falcon. The doors of the limousine slid open and the woman stepped out. As the man briefly rested one hand on the wheel, a massive gemstone glinted on one of his fingers. He turned on the ignition, made a wide U-turn and zoomed off towards Warden Avenue. The woman walked towards 83 Capthorne Avenue. The wavy hair … the curve of her hips …

Nidhi? I thought, surprised and even mildly impressed. She didn't seem the type who would date a doyen in a fedora hat.

A door slammed below. Then, Shailaja's grating voice. 'Sandhya! Are you still up there? Nidhi just got in and we need to lock the terrace …'

I glanced at my watch. It was close to 10.00 p.m. I retreated from the deck and headed back down.

Shailaja was at the stove, frying a dosa.

'This new case is a nightmare,' Nidhi said. 'Just returned from High Wycombe. There was a train delay in West Ruislip on the way back, too.'

'Take it easy,' Shailaja said, flipping the dosa over.

'You must be tired. I'll help out,' I offered.

'That would be nice, Sandhya,' Shailaja said.

I began stirring the batter.

'Walking back here from the station took me forever. I shouldn't have worn those high heels,' Nidhi groaned, massaging her feet.

I was flattening a ladleful of batter on the frying pan when I stiffened. *Why is she lying?*

4 December

With his shifty eyes and phony smile, Jeffrey Stuart gave me the heebie-jeebies. He was the deputy chief executive of SIGNAL, or Society for Inclusive Growth at a National Level, a leading disability charity in the UK.

Charlotte Hale, whose programme I had earlier listened to in Nimmy's car, had featured one of SIGNAL's campaigns as an appeal on her BBC radio show earlier this year. I was awestruck to learn that Keisha knew Charlotte well. We were hoping to get SIGNAL in as a sponsoring partner for Lionheart. Unsurprisingly, Jeff was a lead from Charlotte.

Now, he peered at us over the rim of his crescent-moon eyeglasses. 'I'm not entirely sure of the exact nature of the programme you have in mind,' he said. 'What's more, I'm not at all certain that the media should exploit the condition of disabled individuals.'

'Lionheart is independent of my work for the BBC, Jeff. And the BBC doesn't openly champion any specific initiative,' Keisha answered, unruffled.

Jeff looked dubious. 'What background do you have in dealing with rights and issues concerning disabled individuals?' It was the same question Keisha had amiably asked me a few weeks ago. But Jeff sounded tough as hell. He was no fan of journalists, as far as I could tell.

'I've produced and developed a host of formats and specials for programmes like *See Hear* and *Children in Need*,' Keisha said.

Jeff scratched his greying beard skeptically. '*See Hear*?' he repeated.

'*See Hear* airs on BBC 2 at one p.m. on Wednesdays,' Keisha informed. 'The programme broadcasts content for the deaf and mute community. And *Children in Need* is a fundraising initiative for disadvantaged young people across the country. The BBC uses those funds to ...'

'I've heard of *Children in Need*,' Jeff snapped.

'The idea for Lionheart took shape when I organised a biking event to raise scholarship funds for children at St Ann School and other special needs institutions earlier this year,' Keisha explained.

Jeff nodded, perking up with interest.

'As part of Lionheart, we're conducting interactive workshops to raise awareness of self-protection and street skills among the mentally challenged,' Keisha continued. 'Our target centres are special schools, day-care facilities and residential homes. We're pitching for a national tour to launch our workshops. We would also like to enlist SIGNAL's trainers to provide self-defense lessons to special needs groups that are interested in getting in touch with us after the tour.'

I beamed proudly. My idea. I was flattered that Keisha had incorporated it into her core strategy.

Jeff nodded with an emphatic, 'Ahh …'

Encouraged by his response, I added, 'We're also addressing the need to improve care for the mentally disabled at schools, workplaces, homes and …'

A discreet nudge from Keisha stopped me mid-sentence.

Jeff's clear blue eyes flashed like aquamarines. 'Would I fund an initiative that implicates special schools and daycare centres by suggesting they provide insufficient care?' he said icily.

Uh-oh. Several daycare centres and special schools *were* members of SIGNAL, after all. And what I had just said suggested that I was questioning SIGNAL's role in safeguarding the rights of the disabled.

Why wouldn't you just shut up and listen? You haven't done this before! I reprimanded myself.

'My partner meant to talk about a call for improved public welfare systems, rather than the care fostered in institutions,' Keisha interjected, handing him a slim paper folder 'That's our concept note. I'll send you a detailed brief on our campaign agenda.'

The thunderous expression on Jeff's face dissolved as we shook hands and retreated.

'I-I'm really sorry about what happened,' I mumbled ruefully as we headed south towards Paddington.

'Got ten minutes?' Keisha said, motioning towards a promenade overlooking a warren of waterways and canal boats. My stomach sank. As I followed her, I prayed that I wouldn't be kicked out for my amateurish behaviour.

'Wow!' I exclaimed as we sipped tall lattes outside the Waterside café.

Keisha had just offered me the role of a paid freelance production assistant for Streetsmart, a new television show she had proposed to her team. I didn't dare ask what kind of pay I could expect – I was simply grateful for the golden opportunity.

'Streetsmart is an interactive programme that will teach developmentally challenged children and young adults better life skills for when they're out in public,' Keisha explained. 'If we get the green light next week, broadcasts will begin mid or late Jan.'

'Is it a talk show?' I asked, draining the last few dregs of my latte.

'No,' Keisha replied, signaling at a passing waiter for the bill. 'It's an educational programme interspersed with interviews. My boss, Alfred and I are screening experts and people who face everyday challenges. We need to find a good story to feature on the show.'

'There's always a good story,' I said.

The waiter placed a check before Keisha. I pulled out my wallet.

'No, no …' Keisha protested. 'I'll get it.'

'Thanks, Keisha.'

'To be honest, I got inspiration for this TV show from your ideas for Lionheart. That's why I'm getting you on board too,' Keisha admitted as we walked down the promenade. 'I'll be in touch soon.' We parted ways on the sidewalk.

Minutes later, I jumped into a stuffy carriage on the southbound Bakerloo line at the Paddington Underground. An unusual sight near the farthest set of doors in the train compartment caught my eye. A pushcart was moving towards the doors. It overflowed with electric violet teddy bears.

Right from their bowties to the 'I love you' press-me heart pendants suspended from satin ribbon chains, they were exactly like the one Rosie had left behind at the Sawants' two months ago, although they weren't the same shade of purple. The bowtie and the ribbon chains were a few notches lighter than the teddies' electric violet torsos, but they followed the same pattern of light and shade as I had seen in the purple teddy. A pale, veined hand gripped the handle of the cart. My gaze traveled to the tall, suit-clad passenger wheeling it off the train. I stared at that shock of blond hair – spiked, gelled and parted in the centre. The cartel kingpin guy … who was it? I caught a profile of the man's face just as the doors slid close behind him. *Carl Wright? Nimmy's friend?*

I raced to the nearest window to get a better look at the disembarking commuter.

A buxom woman with shocking pink hair jostled me from the side. 'This is not a cruise on the Thames!' she snarled.

I retreated to a pole near a door to the next carriage. A sense of unease rambled up my throat. Did Carl have something to do with Rosie's unwelcome appearance at the Sawants' last month?

4
The Undertaking

'I saw Carl Wright on a train this afternoon,' I informed Nimmy as we sat in *The Phoenix* with a bottle of Chianti later that evening.

Nimmy laced his arms behind his head and returned my gaze languidly. 'Oh? What did he say?'

'I didn't speak to him. He was getting off the train when I hopped in.' I proceeded to tell him the rest.

Nimmy jerked his head up as if he had been momentarily electrocuted. Then, he broke into guffaws. 'Carl? Violet teddy bears? Why on earth would he push a cart full of stuffed bears in a business suit?'

'I don't know, Nimmy,' I said. 'I have a bad feeling about him.'

Nimmy narrowed his eyes. 'I've known Carl for years, Sandy. He has nothing to do with Rosie.'

I gazed around me, drinking in the soft amber glow of the small, lively pub in Bayswater.

Nimmy reached across the table for my hand. 'We're planning a hike across the Snowdon Mountain in Wales during the holiday season. Rick, Carl, Sal and I. It would be lovely if you could join us. We're staying with an old friend in Flintshire through Christmas. My family will be joining us there.'

'I don't think I can. I have a few course papers and some production work to catch up on over the hols. I'm not an experienced hiker either. And I can get a wheeze easily. Be careful with Carl though.'

Nimmy gave my hand a little squeeze. 'Please do think it over. You could even join us later with my family. They aren't hiking.'

'Is Asha coming to Wales too?'

'Ahhh …' Nimmy shook his head. 'A change of environment disorients her … even if only for a short time. Mum is actually hoping for a vacation herself … she hasn't taken one in years.'

'I guess everyone needs a break,' I agreed.

A sudden flash of inspiration shot through my mind. 'Nimmy …' I began. '… I'm going to be involved in a show called Streetsmart for a TV series producer at the BBC. It's a life skills series involving young people with special needs …' I explained the programme agenda to Nimmy. 'I think it would help Asha if she participated in the show. She could also continue training with the TV host off-air, if she likes. For free,' I finished.

The wine-induced flush on Nimmy's cheeks faded into a ghostly pallor. His tone seemed icy when he intoned, 'Oh, I see.'

'The TV series will be a great platform for Asha to learn a lot more about herself and people around her. You told me she couldn't go to school regularly. Working probably does her good now, but these workshops and some off-air training will help …'

Nimmy leaned towards me and locked my lips with his. All my thoughts melted away as his tongue explored mine with an urgency that made me yield. 'It's Christmas time, baby,' he whispered when we disentangled ourselves. 'You're way ahead of your pace. Don't fuzz your pretty little head up with these heavy thoughts. Sit back and enjoy the wine.'

Later that night, I was idly skimming through an agenda for a lecture programme, when I heard a knock on my bedroom door.

'May I come in?' Nimmy called.

'Yes,' I replied after a moment of hesitation.

Nimmy entered, set for bed in black pyjamas and an old 'Frankie says relax' T-shirt. Something stirred inside me as I drank in the contours of his physique through the faded fabric of the tee.

'Aren't you sleeping yet?' I asked when I found my voice.

'You look beautiful in pink,' Nimmy commented, eyeing me intensely.

I glanced down at my thin, satin nightgown and blushed.

Nimmy scrambled onto the bed next to me. 'I've grown used to having you around. Nine days without you is going to be pretty hard,' he murmured.

'I'll still be here when you're back,' I pointed out, thinking about the two research papers I had to write once LSE let out for the winter break.

'You will, won't you?' he whispered, running his hands through my hair.

Instinctive shudders ran down my spine.

I curled up into a tight ball. 'I'm tired. Let's discuss this tomorrow, please.'

'I'm not here to make you change your mind. Here's what I came in for ...' He slipped a hand into the pocket of his pyjamas and brought out a sheer velvet box. I gasped as he opened it and slipped a simple gold solitaire ring on my finger.

'I love you, Sandy. Will you be mine?' he whispered.

'Nimmy!' I cried. The line between dream and reality was quickly blurring. As our eyes locked, I realised he was the reason I was able to wean myself away from the pain of Saahil's demise and rebuild a promising future in London. Was he proposing to me? I bet he was, but I felt it would be too uptight on my part to seek his confirmation.

'Where did you get the ring from?' I asked instead.

'Ernest Jones,' Nimmy said proudly. 'I found one of your rings on the breakfast counter downstairs. I used it as a sample to figure out your size.'

'I love it,' I said softly.

My stomach fluttered as Nimmy drew me into his arms and planted his lips on mine. I wavered just for a moment as he gently peeled off my nightgown. Soon, we were making love quietly as Polish singer Marek Grechuta crooned *Nie Dokazuj* from my media player in the background. I blanched at the initial discomfort that seized me. For all intents and purposes, my relationship with Saahil had been chaste and I was still a virgin. But Nimmy's tender patience with me laid all my fears to rest.

'Nimmy,' I murmured as we lay spent in each other's arms several hours later. 'It'll help Asha if she participates in Streetsmart.'

Nimmy rolled over and lay facedown on my lap. 'That wouldn't be in *our* best interests, dear.'

'It's okay, baby. Let's sleep now,' I cooed, rubbing my cheek against the stubble on his chin.

I remained wide-awake as Nimmy drifted off next to me. Eventually, I walked over to my window and drew the blinds out. A faint sliver of dawn peeped out from the blanket of a cerulean sky. *Wouldn't be in our best interests? Is Nimmy worried? Is he hiding something? What on earth does he mean?*

~

5 December

The curl of a white rose petal flitted into my line of sight as I opened my eyes next morning. A tiny vase with a long-stemmed rose sat by my bedside. A short note and a steaming cup of coffee accompanied it. The bed dipped in the space next to me. It mustn't have been long since Nimmy returned to his room. I smiled and read the note.

'Had to leave for work early today. Some crappy releases to attend to. Will return home soon to be with you.

Love, N.'

I stroked the gold ring on my finger and stretched with the euphoria of a canary set free to explore the unchartered depths of a straddling horizon. After freshening up, I sipped my coffee and gazed outside the window.

I have to find out what those teddy bears are all about, I decided. Nimmy didn't seem to have a clue about what his friend was up to and I owed it to him to ensure that Carl wasn't playing any hanky-panky with the Sawants.

I glanced at my mobile phone: 8.30 a.m. I whisked open my laptop, retrieved EuroFirst's mainline number from Google and called the office.

I was transferred to Carl's direct number.

'Yes, who's this?' He sounded busy and curt.

'Carl, uh, this is Sandy … from LSE. We met at the Royal Standard a few months ago. I … is this a good time?'

'Sandy?' Carl sounded blank at first. Then his voice came flooding back to me with considerably more warmth. 'Oh, it's you. Nimmy's guest.'

'I'm terribly sorry for bothering you at work.'

'Not at all,' Carl said politely. 'How can I help?'

'Um, I saw you on the train yesterday,' I started. 'On the Bakerloo line at Paddington. You were pulling along a cart full of teddy bears that were *dazzlingly* violet.'

My words were met with a long silence from Carl's end. The faint warble of a morning birdsong whistled through the window into my ears. 'You there?'

I heard a sharp intake of breath before Carl's voice came through. 'Yes.'

'I was just curious, Carl.'

'It's uh … I'm sorry, San. I'm reviewing some data for a deliverable, as I speak to you …'

'No worries,' I replied. 'I thought to say hello to you on the train yesterday, but it was far too crowded. I was surprised to see you with a bunch of teddies though. Violet teddy bears aren't *that* common, huh?'

'I was attending a friend's daughter's birthday party last evening,' Carl replied distantly. 'The teddies were return gifts for all their guests. I got them from a lady in Canterbury. Made to order. She specialises in making teddy bears of colours that you wouldn't find in an ASDA or Superdrug store, if you know what I mean.'

'Interesting. What's her name?'

'Evie Mardling. Up in Kent.'

'So, you got off work early yesterday, huh?' I questioned with deliberate nonchalance.

'Had an afternoon meeting in Marylebone. Headed to Paddington right after.'

'I see. Well, I hear you're going to Wales. Have a great trip. Happy hols!'

'And you,' Carl said.

I hung up. What name had flashed on the departure board when I waited for the train at Paddington, yesterday?

Ah, Elephant and Castle.

Wasn't Marylebone the other way? If Carl had really headed to Paddington from Marylebone, he should have been on a northbound train. Why was he on a southbound service from Queen's Park up north?

I frowned. Carl's story didn't convince me.

~

'Jeff called this morning. SIGNAL is partnering with Lionheart!' Keisha shrieked jubilantly when we met in the BBC Broadcast Centre's sprawling lobby at noon that day.

'That's incredible!' I squealed.

A petite woman in a carmine crew-necked pencil dress joined us in the lounge.

'My colleague, Charlotte Hale,' Keisha introduced. 'Former Valley girl and Albion's Oprah Winfrey. She was an educational research fellow at Cambridge before she founded Topaz, five years ago. It's an educational development outfit.'

'I'm a huge fan of your show!' I smiled as we shook hands. 'It was the first I heard on radio when I moved here.'

Charlotte grinned broadly. 'Why, thank you!'

'Charlotte has also authored a couple of special ed books. I especially loved *Spun Gold*,' Keisha added. '*White Lights* is her latest. I'm going to get my hands on it this weekend. Charlotte is lending advisory support for the Lionheart campaign. We're also hoping to rope her in as an anchor for Streetsmart.'

The supremacy of Charlotte's celebrity stature left me wondering what Keisha could possibly see in a fledgling like me. 'I look forward to working with you,' I told Charlotte meekly.

'Lunch?' Charlotte suggested, jerking a thumb towards a set of glass doors opening out to a row of garden-side cafés and restaurants.

'I'm famished,' Keisha seconded.

We headed towards a Starbucks around the corner and ordered sandwiches and lattes before settling at a table.

'I'm thinking of a week-long national tour involving workshops with special needs groups. Jeff has agreed to fund all expenses,' Keisha said.

'We first need clarity on what themes these sessions will address,' Charlotte advised. 'I'd recommend focusing on techniques to improve survival skills that will help these people live independently.'

'We'll need to identify our target locations too,' I interjected.

'It'd be best to start with special schools, not-for-profits and care centres,' Keisha chimed in.

'Why would care centres be interested if we're talking about de-institutionalising their residents?' I asked.

'A lot of those centres offer outpatient services. Many are owned by local authorities,' Charlotte explained. 'It would be a feather in their cap if they had more residents move on to live independently, don't you think?'

Keisha pulled out a folded A4 sheet from her tote bag and handed it to me. 'That's a list of objectives I've identified for Lionheart and the tour in particular. Feel free to add your inputs to the campaign plan and run them by us. I'm headed to Bergen for Christmas but I'll be available on email. Charlotte will be in town though, won't you?'

'I may be in Prague for a couple of days around year-end but I'm here otherwise,' Charlotte said.

'Okay. I'll do some research before getting started on a proposal,' I said.

'If you're looking at places that may be interested in organising a talk or enlisting volunteer services, I know a bunch of special schools and care centres,' Charlotte offered. 'One of our rookies made that list when Topaz was working on a green paper campaign. We hardly used it though. We had to communicate more with the government. Not that the government is terribly accountable. But I'd definitely recommend reviewing that list.'

'That'll come in handy,' I said earnestly.

Charlotte rose. 'When I get a chance, I'll have my secy, Megan dig it up from our backend server and email it to you then. Got to go now … have a cool Yule, girls!'

My Dad rang me as I headed to the White City Underground.

'Congrats on your first paycheque in London, Sandhya,' he chirped.

'Thank you.' I smiled, remembering the fee that Pinwheel Interactive had credited into my bank account this morning for my work on that CEM summit white paper for Aiden McLeod.

'Yes, it was an interesting gig – and it helps not having to use much from my loan account at one go,' I added.

'Now, this BBC show and that mental health campaign will give you some solid experience outside India,' Appa said.

'It's a campaign for the rights of the disabled, not the mentally ill,' I corrected gently.

'I'm so proud of you, baby.'

'I couldn't have done this without you and Sri,' I said softly.

Then, I excitedly went on about Charlotte and Lionheart's partnership with SIGNAL. When we rang off, I realised that I was glad I hadn't harped on the Sawants' quirks to my Dad since arriving here. The Sawants were good people after all, and I was grateful to Asha for catalyzing my involvement in the Lionheart campaign, which in turn had fetched me this opportunity with Streetsmart.

Now, it is my undertaking to get Asha on the Streetsmart TV show.

~

'Why are you so bent on getting Asha involved?' Ashok Sawant demanded later that night. Shailaja and Nidhi accompanied him in the sitting room, 'Your father's move to send you here was a big decision. Especially with your asthma …' he went on, 'And here you are, getting into the sleazy television business and gallivanting around the city when you should do no more than read for your classes and come right home!'

I felt like an ill-fated employee seated across belligerent managers who were closing in to give the boot under the pretext of unacceptable behaviour. It may have been a tad better if Nimmy were around but he was predictably still in the office.

'How can you call it sleazy?' I replied defiantly. 'The BBC is a public service broadcaster. The production team for this TV show is consulting expert educators …'

'And my daughter will not be a guinea pig!' Ashok roared.

'We can't expose Asha like this!' Nidhi cried, terrified.

I stared at her. My mind swam with an image of the man in the limousine I had seen her with a few weeks ago. Was she really as blinkered as Shailaja and Ashok? Or was she just playing along?

'Is it because anything that isn't "normal" is a taboo to you?' I shot back, beside myself with fury.

'Mind your tongue, especially when you're speaking to elders, Sandhya,' Shailaja admonished.

'That's not the only reason,' Nidhi said reluctantly.

'What else is it then?' I yelled.

Ashok rose from his seat and raised an outstretched palm as he approached me. For a moment, I thought he would strike me. But he dropped his hands to his sides when he stood directly before me.

'That's none of your business!' he said ominously. 'I've been running this family for years. We've had no problems with the arrangements for Asha so far. I don't want an uninhibited chit of a girl to turn our lives topsy-turvy. As long as you're here, you pay your rent to Shailaja on time and keep your nose out of our business. Do I make myself clear?'

I couldn't believe I was living with people who were deriding me when all I was trying to do was help their daughter. I began to feel stifled.

'I hope you see that I mean well,' I said quietly.

'Don't worry about us,' Nidhi said coldly.

I didn't wait to hear any more. I fled upstairs to my room, tears streaming down my face.

I rang Nimmy from my room. He didn't answer.

For a while, I sat fuming. How could he tell his parents about my desire to cast Asha in Streetsmart, especially when he hadn't first told me that he intended to discuss it with them? And what exactly had he told them that elicited such a response from his father?

I would keep brooding if I didn't distract myself. I retrieved my laptop and dropped a note to Aiden McLeod at Pinwheel, hoping he would concede to my request for an interview with Lord Bradshaw, given the work I had done for his other client.

Then I googled Charlotte Hale. I learned that she was a descendant of the wealthy Hale family, known to Hollywood biggies and Broadway junkies as an elite ilk of writer-producers, who were now social impact investors.

A key turned in the lock downstairs. I tiptoed down the stairway.

Nimmy tiredly flung his coat and suit over the banister and whirled around – only to ram into me as I placed my foot on the last step. I shrieked.

'What the hell!' Nimmy exclaimed.

I stared at Nimmy. I desperately yearned to see the man he had been yesterday when he proposed to me.

'How was work?' I inquired, trying to sound casual.

'The usual. Meetings, deadlines, bullshit …' He strode into the sitting room and propped his feet up on the couch. I followed him in and sat on a pouffe. He turned the television on and surfed through channels at remarkable speed, finally stopping at Channel Five. An episode of *Bull Run* was on.

'Had dinner?' I asked.

'A cold turkey sandwich from the vending machine.'

'That doesn't sound like much,' I scolded gently, hoping to diffuse the strain in our conversation.

'What are you doing here, San?' Nimmy sounded irked.

'Nimmy, we need to talk.'

'Not today, San.'

'Looks like you had a tough day.'

'Yeah, and no time at all … I was running from pillar to post, scrambling to convince some morons in Paris about a darned investment portfolio.'

'No time at all? Apparently, you *did* have time to tattle to your folks about what I wanted to do with Asha – some time after last night, I suspect.'

'Last night, I told you it wouldn't be in our best interests to do it, Sandhya.'

This was the first time he was using my proper name.

'And I didn't disagree with you, did I? Now, the point is not about involving Asha in the show … it's about the fact that you told on me to your folks. Have you any idea how they belittled me? What allegiance do you swear by?' I held up my hand, sobbing. The ring he had given me last night shifted colours as it caught the sparkle of a tableside lamp by the settee.

'Allegiance?' Nimmy said coldly. 'Wait a minute, where did that come from? I'm protective of Asha and my family. I'm sensitive to anything that I feel endangers them in any way. I thought I made that pretty clear in the beginning.'

'But how could participating in a show like Streetsmart possibly endanger anyone?' I wailed.

Nimmy's face mellowed. 'It doesn't matter. Their welfare is my sole concern.'

'And mine?' I pouted.

'We just met a couple months ago. You're talking like we're married for God's sake!'

The searing bushfire in my heart diffused to smouldering splinters, giving way to a tide of discomfort. 'What did the ring mean?' I asked quietly.

Nimmy continued surfing channels. 'I can't discuss this anymore.'

I flew upstairs to my room. Did my final act of acquiescence to our union last night dilute Nimmy's respect for me? Or had I misjudged the sentiment behind the ring?

23 February

'Thank you for your story, Linda,' Charlotte said, leaning over to hug a wavy-haired teenaged girl she was interviewing for Streetsmart.

Linda was born with cranial anomalies after surviving a saline abortion. With gentle prodding from Charlotte, Linda had just recounted an incident where she was once left behind in a night bus during a school excursion.

'I hear you're a talented singer. Would you like to sing for us?' Charlotte urged Linda.

Linda giggled and nodded. The pulsating beats of a karaoke began echoing across the studio.

She swayed from side to side and began chirruping. 'It's electric, you can't see it. It's electric, you gotta fee-eel it. It's electric, oooh it's shakin' …'

Charlotte sang along.

Broadcasts had begun mid-January. Today, we were shooting our sixth episode in a BBC Television Centre studio across the Media Village. Over the course of our brainstorming spells for the programme series, I had developed a warm rapport with Charlotte and Keisha. And Keisha and I had now grown close enough for me to call her Kiki.

When the session drew to a close, Charlotte turned back to the camera and announced, 'Off-air, we're training our participants on perception and self-care. Please email us at streetsmart@bbc.co.uk if you would like to sign up for our training sessions or make other inquiries. This is Charlotte Hale signing off. See you next week.' She finished with a smart salute. The camera lights turned off. Keisha and her boss, Alfred Maynard gave her a thumbs-up.

A heavyset bearded man in his late thirties, Alfred was a grumpy producer who had surprisingly grown fond of me, over the past month, when we began working together to produce scripts for each episode and ensure that the series stayed on schedule.

I was disappointed that Asha wasn't participating in the TV show. Nimmy seemed happier, since I had let go of my insistence on her involvement. On his return from Wales, he had taken me out to West End's *Les Miserables.* Despite my better judgement, I continued to sleep with him. Perhaps, I was just lonely for Saahil.

A rotund, middle-aged woman emerged at Linda's side and gave her a big hug. Linda's Aunt, I remembered from my conversation with her before the show. A gopher materialised from our crew and passed around a box of shortbread caramel bites to everyone.

Charlotte stood in a corner, shuffling some papers.

I walked towards her. 'You have a beautiful singing voice, Charlotte.'

'Oh, I used to sing nursery rhymes for Disneyland as a child … back when I was growing up in LA,' she responded, seemingly unfazed with my lionizing.

'Whoa, Disney's darling! You should cut an album!' I exclaimed.

Keisha joined us. 'I think this is one of the best episodes we've shot so far,' she commented.

'I'm off to check out this lovely antique shop with Horace,' Charlotte said. 'A quick breather from work before I head back for a graveyard shift …'

'Enjoy the timeout,' Keisha called out behind her.

I glanced at my watch. Nearly 1.00 p.m.

'Shoot! I have to run too,' I mumbled, remembering the job consultancy fair I was going to film for the LooSE TV network this afternoon. Keisha and I exchanged quick hugs before I followed Charlotte out.

'How did you two meet?' I asked her as we strode across the lobby.

'Horace? I featured him on my show about a year ago,' Charlotte replied. 'I first spotted him at a jazz bar in Chelsea. He was the guitarist of the band that played that night.'

Her tone was even-keel, but her eyes went all glassy as she continued, 'I was by myself that day – chilling out after work, y'know. So, I walked up to him, said hi and left my card. This guy's music is a godsend.'

Huge splotches of rainwater descended on us when we exited the building. Regretting my decision to leave my umbrella behind at home, I tied my hair into a disheveled bun. 'Is he a savant or …?'

'He was living hand to mouth when I first met him,' Charlotte said. 'Working nights in taverns and bars for extra bucks. The combination of that backstory with his talent is what inspired me to get him on my show. It pains me to see all that talent go unrecognised as people slog away in dead-end jobs, live in shacks or fight for their existence.' She pulled an ivy cap over her head. 'Anyhow, we lost touch for some time. But …' A faint smear of crimson appeared on her cheeks. '… the bloke reconnected with me a couple weeks ago with a new piece he'd composed. And boy, did I love it! When I wrote back, he invited me for a cup of coffee, and then we met again … and y'know, one thing led to another …'

'… And you're dating him now, aren't you?' I grinned.

'Nope. I'm interviewing him to research on the medicinal properties of cannabis for my next book,' Charlotte joked. 'Hell, yeah … well, I guess I don't quite know yet … I'm just giving it a shot. Speaking of the devil, he's here now! Bye, San!'

Charlotte strode towards a tall, lanky man standing near a tree. He sure was the eccentric type, all right. Ripped jeans, orange Harrington jacket and the straps of a guitar across his back. Waves of ginger hair peeked out from the canopy of his bright blue umbrella.

I chuckled to myself. Who would have thought a critically acclaimed media star like Charlotte Hale could transform into something of a sparkly-eyed teenager caught by the love bug?

I placed my camera bag on the floor of the Barbican Centre's sprawling exhibition hall and caught my breath. We had just filmed monologues by starry-eyed career contenders and plain-speaking recruiters from the job consultancy fair's corporate glitterati.

'We've got over two hours of footage,' fellow buddy Joey Clayworth informed, hoisting the tripod over his shoulder.

'Not bad for a twenty-minute career show, huh?'

'Nope,' Joey grinned. 'I'll take that camera bag. You look bushed.'

'Thanks.' Sure enough, the rhinestone design on the vamp of my ankle-strap pumps chafed against my toes and a dull throb wormed its way through my temples.

Joey picked up the bag from the floor. 'It's a noisy cavalcade in here. Let's head out and see what we've got.'

Once on the sidewalk, Joey replayed his footage. 'I should have increased the shutter speed a little,' he muttered.

'It looks pretty good. I'm sure Mark will …'

Several yards ahead of me, a pear-shaped brunette walked arm in arm with a tall, slim man in a charcoal grey suit and a fedora hat. I drank in her jazzy haute couture – a sable-collared, midnight blue, mink fur coat over a slinky pink crochet dress that swirled a few inches above her stocking-clad knees. An absurd magenta hat and a pair of black knee-length boots completed the ensemble.

A distinct memory of the limousine on King's Road resurfaced in my mind. That wasn't Nidhi, was it? I was so used to seeing her in understated outfits – mostly tunics and button-downs over trousers or slacks – that I couldn't even imagine what she must look like in the garb of a bohemian Stevie Nicks get-up from the seventies. Yet, the sway of her hips gave me enough reason to doubt the veracity of my logic. The man whispered something in her ear. I caught her side profile as she nuzzled against his shoulder and giggled.

Well, it *was* Nidhi, all right. And it seemed to be the same man I had seen with her in the limousine the other day. But, his face continued to elude my view. If she was dating him publicly, she probably wouldn't mind me stopping by and saying hello. They were heading towards the Barbican Chimes music shop. 'I'll just be back,' I mouthed to Joey.

Then I hustled forward. Alas, the pair ambled up a small flight of stairs around the building and disappeared from view.

I retraced my steps to Joey.

'Everything okay, San?' he inquired.

I smiled. 'Just thought I saw someone I knew.'

5

On The Radar

1 March

I languidly flipped over the dog-eared sheet before me and gawked in dismay at the squiggly lines of the continuing list on the backside. I had been sitting in Keisha's cabin at the BBC Broadcast Centre from early afternoon, making cold calls to several centres from this list to enlist their collaboration for our Lionheart tour.

I was about to call it a night when a peculiar name on the list caught my eye.

Bread Breakers'. Listed on Royal Street in Lambeth. Was it a delicatessen that had accidentally found its way into this list?

I squinted at the tiny font in the description tab. 'We provide nectar to children of a lesser sky.' I knew that the phrase 'children of a lesser God' referred to people born with an impairment or socioeconomic disadvantage. Did 'children of a lesser sky' have a similar connotation?

A Google search on Bread Breakers' didn't yield much and the centre didn't appear to have a website. All I found was a listing of Bread Breakers' Community Residence on a bunch of search directories online.

Scrolling through the list of search results on Google, I spotted a link to a catalogue of phrases that listed an expression of breaking bread. I clicked on a link to a portion of the New Testament, First Corinthians, 11:23. The biblical canon reported that Christ, on the night that he was betrayed, had broken a loaf of bread and passed it around to his disciples with some wine, declaring, 'This is my body for you.'

Today, the phrase 'breaking bread' is associated with strengthening bonds among fellow brethren to make one another feel safe and loved.

'A care centre with a profound philosophy, huh?' I muttered.

A search for 'children of a lesser sky' brought up the lyrics of '*World Hold On – Children of the Sky*' from French DJ Bob Sinclar's album, *Western Dreams*. I grabbed my earphones and hit the play button. Then I switched back to the calling list and moved my finger along the row to locate Bread Breakers' contact information. I didn't see a phone number, but there was an email address.

I logged on to Lionheart's inbox from Keisha's BBC email account on Outlook. A dialogue box jumped out at me. The Outlook server was unavailable due to maintenance work.

'Shoot!' I grumbled. I was sure an update had gone out to BBC employees earlier today but I couldn't be mad at Keisha for not warning me about it. She was overseeing a production this afternoon, which was why she had lent me her cabin today, and a disconnected server was going to be the least of her worries.

I signed into my personal Gmail account. I copied the template of my previous email from Outlook's Sent Items onto the body of my Gmail message. Since the email went from my personal account, I removed the BBC label from any part of the text and hit 'send' before putting my things away.

Nimmy called as I headed out. 'I was really looking forward to watching that movie with you on Netflix tonight, like we'd planned, but I'm going to be late from work today too,' he said exhaustedly. 'Don't wait up for me. You get a good night's sleep alright?'

'That's fine, sweetie. Don't strain yourself.'

I stood on the platform for the westbound Central Line at White City station and munched on a fruit bar. Nimmy and I had both been rather busy these days, and I missed spending time with him. I hoped I would be able to stay up at least until he got home.

I called Keisha after I alighted at Northolt and hopped on a bus. 'Hey, Kiki … How was your shoot?'

'I'm beat. Wrapped up a few minutes ago. How'd the calls go?'

'Do all care centres here necessarily run under the auspices of SIGNAL, the NHS, or any other government entity or charity?' I asked.

'I don't know, San … what's up?' she said, sounding a bit irked.

'Something about an entity I shortlisted. Bread Breakers'. I was just wondering about it.'

'Let's have a detailed update in the office tomorrow, San.'

~

2 March

I was sliding a Belgian waffle into the toaster next morning, when Nidhi appeared in a pair of Khaki trousers and her staple tunic. I hadn't gone out of my way to chitchat with the Sawants since my showdown with them in December. Nidhi, however, appeared to be in high jinks today.

'Hello, San!' she exclaimed cheerfully, pouring herself a cup of tea. 'What have you been up to lately?'

'Busy with LSE work. Student's life,' I mumbled.

My waffle popped out. I splattered some butter on it and sat down at the dining table. Asha, seated across me with a bowl of cereal, pointed at my plate and dropped her tongue out.

'You want some of it, don't you?' I chuckled. I broke off a piece of my waffle and placed it on Asha's plate. She crunched down on it gleefully.

'I saw you one evening last week … outside the Barbican Centre,' I told Nidhi. I had barely seen her at home since then.

Nidhi raised her brows. 'The Barbican?'

'Um, yeah. I thought I'd step up and say hi. But I guess I missed you. You were with a colleague or friend, I think. You were in a pink dress and a blue …'

A snort of laughter caught in Nidhi's breath. Asha looked up from her plate.

'A pink dress indeed! It must have been someone else, dear,' Nidhi warbled. 'I'm swamped with an honour crime case from Greenford. I've been shuttling between the office and the courtroom for the past couple weeks. I really haven't been anywhere else.'

Asha pointed towards my half-eaten waffle and gurgled again. I slid another waffle in the toaster for her.

What was Nidhi hiding?

5 March

At 1.35 p.m. on Monday, I got off at the Lambeth North station and squinted at a street map as I headed towards Hercules Road and passed through a caliginous tunnel. *Creepy place!*

I exhaled in relief when I reached a fenced garden on the other side of the tunnel.

A board wedged between the rails of the fence read 'Archbishop's Park'. I spent a few minutes puttering around in search of the elusive Royal Street, before stumbling upon a leafy residential boulevard peeking out from the far end.

As I approached the Bread Breakers' Community Residence, a pretty white ranch on a furlong of sprawling garden greeted my vision. I walked towards the wooden doors guiding the main entrance of the ranch. The reception area wore a dank look that one would expect to find in the foyer of a quiet old chapel. In the corner, a desk with a faded nameplate declared the presence of an Erica Hamilton who sat not far behind her name.

'Hello! I have an appointment with the communications director, Simon Webb.' I offered with a smile, gulping down the nervousness that surfaced from my recollection of how I had nearly blown my first campaign-related meeting with SIGNAL's Jeff Stuart, even when Keisha was around.

Erica pointed to a row of cushioned chairs lining the wall on both sides of the entryway. 'Have a seat. I'll let him know you're here.'

Before long, I was in a vinyl-floored office with Simon, an angular-featured and balding young man. His single-breasted tan suit looked strangely out of place against the backdrop of the minimalist décor of his cabin. I spoke about my affiliation with LSE, Keisha's work for the BBC, and the agenda of the Lionheart campaign.

'I didn't know that you and your friend work for the BBC,' Simon said when I was finished. 'Well, the programme does sound interesting. I think it'll do us well to be a part of it. It's heartening to know that a pretty young woman like you is steering such an initiative to help the less fortunate,' he added.

Pretty young woman. What an inappropriate thing for the communications director of a care home to say!

'Thanks,' I said aloud. 'Do you have a website? I couldn't find a web page for it online.'

'Our folks are still working on it,' he said with a cryptic laugh. 'What were you hoping to get from the website anyway?'

A guarded response to a perfectly casual question. The slight edginess in his voice made me stutter, 'I, uh, case studies … of people who've recovered, made some progress …'

'Recovered? This isn't a medical centre. We provide accommodation, support and care facilities for the mentally disabled. Our residents can never completely recover at any rate. But they *do* record progress in some areas.'

'Are you a private charity then?'

'Well, ahem, yes … that would be it. The charity sector in the UK is rather complex though.'

Something didn't sit right with me. The fidgeting, the indirect responses to my simple questions, the sharp retaliations to my innocuous statements, the vague mentions of scenarios that did not appear to fall in context with the subject of our discussion …

'The case studies then?' I pressed.

'We don't have case studies here,' Simon said dismissively. 'Sometimes, we publish testimonials in our publications and brochures if our residents grant us permission. In many cases, the residents are unable to take informed decisions. We do have a strict confidentiality policy.'

I nodded. Fair enough. 'If you agree to be part of our workshop, there's an option of signing up for our care home volunteer programme, which is longer-term.' I fumbled around in my bag and retrieved a printout. 'That's a snapshot of our volunteer programme.'

Simon read the overview with inexplicable interest. I wasn't sure if it was my imagination but he seemed visibly pale all of a sudden. He turned the page back and forth, as if expecting to find something more in it.

'You never told me SIGNAL was involved in it!'

'The care home volunteer initiative is optional for participating centres in our awareness campaign. We're enlisting SIGNAL's trainers to coach residents who need help. But SIGNAL isn't directly involved in the workshops. Right now, they're just funding our tour.'

'Very well, then. I'll give it some thought. Thanks for coming by,' Simon said briskly.

'My pleasure.'

As he escorted me to the reception area, I realised I hadn't relieved myself since that morning. I walked up to Erica at the reception desk and requested for the washroom.

'Down that corridor, to your left,' Erica said shortly.

I looked around me. There were two sets of doors on that side. 'Which one?' I asked, confused.

'Those blue double doors there.' Erica pointed at a set of doors closest to her.

I slid through the doors and walked down the ugly green linoleum floors, before waltzing through another set of blue doors ahead of me. I passed a set of rooms on my right, their doors bolted shut and numbered in sequence.

The door to one of the rooms was partially ajar.

The reflection of a woman's shadow on a set of translucent maroon curtains by the bedside ensnared my attention. From that shadow, it looked like the woman was moving her shoulders and elbows as if she were rocking something in her arms. I inched forward to get a better look. The woman had her back to me. The head of a baby peeped out from the crook of her arms.

She's feeding her child. Yet again, I longed for my mother's caressing touch. I heard a metallic screech from that room. I blinked back my tears and tried to focus. The shadows on the curtains had altered. Now, I could see the curve of a wheelchair enclosing the girth of the woman who seemed to be breastfeeding. The contours of another woman emerged on the curtain's reflection. The second woman swung the woman in the wheelchair around to a corner and dusted the bedcovers. My protesting bladder galvanised me towards the ladies' room.

I flopped down on to a rickety toilet seat in a claustrophobic stall. A fresh murmur of voices from a long time ago called out to me. As the voices became clearer, I recognised them as the ululating voices of my grieving family and friends surrounding a bier carrying the freshly bathed body of my deceased mother. The priest was chanting mantras. I clung to my brother, Sri and stared wide-eyed at the flowers … at the sacred ash on Mum's forehead … at the pristine white buds of cotton in her ears and nostrils.

Get out of here, a voice urged. I washed my hands, waved them under the dryer and shuffled out of the washroom. I exited the lobby and trooped down a small flight of steps that opened out to a cobblestoned pathway leading to the main gate. A cornucopia of flowers met my sight in a small garden, off to a side of the main lawn. Swirling concrete footpaths enclosed an open yard. One of these footpaths twirled in the direction of what appeared to be a shed.

A lithe chestnut-haired woman scurried towards the shed along a walkway that possibly emerged from a small passage meandering from a side exit in the main building. Something about the way she moved was chillingly familiar. A beam of realisation nearly knocked me off my feet. Rosie!

I spun on my heel and trotted through the lawns, pausing briefly outside the outhouse. No sign of Rosie now.

Something fishy is going on here.

I suspected that the ghosts of truth reposing behind these closed doors were the antithesis of an overt façade that met a gullible or untrained eye. I took a few steps forward until I stood before a large door reeking of peeling yellow paint. Holding my breath, I turned the brass door handle.

Suddenly, I torpedoed backwards through the air, over a high wall and onto the street beyond … straight into the blinking headlights of an oncoming truck.

~

The truck on the street passed me by just as I grabbed on to the wall when I flew over it.

I looked below me fearfully. A row of thorny shrubs waited to greet my fall. I recalled the sordid experience of tumbling into a bramble bush the same day Rosie had paid a visit home last November. *Serendipitous.* I tried to climb over the wall to the other side, but my arms were no match for the hard concrete of the wall above me – and the pull of gravity from below. After a few seconds of strenuous effort, I just hung from the wall and forced myself to keep my legs still. The lightest wiggle made me extremely precarious.

'Look at that poor li'l chick!' A man exclaimed from below in a horrified tone.

'Bloody 'ell, she's going to bust her arse if she falls in there,' another male voice cried out.

I *was* sure I would topple if I turned around to look at them.

'Help!' I squeaked, hoping they would hear me.

'Hey, you have that fishing rod on you?' the second voice called out to the first.

'Let me get to the car,' the first voice mumbled.

'Hola, just hang in there, all right?' the second passerby shouted out to me. 'Jack's going to be right back with his fishing rod.'

My arms were beginning to give way. Panic rose up my throat. It took every shred of will power to keep still.

The first guy, Jack, came back with his rod.

'This is going to hurt a little,' he yelled. 'But it's the only way we can help ya. Unless you have the Michelin Man pulling you up from the other side, of course!'

Then I felt a sharp stab on my butt. 'Owww!' I squealed.

'Pull yourself up, baby!' the second guy hollered. 'My friend is a six-foot-five giant who's standing on his toes with that fishing rod to reach ya.'

As Jack prodded me, I marshaled every ounce of strength in my arms until I got my chest near the ridge of the wall. Jack began jabbing the soles of my boots.

'Quit using your hands now!' the second bloke urged. 'Use your legs to climb over.'

Taking a deep breath, I swung my right leg. This time, I got my foot on to the ridge of the wall.

'Nearly there,' Jack encouraged. 'Sidle over with that leg!'

After much effort, I managed to drag my right leg over the ridge of the wall on to the other side.

'Thank you, fellas!' I called out.

'You're darn lucky we were out fishing today. Be safe, now!' The second guy said, before they walked away. I looked down below me. The height was daunting, but not too formidable for a five-foot-six person. I jumped off the wall and landed on all fours in the small garden. The thick material of my jeans and the soft Korean grass cushioned the blow of my fall.

A wheeze rode up my throat. I took deep breaths from my inhaler. When I felt better, I scrambled up and padded over to the shed, retrieving my shoulder bag from the ground.

The door to the shed was now slightly ajar. I scooted down to see what had thrown me up in the air like that. There was nothing down below. I pried the door open wide, stood on my toes and peered through the doorframe. I couldn't see much, but the door squeaked horribly. Malfunctioning extension springs. They must have jerked outward with a sudden blow, hurling me over the wall behind when I tried to yank open the door.

Aren't extension springs used for garage doors? I didn't find any safety cables for the creaking doors. Unraveling the mystery of the faulty springs would likely involve standing on a stepladder and surveying the spring connection on the rear door hanger – no mean task for a woman with a moderate mechanical aptitude like me. Nevertheless, a decrepit place with worn-out door springs that screamed of neglect was never a good sign. I swung the door open and walked in.

Several children dotted a spread of interlocking mats on the floor of a playroom, doodling on colouring books, scribbling on blackboards and slates or playing with toys. A toddler in a rocker was fiddling with her rattle. An older boy attempted to console a bawling baby in a potty chair. I quickly counted about twenty children of various races, the identifiable ones ranging from East European to Afro-Caribbean. Not a single one in this room looked older than five.

Wow. A separate place for special kids? Truth be told, I was mildly impressed.

Yet, a prickly sensation overrode my fleeting streak of fascination. The basis for that hunch struck me when I spotted a young child playing with an abacus. For starters, there was no adult supervision here. There was no overt indication that the little boy with the Abacus had any of the delayed milestones that one might expect of a developmentally challenged child in a care centre. While I didn't have the expertise to assess such a situation, it was fairly clear that nothing seemed peculiar about the other kids either. Many of the older ones were speaking in full, coherent sentences and playing board games. I walked up to the boy with the abacus.

'Hey,' I called out. 'I'm a friend of your Mama and Papa. I'm just having a look around.'

The boy looked at me queerly. 'I don't have no Pa,' he said.

'Oh, I'm sorry, sweetie,' I said gently. 'I'm a closer friend of your Mama. And you *do* have a Pa, too. Maybe you just haven't see him for a while.'

'I have a Pa?' the boy asked, wide-eyed. 'Then he mustn't like me very much 'coz he no see me for a loo-o-ng time.'

I was clueless about how I would handle his matter-of-fact statements.

I nodded eventually. 'You do.' My words sounded superficial and hollow, even to my ears.

The boy narrowed his eyes. 'How d'ya know? Who are you?'

'You can call me Sandy,' I said. 'What's your name, young man?'

'Jason.'

'Nice name. Friends?' I extended my hand.

'Friends!' Jason agreed as he smiled shyly and shook my hand.

'How old are you, Jason?'

'Dunno. Think I'm three.'

'You know where your Mama is?'

Jason thought for a while, then pointed towards the nursing home building, visible through a small window across from me.

I followed his gaze. 'Does your Mama work here?'

Again, Jason looked confused. First, he shook his head. Then he shrugged.

'Who takes care of you?'

Jason looked blank.

'Does your Mama take care of you?'

'Mama?' Jason echoed after a beat. 'Some peepul in jeans and skirts. They take care of all of us.'

'What happened to Mama?'

'She no here.'

'Then where is she?'

'There ...' Jason pointed towards the nursing home again.

By this time, a gaggle of kids had gathered around Jason and me. I turned to them with a smile. 'I'm Jason's friend. Jason was telling me about the people who take care of all of you.'

'It's not a nice place!' A tiny English girl shouted.

I knelt down beside her. 'Oh? Why is that, sweetie?'

'Sometimes, a fat lady called Ugo comes here a lot and beats me when I want ice-cream,' the girl said tearfully.

'We have other nicer ladies taking care of us,' another boy offered.

'Where are all your Mamas?' I asked all of them.

Many didn't answer. A few pointed towards the nursing home – just like Jason had.

'My Mama's in heaven,' a taller girl in a skirt said.

I went up to her and took her in my arms. 'I'm really sorry, little one. My Mama's in heaven too.'

I turned to the other children. 'But your Mamas are all there?' I asked, pointing towards the care home.

Some nodded, while others remained mute.

'Where are your homes?' I asked.

'This is where home is,' an older girl said quietly. 'But for me and other kids as old as me, it won't be for long.'

I stared at her. 'Why?'

'We'll be sent away somewhere else.'

'Where?'

The girl shrugged. 'Wish I knew. That's what happened to Ruth, Jamie and Claire.'

'What happened to them?'

'One day, they were all just gone. They were the oldest. I think no one above six is allowed to stay here,' she informed.

'What's your name? How old are you?'

'I'm Nancy. I hear I'm six.'

I froze and wondered what to do. Here were kids left to their own devices in the shed of a special needs care centre, unaware of their origins, birthdays, whereabouts and futures. A soft noise from outside snapped me out of my trance. I knew I couldn't take any chances in case someone came by.

'All right, dears. I'll be back soon,' I promised, hugging some of the kids clumsily.

I peeked outside the door. The coast seemed clear, so I stepped out. A bunch of fruits lay scattered haphazardly at the foot of a tree a few yards away. They must have created that sound when they tumbled down from the tree in the wind. I scampered through the gardens towards the massive white gates and slipped out.

—

A sublime rooftop view of the city met my gaze as I stepped on to the thirty-fifth floor of London Sky Garden, an hour later. After what I had just seen at Bread Breakers', the contrast of the landscaped garden bristling with tropical palms ahead of me was disquietingly palpable.

'Hey, beautiful! The Walkie-Talkie!' Nimmy grinned, spreading his arms to symbolise the expanse of the enlarged glass dome building. 'I love that dress,' he added.

I shyly glanced down at the fitted, maroon scoop neck dress I had changed into in the ladies' room of a bar near London Bridge station while on my way here from Bread Breakers'. The sparkly evening outfit accentuated my décolletage.

Nimmy pulled me towards a terrace sloping down with cycads, African lilies, rosemary and French lavender flowers. Then he kissed me passionately and trailed his lips all the way down my throat. 'I want to do you right now,' he murmured into the cleft between my breasts.

'Oh, Nimmy …' I cleaved to him, the man who had helped me rise above my past – onwards and upwards. I may not have ever recovered from Saahil's death if it hadn't been for him …

Nimmy stroked my arm. 'Come on! Dinner in the sky! You're going to love this.'

We rode another floor up to a pod-like structure, which opened out to Darwin's Brasserie through a panoramic walkway. A trendy restaurant simmering with ornate wood, burnished leather, and saffron-gold sunshine filtering through its regal, floor-to-ceiling windows. Nimmy guided me towards a Scandi wood table by a window, which offered a view of the Thames.

'I feel so lucky,' I whispered, clasping his hands in mine.

He responded with a childlike smile, which melted my heart.

We sipped Sauvignon Blanc and gazed outside the window in comfortable silence for a while, watching the sun sink into the horizon as it cast its pink and orange glow across a blanket of cornsilk clouds.

The food was sumptuous – English asparagus, Yorkshire fettle and marinated olives, and a main course of roasted sea trout and fresh herb gnocchi with truffle and Parmesan fries on the side.

For a change, Nimmy and I steered clear of heavy or intense topics, including those concerning Asha. As we ate, I forgot all about my visit to Bread Breakers' and my grief over losing my mother.

The intimate, romantic dinner and our bouncy, free-flowing conversation culminated into a night of passion in my bed. As daybreak descended, I gently urged Nimmy back to his room.

After he left, the lightness of energy in my being evaporated. I found myself wondering what those kids at Bread Breakers' had meant when they indicated their mothers were in the care home. Not all their mothers were support workers or members of staff … were they?

A distorted image of the breastfeeding woman on the wheelchair played on my mind again. Perhaps, there was a way to find out what was going on there.

By the time I awoke next morning, I knew what I had to do. I hoped Keisha would be equally convinced.

6
The Hotbed

7 March

'What if I'm playing with fire?' I asked myself.

You're not, a voice said from within.

'How so?'

Those children need help, the voice reminded.

'Maybe there's nothing to it, after all. And I could get into big trouble,' I challenged the voice.

Do you want to choose selfishness when a bunch of children may be in trouble?

The second thoughts I was having about my plan dissipated by the time LooSE TV's president Mark Leatherby ushered me into the network's office in LSE's east building. He slid a sleek, black pen cap to me across the desk. I studied it curiously.

Mark laughed at my apparent naiveté. 'It's a pocket spy cam. It's got a 4 GB SD chip. Clip it to the pocket of your trousers, and it'll look like you've slid a pen in there. When you're done recording, all you do is plug it into a computer like any normal USB stick. What's the story behind not using a regular HD or video-cam?'

'I suspect something unusual is going on in a care centre here, and I'm honestly scared … but I really want to investigate it. I can't say more since it's related to some work I'm doing for a BBC producer ...'

But that was definitely not something Keisha had wanted me to do.

'Good heavens, San! You've got to be crazy!' She had cried when I shared my idea with her after noting that something didn't seem right about Bread Breakers'. 'You've only been a newscaster! You don't have any production experience and the BBC certainly isn't going to commission you to undertake something like this. Even experienced producers have got to do boatloads to win the trust of the commissioning team. If you *do* develop a concept plan, design a cost budget, enlist your resources and put forward your bonafides, they're going to think you haven't the slightest bit of experience, San. Do you understand what I'm even talking about?'

'We could mull over a news feature,' I suggested.

'That's not possible, San. This sounds like an exposé. I would much rather have it out as a documentary. Have you heard of *Newsnight* or *Panorama*?'

'Yes.'

'How the hell do you think you will handle it?' Keisha fumed. 'You're wasting your time with this investigative bullshit. The BBC folks would probably put their own in-house team on the chase, if they even decide there's a story in it. You're better off going to the police about it. But even that may be a stretch until you provide some hard evidence.'

The vehemence with which Keisha questioned my experience and investigative skills affronted me.

'Let's do it this way. I'd like to go undercover and find out,' I shot back heatedly. 'There may be something, or there may be nothing at all. Either way, I'll feel at peace for having tried. Something's going on, which I think is unusual and possibly harmful. You've got to give me a chance. I'll hand my film over to you when I'm done, and you can decide what you'd like to do with it.'

Keisha sighed. 'All right, San. Do what you have to. For heaven's sake, just don't get into trouble.'

'The film is top secret until I have a say-so,' I told Mark now. 'Is it illegal to use a hidden cam to …?'

'Not in journalism or the law,' Mark cut in. 'You said you were doing it for the BBC.'

Since I wasn't doing it for the BBC, I had no legal protection. I wasn't even sure how the data protection laws worked in the UK. Of course, I couldn't share those thoughts with Mark.

'On a freelance basis,' I gabbled. 'But … '

'Well, in that case, you should be good so long as you're not capturing activities that are exceedingly private,' Mark intoned. 'Reading up on national voyeurism laws will be incredibly helpful. I'm not suggesting you're a peeping tom, but you want to keep your guard up, y'know? You don't want a hamper of legal bullshit slapping you in the tush 'cause you stumbled upon something unintentionally … see what I mean?'

I nodded. 'Thanks, Mark.'

'By the way, any news on the CEO interview for Career Q&A?' Mark inquired.

'I've been after EGG's PR agency – no bites yet.'

8 March

I re-adjusted the scarf over my curly blonde wig and handed the receptionist, Erica, my business card at the Bread Breakers' Community Residence. It read:

Maya Farmah,

Nursing Sciences Professional,
25, Cumberland Close,
Amersham, HP7 9NH

It listed a mobile number that had once belonged to Nimmy.

With my complexion and heavy makeup, I could easily pass for an English country girl. I had borrowed the wig from LooSE TV's Joey, who was a theatre junkie. I also wore cheap blue contact lenses, thick powerless eyeglasses and a hideous overall over a sloppy old cardigan and a pair of grey jeans. The cardigan belonged to Nimmy. He had last worn it two nights ago and tossed it into the laundry basket in my bedroom before we made love. Afterwards, we had had a heated argument, too. 'You seemed too frozen this time. You're not bored of me, are you?' he asked when we lay spent.

I sighed. 'Just a little preoccupied. And still recovering from Saahil's death.'

Nimmy propped up an elbow on bed. 'Are you in this relationship out of guilt or obligation?'

'Where did that come from? How do you define guilt anyway?'

'Guilt is a necessary emotion, isn't it?'

I disagreed. I went on to share my own definition of guilt and mentioned that I believed instead in Carl Rogers' notion of self-actualization. Nimmy flew off the handle, then.

'Are you citing personality psychologists when I'm the one who has seen, first-hand, all that Asha is going through?' he fumed.

And there he was, bringing Asha up again. *Again.*

'I'm sorry,' I mumbled, hoping to make peace.

He stormed out of my room, slamming the door behind him. I hadn't really spoken much to him after that. And I don't think he was aware that I was wearing his cardigan now as part of this queer ensemble that completed the identity of an out-of-work mental health nurse hopeful.

The unpredictability of what set him off saddened me. I took in a deep breath, now.

Focus, Sandy. Focus on the task at hand.

Erica looked up at me. 'Whataya here for?'

I produced a copy of a fake CV I had crafted the night before.

'I'm Maya Farmah,' I said in a low-pitched Liverpudlian scouse accent that I hoped was different from my own high-pitched voice and my mixed Queen's English-Mumbai accent. 'I'm outta work and I ain't no place to stay. I'm wonderin' if I can find work here. There's my CV.'

Erica looked cross. 'We didn't have any job listings online. For chrissake, we don't even have a bleeding web page. How in hell did you find us?'

'I wouldn't know 'coz I don' have access to the innernet. I'm a friend of Ugo, the support worker who works 'ere,' I said. 'You always need more hands 'round 'ere, she said.'

Erica looked puzzled. 'Ugo said nothin' about it to no one,' she said. 'Anyway, you run along and wait on those chairs there. I'll check with Ugo first and have our manager see if anyone here wants to have anything to do with you.'

I shuffled my weight. 'Could I use the loo, please?' I pleaded. 'I haf come a long way. From Merseyside. I hafn't haf a chance to …'

Erica raised her eyebrows suspiciously. 'This card of yours says you live in Amersham?'

I nearly kicked myself for being so stupid. 'I do,' I said. 'I'm originally from Liverpool, though. I vent to Merseyside to visit ma' ailin' motha and I'm just vack from there now.' I shifted my weight again and planted a hand over my stomach. 'If you don' mind?'

Erica snorted. 'Don't embarrass yourself further, lady. Over there.'

She pointed to the double doors on her left.

I walked past those doors and across the long linoleum corridor before stopping outside the door to the room where I had seen those mystifying shadows during my last visit. I knocked gently. There was no response. I turned the doorknob. It was locked. Was it locked from within or from the outside? Remembering a little trick I had once seen in a Hollywood movie, I whipped out a debit card from my wallet, then hesitated momentarily. I might be on a wild goose chase and I wasn't sure if I would be prosecuted for breaking into a room. Reminding myself of the trouble I had taken to get here, I wiggled my card through the vertical crack between the door and its frame. Tilting my card towards the doorknob, I threw all my weight against the door and bent the card the other way, hoping to force the lock backwards. The door popped open.

'Ow!' I yowled when I tripped over myself and tumbled in.

I looked around me quickly. A single cot with a rumpled white duvet. Translucent maroon curtains gathered to one side of a pelmet halfway across the room. A wooden desk that held a half-eaten bowl of soup on a food tray. A few stuffed toys peering out from a tuck box in a corner. Open shelves bursting with wads of unfolded clothing. A wheelchair folded up in the space between the shelves and a set of white cabinets.

'Hi!' A high-pitched childlike voice greeted me from the bedside. A tiny wan face poked out from the duvet. Mostly Caucasian features. I fixed my gaze on the mildly depressed nasal bridge between her wide-set brown eyes.

I was startled at how young she looked. Not more than eighteen, I surmised. There was no sign of the baby I had seen her breastfeed – if it had indeed been her – a few days ago. 'Hello …' I said softly.

The girl twirled the edge of her pink smock, looked at me intently and giggled. Her behaviour confirmed my suspicions. This woman was mentally challenged.

'I'm sorry to barge in on you. What's your name?'

The girl cocked her head and began picking her nose.

'Nila,' she said finally. I detected a faint British overlay to an accent that could have otherwise been East European.

'I'm Sandy,' I said, extending my hand for a shake. 'I'm here to help you, Nila.'

The girl stared at me. Then she looked outside the window and began picking her nose again. I laid a gentle hand on her shoulder. Nila turned back to face me. I made a cradle with my arms and rocked back and forth. 'Baby?' I mouthed. 'Is that your baby?' I pointed a finger towards her to gesticulate what I was saying.

Nila stared perplexedly. My cradling action seemed to have jolted her in some way. She placed a palm upon her breast and bawled at the top of her lungs. 'My baby, my baby!'

Something about the intensity of the pain and bewilderment in her screams made me believe that the baby was indeed really hers. Flashbacks of my conversation with the children in the playroom, during my visit on Monday, raided my senses. Many had claimed their mothers were in the care home although they didn't work there. I had to get to that playroom next. And fast. Just as I turned to leave, I noticed a few nasty bruises on Nila's arm. They looked fresh.

'How did you get hurt?' I inquired gently, pointing to the contusions on her arm.

Nila continued wailing. I heard a patter of footsteps approaching the door.

'That kid is howlin' her lungs out!' A voice grumbled from a distance.

'Perhaps that whore is in there …' another voice replied back, sounding much closer now. 'Maya Farmer. A nurse who wants a job – indeed!'

A sardonic bark of laughter followed. 'She's spyin' on us!'

My heart flip-flopped. They were already after me.

'Didn't you lock that bloody door then?' the first voice demanded. 'How can anyone get the fok in when you locked the foking door?'

'Sweet Jesus, I did!' the second voice humphed in puzzlement.

I leaped up to the bedside across Nila and raised the window ledge with considerable difficulty. As Nila stared at me, I hastily scrambled over and jumped out of the window. I landed on all fours on a patch of grass outside, just in time to hear two support workers barrel in.

'A pathetic cretin, that one! Cryin' for her sodden baby,' the first worker commented.

'What she needs is a good whack is all. And we need to spruce her up in time for Mr Pedal Pushers,' the other clucked. Her colleague laughed.

'We got to keep her quiet when he gets 'is leg over with 'er. 100 mg of chlorpromazine,' the first worker barked.

A few seconds elapsed before I heard Nila scream again. This time, her wispy childlike voice sounded inhumanly feral with anger and pain. I shuddered on the ground below. Was it some kind of a tranquiliser? Was it even recommended for her? And I didn't quite understand the slang, 'when he gets his leg over her'. Or maybe … I did. I stood rooted to my spot until I heard a squawk from above.

'That window is open! Reckon that 'ore jumped out through it! Get on 'ere, fast!'

I took off, darting madly through clumps of wild bush ahead of me. I scampered down a crooked cobblestoned pathway that led away from the side door. The pathway opened out to the flower garden where I spotted the playroom-shed a few yards ahead. Hoping it wasn't locked, I dashed towards the shed and thrust open the door, careful, this time, of the malfunctioning springs. I shut the door behind me and exhaled.

There seemed to be fewer children in the playroom than there had been on Monday. The baby girl I had seen on the potty chair last time was still on it now, gurgling and playing with her long, golden hair. I recognised the faces of a few other children I had seen or spoken to on Monday. I walked up to Jason, who was fiddling with his Abacus in a corner.

'Hey!' I greeted. 'I'm back to see you. Do you remember me?'

'Hi!' Jason jumped up and wound his skinny arms around my waist.

'She's here!' I recognised the excited squeal as the voice of the petite British girl who had declared she didn't like it here.

Several kids gathered around me as I knelt down, ferreted in my tote-bag and handed them all the little knickknacks I had bought – a few dolls, a Pictionary game set, some stuffed toys, a new colouring book, a pack of crayons, a box of chocolates, a set of fresh chalk pieces, a duster for the blackboard, and a couple of fairytale books.

'You must share these among yourselves,' I told them. If only I could have afforded to get more.

'That's more than we've got in two years!' a pale red-haired boy exclaimed delightedly.

I cleared my throat. 'All right. I would like to see your mamas.'

It broke my heart to be so cut and dry with them. But time was limited and I had to record their words on the spy cam clipped carefully to my Jeans pocket and concealed by my overalls.

'We already told you!' Jason cried in unison with the Hungarian girl I remembered from my last visit. 'Mama is in that place over there. That home,' Jason pointed once again to the care home.

The Hungarian girl wailed, 'My Mama's dead!'

I went up to her. 'What's your name, love?'

'Sandra.'

'What happened to your Mama?'

Sandra hiccupped and began sobbing. A boy, who looked to be about five, slung his arm around Sandra's shoulders and spoke on her behalf. 'They killed her.'

In spite of myself, my blood froze. 'Who killed her Mama?'

'Some big, bad men,' Sandra said tearfully.

'How do you know?' I probed.

'I saw!' Sandra cried. 'Winny and I saw.'

'Winny?'

'That's me,' the boy next to her said. 'I'm Winston.'

I turned to him. 'What did you see, Winny?'

Winston blinked at me, mortified. I ruffled his hair and gave him a light peck on his cheek. 'Don't be afraid,' I said kindly. 'I'm here to help all of you.'

'They put a knife in her pee thing, them bad men,' Sandra said in a broken voice. 'They kept on doing it. And there was blood and more blood, but they were laffing. And they kept on doing it.'

'They were on top of 'er,' Winston said.

I tried to make sense of what they were saying. 'Pee thing?' I said finally.

'This.' Sandra placed a hand on her crotch.

A fresh jolt of shock ran through my system.

Don't throw up now. Be strong for these kids, San, don't mess this up, I warned myself.

Swallowing my revulsion, I gently lifted Sandra's hand away from her crotch and held it in mine. 'Where did you see them doing this?' I choked out.

'There.' Sandra pointed somewhere towards the wild clump of bushes near the pathway I had just passed to get here. 'Winny and I went outside to play … and we saw.'

I hugged Sandra and Winston silently.

'We're never let outside. We're just locked in all day,' another girl mentioned. I remembered her as Nancy, the oldest-looking child in this room.

'The door wasn't locked when I came in today,' I said. 'And on Monday too.'

'They always lock us!' a stray boy yelled angrily. 'The door lock has not been working for some few days now. So they left it like that. But if we goes out, someone always catches us and smacks us.'

I had to marshal the strength to save these poor little souls from the malaise of a care home that was not only ill-treating them but also raping and abusing its mentally challenged female occupants – some of whom had borne these kids. Were those women forced to have sex with several people?

Nancy interrupted my thoughts. 'We're afraid …'

'Please help us,' Jason corroborated, his voice cracking.

'I will,' I said quietly.

A grating female voice from outside reverberated through the air, growing louder with the rhythm of accompanying footsteps. 'What the heck is going on in there? If it's that kid who's gone potty again, I'LL KILL ALL OF YOU!'

I hastily disengaged from the children.

'Run away! She's back,' cried a little girl who had never spoken to me before.

I looked around me wildly. The glass window was tightly locked and grilled. There was no way I could jump out through it like I had done in Nila's room. I darted over to a line of cupboards across the room. Alas, they all had shelves in between, so I couldn't squeeze in.

I spotted an overflowing toy chest a few feet away. I pried it open, tossed an armful of toys on to the floor and scrambled inside. My knees, scraped during my fall from Nila's window, grazed a bed of dolls, broken cars and board games. I brought one of my knuckles to my mouth to keep from yelping in pain.

I heard the woman enter the room with a big brouhaha. I pulled the lid shut over my head as quietly as I could, keeping it open just a quarter of an inch. A wheeze rambled up my throat. I fought the urge to cough. Hiding in closed or low-oxygen spaces had always been out of bounds for me. I yanked out my inhaler and took a sharp intake of breath. Then I unclipped my spy cam, raised it to eye level and peered through the tiny crack between the lid and the rim of the toy chest, hoping to video-record what was happening. The backside of a corpulent African woman in a white ankle-length skirt loomed ahead of me.

'Why are the whole lots of yous makin' so much noise today? And what's all these toys doing 'ere lyin' around?' she bellowed, trudging in my direction. My heart pounded furiously. Just as she reached out to raise the lid of the trunk, Nancy stepped before her.

'Don't put the toys inside yet,' she cried. 'We want to mend these broken dolls. That's why we took them out.' The little girl picked up a one-legged Barbie from the floor. A resounding slap reached my ears. I cringed. Nancy had fallen to the ground. Helpless, I forced myself to stay still. Nancy was holding her stinging cheek. The woman yanked a handful of her wispy golden hair and hauled her up. Poor Nancy squealed in pain.

'Where's the other leg then?' the woman demanded, closing her hands around Nancy's frail throat. 'You nasty harlot! I'll teach you to lie to me!'

Nancy's eyes bulged as the woman pressed her fingers harder against her throat.

A few kids began to cry. Some hurled themselves at the woman and tried to bite her. The old dame swung her arm wildly with her free hand, knocking the angry children to the ground. She released her hold on Nancy only when the little girl's eyes began to roll backwards.

'That'll make yous remember what'll happen if yous lie again!' she growled.

Nancy slid to the ground, gasping and coughing painfully. A wisp of a kid trying to protect me and getting banged up for it.

'I want Mama. I don't know what you did to her. I want Mama!' Nancy wailed in a broken voice. A group of kids helped her up.

I re-clipped the spy cam to my jeans pocket and swiped away my tears. I found an old Halloween mask and a boomerang when I dug around in the toy chest. I slipped the mask over my face, rearranged the scarf around my head and jumped out of the box.

Flexing my foot, I raised my leg, leaned backwards and landed a well-aimed kick at the woman's butt. She stumbled forward a few feet from the impact of my boot, then whirled around to face me. I hurled the boomerang at her and fled to the door. The tool hit her on the shoulder and flew back towards me, landing somewhere near my feet. She jerked backwards with an angry roar.

'Dare you touch any of these kids again and I'll have you in a trice. Or the police and social services will!' I cried.

With a bark of fury, the woman began to charge at me. No matter how frightened and guilty I was to leave these kids behind with a wretch like her, I took off on my heels. The woman gave me chase. As I raced across the lawns, I thought about running to the main gate, but believed that she might hunt me down the street too. Just as I approached the front-side gravel that led to the gate, I deflected rapidly to a narrow alleyway on my right. The alleyway snaked through a backside porch. The woman's overblown girth was no match for my lithe build. She lost me somewhere during the time I made the swift turn. I juddered to a halt and looked around. I was in an entirely new area lying north of the main vestibule and the care home out front.

Ahead of me was a quadrangle strewn with dead leaves. A wooden bench and table stood under the shade of a gnarled tree. A pathway before me led to a wooden backdoor. An overflowing trashcan and a crate of boxes stood haphazardly beside it. On either side of those boxes was a glass window about eight feet from the ground.

My suspicion and horror got the better of me. I tiptoed towards the door and attempted to turn the handle. It seemed to be locked from inside. The crate of boxes looked sturdy enough to bear my 128-pound frame. I gingerly placed a foot on the crate. It didn't seem to give way. I climbed up on it stealthily and leaned over sideways to peep in through the window on my left. Both windows were closed. Through the glass, I strained my eyes to trace the contours of some hazy objects, which indicated that the room I was viewing, might be a consulting office or clinic. There was a small, empty waiting area outside a curtained partition that I presumed was a doctor's cabin. The door to the cabin was open. A narrow corridor in the far corner led up to a room shielded by a screened divider below a flaking board marked with a word I identified as 'Surge'. 'Surgery' was more like it; the last two letter stencils seemed to be missing.

I was just about to step down when a lurking image on the cabin's doorsill arrested my attention: the shadow of a tall woman holding on to the bar of something that looked like a pushchair. When the source of that shadow materialised from the recesses of the consulting cabin, I nearly toppled over the boxes I stood on. The biggest shock had arrived. It was inconceivable.

Shailaja emerged from the cabin, pushing a pale and tear-streaked Asha on her pram. A tall man in a lab coat followed them towards the door. What in Pete's name were they doing here of all places?

I realised Shailaja would see me spying on them as soon as she stepped out. She might not instantly recognise me as Sandy, but she would certainly make out Nimmy's cardigan. They would be out of that door in seconds. I had no time to scoot. My eyes darted wildly around me scanning for a place where I could hide. I climbed down from the boxes I stood on as swiftly and gracefully as I could. I shuffled a large box in front of me and crouched as low as I could, behind it. The door swung open.

'It'll be all right, little one,' The doctor said, patting Asha's head gently. Then he straightened himself and looked at Shailaja. His angular features and Aryan complexion indicated a Persian or Iranian ethnicity. 'Having to manage her periods will soon be a thing of the past. And a pap smear won't have major side effects,' he assured. 'There may be a …'

A call on his cell phone interrupted him. He answered it with a frown. 'Simon, I'm just seeing a patient off now. I'll call you back.' His expression changed. 'A blonde with thick glasses, and a woman in a Halloween mask?' he exclaimed, raising an index finger to excuse himself. 'All right. I haven't seen anyone like either of them but I'll certainly keep my eyes peeled now.'

My stomach sank. Obviously Erica and that monster of a woman in the playhouse-shed were alerting everyone on the premises. I had had many narrow escapes today and I was afraid I had pushed my luck just about as far as I could.

'Pardon me, Mrs Sawant,' the doctor apologised, reappearing at the door. 'As I was saying …' he paused, as if he didn't remember where he had left off. Then, he continued, '… there may be a slight stretch of spotting for a day or two. But that's hardly anything to worry about. I'll call you with the results in three days.'

'Thanks, Dr Tahseen,' Shailaja said. 'I'll confirm the dates for the hysterectomy.' I detected a tinge of hesitation in her voice, 'It's not just her menstrual hygiene, you know. That incident two years ago …' She swallowed with considerable difficulty and went on, '… was a nightmare for all of us. I really don't want a repeat in the future. I'm afraid it will …'

'We've discussed this before. We'll have all of it out,' Dr Tahseen smiled crisply. 'Take care.' The door closed behind them.

A hysterectomy? A distant memory came flooding back to me.

An ex-colleague in Mumbai had once mentioned that his aunt had undergone a hysterectomy after being diagnosed with ovarian cancer. The colleague had mentioned that his aunt wasn't planning on having more kids anyway. Were they considering a hysterectomy for Asha because she had some form of cancer? I shook my head. That didn't make any sense. If Asha had developed a cancerous cyst or fibroid, Shailaja would have taken her to the NHS or another reputed private hospital. No, this had something to do with whatever happened two years ago. What was it?

Shailaja walked past me, then paused to retrieve a juice carton from Asha's pram. She fixed a straw and held the Tetra Pak to Asha's lips. For a moment, she looked anguished. But that look was gone almost as soon as it appeared. Asha was gurgling from the straw. Shailaja pushed Asha along in her stroller until the pair camouflaged into the paddock of the main lawns around the corner. A paroxysm of claustrophobia was fast scaling my solar plexus, accompanied by its allegiant friends: the dreadful wheeze and a loud sob that threatened to wrench my gut. I uncoiled myself from my crouching position and took a few deep breaths from my inhaler, wondering if the doctor would reappear and search around the yard for 'the blonde with thick glasses' or 'the lady with the Halloween mask'.

The door did not open. I slung my bag over my shoulder and sprinted across the quadrangle towards the lawns. I heard angry voices behind me as I ran. I didn't dare look behind. At the gates, I fumbled for the latch and tumbled out onto the street. As I dived into the dark tunnel towards Hercules Road, my mind began to absorb the implications of every word Shailaja and the doctor had exchanged while poor Asha lay sobbing in her pram.

The Lambeth North tube station loomed ahead of me. A tall grey façade of the Christ and Uptown Church stood to my right, its cone-shaped turret shimmering in the effulgence of the mid-day sunshine. I blindly traipsed over to the church, flung myself on to one of its cold stone steps and nestled my forehead against the balls of my palms.

A steady stream of recollections from the Sawant household spilled into my mind, along with random spotlights on the behavioural patterns each Sawant member had manifested.

The Sawants' dogmatic adherence to taboos … the raging protests they had staged when I wanted Asha to participate in Streetsmart … Nimmy's frightful sensitivity to any matter concerning Asha … Rosie's eerie visit, Nidhi's hard-hearted response to Rosie's entreaties and Asha's subsequent disappearance … Asha's claim that Rosie was a bad sign … Ashok Sawant's apparent lack of involvement in situations or chores that revolved around Asha …

At twenty-two, she was a pretty woman. She may have been pregnant two years ago and had an abortion. And the Sawants, in their anxiety to preserve their honour, wanted to now sterilise her, without her knowledge or consent, so that she would never again be with child. That was the only plausible line of reasoning against the backdrop of the schema I had mapped out in my mind.

And then, a distant memory, from my early days with the Sawants swept ashore. A haunting image of Asha crying out to feed Sunny milk, the night she had a seizure. That scene seemed to fit with the ease and pulchritude of a stray bead that completed the link in a chain of concatenating events and responses. Maybe Sunny wasn't a hallucination. Maybe Asha hadn't even had an abortion. The possibility struck me with the force of a gavel in a courtroom. If my hypothesis was right, Sunil wasn't Jyoti's son as everyone had made him out to be. He was Asha's.

7
The Tram Tunnel

Keisha was rather quiet after she viewed my ninety-three minute video in stricken silence.

'I didn't expect this,' she said finally. We were seated on wooden benches facing each other across an adjoining table in the BBC Media Village gardens. My spy cam peered out from a USB port on Keisha's MacBook.

'This video clearly unleashes the abuse going on there … and raises many more questions. This looks like an exposé, but we'll have to investigate it further,' Keisha added. She transferred the film to a fresh folder on her laptop and made a backup copy on a 16 GB SanDisk Connect flash drive dangling from a red text-label keychain. She scribbled 'High Priority' on the keychain label and ran an encryption code for both folders.

'Is the encryption necessary?' I asked.

'Yes. This is highly sensitive information and I want to keep the film extremely safe,' Keisha replied. 'I don't want you talking about this to anyone under any circumstances until I say you can. D'you hear?'

'You're the boss, Kiki,' I said simply. 'There's the proof now. Whatever I could manage.'

Keisha looked me in the eye. 'I don't know how you managed to get hold of this on your own, but it's a jolly brilliant job, San,' she said sincerely. 'I'll get this out to our team at the earliest. They'll probably want to investigate it further and slot it in the current affairs segment. I'll talk to Alfred about hiring you as a paid production intern once you graduate. We'll have the police raid that care home once the story is out. But that will take at least a few more weeks.'

'Do … do we really need to let the abuse go on while we wait to do an exposé? Can't we inform the police right away?' I spluttered.

Keisha laughed. 'You really *are* a newbie, aren't you? How can we get more materials for an exposé if we have the police step in, right away?'

'But … a few more weeks?' I squeaked. 'What if some children and residents are traumatised so badly that they die by then?'

Keisha shoved her Mac into its case and sighed. 'I know, San. But journalism is what it is. Sometimes, there's no room for emotion. A lot of ungodly incidents like the Kabbalah Centre Scam or the Israeli Attack on the USS Liberty reached the public only through media-driven exposés, not through the police or not-for-profits or social activists. To do that kind of work, you've got to be thick-skinned and cold-blooded. That's something that'll grow on you with experience.' She rose from the bench. 'I have to leave now. We're wrapping up a high-pressure production. Go home and run a warm bath. You look like shit.'

As I walked out of the BBC complex, my mind spun with memories of the West Harrow police's lackadaisical approach to the Sawants' report of Asha's disappearance the day Rosie had visited. I sighed. Keisha was right. Tipping the police off would not only have a bearing on our own investigation but also be substantially less impactful than the potential long-term benefits of running a bone-shattering exposé. Those residents and children would have to brave it until our story raked public attention.

I bought a sandwich from a confectionary store at the White City Underground. I ate while waiting on the platform for the tube, mindlessly sifting through a horde of emails on my phone. Committee meeting reminders from Lanong, a midterm report brief from Mark, a conference invite … something jumped out at me from the muddle … oh, wait … I wasn't sure I had seen it right. I squinted into my phone and zoomed in the text. It was a note from Aiden McLeod all right!

I headed to LSE. Dissolving into the whorls of its scholarly lair was just what I needed right now. After what I had just discovered, I couldn't have stomached returning to the Sawants'. In the offices on campus, Mark was logging videos as he did most Thursdays. 'The spy cam was a godsend,' I greeted, returning the gadget to him.

Mark pulled at one of his sideburns and grinned. 'I'm glad it helped.'

'EGG's Lord Bradshaw has finally agreed to a fifteen-minute interview with me, thanks to Aiden McLeod!' I burst out. 'It's on Twenty-eight March. 10 a.m.'

'Kudos, Sandy!' Mark came around to my side and thumped my shoulder in exultation.

'Aiden has already asked for a briefing document,' I informed. 'So, I'll put together an interview guide.'

'Sounds good.'

It was nearly 7.30 p.m. when I swiped my card at the turnstiles in the LSE library and lumbered through a sloping corridor to the third floor. A voice boomed out at me from behind.

'Ahoy there, San! Haven't seen ya 'round in yonks. An all-nighter for those horrid papers, eh?'

I turned around to find Ritchie. This time, he wore spiked hair with faint blue highlights. His felt-brown trench coat rumpled a little around his shoulders under the weight of his enormous bag. 'You're beginning to sound quite English. What the devil have you done to your hair?' I exclaimed, despite myself.

Ritchie flashed a grin. 'A new style I'm experimenting with. How've you been?'

An incomprehensible cloud of comfort evolved in his presence, enveloping me in its snug entirety. 'I'm not feeling that great today,' I admitted, as we headed upstairs.

'Out to solve a mystery and such, Wonder Woman?' Ritchie chortled amusedly.

'Something like that,' I said wryly.

We found adjacent carrels on the third floor. 'So, what's up?' Ritchie asked seriously.

As I gazed into his eyes, something stirred in me enough to kindle a desire to open up to him.

In hushed whispers I told Ritchie everything, right from my work for Lionheart and the Streetsmart TV show, to the events that had unfolded at Bread Breakers'. I left out my return to the care home as an undercover videographer, since Keisha had warned me against mentioning it.

I spilled out details of my volatile relationship with Nimmy as I recalled our argument over his question about whether I was with him out of guilt or obligation. Finally, I admitted how perplexed I was at the prospect of facing the Sawants now and deciding what to do.

Somewhere along the way, the dam my defenses had carefully cobbled up burst open and I was sobbing hard by the time I finished.

'I can understand it's been a lot for you,' Ritchie said after a spell of silence. 'For the moment, let's keep aside your campaign work and take a better look at you. How can you let yourself in for that kind of behaviour from Nimmy?'

'I slept with him, Ritch.'

'So he owns you now?'

I sighed. He had a point.

'You're here to do what you believe in, as long as you're mindin' your own business or helpin' others rather than harmin' them,' Ritchie went on. 'And this time, I'm afraid you're only hurtin' yourself.'

Subconsciously, I knew I would be a fool not to trust Ritchie's judgement. But the love and affection I had developed for Nimmy and Asha were hard to let dissipate. And what was happening with Asha now would only complicate matters further.

'About what happened this afternoon, it sounds like this care centre has a surgery clinic that illegally sterilises their female residents. For the life of me, I can't imagine how your host family got involved in it,' Ritchie said quietly.

'You think so?'

'I think there's actually more to it than that, San. What are those kids doing in the shed of a home for the mentally challenged?'

I hadn't thought that the answer to that question might have anything to do with how the Sawants were entangled with them. 'I don't know what you're getting at,' I snapped.

'Think for yourself, San,' Ritchie said. 'It sounds like you stumbled upon a dangerous mystery. And now that you have, you need to be three steps ahead of your antagonists.'

I smiled weakly. 'You sound like you're plotting a film.'

'I'll leave you to chew on it for a while, then.'

As Ritchie turned back to his computer screen, I harked back to the events of that afternoon. Indications from many children in the playroom-shed pointed to the possibility that their mothers weren't support workers who left their children in the play area during their work shifts. And the mother of that Hungarian girl, had most certainly been raped and murdered. I recalled my brief interaction with Nila and her screams as the support workers stormed in, gave her an injection and joked about getting her ready for a Mr Pedal Pushers. The sequence of events I had seen began to yield the contours of a horrifying but plausible image. Were many Bread Breakers' residents the mothers of the children in that shed? If my hunch was correct, there was a story behind their pregnancies: a cold-blooded tale of sexual abuse and exploitation.

But my mind drew a blank. I couldn't think further.

I signed into my LSE terminal and launched Google Chrome. What was that tranquiliser the support workers had given Nila? Was it 'chlorophomazin'? I typed out the word in the search tab. Numerous results turned up for chlorpromazine.

An anti-psychotic drug prescribed mostly to treat symptoms of schizophrenia. But Nila had hardly seemed psychotic or schizophrenic. She was just a few years behind her biological age. Why the hell were they giving her chlorpromazine?

I opened a new window and researched on hysterectomy. What did Dr Tahseen mean when he told Shailaja they would have "*all of it out*"? Given that Shailaja had mentioned the hassle of maintaining Asha's menstrual hygiene, it was likely that they were considering removing her uterus, ovaries and fallopian tubes. An irreversible process that had indelible long-term health effects. Recommended for intractable medical conditions, only if no other treatment options were available.

An email from an unfamiliar address popped up on my Gmail. I clicked on it. The hiss of a rusted harmonica hit my eardrums. It took a second to realise that the sound was a choked gasp from me.

'What's wrong?' Ritchie demanded when he saw my expression.

I wordlessly pointed to the email on my screen. The subject line danced with three ominous words: *I see you.*

Ritchie leaned over and followed my gaze.

Signorina,
Do what u came here to do. Graduate with respectable grades and go back to ur own fucking country. Don't forget to mind your own fucking business while u still here. If u do, u wish u were dead. So long, love.
Yours,
Bloodfonso

SMS language. It had come from alfonso@bloodfonso.com. The time stamp said 6.15 p.m.

'This looks serious, San,' Ritchie muttered. 'Bloodfonso? Who calls himself that? Looks like the chap needs an English lesson too.'

I searched for Bloodfonso on Google. All that stared back at me was a message from Google: *No results found. Did you mean: Blood Font?*

'Someone's kept a screen name to scare me off,' I mumbled.

'Signorina is an Italian term of address for an unmarried lady,' Ritchie told me. 'Alfonso is an Italian name too.' He returned to his laptop, wiggled his fingers on the keypad and squinted into the screen before turning back to me. 'Here we go. Alfonso means "ready for battle".'

'Italian?'

'This seems too much like *Godfather* to me ... I doubt the sender is even close to being Italian,' Ritchie stated grimly.

'Well, he can't be Indian,' I muttered. 'I don't think Indians would use expletives of that sort in the context of their own country.'

'Don't be so sure.' Ritchie warned.

'There's not a lot to go on,' I agreed. 'I'm sure this threat is related to what I did this afternoon.'

'Methinks you'd have received this threat even if you hadn't scaled windows and hidden in boxes today,' Ritchie said suddenly. 'Whoever it is knows about your Lionheart campaign and is after you 'cause he or she's afraid you'll uncover something that isn't meant to be found. That means this person also knows you recently arrived from India to attend LSE. They probably even know where you live. Watch out, San. It wouldn't be hard for this person to find you.'

A steady swell of panic squeezed my chest. I began gasping for breath.

'There, there ...' Ritchie said. 'Get a hold of yourself now.'

He held me tentatively as I leaned against him. Focusing intently on the steady rise and fall of his chest trounced the mad rush of adrenaline coursing through my veins.

'Should I report it? And what I saw in that centre and everything?' I murmured, calmer now. 'I can remain anonymous if I talk to Crimestoppers.'

'Do it right away,' Ritchie ordered.

Then I remembered that I couldn't go back on my word to Keisha. 'Forget it, Ritch … it's all right. I don't think it's worth it.'

Ritchie raised his eyebrows. 'Why?'

I took a deep breath and fixed my gaze on the iridescent glimmer of his eyes. An inner voice reassured me that I could trust him enough to answer that question.

'I'm not in a position to inform the police, Ritch,' I whispered, leaning forward. Then I briefly explained my undercover work and the care home footage that sat in the BBC's alcoves now.

Ritchie's face puckered into a half-smile. 'Whoa! You took a hell of a risk. It must've taken a lot of trust and courage for you to decide to share it with me. Let's keep the police out of it then … at least for now. You'll need to stay safe though. I don't imagine you'll have protection from the BBC at this point, right?'

'Nope.'

Ritchie stretched his arms and sighed. 'I think we could both do with a shot of caffeine. All campus cafés are closed. I was going to hop along to Café Nero. Care to join?'

The decadent aroma of freshly brewed coffee sounded like just what I'd need right now.

'Sure.' I stuffed my inhaler into my jeans pocket. Grabbing our phones, wallets, coats and scarves, we took the elevator downstairs. A security guard hovering near the turnstiles glared at us suspiciously.

'Darn! That's quite a downpour,' Ritchie grumbled, picking up an old English umbrella from the library foyer on our way out.

It was a cold, windswept and rainy night. Huddling together under the umbrella, we hurried towards the underpass on Kingsway. At the mouth of the reeking tunnel, I tripped over what felt like a hand. A shrill scream fought its way out from the hollow of my throat.

'What happened? You okay?' Ritchie cried, pulling me back towards him.

Frozen, I pointed at the ground. We jerked our heads down to see a bedraggled figure sprawled at my feet in a lumpy coat. It was really too dark to see much, but I felt the figure stir as I stood there and hyperventilated.

'It's just a hobo, San.' Ritchie laughed. 'A drunken one. Let's haul him away from the frigging dark.' He tugged at the coat sleeves of the scruffy tramp. A moan escaped the vagrant's lips.

That voice sounded oddly familiar. A shingle of light reflected on to the tramp's face from a nearby sidewalk store as we steered him towards the entryway in the direction of the Holborn station. My hands jumped to my mouth on instinct, and the tramp went crashing down to the ground once again with a sad groan.

'N-N-Nimmy?' I spluttered. 'What happened to you?'

I was all over him – brushing the dust off, going around him to see if he had been stabbed or shot, straightening his coat and dusting his trousers. He didn't appear to be hurt, at least visibly. As if on autopilot, I vaguely introduced Nimmy and Ritchie to each other, standing in the pouring rain. Ritchie, who was not impressed with what he had heard about Nimmy from me earlier that evening and even less so when he saw him in a drunken stupor, shook his hand limply.

Nimmy's hand flopped in Ritchie's. Ritchie's eyes met mine over Nimmy's shoulder. 'Sandy, I don't think he's even looking at me.'

As Nimmy began to adjust to the lights and sounds of twilight, I leaned forward and brought my lips to his. Ritchie stood by, now looking annoyed.

Nimmy squinted at me in bewilderment. Then, to my horror, he swayed unsteadily and burst into peels of grotesque laughter. I gasped when he turned around slowly to face me. Nimmy didn't seem like himself at all. His eyes, sunken and bloodshot, rolled upward slightly. Purple bags lined his cheekbones. His arms and legs were loose and wobbly. Scuttling passersby peeked out from their hoods and umbrellas to stare as Nimmy continued cackling like a lunatic.

'Ritch!' I panicked. 'I don't know what's happening to him!'

I grabbed Nimmy's arm. 'Nimmy? Can you hear me?'

Nimmy's laughter stopped abruptly. All of a sudden, he clung to me as if he would fall to his death from a cliff top if he didn't hold on. 'I can't feel anything. I think I'm dying,' he groaned. His disembodied voice rose to a crescendo as his last few words curled into a scream.

'Nimmy!' I screeched, looking at Ritchie helplessly.

Ritchie lost no time in dialing triple nine. 'My friend is in danger,' he began shakily. 'I found him spread-eagled in the underpass on Kingsway.' I could hear only his side of the conversation. 'No, he's not visibly hurt … yes, it could be life threatening. I'm not sure if he's drunk or drugged … yes, like a psychotic … all right. We'll get to somewhere warm … yes. Costa café. Right next to the Holborn Underground. On the same side as Carphone Warehouse. Thanks.'

As Ritchie hung up, he resembled a little boy who had lost his way in the woods. A veneer of authority replaced his glazed look instantly. 'C'mon,' he barked urgently. 'This rain's a frigging pest. Let's wait at Costa till the medics arrive.'

'Okay,' I said, forcing myself to remain calm.

I staggered when Nimmy leaned and shifted all his weight onto me.

'Easy, San!' Ritchie said, springing forward to give me a hand. We teetered from side to side as we prodded a floundering

Nimmy down the road towards the Holborn station. At a height of six feet, Nimmy must have weighed close to two-hundred pounds and egging him along was no mean task.

Someone rapped me on my shoulder. 'Would you like some help?' a stocky Asian man in an anorak inquired, shuffling a bundle of *London Lite* tabloids in his arms.

'Aren't you a godsend ...' Ritchie said gratefully.

The bloke placed his bundle of newspapers by the foot of a flower shop across the Holborn station before scurrying back to us. 'Don't be sweating, lady,' he told me kindly. 'Oye, there! We need a hand 'round here,' he hollered to a fellow newspaper distributor. Another Asian guy in a sports jacket emerged from a corner. Ritchie and the two men carried a burbling Nimmy towards the Costa around the corner.

'Sandy!' Nimmy howled, twisting against the firm grip of the three men who held him. 'I'm right here, sweetie,' I called out.

The men set a drenched Nimmy down on a bar stool in Costa a few minutes later. A lone bespectacled cashier at the counter looked on, puzzled.

We thanked the lads. 'Glad we could help, lady. Now, take care,' the larger of the two men said before they walked out.

Ritchie retrieved some napkins and ordered three cappuccinos, while I mopped Nimmy's soaked face and hands with paper towels and coaxed him to tell me what had happened.

'Um b-b-being ...' Nimmy sniffled, swiping his nose against the back of his shirt. The stuttering that had claimed an otherwise articulate tongue did nothing to quell my escalating anxiety. I looked behind me to ensure that Ritchie was still at the counter waiting for our coffees.

'Go on ...' I urged gently. 'It's only me.'

'Um b-b-being f-followed ...' Nimmy whimpered.

I narrowed my eyes. 'Followed? For how long? What happened?'

Ritchie came back with a tray. 'This'll make you feel better,' he grunted, pushing a cappuccino to Nimmy. Nimmy slouched back in his seat and took a long swig.

'You rem … you … Rick, Sal, Carl … guys?' Nimmy slurred to me.

'Tell me everything from the beginning,' I pressed firmly. 'Did you take drugs?'

Nimmy suddenly lurched forward. His back arched as he began to tremble.

'The docs will be arriving soon,' I said. I sprang from my chair and reached out to touch Nimmy's shoulder. He violently shrugged me off. The force of his movement sent me flying back against my chair. The chair slid sideways, screeching against the floor. I skidded along with it. Ritchie jumped to my side at once and took me in his arms. 'You okay, San?'

I nodded faintly.

Nimmy's growling gave way to laboured breathing. Despite himself, Ritchie gave a brotherly pat on Nimmy's shoulder. I groped around in Nimmy's trouser pockets, retrieved his phone and scrolled down his contacts list for Carl's mobile number. Then I called Carl from my phone.

From the corner of my eye, I saw Nimmy blow out his cheeks and double over. My heart twisted in agony to see him trapped in such a gruesome spiral. Ritchie asked the cashier if there was a washroom. The cashier looked at us disgustedly and waved them towards a McDonalds across the road.

Carl picked up on the sixth ring, sounding curt. 'Yes, who's this?'

'Carl, this is Sandy …' I said. 'Uh, how're you doing?'

'Oh … well, hi!'

'I found Nimmy sprawled in the tram tunnel at Kingsway. Dead-drunk, drugged … I don't know. He isn't coherent and he's probably throwing up now …' I reported.

'Where are you guys now? Would you like me to come over?'

'Did you, Rick, Sal and Nimmy meet after work today?' I inquired.

'Yep, we met in Corney and Barrow for a round of drinks after work.'

'Oney and Bara?' I echoed blankly.

'Corney and Barrow,' Carl said. 'It's a wine bar on Liverpool Street, around Broadgate Circle.'

'I'd like to know what happened this evening,' I pleaded. 'Every little detail. This is important. Nimmy isn't even talking coherently.'

'I … Sal met me after work around quarter to six and we took the tube from Blackfriars to Liverpool Street,' Carl spluttered. 'Nimmy and Rick joined us some time later. Nimmy seemed stressed out. He didn't say what was eating him. But he definitely looked like he could do with some chilling out.'

'And?'

'We sat in the patio upstairs. Had a couple of beers, ciders … stuff like that. Nimmy got Prosecco, I think. Then he asked for a refill. We sat and chatted for a while. Rick left early but Nimmy, Sal and I hung around. Nimmy dashed to the washroom after his second drink, I think. He was complaining about a headache and nausea. I offered to accompany him to the washroom, but he insisted he'd go on his own. I imagine he threw up in there. We hoped he would feel better after that, but he just got worse.'

'What did you guys do then?' From the periphery of my vision, I saw Ritchie return with a paler Nimmy. Ritchie sat him down and appeared to be engaging his attention in some contrived way.

'Sal phoned a cab. We all left in about fifteen–twenty minutes. Nimmy was dawdling and unsteady, so we thought the Prosecco really did him in.'

'Where was Rick?'

'I told you … Rick left early.'

'Early? Did he say why?'

'He had to go see his girl.'

'Oh!'

'He, uh, doesn't know about what happened I guess. He left before any of this shit happened,' Carl mumbled. 'We were really surprised. Nimmy usually holds up many drinks. Four spirits, six Beefeaters, a glass of wine and he'd still be good to go. Can't fathom how two glasses of sparkling wine sent him topsy-turvy today.'

'Go on.'

'Sal and I asked the cabbie to take Nimmy straight home. We got off at Bank. On the DLR from Bank, Sal called Nimmy to check if he was okay. I don't think that call went through. We thought his phone ran out of juice.'

'How could you be so stupid?' I hissed.

'Sorry?'

'Your friend is sloshed and you just leave him alone in a cab?'

'Well, Nimmy said he'd be fine and …'

'You should know better than to let a cabbie drop him home or listen to a drunken friend who's blathering on about conquering the world. What's wrong with you guys?'

'Look, Sandy,' Carl said. 'I had a conference call at nine-thirty with folks in New York. I had to get home soon.'

I sighed. 'I … Well, all right, Carl. Thanks.'

'No problem. Let me know how Nimmy's doing, all right?'

'Will do. And call me if you remember any other details, okay?'

Carl grunted. 'Sure.'

I hung up and stared at Nimmy. He seemed to be nodding off to sleep.

I looked at Ritchie. 'Ritch?' I whispered.

Ritchie had his head in his hands. He seemed equally exhausted. 'Hmm?'

'Nimmy said he was being followed,' I began anxiously. 'But that's about all he said. I really don't know if that's related to the threatening email I got today, though.'

'It looks like he's been hallucinating, San,' Ritchie said. 'But we can't rule out any possibilities now.'

I closed my eyes to blot out the cumulative effects of stress and exhaustion now settling in my chest.

Ritchie's phone buzzed. 'Yes?' he barked. 'Yes, we're in here ... no, he can't ... that would be just fine, thanks.' He looked at me. 'We'll soon know what the hell happened to him.'

Two A&E paramedics barreled in with an apologetic look at the cashier who looked on, stunned. Nimmy opened his eyes weakly and began flailing his arms wildly in his semi-conscious state as they strapped him into a collapsible gurney.

'Is he having trouble breathing?' one of the paramedics inquired, raising the head of the gurney.

'He's been gasping for breath.' I launched into a brief description of what had most likely happened that evening.

'Looks like his drinks were spiked,' one of them said gravely as they began to wheel Nimmy outside.

My stomach churned. *Spiked?*

Ritchie sat in the front of the ambulance, while I climbed in the back with Nimmy and the A&E support crew. The medics checked Nimmy's vital signs and tested his blood sugar and blood pressure. 'His BP and blood glucose are on the lower side,' one whispered to the other.

'Just give me the numbers,' the other snapped.

'The BP's eighty-six/fifty, BG sixty-one.'

'That settles it then.'

Nimmy screamed as one of the medics promptly ran an IV on him and put him on saline and glucose.

'I'm right here, darling,' I said, squeezing his other hand as the ambulance hurtled down the road, its sirens wailing ominously.

~

An hour later, a casualty officer in a plastic apron approached Ritchie and me in the waiting lounge of University College Hospital's A&E unit.

'I'm Dr Baumler. We've detected traces of phencyclidine and ketamine in his blood,' he informed gravely. 'He has a BAC of 0.16 and his serum indicates levels of 0.08 mg and 0.12 mg of PCP and ketamine. It's likely that high doses of K can make the test for PCP positive, especially if he just consumed it a few hours before … but the level of ketamine in his blood is something to pay attention to. Are you aware if he snorted Cat Valium, LSD or anything else?'

All these terms sounded alien and scary as hell.

'N-no,' I said, when I found my tongue. 'Nirmal would never do drugs. I doubt he even knows the difference between coke and Coke …' I jerked my thumb toward my mouth to demonstrate the act of drinking from a Coca-Cola bottle.

Dr Baumler nodded grimly. 'To be sure, I just wanted to eliminate the possibility that he had consciously ingested those drugs. His BAC is phenomenally high for just two glasses of sparkling wine … if he really did have only that much. It's quite likely his drinks were spiked with alcohol and Cat Valium. We'll need the police to run an investigation, I'm afraid.'

'Will-will he be all right?' I stammered.

'His vitals are good. The drugs should leave his system in three to four days,' Dr Baumler said. 'His tendon reflexes are poor right now. He's also having electrolyte imbalances. His chloride and potassium levels are very low, and we'll have to monitor him overnight. If all goes well, he can go home tomorrow. We'd like to have one of our psychiatric residents conduct a partial cognitive examination on him at the emergency ward, when he comes to.'

'What will I tell the Sawants now?' I groaned to Ritchie.

'We'll worry about that later,' Ritchie said shortly.

'Your friend should be okay,' the doctor managed.

I completed some formalities to admit Nimmy overnight. A ward bed was arranged for him.

'Here's the Camden Borough police home page,' Ritchie said, leaning over to show me his phone screen once I sank back into the seat next to him. 'They serve the Holborn area too, so we should report this incident to the Holborn station.' he jabbed a stubby finger at the area of the screen which showed a link to the Holborn police station along with its telephone number and working hours. 'They're open twenty-four seven.'

I called them. 'Yes?' a police officer barked gruffly.

'My friend's drinks have been spiked,' I began nervously. 'I found him ...'

'What's his name?' the officer interrupted.

'Nimmy ... I mean Nirmal Sawant.' I then spelled it out.

'Right,' the officer said. 'Continue ...'

I recounted what I had heard from Carl and what the doctor had just said.

'Were you at the scene when this happened?' the officer asked when I finished.

'No … what I described was what one of Nirmal's friends told me. He was there with Nirmal.'

'What is Nirmal's friend's name?'

'Carl Wright. I don't know him very well.'

'Well, I'm afraid there's not much we can do unless Nim …' the officer struggled to pronounce Nimmy's name. '… Unless your friend himself comes down here and gives us more information. It would be best if Carl came down as well. Your friend wouldn't be likely to remember much.'

I fixed an appointment and rang off. Ritchie was reading a course paper.

'You should head home, Ritch,' I said. 'I feel bad keeping you cooped up in here with me.'

A light furrow creased Ritchie's forehead. 'Sure you'll be all right, San?'

I nodded firmly. 'Had it not been for me, you'd have reached an epiphany by now.'

Ritchie laughed. 'Aw, I ain't so sure about that.'

As he rose and shrugged into his coat, I realised that a part of me still yearned for his companionable presence through the night. But it wasn't appropriate for me to hold him here any longer.

'If those pesky Sawants raise a question, you could just say Nimmy worked late last night and fainted. Don't know how they'd respond to Nimmy getting mullered out of his mind. Not very kindly, I'd imagine.'

'You're a brick, Ritch,' I said quietly.

He was gone before I could say more. I glanced at a wall clock ahead of me. 12.47 a.m. I wanted to inform one of the

Sawants that Nimmy and I weren't going to make it home that night. But it was way past their bedtime.

'Would you like a cup of tea?' a triage nurse in the area asked me politely.

I nodded. 'That's very kind of you. Thanks.'

As I waited for the tea, I dialed Carl's number from Nimmy's phone.

Carl must have thought it was Nimmy calling him. 'Yo, mate! What an ungodly hour this is. Wazzap?' He mumbled groggily.

'I'm sorry to disturb you again, Carl,' I began curtly.

'Yes! Uh … how's Nimmy doing?'

'They've detected traces of PCP and ketamine in his blood. His BAC is way too high for two glasses of Prosecco. Is there something you might have forgotten to tell me last night, Carl?'

'Ket-what? You mean they found traces of drugs in his body?'

'Did Nimmy leave his drink unattended at any time?' I asked firmly. 'Please try to be as accurate as you can. If a bartender or waiter spiked a drink, the pub can be screwed big time.'

'We watched the maître d' pour out our drinks. And the table was never left unattended,' Carl replied after a beat. 'But …' He seemed to have just remembered something.

'What?' I probed.

'Well,' he began uncertainly. 'I'm not sure if this matters, but …'

'Everything you say matters, Carl,' I reminded him.

'Right. Um, Nimmy did leave our table to attend a work-related call … halfway through his first drink.'

'Where'd he go?'

'Stepped to a corner of the patio. He returned to the table in a couple of minutes. After some time, Sal and I went to the washroom together. But Rick was around attending the table. I think Nimmy was there too.'

'Why didn't you tell me this earlier, Carl?' I demanded.

'I just remembered it when you mentioned his high BAC.'

'Carl, someone likely put more alcohol in Nimmy's drink and slipped in some Cat Valium too.'

'As long as I was around, I didn't see anything unusual going on when he was outside or otherwise,' Carl said in a bewildered tone.

I blew out my breath. 'Could you come along to the Holborn police station tomorrow and report what happened yesterday?'

'The *police*? Why, I ...'

'Just to tell them what you've told me, Carl.'

'I, uh, have an important client meeting tomorrow.'

'What's important to you, Carl?' I burst out angrily. 'A meeting with a client or justice for a friend who could have even lost his life?'

'When is it?'

'Eleven a.m.'

Carl sighed. 'I'll be there.'

A spate of hard-hitting images barraged my mind after I hung up. Rosie's arrival at the Sawants' doorstep with a purple teddy bear; Carl getting off the train with a cartload of identically patterned, electric violet teddies; spotting Shailaja at Bread Breakers'; the threat from Bloodfonso; Nimmy's spiked drinks; Carl's failure to divulge every detail when first asked; his reluctance to accompany me to the police station ... I noticed a cup of tea on the table next to me. Cold rivulets of dread iced my jaw as I sipped the tea. Was Carl somehow involved in this bizarre matrix?

8

Victims of Honour

9 March

'I was shoved from behind,' Nimmy told Chief Superintendent Gary Thompson as he, Carl and I sat in the Holborn police station, next morning.

Gary raised a bushy eyebrow in response to Nimmy's statement.

After a client meeting last evening, Nimmy had walked over to Corney and Barrow from his office. Carl and Sal were at a table in the patio, and Rick had just arrived. After their usual badinage, the four lads ordered a round of drinks. When Sal and Carl left for the washroom together a few minutes later, Nimmy vaguely remembered bending down to re-tie his shoelace, but he had otherwise watched the maitre'd pour out their drinks. Neither Rick nor Nimmy had seen any suspicious characters lurking around. But Nimmy threw up in the washroom, shortly after. The only memories he could recollect after that were his adamant insistence on alighting from a cab at Holborn, and the shove he received while staggering through the underpass towards LSE – his inebriety had triggered a random thought of approaching me at the university.

'You were pushed? Is that the most recent memory you have of last night?' Gary pressed.

'Yes,' Nimmy affirmed. 'The next thing I remember is waking up in the hospital.'

'Can you describe what exactly happened at the underpass?' Gary inquired.

'I was already wobbly,' Nimmy recalled. 'Then I felt someone dig into my back. I tumbled over and fell.'

'Do you know if the person who pushed you was a man or a woman?' Gary inquired promptly.

'Couldn't say,' Nimmy said.

'Someone may have bumped into you by mistake, and you could have fallen since you were already unsteady,' Gary suggested.

Nimmy fidgeted agitatedly in his seat. I wondered if he wanted to say more, but he didn't. I squeezed his hand reassuringly.

Gary scratched his chin thoughtfully, studied Nimmy's medical report and shifted his gaze to the pile of notes he had made during our interview.

'It's evident his drinks were spiked,' Gary said. 'But we have no clear suspects in this case. It's quite likely this was no more than a prank by one of your mates.'

'That's hardly likely!' I hissed.

'No one from our group touched anyone else's drinks yesterday,' Carl added.

Gary ignored Carl and turned to me. 'And why would that be so?'

'I, uh … I received a threat myself. On email!' I stuttered. 'By someone who signed off as Bloodfonso. I got that email, the same night Nimmy's drinks were spiked. I believe someone is threatening …'

Nimmy and Carl looked befuddled.

'Miss, we get numerous complaints out here from people who *think* their drinks were spiked,' Gary boomed. 'We've wasted our time contacting pubs and clubhouses for CCTV footage, only to find that the whole spiking business people rattle to us about is usually not the case. I know your case is different because you brought a medical report in here. But we have many other heinous offenses we're dealing with … and the case of a spiked drink or an anonymous note just isn't as high on our priority list right now.'

'What about the fact that I was pushed yesterday?' Nimmy challenged.

'We don't know that that's a fact.' Gary turned the medical report over in his hand. 'Those could have been drug-induced hallucinations. People who are drugged tend to remember and imagine things that were either innocuous or never happened at all.'

I slumped in my seat. This man didn't seem to be cooperating.

Gary caught my expression. 'Look,' he intoned in exasperation. 'I'll try to have that pub get us a copy of last evening's CCTV footage … but I can't promise it'll be done soon enough. It's all we can do, unless you have some hard evidence to substantiate your claims. I'll get in touch if anything comes up.'

He rose from his seat, indicating that our meeting was over. I was too furious to even swallow. To add insult to injury, he chuckled, 'Be careful next time you hit the bottle!'

~

On our way back in a cab from Holborn, Nimmy phoned his mother at university and corroborated my story that he had pulled an all-nighter at work for a client presentation while I burned the midnight oil at the LSE library.

I had a quick chat with my father, too. It had been days since I'd spoken to him; I wanted to check in and ensure that he wasn't feeling too lonely. Of course, he had been by himself in Tanjore for a good while now, given that I was in Mumbai at least for a year before moving to London. But, now that I was in another country, it was different.

When Nimmy and I got home, I was relieved that no one else was around, except Pandy who greeted us with licks. After what I had seen at Bread Breakers' yesterday, I wasn't ready to face the other Sawants – including Asha – yet.

'Let's get you sorted,' I told Nimmy, leaning over to kiss him.

'Thank you, San,' he said tiredly.

I ran a bubble bath for him upstairs. I was stirring some okra pieces in a pan on the stove when Nimmy arrived in the kitchen, clean-shaven and a lot more tranquil in lounge pants and an undershirt.

'Sandy, I have to talk to you,' he said.

I perked up. Wasn't I supposed to say those words to him, confronting him about what I had seen at Bread Breakers'?

Remembering our guilt/obligation argument earlier this week, I wondered if he was going to address issues concerning our relationship.

'What's up?' I inquired, once we were seated comfortably at the table. As Nimmy talked, I realised he was trying to tell me what he thought had really happened last evening.

He had felt someone's presence while walking to Corney and Barrow from his office at around 5.00 p.m. yesterday. But, whenever he turned back, he saw no one.

'I'm sure I wasn't imagining it,' Nimmy said. 'You do believe me, don't you?'

I reached out for his hand across the table. 'Of course I do.' I wondered how I could diplomatically broach the subject of yesterday's events at the care home.

'Why didn't you take the car out yesterday?' I began.

'The BMW was taken to the dealer for service. Mum needed the VW for some work that afternoon. Besides, I couldn't drink and drive anyway.' He was still slurring from the effects of the dope.

'So, Corney and Barrow wasn't a spur-of-the-moment thing, was it?'

Nimmy shrugged indifferently. 'I guess not. Carl called. Wanted to get everyone together for a rounda drinks, y'know.'

'Why didn't you tell the police you were being followed?'

'They'd have put it aside as a drug-induced hallucination, San.'

This was going nowhere. So, I took the plunge. 'Nimmy, I have something to tell you.'

Nimmy raised his brows, looking like he couldn't fathom what on earth I would have to say to him when he had been the nucleus of yesterday's drama. He leaned back against his deck chair and gazed up at the sky with a jaded expression, evidently deciding that I was only going to preach about something.

I filled him in on the sequence of events that had unfolded since late February, tweaking my story to exclude the fact that I now had an incriminatory video that sat with the BBC. Nimmy's eyes widened when I mentioned his mother's conversation with Dr Tahseen.

'Mum was in the surgery clinic there?' he squeaked.

I nodded and cleared my throat nervously. 'I think Sunil is Asha's son. I'm not sure about it, but it's a hunch. I need you to tell me if that's true.'

Nimmy lifted his face from his hands. 'Oh, Lord,' he mumbled more to himself than to me. 'Tell me this isn't really happening!'

'Nimmy?' I prodded gently. 'Was Asha raped two years ago?'

Nimmy's eyes bled with anguish. 'Good heavens! You're smart up there, aren't you?'

'What's going on, Nimmy? Are you aware of any of this?'

'The Bread Breakers' and the hysterectomy thing … *no*!' he said. He didn't offer to say more.

'Was Asha raped?'

Nimmy nodded heavily. 'None of us knew about it until much later. Asha was losing weight, retching a lot, throwing tantrums and having stomach cramps. Then Mum found out Asha wasn't having her periods.'

'And then?'

'Well, my Mum and Aunt Nidhi took Asha for a check-up and found that she was already four months pregnant,' he confided. 'Mum, Nidhi, my grandparents … everyone wanted her to have an abortion … but the doctors said Asha's life would be at risk, especially when she was almost four months along. So, just going with it, praying for a healthy baby and embracing it into our lives seemed like the best thing to do.'

Nimmy's voice dropped a few notches. 'This incident is a big shame to everyone in this family. Not me, of course. But to everyone else.'

I came over to his side and took him in my arms.

His eyes took on a ghostly glint. 'Mum and Dad are from different states,' he said quietly. 'They speak different languages, Tamil and Marathi. They didn't let that prevent them from getting married to each other. But you know what? They are hypocritical – at least, Mum is. They're about honour and all that bullshit. No one really understood or cared, that what happened to Asha was something she was vulnerable to. Everyone thought Asha brought shame upon the family. I tried to make them see sense. But they would tell me it was a 'woman thing'. He paused and gazed unseeingly at a spot on a tree, somewhere behind me. 'None of them really spoke about the rape and her pregnancy. They didn't know what had actually happened and didn't care to find out either. When the time came for the baby to arrive, Asha had a caesarian and nearly lost her life for it.'

He sighed heavily. 'Jyoti had just come in as a caretaker then. So, the baby was passed on to her and she's been calling him her son ever since. I tried to protest but I eventually gave up that battle. Dare I question the so-called beliefs floating round here and I'll be tagged a misfit. There's so much I want to do. But I don't have the courage.' Nimmy laid his hands on the table and nestled his head in the crook of his arms. My heart went out to him. But there was little I could say.

'Honour is such a big fucking deal,' he ranted. 'It eats your soul! It has no beginning and no end. Question it and you'll be damned forever. Good Lord!' He looked dead as he said it.

Tears streamed down my face as I held his hands and stroked his hair.

'What's the family's history with Rosie?' I urged.

Nimmy had now opened up to me so much that I knew he was being honest when he muttered, 'I don't know much, really. Just that Asha first met Rosie at the hospital … Portland hospital I think. It was after she delivered her baby. Asha was in a nursing home for a while – a few years before she got pregnant. Around in Lambeth I think …'

Oh God! Asha had once been a Bread Breakers' resident herself! I wondered how long she had been there. But I didn't dare to interrupt as Nimmy continued, 'So, somebody from Portland hospital called up that nursing home, for general care and stuff, and Rosie came over from there to visit Asha in the hospital. After delivering her son, Asha went to that nursing home again for a while to recover. Rosie must have seen her a lot more then, I don't know. I didn't like Rosie very much. She was trying to convince us to let Asha leave her baby behind in the care home, so that they could take care of him or whatever. Rosie once visited me at home – when Asha was still in that care centre I think – to talk me into letting them keep the baby and put him up for adoption when he was about five or six ...'

My heart skipped a beat as he went on.

'Rosie said their nursing home had a crèche and they'd bear child-related expenses and take care of him in that facility and ...' he pecked at the remains of his lunch. 'I raised a stink and Dad kind of supported my decision. So, Sunil came right home with us. Everyone at home, except Dad, was miffed about it.

'I think Rosie went to Nidhi's office in Southall a few months later ... my aunt wasn't too pleased to see her, you know, because she'd just wrecked all that havoc ... and no one wanted to be reminded of it. But Rosie insisted on seeing my aunt when she visited the SBS offices and claimed she was being abused where she worked ... she had 'nother job I think. My aunt just referred her to another caseworker at Southall. We never saw her again until last November.'

I exhaled. I was surprised to hear that Ashok had played a role in ensuring that Sunil wasn't stuck in that little shed at Bread Breakers'. Why wasn't he involved in Asha's care then? Or even Sunil's, for that matter? Was he really upset with Asha? Or was it his way of silently protesting against the family's anger with Asha?

Now that I thought about it, it occurred to me that Shailaja hadn't been deeply involved in Asha's care either. Not unless there was a crisis, or a major task that required her involvement. It was Jyoti and Nimmy who attended to Asha a lot more than her mother did. Was Shailaja still embarrassed about Asha's rape and pregnancy? Did Asha have a history with Rosie even before they met at the Portland hospital? Where were all those Bread Breakers' children sent when they got older? These questions ricocheted in my mind like a haunting echo from the crevasse of a dungeon.

'Asha doesn't know what happened to her,' Nimmy growled like a wounded animal.

I grabbed his arm. 'Your mum wants a hysterectomy for her now. Based on what I heard, it is most likely a surgery that involves removing her uterus, ovaries, fallopian tubes and everything – so that she doesn't menstruate and never gets pregnant again.'

Nimmy looked blank.

'Such a hysterectomy is usually done only when there is a serious health issue and there's no other way to treat it. Asha doesn't need hormonal imbalances to compound the problems she's already having ... and that's what will happen if a hysterectomy is done.'

Nimmy nodded vaguely.

'We want justice for Asha,' I went on in vengeance. 'Her rape is a crime and we need to release that news. To the law. To the media. To the goddamned public!'

Nimmy reached forward and clamped both my hands like a vise. 'No, Sandy, no! You must do no such thing. No media, no public ... *please!*'

'Why?' I protested. 'I love you and Asha. I only want what is best for you.'

Breathing heavily, Nimmy grabbed my shoulders and looked at me with bloodshot eyes. 'You received a threatening email and I was being followed yesterday … and my drinks were spiked. I think whoever is involved in that Bread Breakers' racket is after us now.'

~

'Keisha showed me that video. Splendid job, San. I reckon the sooner we get cracking on it, the better,' Charlotte said when we were sat at the BBC Broadcast Centre lobby that evening.

'Alfred saw the video too,' Keisha said. 'We're contacting the *Panorama* team first thing Monday.'

'Good show! It'll save those kids and residents if we can get it out soon,' I said.

'You look beat,' Keisha remarked as I poured myself some tea. 'What happened?'

'My boyfriend was rushed to a hospital last night. His drinks were spiked.'

'Gosh!' Charlotte exclaimed.

'Will he be all right?' Keisha asked contritely.

I smiled wryly. 'Getting better. He said someone was stalking him. I think it's related to the Bread Breakers' events I taped yesterday.'

Charlotte raised a eyebrow. 'What makes you think so?'

'Well, I got an email last evening too. Just an hour before I found my boyfriend passed out on the underpass outside LSE. It came from alfonso@bloodfonso.com.'

Keisha frowned. 'Alonso Bloodfonso?'

'Alfonso. His note said I'll wish I am dead if I don't mind my own business.'

Suddenly, I remembered that I had first contacted Bread Breakers' from my personal email account because of maintenance issues on the BBC server. The signature on my personal email account mentioned I was a student at LSE. Perhaps, that was why Simon Webb had agreed to meet me. He may have alerted the staff when he learned of the BBC's involvement during our meeting. And they would have connected my first meeting to Maya Farmah and the lady with the Halloween mask spotted yesterday. Now, it made sense … all of it.

'I think Bloodfonso is aware of my involvement in this campaign,' I continued. 'So, I'm pretty sure he knows you two are behind it, too. Not to mention the fact that you both work for the BBC.'

The momentary cloud of unease on Charlotte's face dissolved into an amused expression.

'It's probably nothing to worry about, San,' she reassured. 'Must be some nut who watched our show or somehow got tipped off about the campaign.'

'Lionheart's all over Twitter and Facebook anyway,' Keisha pointed out.

'That's the point, Kiki,' I said. 'It wouldn't have been hard for them to figure out that you and Charlotte are running Lionheart too.'

'Many of us have received a menacing note now and then. Turned out to be nothing more than a desperate attention-seeker or a deranged fan!' Keisha said. 'It's all harmless, really.'

'The BBC have enough security to give the FBI a run for their money.' Charlotte chuckled.

Keisha ran through our tour agenda and listed all the schools and care homes that had agreed to participate in the first leg of our workshop series. 'For apparent reasons, we're leaving Bread Beaker out of this,' Keisha said as we were wrapping up.

'Bread Breakers',' I corrected.

'I've got to scoot now.' Charlotte said. 'My show's on in fifteen minutes and I still have to do my hair.'

We exchanged hugs and parted.

I spent the next hour in Keisha's cabin, updating the Lionheart campaign mailing list. Keisha sat at her desk, reviewing some propositions for an onslaught of new kids' programmes.

As I packed up to leave, Keisha waved a paper before her. 'I'll see if I can speak to Alfred about having you develop content for one of these kids' shows. I've received a compelling proposal on music therapy for pre-teens recovering from brain illness. You interested?'

My heart jumped at the opportunity. 'I'd love it! I could discuss it with Alfred on Monday.'

'Good. That's settled then.'

I hesitated at the door. 'Kiki, please be careful.'

12 March

'Char is never late!' Alfred Maynard grumbled, glancing at his wristwatch as we waited to start shooting the next episode of Streetsmart on Monday afternoon.

The show guests were getting fidgety and the crewmembers were growing impatient. Keisha had been flapping around like a mother hen, engaging everyone until Charlotte's arrival – but now, she stood next to Alfred, as tense as the wire rope of a suspension bridge.

I gazed around me in dismay. Keisha's promises to talk to Alfred about an opportunity for me on one of those kids' shows had long since been forsaken. We were running on a tight schedule. Calls to Charlotte's mobile were going through to her voicemail and she hadn't responded yet.

Alfred punched some numbers on his phone.

'Afternoon, Meg,' he began tersely. 'Charlotte was supposed to be here at three. She hasn't arrived yet. I hope she's okay.'

I saw Alfred's face pucker with surprise as he listened.

'Oh … okay, thanks. Beats me. Well, it must be traffic then, right? Cheers!' He hung up and shuffled uneasily.

'Char's secy says she left for our shoot with some props over an hour ago,' he reported.

Ten more minutes whizzed by. Keisha stepped to the centre of the studio and clapped her hands for attention. 'We're rescheduling this episode as our host, Charlotte has had an unforeseen emergency and is unable to be with us today,' she said into a microphone. 'We'll send you an update on the Streetsmart mailing list and keep you posted on when the next episode will be scheduled. Please accept our sincerest apologies.'

Everyone rose to leave. The videographers were folding their tripods when Alfred's phone rang. He disappeared through an exit door. He returned two minutes later, white as a sheet.

'That was Meg. She just received a call from Kings College Hospital,' he informed solemnly. 'Char has been gravely injured in a car accident.'

'They've taken her to surgery,' Megan reported in a flat monotone as Alfred, Keisha and I ploughed into the waiting room outside an intensive care unit half an hour later. A frightful wheeze jostled its way up my throat. I hurriedly reached for my inhaler and took a few deep breaths.

Keisha turned to me. 'You okay?'

I swallowed my tears and nodded. I couldn't get rid of the feeling that I was inexplicably responsible for Charlotte's 'accident.' An hour later, Alfred patted Megan's shoulder silently and took his leave. I surmised he had shitloads of work to get done. Keisha and I didn't move. Nearly two hours passed before a doctor came in.

'Your friend is in a coma,' he stated somberly. 'It's premature to say if she will make it … she has skull fractures, a crushed sternum, a swollen brain and other internal injuries. She was in a semi-conscious state in the emergency ward, though barely breathing.'

I felt faint. Megan and Keisha remained dazed with shock.

'She kept saying something. Sounded like *"horse"*,' the doctor added as an afterthought.

I frowned. *Horse*?

'Did you say she said something that sounded like "*horse*"?' I repeated.

The doctor nodded. 'Indeed. Would you know what that might mean?'

Megan rose unsteadily from her chair. 'I don't know.' She clasped the doctor's hand. 'Will she be all right?'

'We'll do our best,' the doctor said grimly.

Jumping out from a TV screen in the LSE library foyer was the image of a cordoned-off section at Blackfriars Bridge, clogged with a monstrous traffic jam around the scene of a blood-spattered truck with a smashed-in grill and a wrecked Skoda Octavia surrounded by shards of broken glass and amorphous pieces of metal.

'A devastating road accident occurred on the A201 in Blackfriars at two-thirty p.m.,' an off-camera BBC News commentator reported on the seven o' clock news. 'Thirty-two-year-old Charlotte Hale was the victim of this collision. Hale is a renowned education entrepreneur and a popular radio and TV host for the BBC. She was rushed to King's College Hospital with severe injuries. She is in a coma. Prayers for her speedy recovery are pouring in from across the island. Christina, our reporter at the scene spoke to a few eyewitnesses about the accident …'

The static image of the wreckage dissolved into a moving scene of frenzied people. I heard a smatter of excited comments.

'I hope she recovers.'

'I was driving through the A201 from Victoria Embankment and I saw a crowd gathered around there. Never expected it'd be so bloody …'

'We need better traffic regulations in this city …'

'She drove into the median and toppled over – right into an oncoming lorry from the other side.'

A lone female voice emerged from the cacophony. 'That's not true! It was a hit-and-run!'

I stared in stunned disbelief as the reporter thrust a microphone towards the young brunette who had spoken. She appeared to be in her late twenties.

'What's your name?' the reporter yelled over the din.

'Harriet Blue.'

'What makes you say it was a hit-and-run?'

'I was just about to get into the Blackfriars Underground when I saw a big black jeep speeding towards that car. The signal at the corner was still a fair distance. I first thought the jeep was just trying to overtake her on the wrong side. But I saw the jeep ram into the side of the Skoda and push it into the median barrier. The car hit the median and toppled over on to the other side – into a lorry. The jeep sped away in a trice and disappeared around a corner. Blimey, I was gobsmacked! I dialed triple nine in panic … there was already a huge crowd by then.'

'That's ridiculous! She drove into the median herself!' another bystander shouted.

The newscaster's sonorous voice came on again. 'We are being told that the traffic police will record Ms Blue's testimony. If her story is true, what appears to be an accident might in fact be an act of homicide. We will follow up with more details as they develop.'

My hand trembled as I phoned Keisha.

'If that eyewitness' statement is true, it means Char's car crash has something to do with my Bread Breakers' investigation!' I cried breathlessly when she answered. 'Whoever's on our trail knows that Char is part of Lionheart too. And it doesn't help that she's the face of Streetsmart!'

Keisha remained silent before bursting out, 'What a wild theory, San. What would they have against Lionheart or Streetsmart? All this while, the show has been doing well on its own, too.'

'Kiki, your life could be in danger!' I hissed, struggling to rein in my anxiety. 'Can you tighten security at home and work? We can lie low on the campaign for some time.'

'Let's see.' Keisha sighed. 'It may be a while before Char recovers from her coma. Her Mum is on her way here from LA.'

'What about her Dad?'

'I've no idea … the Mum and Dad divorced some time ago.'

'Okay, I'll let you get on now. Do be careful!'

I called Nimmy next.

'I watched the news too,' he said. 'It's pretty awful. I hope she makes it.'

I took a deep breath. 'I suspect it's related to everything that happened last Thursday – the day I visited Bread Breakers', the day I received that email threat, the day your drinks were spiked … Someone's after everyone who's involved in our campaign. I'm worried for your safety and Asha's too. Can Asha take it easy at work and stay home for the next few days?'

'Let's discuss this at home, San. I've been lounging around in the house all day. I feel loads better. When are you getting back?'

'In an hour or so.'

Nimmy's voice rang with concern. 'Sandy, you're no safer. Just cab it home today, all right? I'll take care of the fare.'

After I hung up, I took in my surroundings with conscious awareness for the first time since that morning. Students clad in jeans, sweatshirts and puffy windcheaters bustled in and out through the library's main doors with brimming book bags and laptops. For a split second, I envied them. Their biggest source of concern was meeting course paper deadlines.

My biggest source of concern? Keisha. Nimmy. Asha. Me. All our lives were in danger.

9
Fracture

'You seem tense, honey,' Nimmy remarked when we were in my bedroom that night. 'If you're worried about me, don't be. I've rested most of the day and I feel fine now. Rick, Sal and Carl called to ask how I was doing. We've sworn not to touch drinks for a while.'

He took me in his arms and brought his lips down on mine with a crushing force. I tossed my head back and closed my eyes, savouring the tingle of his kiss on my tongue. He pulled off my camisole, traced my collarbone with his tongue and fondled my breasts longingly.

'Nimmy, I just want you to be safe. Asha too. I love you both too much to ...' I trailed off and leaned back with a moan as he suckled my breasts tenderly.

'You're gorgeous, Sandy,' he breathed. 'Do you know that? You would drive most men insane. And you're beautiful inside. Oh, my sweet little one.'

Our union was slow, tender and sweet. He came inside me with a shuddering sigh that I hoped my soundproof bedroom door would ensure was out of earshot of the other Sawants.

'Nimmy ...' I whispered as we lay spent in each other's arms.

'Want to go again?' he murmured, fingering my navel with unrepressed desire.

'I'd like to show you something.'

He sat back on his heels in bed. 'Go on.'

I hopped off the bed, yanked a printout of Bloodfonso's email from my bag and handed it to Nimmy.

'Good heavens!' he exclaimed after reading it.

'Nimmy, I know Gary at the Holborn police station wasn't all that helpful when we reported the spiked drinks to him. But it may be worth showing Bloodfonso's email to him and telling him our suspicions that you were being followed yesterday. When we saw him the other day, you never did tell him what you told me: that you were being followed from your office. Did you tell him that?'

Nimmy shook his head.

'To be fair, Gary did finally say he'll try to get a copy of that CCTV footage from Corney and Barrow to look into who spiked your drinks,' I went on. 'I'm considering seeing him again, because …'

'I'm not sure that's a good idea,' Nimmy said.

'Why not?' I protested. 'Because, at this point, the situation is different. Charlotte has become the next victim now. No one knows whether she'll make it. Do you think these are all coincidences? Come on, Nimmy … it's a no-brainer. They're all related. Someone's afraid we'll discover something. I don't want anyone else to get hurt. There's something fishy going on at Bread Breakers'. And now they're going to sterilise Asha. I'm dying to report that care home as well.'

Nimmy flew across the bed and clasped my shoulders with surprising strength for a man who was just recovering from a drug overdose.

'I wouldn't do that if I were you,' he snarled, rattling me back and forth like a poker chip. He brought his face close to mine and grit his teeth. 'If you must go to the police, do *not* bring up Asha.' He released his hold on me. In a second, his hardened expression transformed to that of a little boy who had just lost his puppy.

'Please,' he whispered. 'You know why I'm not in favour of that. Our family has gone to great pains to keep what happened to Asha under wraps. If it's ever released to the public, even the police, and if my parents find out I was party to that, they'll blow their fuse and disown me. No holds barred. And you know how the police are. They'll dig for information, search for witnesses, interrogate people and it'll all come out in the open.'

'I ...' I was at a loss for words. 'Well, I don't know how receptive the police will be, but we must at least try and alert them for our own safety, if not anything else. I won't bring Asha up. But I do think I must report what I saw at Bread Breakers'. I don't know how safe those kids are or where the hell they're taken when they get older.'

'If you must,' Nimmy sulked, drawing his legs to his chin as he sat back on the bed.

I reached out for his hand. 'I'd like you to come along.'

He swatted my hand away. We both sat silently for a few moments.

'I suppose it does make sense to tell Gary that someone was on my heels the other day,' he agreed at last.

'Thanks, Nimmy.' I slid off the bed and slipped into my camisole. 'What did Rick and Sal say when they called you today?'

The question caught Nimmy off-guard. 'Huh? Why?'

'Well, I'm wondering what they said to you after leaving you alone in a cab when you were in that state.'

'What are you suggesting?'

I walked up to him and held his face in my hands. 'Be careful,' I pleaded.

'Rick called and apologised over and over again for leaving early and not being around,' Nimmy admitted. 'But it isn't his fault anyway. He was completely shocked when he heard about it from Carl. Sal and Carl said they were pretty high themselves. Carl had brought some E from a house party he'd attended last week. And he and Sal downed one each with their drink. So, they couldn't think clearly enough to understand that I might've had to have someone with me.' He sighed. 'Anyway, I'm feeling sleepy. I'll head back to my room now. Nighty night.'

Feeling high on E, were they? I thought as Nimmy slipped out of my room. *Carl didn't tell me that.*

13 March

At the Holborn police station next morning, Gary Thompson glanced at a copy of Bloodfonso's email on the desk before him and scratched his chin thoughtfully.

'I can have the tech guys trace the IP address,' he suggested. 'Since there's no actual crime involved, I can't say how much attention it will receive though. That note could just be an inane prank.'

There we go again.

Well – at least, I was trying to see if he would be more serious about my case after what had happened to Charlotte.

'This could lead *to* a crime. A big one. Especially since it seems to be related to the Corney and Barrow incident,' I said aloud.

Nimmy, who had just revealed his suspicion that he had been followed to Corney and Barrow, looked exhausted.

'We don't have solid evidence of that,' Gary said. 'But I'll see what I can do.'

'What about Charlotte Hale's car crash?' I began.

'The Westminster police are working on it,' Gary cut in tersely. 'We have Ms Blue's testimony. The security guards played back CCTV clippings of the car crash. The traffic police have seen it in-situ. They're tracing the owner of the vehicle that rammed into Ms Hale's car. I'll have an officer contact that pub for CCTV footage. That should take about two-three weeks.'

'Thank you, Officer,' I said. The possibility of foul play hammered into my thoughts with renewed persistence. 'I think it's all related. The death threat, the spiking incident and Charlotte's car crash,' I added.

Gary rose from his seat and shook our hands crisply. 'We'll find out.'

~

14 March

The despondence in the air belied the colourful décor in Topaz's office lobby when I stepped in next day at noon. Paintings of Rembrandt, Raphael and Hans von Aachen dotted the bright yellow walls, and a mini-fig scale desk, designed like a Lego set, sat across the entrance. A stocky receptionist ushered me into Megan's cubicle.

'Charlotte has stabilised but her condition may remain unchanged for weeks,' Megan reported.

'How are things at the office?' I inquired.

'Not pretty. Our co-director, Becka is handling most of Charlotte's affairs now.'

'You remember what that doc said when we were outside the ICU on Monday? He said Char was mumbling something that sounds like "horse" – when she was wheeled into the emergency ward,' I mentioned gently.

Megan nodded.

'Well, the doc asked if we knew what Char may have been trying to say. Did you figure out what she may have meant?'

Megan raised a brow querulously. 'How will that help anything?'

'It could,' I said uncertainly. 'Maybe the guy who ran her down is a horse-rider, you know …'

Megan's eyes widened. 'I haven't the foggiest,' she admitted finally. 'And she won't talk anytime soon either. Not as long as she remains in a coma.'

'All right, let me know if you need anything,' I managed, hoping I hadn't sounded like an idiot.

'Thanks, San.' She saw me out.

I walked across the Southwark pier, staring absently at a mariner mooring a boat on the banks of the Thames. A deadly thought struck me. I spun on my heel and retraced my steps to the Topaz building. The receptionist looked on, puzzled, as I mumbled a hurried apology at the desk and hustled back into Megan's cubicle.

'We need police security at Kings,' I said. 'Charlotte might still be on the attacker's radar.'

⁓

'We have a police liaison officer and some security folks patrolling Charlotte's ward at Kings,' I updated Keisha on the phone later that evening.

'Blimey,' Keisha mumbled.

'Have we begun work on the exposé yet?' I prodded, glancing around me at the steady flow of traffic on Kingsway as I proceeded towards the Holborn Underground after classes at LSE.

'We're starting next Monday. Nineteenth March. By the way, I'm just came back from a meeting with Jeff Stuart from SIGNAL. He's cheesed off that we're delaying the tour for a bit.'

'All well with Jeff?'

'I guess he needs some pacifying,' Keisha replied.

'About what? Did we tell Jeff about Char's accident or the Bread Breakers' incident?'

'I don't see how or why the Bread Breakers' incident is relevant,' Keisha pointed out. 'Anyway – Alfred wants me to step into Charlotte's shoes and run the show now.'

'Wow. You don't sound too happy about that though. What's eating you?'

Keisha sighed. 'I don't know. Charlotte is the face of Streetsmart. I'm not sure how the public will respond to a new person … even if it's my own show.'

I approached the Holborn station. I ducked into an adjacent confectionary store to carry on our conversation in case the phone reception waned when I stepped underground.

'Don't be silly, Kiki,' I chided.

'If I'd had my way, I would've jumped in on the Bread Breakers' story right away,' Keisha said. 'But this film I've been busy with was keeping that on hold for a few days. We wrapped up the final shoot this morning. It goes on air next week. The Bread Breakers' story is my highest priority now. I'm done playing the role of a minion and pandering to people's egos.'

I didn't know what to say. The fact that she had just concluded a major documentary should have given her a reason to celebrate. Instead, she sounded overworked, jaded and dejected.

'Kiki, are you safe?' I began, but Keisha cut in.

'I'm getting away for a bit. Ken and I are leaving for Cornwall tomorrow morning. We'll be back Sunday night. Might do me good to clear my head for a while.'

'Ken? Your boyfriend?' I didn't mean to pry, but she didn't sound like herself.

'Hell, no. He's a guy I just met.'

'Whoa, where did you both meet?'

'At The Globe. He's an investor relations manager at IBM,' Keisha said, sounding relaxed for the first time since her call. 'Some school kids were attending a special performance of *Macbeth*. We were doing a short feature on it for the BBC. IBM sponsored it.'

A pang of uneasiness engulfed the pleasant sensation of being a part of Keisha's fantasy story. 'Why're you going away with him for a weekend when you've barely known him for a few weeks?' I spluttered.

'I think you should mind your own business, San,' Keisha said coolly.

'I'm concerned about you, Kiki,' I said, taken aback. 'Does he know anything about Lionheart, Bread Breakers' and whatever else?' I cringed when I realised that it was I who sounded like the boss now.

'Just this and that about Lionheart …' Keisha said dismissively. 'If Jeff emails, mention that some unexpected contingencies are causing a mild delay in the tour. I'll handle the rest when I return from Cornwall.'

Asha Sawant's hysterectomy was scheduled at 3.00 p.m. on Twenty-ninth March.

'She's made up her mind,' Nimmy said sadly when we were in my bedroom that night.

Shailaja had herself told Nimmy about it after he returned home from work this evening. He had tried to dissuade his mother from putting Asha through the surgery and proposed alternatives. But Shailaja threatened to disown him if he kicked up a racket about it.

'I don't think I can do much more without incurring their wrath,' Nimmy added.

'Are they—are they, you know ...' I spluttered for the right words. 'Is it a surgery where they're removing her uterus, ovaries, and fallopian tubes?'

Nimmy nodded 'As far as I understand it, that appears to be the case, yes. All we can do is pray that her surgery goes well and hope she gets better after it.'

'What does that mean?' I demanded sternly. 'Did you read up on the effects of such a hysterectomy?'

'I did,' Nimmy said, curling his toes uncomfortably.

'Then?' I demanded. 'Are you saying you're going to let them go ahead with that plan? Do you think they're doing this so that Asha gets better? Don't kid yourself, Nimmy. If menstrual hygiene is really their biggest concern, there are other alternatives to manage that. They probably give a tinker's damn if she gets raped or not, so long as no one screams blue murder. But they're certainly afraid their honour will be tarnished if she gets pregnant again. So, of course – they'd rather have "all of it out", if that also means not having to deal with her period in the process. It's no different from an honour killing.'

Nimmy jumped up from the bed and stood before me, glowering furiously. I scrambled to the other side of the bed. 'Are you calling my parents murderers?' he snarled, hauling me towards him. I struggled to pull myself away, but he gripped my arm tightly. I dissolved into a bout of coughs. 'Nimmy, I-I'm asthmatic ...' I gasped, straining across the bed to reach for my inhaler.

'I don't care!' he said coldly, but he let go of me.

I massaged my chest and grabbed my inhaler. 'You—you had no right to grab my arm like that, no goddamn right,' I wheezed in between puffs. 'How dare you? I'm trying to say a hysterectomy for ... for someone who's already suffering so much ... without her consent and awareness ... that's a human rights violation. I didn't call your parents murderers.'

Nimmy glared at me. 'You just did. And you do know Asha is in no position to take informed decisions.'

'That doesn't matter. No licensed gynaecologist would recommend such a surgery for Asha. Even in a genuine case where such a surgery *is* required for a person who can't provide an informed consent, a court approval is required.'

'Are you a lawyer?' Nimmy jeered.

'Well, you lead M&A advisory in some lousy sector at Deutsche. Don't you know anything about your own country? I've been here less than a year, I'm not even out of my teens yet, and I'm a freaking student. And I seem to know much more about these things than you do. Are you mentally retarded?'

A searing blow stung my jaw. I flew backwards and slammed against the wall behind me. A pile of books and CDs on top of the bookshelf next to me crashed down, missing my head by inches. A flurry of stars danced before my eyes. I remembered the blazing resolve with which Ritchie had held me in his arms in the LSE library after we read that email from Bloodfonso. And here Nimmy was, pummeling the daylights out of me when all I was trying to do was convince him that a hysterectomy wouldn't be in Asha's best interests or the Sawants'. Both events were unrelated, but my recollection of Ritchie's courage and reassurance kindled a violent pang for him. I lay rumpled on the floor and sobbed. Nimmy knelt beside me and stroked my hair, mumbling apologies. I swatted his hand away and edged along the wall tremulously.

'What can I do, Sandy?' Nimmy wailed. 'I feel like I'm being stretched taut between you and my family. And my love for Asha is the line that's being stretched to its limits. Everything you say makes sense … but I'm afraid to break the yardsticks my parents have put up to preserve their bloody honour. I'll lose their love if I go to the cops or raise a hue and cry about Asha's surgery!'

I rose unsteadily to my feet. 'You hit me. Do you realise that?'

'Good heavens, I didn't mean to,' Nimmy spluttered.

I slid out of my camisole and shrugged into my jumper. 'I've a good mind to report you to the police too, for what you just did.'

'Gosh, Sandy.'

'I'd bloody slap you myself, but I just won't stoop down to that level. You're fucking pathetic. A person who can't face himself. A coward. Now, that stings, doesn't it?'

'Where are you going?'

'That's none of your business. At any rate, I need to re-think things.'

'Think … think about what?' Nimmy sounded increasingly panicked.

'For starters, you just assaulted me physically. You have no fucking excuse for what you just did. I don't want any further association with you. You don't have enough courage to stand up for what you believe in. You claim to love Asha, but you can't stand up against your parents even when you know what they're doing isn't right. You're really a confused man. And I won't tolerate abuse from you or anyone else under any circumstance whatsoever. I'm out of here.'

At a small pub on Alexandra Avenue, I ordered a glass of sherry, sank into a wing chair and called Ritchie. 'You were right about Nimmy,' I sobbed to him. 'He got physically violent with me tonight. They're going ahead with Asha's surgery and there isn't a damn thing I can do to prevent it.'

'Good Lord, San!' Ritchie said. 'Are you all right? Would you like me to come over?'

'I'll be fine.'

'Did you report Nimmy to the police?'

'I don't know. To be fair, he grabbed my arm, then slapped me once.'

'That's no excuse for what he's done. You should probably consider moving out. Anyway, where are you right now?'

'In a pub across the Rayner's Lane station.'

'Have you gone nuts?' Ritchie bellowed. 'After Nimmy's drink-spiking incident and Charlotte's car crash, you may well be next. And you have the balls to walk out at this hour?'

'Balls? The last time I checked I was a girl.'

Ritchie broke into guffaws. My tension began to dissipate.

'Darn you,' Ritchie said. 'You're being foolish right now. Get your ass home at once. Call a cab. NOW. And keep away from that pig, do you hear?'

I hailed a cab home. When I got in, Nimmy was nowhere in sight. In my room, all my books and CDs were back on the bookshelf. My camisole had been folded neatly on the back of my chair. I wrenched it from there and tossed it in my laundry bag in the corner. I put on a beige flannel nightgown and trotted downstairs to the kitchen to make a cup of coffee.

Returning to my room, I set the steaming cup on my bedside table and glanced at my phone. 11.15 p.m.

An unfamiliar number flashed on the screen. I hit the answer button, hoping it wasn't Bloodfonso or any other creep.

A baritone male voice resounded in my ear. 'Hello, am I speaking to Ms Sandhya Raman?'

'Yes. Who's calling?'

'This is Inspector Tim Herbert. I'm a Senior Investigative Officer with Scotland Yard.'

By now I was wide-awake.

'Scotland Yard?'

'The Criminal Investigation Department of the Metropolitan Police Service,' Herbert explained.

I tried to understand what was happening.

'Miss, I'd like to know about the nature of your relationship with Ms Keisha Douglas?' Herbert inquired carefully.

'I work with her on a BBC show and a campaign for the mentally disabled,' I replied nervously.

'How long have you known her?'

'Uh, about four and a half months.'

'How did you two meet?'

'Is something wrong?' I spluttered, wondering where this conversation was heading.

'Just answer my questions for now, please,' the officer snapped.

'I met her at a media career fair at ExCEL London Centre last November. She was representing the BBC. I'm a student at the London School of Economics. I attended the fair to explore career opportunities in my field.'

'What sort of campaign were you and Ms Douglas involved in?' He sounded less surly now. I wondered if the LSE name-dropping had anything to do with the reduced animosity in his tone.

'It's a drive to integrate special needs people into mainstream society.' The tug of trepidation in my chest rose to a crescendo. 'Wh-what happened? Is she okay?'

'Ms Raman,' Herbert said gravely. 'Keisha Douglas has been found dead in her apartment.'

Keisha's residence was a split-level sixth floor conversion apartment in Beacon's Bow Enclave, a gated community overlooking the Victoria Park Square in Bethnal Green. From Keisha's tastefully designed drawing room, I had a partial view through the open door of an adjoining bedroom. I stared in horror at Keisha's still form on her four-poster canopy bed. A crew of people in blue suits hovered around in the bedroom and an adjacent balcony taking photographs, fingerprints and DNA samples.

Keisha was in a short yellow nightdress. A half-empty bottle of sleeping pills sat on the nightstand next to her. A few capsules lay scattered haphazardly on the table.

Inspector Herbert and a trainee forensic investigator, whose name no one bothered to mention, puttered around anxiously in the living room, scrawling down notes and inspecting various articles. Another investigating officer, who curtly introduced himself as Ben Reynolds, was barking instructions on his walkie-talkie. My heart lurched when I emerged from my dazed stupor. Jeffrey Stuart from SIGNAL sat on a pouffe ahead of me, wearing a troubled expression. What was *he* doing here?

My gaze shifted to a middle-aged, pyjama-clad woman, huddled in a settee and crying. A tall young man with wavy titian hair slumped on a chair by the dining table at the far end, holding his head in his hands and repeatedly gasping, 'Oh, God … I can't believe this.'

'Inspector, can I go inside?' I asked tearfully, when I found my voice.

'No,' Herbert said shortly. Then he turned around and hollered to everyone as a general warning, 'Everyone is to be seated here in the sitting room. None of you can go inside the bedroom – including us. Reynolds and I are here solely for interrogation purposes. The rest of the folks 'round here are forensic guys and they're wired up studying fingerprints, taking shots and investigating the scene and the body.'

I cringed at the mention of the word *body*. Had Keisha become no more than a body now?

My knees buckled under me and I slid down to the floor, racked by gut-wrenching sobs.

'Oh, God … Kiki … noooooo!' I wailed.

Reynolds, who was finished with his walkie-talkie, bent down and patted my shoulder.

Inspector Herbert towered above me, waving a note in front of my face. 'We found this slip of paper on the bedside table. Would you recognise it as her handwriting?' he asked.

I gawked at the lined yellow memo paper. Penned in a neat, pearly handwriting were the words:

'Life has become more than I can ever cope with.

Father, into your hands I commit my spirit.'

The note was signed off as 'Kiki'. I stared at Inspector Herbert, astonished.

'I don't know,' I managed. I had never seen Keisha's handwriting.

'We'll have to inspect Ms Douglas' handwriting then. Do you have those handwritten notes Ms Richards provided?' Herbert barked at Reynolds, who nodded compliantly.

Herbert and Reynolds asked me a few more questions. I debated whether to share my suspicions of all the events that had been going on lately. As I gazed at the trio before me, I decided that I would do so later in private, if I needed to.

Jeff scowled at a coffee table that held a phone and a sleek black USB flash drive. The woman dabbed her eyes and the man, who I thought must be Ken, was crying openly. Jeff attempted to reach for the flash drive on the table.

'No!' Herbert barked. 'You don't touch anything in this room either.'

'But all my data …' Jeff choked out.

'Did you hear what I said?' Herbert roared.

Jeff quailed as if he had been struck with a belt. He glanced at me before lowering his gaze.

The forensic investigator emerged from the bedroom.

'Sir,' he announced to Herbert and Reynolds, breaking the stiff silence in the room. 'Ms Douglas doesn't appear to have been touched. There's no sign of any physical injury. But she seems to have consumed an entire bottle of sleeping pills. I found the empty bottle on the floor by her bedside. There is another half-empty bottle on the bedside table.'

'Take a sample of each with you,' Herbert instructed. 'Also, cut a piece of her clothing for DNA testing. We'll have Tony inspect all of them back at the lab.'

The forensic investigator repeated the orders to his team and turned around to us. 'Would you know if she was prescribed drugs for insomnia?'

Ken shook his head jadedly. 'I-I've been dating Kiki only for about a month,' he croaked. 'I knew she was a nocturnal person but never an insomniac.'

'As of now, it appears to be a suicide,' Herbert said grimly. 'The autopsy will verify it. Did she say or do anything that indicated she might have contemplated taking her life?' Herbert questioned me, as the forensic investigator disappeared into the bedroom again.

I stole a peek at Jeff. Catching my gaze, Jeff shrugged ruefully.

'No,' I shot back at once. 'Keisha was a fighter. Our campaign was picking up steam. She was excited about the release of her next show and we were going to do an ex ...' I bit my tongue. I had been on the verge of saying *exposé*. '... clusive for our show, Streetsmart,' I managed somehow. 'It was all going well ...' My words suddenly drew to a halt. I remembered she had seemed dejected earlier this evening.

Reynolds picked up the cue. 'What is it?'

'Well, I ...' I didn't know where to begin. 'The TV host for Streetsmart had an accident earlier this week. Our campaign tour was delayed because of that. And ...' I shifted my gaze to Jeff, who was staring at me. '... And Jeff didn't seem happy about it at all ...'

'I wasn't unhappy about it!' Jeff protested. 'I was just concerned. I told her ...'

Reynolds held up a hand. 'Let her finish, Mr Stuart,' he spoke sternly.

'... Jeff seemed quite 'cheesed off' about the delay. That's what Kiki—I mean, Keisha, told me on the phone when we spoke at six-thirty this evening,' I continued, glaring at Jeff. 'And Keisha's boss, Alfred asked her if she could replace Charlotte on Streetsmart, at least for the time being. She didn't seem very happy about that, either.' Herbert nodded, as if what I had said confirmed their hypothesis.

'But she'd never go to this extreme for something like that!' I yelled.

'Calm down, Ms Raman,' Reynolds said. 'We're only asking standard questions.'

'How did you get my number? What exactly happened?' I demanded.

Herbert exhaled. 'Well, you were among those whom Ms Douglas called this evening. And Ken here,' he pointed at the disconcerted man at the dining table, 'is the person she last called at around nine-fifteen. Now, the flash drive you see on the table here belongs to Jeff. He appears to have called her many times between seven and nine in the evening today. He claims that drive has some important data related to one of SIGNAL's initiaitives. But we don't know how it turned up on Keisha's bedside.'

'I told you!' Jeff yelled. 'Keisha met me in my office this evening. She mistook my USB drive for hers. Her own pen drive is in my office right now! I was trying to contact her because I needed my pen drive this evening. But I never came to this house until I got a call from you.'

Reynolds shushed him. Herbert waved his arm towards the middle-aged woman who was dabbing her eyes in the corner. 'Now, Ms Douglas' neighbour, Ms Sofia Richards, who lives on the floor right below ...'

Sofia, who had earlier been grilled by both officers, lost no opportunity in recounting her story once again – for our benefit, I presumed.

Most residents at Beacon's Bow commended Sofia for her culinary expertise. Keisha had arranged to feature Sofia in a cooking show on the BBC's kids channel, CBeebies, last year. Since then, Sofia had never failed to check up on Keisha or drop in for a cup of tea on her rare evenings home. Keisha ran into Sofia in the elevator on her way to her apartment at 6.30 p.m.

'You look beat,' Sofia greeted. 'All well at work?'

Keisha smiled tiredly. 'The host for one of our shows had an accident. And some issues have put the campaign on hold.'

Sofia raised a brow quizzically. 'Oh, *that* campaign? Is it stirring up controversy?'

'Well, there are people who aren't happy with it,' Keisha mumbled.

'Oh?'

'I'm taking a breather for a bit. Leaving for Cornwall tomorrow morning … with Ken.'

Sofia winked knowingly. 'That gorgeous hunk I've seen slinking around here a lot lately? I think the doorman's taken a liking to him, too. By the way, I made some cheesecake this afternoon. I can leave some of it with you later tonight.'

'You're a peach, Sofie,' Keisha said. 'I'm not going anywhere tonight. Do drop by.'

At 8.30 p.m., Sofia rang Keisha's doorbell with a carefully wrapped parcel of blackcurrant and crème fraiche cheesecake. The door remained unanswered.

'I guess she did step out after all,' Sofia mused disappointedly after a few minutes. As she turned to leave, the faint sounds of a TV news programme emerged from inside the apartment. Deciding that Keisha had left the TV on and slipped out somewhere in a hurry, Sofia headed back to her flat and flipped on the telly. An hour passed before she tiptoed upstairs and rang Keisha's doorbell again. The TV in the apartment was still on. Perplexed, she dialed Keisha's cell number from her mobile. The tinkle of a phone resonated from within the apartment.

Didn't she take her mobile with her? She wondered, bewildered.

After trying Keisha's cell a few more times, Sofia called her on her landline. All she got was Keisha's voicemail. When she put her ear to the door, she heard the answering machine.

Any lack of responsiveness from a woman who was on call 24x7 was unusual. A vague misgiving urged Sofia to dial triple nine.

'Keisha used to leave little post-its on my door before heading out at dawn for a TV shoot or crew emergency, usually requesting me to collect a parcel or spare keyset or some milk and stuff like that. I just gave you those notes as samples of her handwriting – the ones I still have with me anyway. I hope we can figure out if she really wrote that suicide note,' Sofia finished, looking at the two officers.

'That can't be right!' Ken protested. He turned to the officers with tears in his eyes. 'I've already told you my story. I was going to stay here tonight before our drive to Cornwall next morning. I came here at around seven o'clock but she wasn't in. So, I rang her and couldn't get through. I waited for a while before calling her again. She answered my call then, and said she was out. So, I left from here around seven-forty-five and did some shopping.'

'You went shopping at Sainsbury's in Bethnal Green. Is that correct?' Herbert interrupted.

Ken nodded. 'When I was done, I phoned her again at eight-thirty, but she didn't pick up. She called me a little after nine, and asked if we could meet at Liverpool Street for a quick bite and drink. She was out on a work emergency, she said. She didn't tell me what the issue was. But she said she was raving hungry when she called me.' His voice cracked as he went on. 'I waited at the Liverpool Street station till ten-thirty. She didn't show up. I called her several times. I decided to check in on her and see if she was all right. I got a call from you when I was on my way back here.'

He sank to his knees and began panting for breath as if someone were choking him.

'That's all right, Mr Butler. 'Here.' Tim Herbert produced a Kleenex box.

Sofia and Jeff glared at Ken.

'How could she have called you after nine?' Sofia yelled. 'I was right here at eight thirty and the TV was on. At nine-thirty, she wasn't answering either of her goddamn phones and I was standing right outside this door and her cell phone was ringing from inside when I called her!'

'She wasn't taking my calls either,' Jeff corroborated.

Reynolds looked at Sofia and Jeff. A cloud of suspicion wafted over his face. 'For now, Mr Butler's story appears to be accurate,' he told them sternly. 'As I earlier mentioned, Mr Butler called Ms Douglas at seven-forty and eight-thirty, this evening. The doorman's testimony coincides with his story, too. The doorman buzzed Mr Butler in at five past seven. Mr Butler was seen leaving at seven-forty-five. He rang Ms Douglas at eight thirty and it turned up as a missed call on Ms Douglas' phone. She returned his call at nine-fifteen. Mr Butler called her several times between nine-thirty and ten-thirty, both on her mobile and landline. We happened to speak to the doorman and check the call lists on both phones,' he added emphatically.

'No, no … don't go anywhere near there!' Herbert yelled, as Sofia unexpectedly sprang from the settee and darted to grab Keisha's phone from the coffee table to see if she had really phoned Ken at 9.15. Sofia sat down again, her eyebrows raised in disbelief.

'And what were you doing between seven and nine this evening?' Herbert demanded of Jeff. The chip in Jeff's front tooth caught the light of a side lamp as he shuffled in his seat and blanched.

'I-I was in the office,' he parried. 'Working on a proposal to the government.'

'What proposal?'

'A proposal to expand the employment budget for the disabled,' Jeff said sullenly.

'But the presentation we studied on your flash drive seems to address an entirely different subject,' Herbert said. 'Why were you in a hurry to get that flash drive back?'

Sofia snorted. Jeff's beady eyes flitted around from one end of the room to the other.

'I'm working on that too. Or rather, one of our managers is,' he blathered. 'We were approaching British Telecom with a proposal for an assistive technology device. All the stats and data are on there.' He pointed to the flash drive on the table. 'That proposal is due tomorrow.'

Herbert harrumphed. 'And the manager's name?'

'Gretchen Friedland.'

'We're going to cross-check all that you've told us,' Herbert told Jeff in a formidable tone.

Reynolds cleared his throat. 'Right now, it's likely she may have committed suicide. The suicide note and all …' he said to all of us.

I looked at the blasted note in Herbert's hand. I couldn't argue with what they were saying. The note didn't show that she had scrawled out a string of words haphazardly in duress; her handwriting was neat, smooth and contemplative.

'But we want to rule out the possibilities of a homicide here,' Reynolds was saying. 'The scene is being thoroughly investigated.'

'Not a word to the media,' Herbert added warningly.

While in a cab back home, I thought about how full of life Kiki had been when we spoke just a few hours before. Now, I would never see her again. Good Lord. Why was I losing people I loved? First, my Mom … then Saahil … and now Keisha who had taken me under her wing like an older sister in the big, bad media world. A shard of intense pain clutched my stomach. I wrapped my topcoat around me more tightly. The events unraveling in my life seemed to carry a damning ring of unpredictability. And I felt entrapped in that ring. As I went over Jeff's half-baked explanations, a dreaded question fought its way into my train of thought. Was he behind the mystery at Bread Breakers'? Was he involved in Keisha's death?

10

On the Skids

15 March

Dr Edwin Hardy, known to many as Eddie, had been a barrister for the Crown Prosecution Service for five years before deciding that prosecuting criminals wasn't his cup of tea – a move that urged him to enroll in medical school. Today, he was a home office pathologist held in high regard for his astute observations. Unsurprisingly, Eddie was Herbert's natural choice for Keisha's inquest.

'There are no signs of a struggle,' Eddie reported to a grim Herbert at 8.00 a.m. on Thursday, as he and his toxicologist, Rodney Pike, finished their post-mortem examination on Keisha's body in London Chest Hospital's dingy mortuary in East London.

'Acute barbiturate poisoning was the instant cause of death,' Eddie added. 'She consumed 100 mg of chloral hydrate and 40 mg of ametyl sodium. She appears to have been in generally good health. She did not have sex before she died.'

'We found small portions of food residue and an odour of champagne in her stomach,' Rodney said. 'There was also a BAC of 0.2 in her blood.'

Herbert raised a brow in surprise. 'Alcohol?'

Rodney nodded. 'Didn't you locate traces of alcohol in her chambers?'

'No,' Herbert said, puzzled. 'We never even found a champagne flute anywhere.'

'I'd check again if I were you,' Eddie advised. 'Quite likely she consumed alcohol and food, trashed them out and overdosed on the pills about an hour later. We estimate the approximate time of her death at eight p.m. yesterday.'

Herbert exhaled tensely. 'You sure 'bout that?'

Eddie nodded. 'I can't give you an exact time. But, dead sure it was before nine.'

Herbert's suspicions began to mount. This revelation made Ken Butler the prime suspect.

'Well, I don't wish to eliminate the possibility that she could have been injected with those chemicals,' he said aloud.

'We'd have identified a needle mark even from a subcutaneous insulin injection, Sir. We haven't found any needle marks on her. It was an oral overdose,' Rodney said.

'Would you be able to tell me if that was self-administered?'

'I'm afraid we can't say that, Tim,' Eddie stated candidly. 'Is the lab testing the fingerprints on those bottles?'

'Yes,' Herbert said shortly. 'And the fingerprints on the note she wrote, too.'

Eddie gave a brisk nod.

'Thanks, Eddie. For the most part, I'd say it still looks like suicide,' Herbert said.

Eddie nodded again, though decidedly less certain this time.

'It's a wonder how many fruitcakes pop up like this one,' Herbert remarked pensively. 'Young and alive and healthy. The minute they decide they can't cope with their lives … boom!'

He snapped his fingers. 'They snuff themselves out. Just like that, Eddie.'

'I'd like to consult a bacteriologist and run some special tests,' Eddie said somberly. 'I also need to do more blood work. That'll take some time, but the autopsy report will be ready in a week.'

Herbert left the hospital with a nagging doubt.

This champagne business needs to be investigated, he thought.

Despite my efforts to keep the media at bay, news of Keisha's death spread like wildfire by Thursday afternoon. I barely slept a wink last night. Just after dawn, I called Charlotte's office and delivered the news to a devastated Megan. After that, I spoke briefly to my father and brother. Both of them picked up on my low energy. Citing preoccupation with LSE coursework and my other ongoing activities, I managed to brush their questions aside. Although they knew about my work for Lionheart and Streetsmart, they weren't aware of what I had seen at Bread Breakers', and I wasn't intending to update them about the drama going on here. But just hearing their voices and listening to Sri prattle on about his new girlfriend calmed me down a bit.

By mid-morning Alfred rang me, panicked.

'Would you know what exactly happened to Keisha?' he demanded. 'I can't believe she'd really go out there and commit suicide.'

I briefed Alfred about my visit to Keisha's apartment on Wednesday night and Herbert's update of his meeting with the pathologist this morning. 'I suspect foul play, Alfred,' I finished. 'We need to …'

'Let the police do their job,' Alfred completed.

'I know, but …'

'Will you do the show?' Alfred chimed in suddenly.

I wasn't sure I had heard him right. 'Wh-what?'

'Streetsmart. I know you're no expert but I do think you can pull it off with some guidance. If you can't, we'll find someone else. We need to find a replacement soon. Dear Lord ...'

In sunnier circumstances, I would have pounced on the opportunity to host a top-rated BBC show. Now, I was miffed that all Alfred could think about was how Keisha's demise would be detrimental to his show. 'I'll think about it,' I said tightly.

'We'll assign a murder squad to investigate Ms Douglas' case. And we'll need concrete evidence to conduct a raid on that care home,' Herbert said grimly, after I reported last week's incidents to him, including what I had seen at Bread Breakers', in his dilapidated office at the Bethnal Green police station, an hour later.

'I've recorded instances of abuse there,' I revealed. 'It's all on video.'

'That'd be pretty solid,' Herbert intoned. 'Where's it now?'

I realised I had no copy of it. 'The film is on Keisha's computer. The file is password-protected. I don't know what the password is. But I'm sure we can find a way to open that file and make copies. Anyhow, her boss, Alfred has seen it. Maybe he has a copy of it.'

'You should have made copies and reported it to the police right away,' Herbert barked.

I stared down at my lap.

'Let's do it this way ...' he said finally. 'We'll contact the murder investigation team. They'll touch base with you soon. Meanwhile, get hold of that film.'

I hesitated as I rose from my seat. Herbert caught on. 'What is it?' he inquired.

'Well, I think Jeff is hiding something,' I admitted. 'I don't know him anymore than you do. But that's the hunch I've had since last night.'

Herbert's face darkened. 'Well, he certainly wasn't in his office last night. Guy gave us a cock-and-bull story.' He rose from his seat and shook my hand stiffly. 'Leave Jeff to us.'

I marched into Jeff Stuart's office later that afternoon.

'How can I help you?' Jeff rumbled.

I gingerly took a seat. He reached for a Zippo lighter. I lost my nerve.

'Keisha was pretty upset about your response to the tour delay,' I began lamely.

Jeff blew out a ring of smoke and tapped his cigar into an ashtray that sat beside him.

'Yes. And I'm afraid we're withdrawing our funding for Lionheart,' he informed decisively. 'With Keisha gone, I can't imagine how we can proceed further. I also understand the police may be raiding a nursing home on Lambeth and that you happen to be involved,' he added.

I froze. Why had Herbert told Jeff about my investigation when he had agreed that Jeff was acting suspiciously?

Jeff smiled coolly. 'Whatever's going on in that care home,' he went on, 'I'm glad it's being looked into. But SIGNAL can't endorse this campaign any longer. We don't want to stir up any controversy with it. No hard feelings. It's a business decision.'

He blew out another puff of smoke in my face. I coughed and pulled out my inhaler.

'A care home is exploiting its residents to the core!' I cried indignantly. 'I thought SIGNAL would step in to investigate this rather than back out.'

'The police will look into it and the Mayor will review mental health care policy if it comes to that,' Jeff said slickly. 'That's their job, not ours.'

As I rose to leave, three champagne bottles on a shelf behind Jeff's workstation caught my eye.

I remembered what Herbert had told me about the champagne traces they had found during Keisha's post-mortem. I fled from his cabin, terrified.

Ritchie called me worriedly that night.

'I'm sorry about Keisha, San,' he empathised. 'It's all over the media now. Even NPR in New York has picked it up. Hope you're doing okay.'

'Barely,' I moaned. 'I suspect it's homicide, Ritch. First, Nimmy was the target, then Charlotte … now Kiki …' I began sobbing.

'Stay cool and strong, San,' Ritchie said. 'I know it's tough …'

'… Everything's turning into a nightmare,' I wailed. 'SIGNAL has withdrawn funding for Lionheart. I have to answer to fifteen schools and care centres that have signed up for our workshops … the media will sniff on it and my name will be floating around in newsrooms. Streetsmart is hanging in the balance and my only source of income from that show could be gone. All I'm involved in right now is a controversy with Bread Breakers'. And I lost a dear friend. I don't even know if Charlotte will make it. My relationship with Nimmy is on the rocks and Asha will be sterilised very soon. God knows if they're safe too. And my life is at stake. Good heavens, Ritch ...'

'Your fears are baseless, San ...'

'I suspect Jeff is behind all this,' I cut in. 'And in some bizarre way, Carl Wright too ... that friend of Nimmy's.

Ritchie chuckled. 'That's a good thing, isn't it?'

'Excuse me?'

'Isn't it good that you're getting closer to nailing the offenders?' Ritchie clarified.

I sighed. 'I don't know. Nothing makes sense anymore.'

'You remember the Gregersen International Scholarships I told you about?' Ritchie said suddenly. 'I think you should apply for it. I know it isn't much, given the mess you're in right now ... but it'll ease your purse strings a bit.'

'I'll put that on my to-do list,' I muttered.

'Fight for it, San,' Ritchie advised. 'The dust will settle soon.'

I hung up and sat exhaustedly in bed.

Nimmy poked his head in. 'I'm really sorry I ... I ... well, you know, about last night ... about me hitting you ...' he began.

'That's the least of my concerns right now,' I snapped. 'Kiki is *dead* and there are a zillion things I need to sort out around me or I'll go crazy. If I don't, someone else will. Get out of here.'

Deciding that I needed my own space, Nimmy retreated hastily. When I checked my emails, my inbox flashed with another note from alfonso@bloodfonso.com:

Enjoying the drama, aren't you?

20 March

'It's a pretty complicated case,' Inspector Craig Davenport stated emphatically on Tuesday morning as I sat in his office, sipping stale coffee.

Tall, green-eyed and well into his fifties, Detective Chief Inspector Davenport, appointed by Scotland Yard, was investigating Keisha's murder on behalf of the Homicide and Serious Crime Command of the Specialist Crime Directorate as part of the East London Murder Squad. The former Merchant Navy officer had once worked closely with the Home Office to help revise criminal justice legislative clauses. Stepping into the role of a victimologist with natural ease, Davenport was burning the candle at both ends to fit the jigsaw pieces together, just as soon as the case of Keisha's mysterious death fell on his lap on Thursday evening.

Keisha's family had flown down to London in an inconsolable state on Thursday night.

'My girl would never do anything like that!' Mrs Douglas cried when she and her husband were questioned on Friday morning. 'As a child, she always loved movies, documentaries and writing. She believed there was so much more to life than what most of us tend to live for.'

'We don't think what happened was a suicide or an accident. We want justice for our daughter,' Mr Douglas seconded in a shaky voice.

The Douglase' tearful avowals drove the squad into the inquiry with stoic resolve. By Friday noon, the investigation, launched as Operation Douglas, was in full swing.

Jeff was summoned on Friday afternoon for further questioning. I heard he had come up with a revised story when a detective pointed out that, contrary to his claims, he hadn't been in his office on Wednesday night. The modified explanation was some hogwash about working in an undisclosed subsidiary office because his British Telecom proposal was top secret.

Even as detectives were speaking to Alfred and Keisha's friends, associates, and colleagues, Ken Butler, who was on Davenport's radar as a prime suspect, had simply vanished – as it turned out – the morning after Keisha's death. A background check in his name yielded no results. He didn't have a national insurance number either. A sales receipt at the Sainsbury's store near Keisha's apartment revealed that the name on his credit card account was Dario De Luca.

A UK driving license had been issued in that name, five years ago. By early evening on Friday, a bunch of detectives had alerted airports, train stations, and border officials about Dario's disappearance.

By Monday morning, a scruffy picture was shown around to everyone from security guards to the senior management of his professed employer, IBM, but no one had seen anyone who looked like him. Neither had they heard of a Kenneth Butler or a Dario De Luca.

Davenport had called me last evening with a request for information on Keisha and the Lionheart campaign. Now, I had just spilled out everything in my list of concerns to him, including the incident of Asha's rape two years ago, my limited knowledge of the Sawants' history with Rosie at Bread Breakers', and my misgivings about Carl and Jeff.

'Thanks for listening to my story. You've been very patient and kind,' I said in response to his statement on the perceived level of complexity in this case.

Davenport smiled benignly. 'You've been incredibly helpful yourself. You might soon become an important witness in this case.'

'I received another threat last night,' I reported, turning in a copy of both emails I had received from Bloodfonso.

Davenport studied them squarely. 'We'll need to trace the IP address for both emails.' He hastily clicked away on a small tablet on his desk.

'I just emailed the team an update on Bloodfonso,' he informed after a minute. 'We'll keep these printouts with us. I'd advise you to be careful.

'Jeff's evasiveness and the boyfriend's disappearance have put us on high alert,' he added darkly. 'The boyfriend said that Keisha told him she was out on a work-related emergency when he rang her at five past eight last Wednesday. But the CCTV footage we've got doesn't show Keisha stepping out after she entered her apartment at seven-thirty. If he's on the run now, I'm hoping a border agent hands him to us. They've got his picture on their system. And Jeff is lying to us. The British Telecom guys claim they had no idea an assistive technology proposal was coming their way.'

'What about Carl Wright and the teddy bears?' I reminded.

Davenport cocked his head. 'Did Carl know Keisha directly?'

'I don't know,' I said. 'But I think he spiked Nimmy's drinks after my care home investigation.'

'Okay, let's take it one step at a time, Ms Raman,' Davenport said firmly. 'Investigating Ms Douglas's death is top priority. Unless we have something that proves Carl is directly related to it, we're focusing only on our immediate suspects.'

'Who are the other suspects, besides Ken and Jeff?' I asked curiously.

Davenport crossed his arms on the table before him. 'We can't disclose every detail at this juncture. All I can say is that there could be alibis or accomplices.'

He raked a hand through his balding head. 'By the way, one of our detective constables mentions that a receipt for a four-month membership contract at Fitness First in Shepherd's Bush was found in Ms Douglas's handbag. Would you have any idea if she frequented a health club?'

'I'm sorry, Inspector,' I said apologetically. 'I didn't know much about Kiki's personal life.'

Davenport looked pensive. 'I'd like to get my hands on that piece of film you were talking about,' he said suddenly. 'If your theory on these events being related is consistent with what we find, we'll investigate the care home and bring Carl Wright in for questioning. But the squad will need to see the film first. I'll put you on to my colleague, Sergeant Dennis Wheeler. He likes to be called Wheeler. Can you direct him to the care home videotape?'

I swallowed tensely. 'The videotape is on Kiki—Keisha's Mac, and the folder is password-protected. Can we retrieve the password?'

Davenport chuckled. 'That's not a problem. Wheeler has been with the Interpol before. He's an expert with computers.'

22 March

'Are you sure you're right about this, Ms Raman?' Dennis Wheeler inquired, hunching over Keisha's MacBook in the Bethnal Green police station at 3.00 p.m. on Thursday.

'Of course I am,' I said. 'What's wrong?'

'There are no traces of any file or folder that matches your description,' Wheeler replied. 'I've cracked open the password for the Mac. And I'm pretty sure one of us would be able to tap into an encrypted folder with an open-source cracking tool. But it just isn't here.'

A blare of disjointed voices billowed in my head like echoes from the walls of an uninviting morgue. Where the hell had it gone? Without that film I couldn't prove that these baffling events were all connected. 'Can I have a look?' I requested. 'It *must* be in there somewhere.'

Sure, she's all yours.' Wheeler slid the laptop across the table towards me.

His Blackberry buzzed. 'I'll be right back.' He fixed a Bluetooth device on his ear and strode out swiftly, booming into the phone.

Peering into the screen of Keisha's sparsely populated desktop, I searched the contents of all her documents, opening each folder and file to be doubly sure. I found a bunch of music files, picture folders, audio and video clippings of various news stories and documentaries, and half-written programme formats, presumably recent. My face steamed up. Many of her unfulfilled dreams and creative energies were stashed away here. And she was stabled in a mortuary, rotting flesh and all. A life unlived.

'You find it?' Wheeler demanded, returning to his desk.

I shook my head disconsolately. 'Do you think Kiki's killer removed that folder from her Mac?'

Wheeler chortled. 'You're over-imaginative, aren't you?'

'I saw her move the film on to her Mac from my spy cam!' I cried.

'Where's that spy cam?' Wheeler asked sharply.

'I borrowed it from the LSE TV network,' I said. 'I had to erase my video before returning it.'

'Well, she probably moved it elsewhere to keep it safe,' Wheeler surmised with a sigh. 'She didn't transfer that file to her office laptop. We've had that checked too. Mr Alfred Maynard said he viewed the video and he described it to us. And that secretary Meg said Charlotte had seen it too. But neither of them has a copy of it.'

'She backed the film up on a flash drive,' I remembered. 'A SanDisk Connect, I think. It was attached to a red keychain with a label on it. She kept it in her briefcase in a side compartment. It should still be in there.'

Wheeler stared at Keisha's purple laptop case on the desk. 'That film is a strong source of evidence and not just for raiding the care home. It'll also come in handy when we develop a case for the Crown Prosecution Service in the event of a murder trial, should we be able to convict Keisha's murderer. Keisha's briefcase is in the BBC offices. It's being investigated right now. I'll drop a note about the flash drive.'

I nodded. Wheeler picked up his phone and rattled a few instructions to the detectives who were interrogating BBC officials and searching the contents of Keisha's workstation in White City.

'I have some updates for you,' Wheeler told me when he hung up.

'I hope they're positive.' I muttered.

'That's what an update is, I'd reckon,' Wheeler grunted. 'We spoke to the traffic police in Westminster. It turns out that the owner of the Wrangler that hit Ms Charlotte Hale's car is a David Cooper who runs a drycleaner's shop in Moor Park. He reported it missing after it was stolen from the car park at the Moor Park tube station.'

'Moor Park?' I echoed. I wasn't familiar with the area.

'Yep. Up in the northwest. The Wrangler was found broken into and abandoned in a shopping arcade in Green Park. Fingerprints and DNA samples have been taken from wherever possible. Since the driver wore gloves, the search hasn't brought up much yet. But we did hit some pay dirt. The driver smoked a cigarette and stubbed it out on the floor of the car. We've taken DNA samples from it. That little ciggy is a Drina special filter, a domestic brand in Bosnia and Serbia. Cooper is a British national and does not smoke. He is being questioned right now. So, here's our best bet: our suspect isn't a Brit.'

My stomach churned. I recalled Jeff Stuart blowing swirls of cigarette smoke into my face in his office. Did he smoke this particular brand or a different one? One could never be sure.

I struggled to focus on Wheeler's commentary.

'Our constable has also identified the IP address of the first anonymous email you received,' he was saying. 'He's traced it to Café Forever in Crossharbour down south. Davenport emailed us as soon as you showed him those threats yesterday. We're working with the cafe to determine who could have sent that email. But none of this is much to go by at this juncture.'

Up north, down South … my head began throbbing again.

'This squad sees you as an ally on this case,' Wheeler was saying. 'But we don't have enough evidence to make any conclusions unless we get that film.'

⁓

'You want Asha to stay cooped in all day like a caged animal? Have you gone out of your mind?' Nimmy bellowed to me on the phone from his office at 4.45 p.m.

I was sitting in a café at LSE, reviewing some notes for next week's seminar. I sighed. I didn't want to have anything to do with Nimmy at all after he had hit me that night, but I couldn't live with myself if I let someone undergo something I knew was neither legal nor justifiable. So, speaking to him was something I *had* to do if I wanted to avoid the alternative route: explaining the situation, or a modified version of it, to a family of livid Sawants.

'Nimmy,' I began. 'Listen. I ...'

'What would Mum and Dad say to that, huh? Have you thought about that?' Nimmy fumed.

I shuddered to think of how Nimmy would respond if I told him I had discussed Asha's sterilisation with Inspector Davenport.

I took a deep breath. 'Listen, Nimmy. Asha's life could be at risk. Last week, Charlotte had an accident. Two days later, Keisha was found dead. I've been getting death threats. Someone's after all of us! I thought we both agreed with all that when you told me about Asha's pregnancy last week.'

Nimmy exhaled. 'What's the proof that all those events are connected?'

'We're figuring that out,' I said. 'But Asha ...'

'Asha, Asha, Asha! It's always about her. Good grief, San! What do I do with you now?'

'Perhaps we could at least make everyone at home understand that it would be best to keep a watch on Asha, just for the time being, since the police are searching for an offender who's pandering to his—or her—vendetta against special needs people,' I said tentatively. 'That's all. Nothing more. Is that acceptable?'

To my surprise, Nimmy seemed to hunker down.

'All right, San. We can do it that way,' he agreed.

Perhaps, my persistence had gained me some kind of an allegiance from him. He might be confused about his ideals but he really did have a good heart.

'Thanks, Nimmy.'

'That's fine, Sandy. You do mean well,' he said. 'I'll see you at home.'

Shailaja and Ashok were glued to the TV when I returned home. Asha sat in an armchair at the other end of the sitting room, trying to watch the telly. The six o'clock BBC news was on. Pandy was slurping up soup from a bowl in the kitchen and Jyoti was at the stove, cooking dinner. I leaned against the banister and sipped my tea. It was a family scene of reasonable normalcy – the first-of-its-kind since I arrived at the Sawants' six months ago.

The newscaster's voice resonated from the sitting room. 'A young woman was knifed to death outside The Anglesea Arms pub in the South Kensington area of Chelsea. The murder victim, Harriet Blue, was an eyewitness to the accident of TV show host, Charlotte Hale last week ...'

I hustled over to the sitting room and froze. The channel replayed a segment from last week's news, including a report that Blue had spoken to the police, insisting she had seen a mysterious Wrangler push Charlotte's Skoda Octavia into the median barrier on the road. The anchor carried on about the murder, but I wasn't listening anymore.

I decided to share my theory with the Sawants. It was now or never.

I turned to Ashok. 'Um, Uncle ...'

Almost at the same moment, Ashok cleared this throat and boomed, 'Sandhya, we'd like to speak to you.' The short speech I had rehearsed faded away under the thriving sway of Ashok's unanticipated words.

'Yes?' I said meekly.

'We understand you want Asha to stay home,' Ashok said.

Nimmy has kept his word after all, I thought, grateful that he had broken the ice for me.

My fleeting relief ruptured into a million shards when Ashok snarled, 'What the hell are you doing with my daughter?'

Even as he spoke, Shailaja jumped up from a seat and came right before me. Exchanging a concerned look with his wife, Ashok motioned for her to sit down.

'U-Uncle …' I spluttered. 'Asha's life … well, it's … Keisha Douglas, my friend and a TV producer at the BBC … she's dead. I was working with her on a skills' campaign for special needs people …' My words were met with stony silence.

'Charlotte Hale, who's hosting Streetsmart – the TV show I thought Asha could participate in … she had an accident last week. The police are investigating both cases,' I continued, cowering in my seat. 'They believe someone is against the mentally challenged – or people supporting their cause. They say Asha and everyone like her should lie low until these cases are solved …'

A blend of horror and disgust settled on Ashok's face. Shailaja adroitly took the baton from him.

'That's because you were involved in that sleazy TV show and the campaign! Your thoughtlessness has resulted in an accident and a death,' she said quietly.

'No, I …' I was helpless in my efforts to create a bridge that would connect our vastly different mindsets and perspectives. But I couldn't refute what Shailaja said. The guilt had been gnawing at me from within – and now, I felt queasy.

'We're from a respectable Brahmin family, Sandhya,' Shailaja went on. 'We've welcomed you into our home and hearth. We've tried to lead normal, happy and productive lives. But you've been a source of various problems since you moved in. You kicked up a great deal of tension with your insistence on Asha's involvement in some dodgy TV show and that anchor was the subject of a hit-and-run accident. Your friend was murdered and Nirmal who's usually focused, has been quite distracted lately. We've been kind enough to tolerate you despite your asthma. We've respected you and given you your space. We've been keeping quiet for everything you've done: returning home late nearly everyday, making coffee in the dead of night and disturbing everyone's sleep when they need to wake up early next morning and go to work, unlike you. You've been talking to all kinds of men on the phone, you haven't been closing the showerhead properly, you've been leaving your inhaler and hair clips in random places across this house … I could go on for hours! But your behaviour doesn't stop with the recklessness of a lazy and inconsiderate paying guest. You drag your feet in the media, an entity that glamourises one's personal turmoil, intrudes into one's privacy and cashes in on tragic incidents to sensationalise and sell content. Do you really believe what journalists do in the name of social justice is real?'

'I think there's a misunderstanding …' I began.

'You didn't even stop there,' Ashok spat accusingly. 'Now you're bringing the police to our doorstep because of that campaign and the TV show and all that nonsense. Asha is a sweet little girl and you dare to exploit her disability and flaunt her to the media?'

Shailaja cut in, 'And you're not only discrediting yourself and your family, but also tarnishing our name, caste, honour and everything we hold dear to our hearts!' Her voice rose in octave as she finally shouted. 'And, to top this off, you've been sleeping with our son!'

A loud gasp escaped from my gut, as if I had been stabbed. Now, I understood the motive behind Nimmy's unusual acquiescence to my suggestion this afternoon – rattling on me to his parents about everything, including the nights I had spent with him. I recalled my tirade with the Sawants when Nimmy had told them about my insistence on Asha's participation in Streetsmart – without consulting me about it, of course. He had done this before. Why wouldn't he do it again? And now, after instigating this diabolical blaze, he was nestling in the comfort of his office to absolve himself of all the dirt and grime this encounter was spewing out.

A key turned in the lock. Nidhi bounded in with a singsong, 'Hello!' When she saw us in the sitting room, she halted in her tracks like she'd been shot.

'Is everything okay?' she inquired when she found her tongue.

'We're discussing Sandhya's behaviour in this house,' Shailaja said shortly.

Nidhi tossed her handbag over the kitchen counter and retraced her steps to the sitting room.

'Who's sleeping with whom?' she asked quietly. I gazed down at my lap, wishing the floor would swallow me up. Nimmy had desecrated our relationship and my love for Asha to ward off his personal dilemma and save his own skin. He had not only had his lay, but also made a fool of me. I would be a bigger fool if I didn't acknowledge the clarity of his purpose now.

'Sandhya has been sleeping with Nirmal and she's turning the public eye on Asha now,' Shailaja reported to Nidhi, bursting into sobs. Nidhi knelt down before Shailaja and draped a comforting arm around her. Ashok wore a troubled frown. Asha sat in the armchair and doodled on a colouring book in her lap, oblivious to the realities of the world. Jyoti squatted at the doorway to the sitting room, watching in wordless shock.

'You've violated your role as the daughter of a Brahmin priest!' Ashok avowed scornfully. 'A priest who fathered a scrawny slut and a real estate developer who's funding her. Both of them think their woman is a Goddess.'

That did it. Hearing Ashok taint the names of my father and brother snuffed out any iota of respect that remained for the Sawants. 'How dare you talk about Appa and Sri like that?' I shrieked in a voice I didn't recognise as my own. They had already denigrated my personality, character and everything I stood for. How did it matter what the hell I did now? I squared my shoulders, drew in my stomach and thrust my sizeable breasts for all to see. One of my blouse straps slid off my shoulder.

I felt like I was in the midst of a psychic vibration as I screamed, 'Do I really look like a scrawny slut?' Expectedly, there were pants of horror everywhere around me. Even Jyoti gasped and ran for cover – away from the sickening scene in the sitting room – to the relative safety of the kitchen.

'She's gone mad!' Shailaja wailed. 'Get her out of my sight!'

Ignoring her, I walked up to Ashok and extended my outstretched palm. 'Nirmal gave this ring to me,' I choked. 'Not that I blame him – because I admit I had feelings for him too. I loved him from the bottom of my heart. I thought this ring was an avowal of his intent to marry me.'

Shailaja's brow cocked in unbridled hostility. 'Marry *you*? Heavens forbid!'

'That's why I slept with him!' I yelled. Sliding to the floor, I buried my face in my hands and allowed myself the luxury of sobbing aloud.

'All right … that's enough,' Ashok told his wife.

Shailaja called out to Jyoti in a pained voice. 'Take that poor girl away from here, please.' She pointed towards Asha. 'She doesn't have to watch all this.'

Fortunately, she wouldn't understand it either. Jyoti reappeared at the threshold with a frightened look and quietly led Asha away from her armchair.

'Poor girl, huh? I can't believe the extent of this hypocrisy!' I raged. 'What about the baby she had after she was raped two years ago? Why didn't you report the rape? What about the hysterectomy you want to put her through now in a nefarious care home? You want to inflict additional lifelong pain on her, don't you? Would a parent sterilise a daughter who had the capacity to make informed decisions herself? And you're accusing *me* of exploiting Asha's disability? What a bloody irony! Would I be sticking my neck out if I didn't love her?'

Besides collective coughs and gasps at various stages of my diatribe, there wasn't a single word from anyone while I spoke. Nidhi rearranged her expression from one of shock to a countenance that was more neutral. It seemed like she hadn't known about the hysterectomy that Shailaja was planning for Asha. Ashok was too staggered to move. Shailaja broke the catatonic silence after what seemed like a full minute.

'Where did you hear all that from?' she asked me sharply.

'I heard the conversation you had with Dr Tahseen at Bread Breakers' on the Eighth of March,' I divulged.

'Is that all?' Shailaja asked when she regained her composure.

'That's all!' I said tartly. Although Nimmy had betrayed me, I wouldn't give him away by admitting that he had shared the story of Asha's rape and pregnancy with me last week.

'Pieces of that conversation led me to reason that Sunil is Asha's son,' I added.

'Why were you there?' Ashok demanded.

'They were one of the care centres I approached for my campaign,' I said. 'I suspected they were doing things they weren't supposed to. So, I videotaped them secretly. I came across several scenes that are just too horrible for me to mention now. We were going to break it as an exposé on the BBC.'

'Good heavens, you went undercover for the BBC?' Ashok roared.

I shook my head. 'No, I did it on my own. But we were going to feature it on *Panorama*, just before Keisha died.'

'You stupid bitch, you've killed a BBC producer and put everyone at risk!' Ashok raged.

'Dear Lord, you went into the care home with a camera all by yourself?' Nidhi exclaimed at the same time. 'You'll be prosecuted for breach of privacy.'

'The police are investigating the case now,' I said calmly. I turned to Shailaja. 'Anyhow, I accidentally overheard your conversation with Dr Tahseen.'

'Dr Who?' Shailaja asked. Ashok was shaking his head.

'You know what I'm talking about,' I said.

'No, we don't,' Shailaja shot back at me. 'Asha never did become pregnant. Sunil has always been Jyoti's son. I never spoke to Dr Tessie or whoever it is. No one from our family has ever been associated with rape, pregnancy, an illicit affair or an illegitimate child.'

'We don't know where you're getting all your wild theories from,' Ashok retorted.

I felt like every gust of wind had been whipped out of my sails. I was trying my best to make them see some sense in all my actions and they were just flatly denying it all!

Shailaja took advantage of my momentary speechlessness. She rose decisively from her seat and clapped her hands for everyone's attention. 'We've had enough of you and all your crazy histrionics. Get out of the house, Sandhya.'

My blood froze. 'Wh-what?'

'Get out of my house,' Ashok repeated firmly. 'We don't want you here any longer. We don't want you to keep in touch with Nirmal, Asha or anyone in this household ever again, under any circumstances whatsoever.'

'Well, I don't want to be in touch with Nimmy either,' I shot back. 'He hit me last week.'

'Not another word from you!' Ashok thundered. 'You've made a fine nuisance of yourself when we've been trying to lead upright lives.'

'Isn't there at least is a one-month notice!'

Ashok stormed over to me and shoved me against the wall. 'None of the rules meant for sane people apply to you, Ms Raman,' he snarled. Then he looked over his shoulder and bawled at Jyoti to get my things from upstairs. Jyoti hitched up the skirts of her sari and compliantly flitted upstairs to my room.

'You wouldn't be evicting me if I'd signed an official agreement with you,' I yelled.

'Sandhya, this was a word-of-mouth arrangement made by your brother. There are no written agreements for such informal arrangements,' Shailaja said in a tone that would have you think she had always been extremely fair, just, and reasonable.

'Could you give me a week, please?' I begged.

'No. It's come to a point of no return,' Ashok said.

'Can I stay here just tonight then? I'll visit the LSE accommodation office first thing tomorrow and move out in a day or two.'

Pandy, who had woken up, wagged his tail and ran over to me. 'Don't go near her!' Shailaja yelled at the dog.

Nidhi quickly darted over to the alcove under the banister, fetched a leash and led Pandy away to chain him somewhere near the lawn garden. Pandy didn't put up much of a resistance, though he did bark ferociously.

'I'm sorry, we just can't have you here any longer,' Shailaja stated with finality.

I sobbed into my shirtsleeve. Jyoti returned downstairs with some of my bags. Ashok was right behind her. He carried one of my heavier suitcases and flung it all the way down the stairs. The suitcase burst open as it landed with a reverberating thump. Some of my contents, which they had haphazardly shoved inside, spilled out on to the floor. I blushed furiously as I glimpsed a box of sanitary pads on the floor. From somewhere under the heap of things in my suitcase, the sharp edge of my laptop peeked out through a slit in the torn zip. I lurched forward, knelt down and turned my laptop this way and that, praying that it hadn't been damaged.

'Where is its case?' I shouted desperately. 'That laptop cost me a bomb and it has all my data!'

'Keeping you here has cost us a bomb, too,' Shailaja spat out unfeelingly.

Ashok reappeared on the stairway with my other suitcase and tossed it towards the door at the end of the stairwell. I jumped aside with a shriek. The suitcase missed my shoulder by inches and landed on the floor with an earth-shattering thud. This one was zipped up fully though.

I sat on my heels on the floor and began organising my things into a manageable mess. My ideals had now been striped down to an amorphous state where my life hinged on the basics.

'Where will I sleep tonight?' I yelled.

'In the streets for all we care,' Shailaja said.

'Can I … can I see Asha? Say goodbye to her?' I sounded pathetic, but I didn't care.

'Do you want me to call the police?'Ashok warned.

Jyoti hurried over to me and placed a comforting arm on my shoulder. 'Baby, it's really best you take your leave now,' she whispered in Hindi. 'I'll call a cab for you. See if you can stay with a friend for a few nights.'

'You have all your things. What're you waiting for? Get out now!' Ashok bellowed.

'Can I take my coat?' I croaked pathetically. Nidhi retrieved my coat from the rack under the banister. Shailaja grabbed it from her and flung it at me. I quickly shrugged it on and shoved my feet into my sandals, which lay invitingly below the shoe rack in the foyer. Jyoti scuttled to a landline phone in the foyer and called a cab as discreetly as she could. Then she turned to one side, reached into the depths of her blouse and pulled out a wad of cash. Balling the notes up in the palm of her hand, she walked over to me and pressed them into my hand. 'The cab will be here in ten minutes,' she whispered as inconspicuously as possible in everyone's presence.

'Let go of that rascal!' Shailaja screeched. 'I hope you haven't given her any money!'

'Of course not,' Jyoti lied. 'I was returning a bobby-pin she left in the kitchen.'

'Th-thanks,' I stuttered, touched that Jyoti was doing what she could to protect me from the irate Sawants.

'Now get off our property!' Ashok hounded. 'Don't hang around in our porch if you're waiting for one of your boyfriends to fetch you from here.'

Flaps of wind screeched gleefully in my ears as I dragged a suitcase out into the freezing night. A topcoat over a nightshirt and pyjamas did little to keep me warm. A streak of lightning rent the sky like a wildcat. An ominous clap of thunder followed. An unforgiving downpour began as I hobbled back and forth to pick up my other suitcase and all my bags.

The door slammed on my face. The last words I heard were Shailaja's.

'Don't ever come back again.'

11

Eating Humble Pie

'Where to, Miss?' The cabbie inquired, revving up the engine of his Fairway.

'I'm trying to figure that out,' I said ruefully. 'Would you, uh, have some water with you?' The bottle of water I always carried with me on the go was back at the Sawant residence.

''Fraid not,' the cabbie said. 'We'll find you something in one of those stores next to the station.'

'Okay. I'm, uh, making some calls. I'll let you know where to go in a few minutes.'

'There's a whole lot of turns on Westway, Miss. So, I'd better know right fast.'

His tone became less brusque when I began weeping. 'Hey, you all right, Miss?'

'I just got thrown out of the house. Right now, I have nowhere to go.'

'There, there.' He handed me a box of Kleenex from the glove compartment. 'When we long for life without difficulties, we must remind ourselves that oaks grow strong in harsh, contrary winds. If you think about it that way, it'll be easier to get by such situations.' He pulled up near the Rayner's Lane station and pointed to an adjacent Asian produce store. 'Here we are.'

The store bustled with cheerful customers, mostly middle-aged Indian women and men in salwar suits and pyjama-kurtas under sweaters or jackets. A family was noisily carting around a trolley brimming with plantain chips, potato crisps and bags of fresh vegetables. Oh, what wouldn't I give to be part of such a sane, happy and homely scene.

Memories flooded me. Eating temple food and playing with the neighbours' children during my last few days with Appa in Tanjore … my delight in having Sri join us from Pune after he had taken a few days off work, just to be with us before I left for London … Our visit to the Tirupati, where Appa had arranged a special darshan for me, the weekend before I was due to fly out … Swarms of people gathered around the temple, where Appa worked, to bid me an earnest farewell, the evening before I left.

I picked up a bottle of water, a loaf of bread and a packet of biscuits. As I waited to have my items billed, I wondered if my move to London had been a good idea after all. I had put up a fight with Appa and Sri to get here. But, when I had joined ABP News in Mumbai two years ago, I had their blessings right away.

A glissade of images from Mumbai resurged on my mind. ABP News' offices with its colourful backdrops and walls filled with newspapers … the cheerful face of my boss, who had wanted me to stay on with the team when I announced my resignation … the refreshing sweetness of fresh mango juice that I used to slurp up from a tall glass amidst throngs of people outside the Haji Ali Juice Centre … the shimmer of lights along the mouth of the queen's necklace whenever I strolled down Marine Drive after watching a Bollywood masala movie at the Inox theatre …

Tears eclipsed my vision. In Mumbai, I had shed the garb of a small-town girl from Tanjore. And my coverage of those gruesome train blasts had made me a poster girl for reporting on terrorism. In London, I was a dispossessed soul riding an unknown carriage to an unknown destination.

After I hopped back into the cab, I considered calling Nimmy and howling. But my more rational self warned me to first arrange a place where I could stay the night.

As I fiddled with my phone, I realised that I hadn't interacted with my classmates that often. I had been too embroiled with the Streetsmart crew. Ritchie and a few LooSE TV members were all I had really hung out with at LSE.

I hesitantly dialed Megan's cell number. Her phone was switched off. I remembered that she had been working late since Charlotte's car crash. When I tried her work number, a voicemail said she was out of office for a few days.

Next, I phoned Mark Leatherby from LooSE TV. Another dispassionate voicemail walloped me. I couldn't marshal the courage to leave a message.

I remembered how considerate Joey Clayworth had been during our Barbican filming expedition. I rang him next, hoping he would understand my situation now.

'Yo, what's up?' Joey sounded puzzled that I had called him out of the blue on a weekday night.

'Joey, I ...' My voice caught in my throat.

'You sound like you've been crying!' Joey interjected. 'What's wrong?'

'Joey ... I ... could I stay over at your place tonight?' I winced as I said it.

'Tonight?'

'I know. I'm sorry. The thing is I just got evicted. I'm hoping for a temporary arrangement, y'know ... a day or two, until I figure something out.'

'Isn't there usually a one-month notice? Or at least two weeks? How can ...?'

'My host family decided things weren't working out and threw me out.'

'Gosh, I'm sorry, San. Just like that?'

'Yes.'

'You need to report them to the police.'

'I didn't sign any agreement with them when I moved in.'

'Sweet Jesus, you're a big fool, San. How can you move in anywhere without signing a lease?'

'Staying with the Sawants was my family's suggestion. I couldn't have come to London if I hadn't agreed to it.'

Joey sighed. 'I wish I could help you. But my roommate's girlfriend came over from Paris just this afternoon. She's, uh, campin' out here for a few days. We had to dish out an extra mattress. I personally wouldn't mind at all. But with my roommate ...'

'I understand.'

'Why don't you approach the LSE accommodation office?' Joey began, but I cut him off.

'I'm doing that tomorrow. The question was where I would stay *tonight*. I just got thrown out into the street – lock, stock and barrel. Thanks, anyway. Goodnight!'

'Any luck, Miss?' The cabbie asked. 'I'm approaching South Harrow now. I need to know before we hit the A40.'

'I'm still trying.'

It's time to call Ritch and Lan, I told myself. I was too embarrassed to make Ritchie my first choice for getting me out of another scrape. I dialed Lanong. Before my call went through, I heard an overbearing warning that I had exceeded my airtime credit limit.

'I'm pulling an all-nighter in the library, Sandy,' Lanong groaned when he heard my voice. 'My roomie just turned in his last coursework paper today. He's now waltzing up a storm out there. He's invited practically everyone from Butler's Wharf for the party. They're crawling all over the kitchen and our room. And I have a shitty paper due tomorrow.'

I hated to say it, especially when Lanong sounded so stressed, but I couldn't help myself.

'Lan, I'm in trouble.'

'Good grief! What happened?'

I explained my situation.

'Christ, San! Several months ago, I told you to get the hell outta there. You didn't listen.'

'Please, Lan,' I begged. 'I'm so knackered I'm pretty sure I'd sleep through all the noise in your place.'

'I'm sorry, San. I tried to guide you before but I can't help you, right now. Hope you'll get this sorted.' I heard a click, followed by the buzz of the dial tone.

'I'm already on the A40,' the cabbie announced.

'Just a few more minutes, please,' I pleaded, dialing Ritchie's number.

My call to Ritchie didn't go through. I sat dazed for a minute. *Murphy's law,* I cursed to myself.

A dull ache in the pit of my stomach reminded me that I hadn't eaten. I tore open a loaf of bread from my grocery bag and chomped on it like a hungry deer as I dialed the number the message told me to contact to get rid of the bar on my calls. My call went through to Carphone Warehouse, where I had signed my contract with T-Mobile.

A female customer service representative answered my call after a five-minute wait. 'How can I help you?'

'My number is 079 859 125 84,' I slurred between munches. 'I need to make an emergency call. My outgoing calls have been barred. Can I have it lifted please?'

'You've exceeded your credit limit by 150 pounds, Ms Raman,' she informed. 'You'll need to clear that amount before your bar can be lifted. That works out to 321 pounds.'

'Why didn't I get a warning message earlier?' I demanded tearfully.

'I'm afraid we cannot answer that, Ms Raman.'

'I'm homeless as of today and I can't pony up right now!' I shouted. 'I need to get through to a friend!'

'I'm sorry, Ms Raman. You need to clear that amount before the bar can be lifted.'

'What the hell!' I protested. 'That's a rip-off.'

'Look here, Miss,' the cabbie interrupted from the front. 'I'm entering Westway soon. Where the hell do I go? Addison Lee always records its customers' destinations in advance. I cut you some slack. Now, I'm afraid there'll be a double charge if I don't know where I'm going. And if you ain't paying up, I'll drop you right here.'

'Please hold on,' I said on the phone before turning to the cabdriver, harried, distressed and confused. 'Can you, uh, head to the London School of Economics library, please? On Holborn. Uh, Houghton Street. Actually, I think the Holborn station will do – the underpass …'

'Got it,' the cabbie grunted.

I went back to the phone.

'We can raise your credit limit and lift your bar, Ms Raman,' the agent offered.

That would do so long as I didn't have to pay up right away. 'Yeah, uh, okay.'

'How much would you like to increase it to? Three hundred?'

I couldn't think clearly. 'Three hundred pounds?'

'Yes, ma'am.'

'Yes, please,' I snapped.

I heard a few clicks before the agent piped up, 'All done.'

'Is that bar off now?'

'It'll take between two and twenty-four hours.'

'Please activate my calls now!' I shrieked. 'This is an emergency. Make a special request!'

'The system automatically places a bar on your number when you exceed your credit limit. It isn't amenable to new data. I'll do what I can.'

'Do it!' I hung up, fuming.

A jagged wheeze scaled the walls of my throat, feeding an indistinct sense of disconnect between my body, mind and reality. I sniveled into my inhaler and drifted into an unsettling sleep until a warble of music trilled into my eardrums.

I rubbed my eyes blearily. A tube sign flitted into my line of sight as we sped by. We had reached Baker Street. There was that incessant buzz again. I think I was getting a call. I answered the phone with a weak hello.

'Sandy, is that you?' Ritchie's voice demanded.

'R-Ritch?'

'Sandy, I've b'in trying to call you for ages!' Ritchie said angrily. 'Your line was constantly engaged. You sound like shit. What's goin' on?'

Despite how angry it sounded, that proverbial baritone was a familiar strand in the vast sea of nothingness engulfing me now. Before I knew it, I was blubbering, coughing and sniffling into the sleeve of my coat.

'Whoa! I'm sorry if I said anything,' Ritchie exclaimed. 'Hell, I …'

'No, no,' I wailed. 'I'm, uh …'

'I hear horns blaring. Where the hell are you?'

'I … don't … know,' I sobbed.

'What in Pete's name do you mean?'

There were a few moments of silence as I continued weeping. From the corner of my eye, I spotted the contours of a spiked gate enclosing Regent's Park.

'San, are you safe?'

'I … don't … know,' I panted amidst gut-wrenching sobs. 'I'm … in a cab … I guess … you …' I broke out, sniffling into the sleeve of my coat. '… huh-huh … you see, I got … I got … huh … kicked out … huh-huh, of the … huh … house tonight. Huh-huh …'

'I can't understand what you're saying. Are you in a cab?'

'Huh-huh.'

'Where are you going?'

A fresh bout of coughs and sobs gushed out from my bosom. 'I dunno …'

'Why the fuck didn't you call me right away?'

'R-r-ran out of credit …'

'I don't want to hear you talk anymore. Give the phone to the cabbie, NOW!'

I nearly lost my grasp of the phone as I passed it on to the amused cabdriver.

'We were heading to Holborn, Sir … we're on Euston Road at the moment. I have to take a detour to come to your place …' he complained. After a few moments: 'All right. Through Camden High? Spot on. And the postcode?' He punched some buttons on a navigation device before him. 'NW5 4QA. All right. I see that I have to take the A4200. I'll be there in twenty–thirty minutes, depending on the traffic.' As he handed the phone back to me, it blacked out with a huge beep of protest. The battery had died out.

'You look like crap,' Ritchie commented when I tumbled out of the cab at Gilden Crescent. I vaguely noticed he had changed his hairstyle again. The blue highlights were gone. The sideswept bangs over his forehead made his face softer and fuller, giving him a preppy, little-boy charm. When I caught myself goggling at him, I lowered my gaze in embarrassment. He was seeing me at my absolute worst. I fought through the cloud of disorientation and fumbled for my wallet.

'That'll be sixty-two pounds,' the cabbie said crisply.

I didn't even flinch at the fare. All I could think of was a comforting hug.

'Could you, uh, help me please?' I requested, pointing towards my luggage in the trunk.

'It's not customary for us to do that,' the cabdriver said matter-of-factly.

Ritchie gave him a thumbs-up. 'No worries, mate.' I spun around to see him hauling out my luggage from the boot. The cabdriver hopped out as an afterthought and assisted him.

'Half an hour ago, she had no clue who the hell she was and where she was going,' the cabdriver told Ritchie as we waited for the elevator. 'I've never faced such a bizarre situation before.' He gave me a swift nod and retreated to his car. 'Take care, lady.'

The elevator opened out into a narrow hallway. Ritchie placed an airbag on one of my suitcases, slung my other airbag on one of his shoulders, grabbed my grocery bag and two stray overnight bags with one hand, and wheeled the suitcase with the other. I listlessly followed Ritchie down the hallway, taking long deep breaths with my inhaler as I dragged my other suitcase. Somewhere en route, I tripped on one of the wheels of my suitcase, lost my balance and smacked my hip into a wall beside me.

Ritchie turned around. 'Jesus, San … drop the bags!' he growled.

I left my suitcase on the corridor and hobbled along. Ritchie dropped my bags, unlocked his door and retraced his steps to fetch my other suitcase. A flood of soft amber light greeted me when I stepped in. I shrugged out of my cumbersome coat and let it fall to the floor. Ritchie pointed to a comfy old plaid couch in a carpeted living room.

I staggered in and sank into it. He arranged all my bags by the hall closet, picked up my coat from the floor and brushed it before placing it in the coat rack. I was half-dozing when I felt a hand on my forehead. Then, Ritche's voice. 'Christ, San, you're burning up.'

My chest began constricting once again. An unpleasant sensation of soreness scratched the back of my throat and all my joints ached. I reached for my inhaler and gasped into it.

'D'you want to go to the doc?' Ritchie asked.

I waved my hand to indicate that I didn't want to go anywhere.

Ritchie disappeared for a few minutes. I was nodding off to sleep again when I felt a gentle shove on my shoulder. 'Sandy!'

'Ouch!' I grumbled when sprinkles of cold water splashed my face.

'Have this,' he ordered, thrusting a glass of hot water before me. 'I put some garlic in it. It should bring down the fever.' He pointed to a mug on the coffee table before me. 'And that's a glass of warm milk. I put some honey in it. It'll help your wheeze.'

I drank the water and reached for the glass of milk. I hoped he would sit next to me but he bounded into his room and closed the door behind him. I didn't realise I had begun crying again until I reached out to brush a few tendrils of hair off my face.

Ritchie reappeared with a book bag on one shoulder, a comforter on the other, and a bundle of pillows in his arms. 'I've straightened out my room for you,' he told me shortly. 'I have coursework reading to do and a tonne of emails to catch up on. There's a bowl of curry in the fridge, if you're hungry. Goodnight!'

I tried to process what he was saying, but all I could think of was how cold and aloof he sounded.

'Wh-where will you sleep?' I rasped.

'On the couch here,' he said curtly. 'Call me if you need anything.'

'Okay,' I said in a small voice.

I gathered my shoulder bag, waddled into his bedroom and plugged my phone into a port near the fireplace. A set of unfamiliar clothes lay at the head of a round-design bed. Satin blue pyjamas and a matching nightshirt with a nude-shade free-size bra to boot. Were these for me? What was the *bra* doing here?

For a reason that defied all sense of logic and gratitude, I wondered if he had a girlfriend. Before I could brood further, the intensifying pressure on my bladder drove me to the washroom.

I relieved myself and peered into the mirror. The first two buttons of my blouse had fallen off, presumably during my scuffle with the Sawants. My face was swollen and puffy, my hair was half undone, my nose was runny and purple rings circled my tear-streaked eyes. I opened a maple raised-panel door on the front-side of the bathtub and found a bathing gel.

I ran a bath, sat in a tubful of warm, foamy water for a while, then fell into bed and switched my phone on.

Nimmy hadn't called me yet. I pressed a random number on the speed dial. The bar on my outgoing calls had been lifted by now. I punched a local access number and called my father in India, mollifying myself with a recollection of the old-fashioned green rotary dial phone that had been around for a long time at home in Tanjore, until a maroon push-button telephone replaced it, four years ago.

'How are your studies coming along, Sandhya?' Appa greeted chirpily.

'I've submitted three papers this term, Pa. I have two more due in …'

Appa's tone changed. 'Sandhya, what's wrong? You don't sound good.'

'Things have been a little strange here,' I began euphemistically. Then, I let my floodgates open and filled him in on all the events unfolding in my life, excluding only the portion where I was receiving death threats; I didn't want Appa hyperventilating at the prospect of my personal safety in jeopardy.

He was silent for a long time. Then he sighed heavily. 'Are you safe?'

'I'm in good hands – for now, at least,' I replied diplomatically.

'We sent you there with so much faith, Sandhya,' he said softly. 'We arranged a good family for you to stay with. You shouldn't have interfered in their personal affairs and …'

'But, what the Sawants are doing to Asha …'

'Sandhya, I understand what you're saying. What you did wasn't wrong – but, look at the mess you're in now. Having moved to a different country, you should have concentrated on your studies and saved money, wherever possible. Graduating with flying colours and getting a good job in the UK should have been your main priorities. You can't pay off your loans with the salary you would get as a media professional here in India, if you even do get a job at that. And I can't help you repay your loans. Not with my earnings as a priest. Sri has to pitch in and it'll take a huge toll on his health. Or we'll have to forfeit this house we pledged for your loan.'

Tears swam over my face as I listened.

'By the looks of it, I'm not even sure you'll complete your degree. Your decision to attend LSE carries far more risks for Sri and me than it does for you. It was a decision we took on the soil of my home and the foundations of our blood, sweat and desire to see you thrive and be happy. I can't really do much from here, except pray ardently for you. I hope you'll come to your senses soon.'

'I hope to make you and Sri proud one day,' I choked out.

'It's raining heavily in Tanjore right now. Your mother is crying piteously for you from the skies,' Appa said sadly. 'She sees where you are now and she's deeply saddened with the turn of events, your lack of focus, your impractical and over-ambitious nature, your emotional immaturity and vulnerability, your sufferings and the toll it is taking on us here. You'll realise the impact of your foolishness only when I'm no longer here.'

I threw myself facedown on the bed. 'Don't say that, Appa. I love you!'

'What are you going to do about your accomodation now?'

'I don't know.' I explained the general housing situation in London – the expensive rents, the council taxes, the fees for letting agents, the challenge of squeaking through checks on the rental history of prospective tenants, and everything else that made house-hunting difficult for an international student on a shoestring budget in the middle of an academic year.

'I left the government years ago, dear. Since joining the temple, I've lost contact with most of my ex-colleagues,' Appa said. 'Even if I make inquiries about whether any of the temple's hereditary trustees knows someone in London who can take you in temporarily, they will be preoccupied with activities far more important than helping a priest's daughter find a place to stay in London because she mismanaged her affairs there. You should inquire within your own networks.'

'I understand. I ...' A tight ball of shame clutched my entrails. '... I need some money. For a fresh rental deposit and such. And I don't think the Sawants will refund the 800-pound deposit we wired from India ... maybe Sri could talk to them and request them to pay it back.'

'We have too much dignity to approach them for that money especially after what they did to you,' Appa cut in. 'We'll send you more money from your loan account here. You've used up nearly 80 percent of it, but you can discuss the details with Sri. I'm leaving for the temple now.'

Fumes of guilt seeped into the morass of loneliness and despair in my heart. I had let my family down badly. And here I was, selfishly upset with Nimmy's betrayal – a man I had met just months before. Hadn't I betrayed my family? Nimmy's betrayal was my karma.

Ritchie was probably the only rock in this tempest. I yearned for him now, but I was too spent to call him to my side. I lay in bed and waited for ages, willing Ritchie to check in on me – but to no avail. In spite of the abuse my lachrymal glands had seen all evening, fresh tears crisscrossed my face until I curled into a foetal position and drifted off. I must have been out cold for hours when I felt a caress on my face and a pair of strong, gentle hands stroking my hair. Through a film of hazy consciousness, I saw Ritchie gazing down at me with unspoken fondness. That sublime moment was fleeting. The lights in the room turned off and the door closed with a gentle thud. I was alone once again. But this time, the darkness brought with it a faint glimmer of hope.

23 March

My mobile phone shrieked from somewhere near me. I smacked a pillow over my ears. then sat up slowly and stretched. My head throbbed as I flipped open my phone.

'Sandy, where the hell are you?' Nimmy's frantic voice.

'Hummph,' I grunted, my voice unidentifiably thick with sleep. And then fragments of last evening's drama ricocheted off my mind, like a salvo of hailstones bouncing off a frail vineyard roof. 'Uh, I'm in a friend's place. He took me in on short notice.'

'How could you sleep over in another man's house?' Nimmy snarled.

I yanked the phone away from my ear, aghast.

'Answer me!' Nimmy growled.

'What the hell? Are you real?' I rasped.

I heard Nimmy swallow. 'I was so worried. You suddenly vanished. No one at home would say a word. It was as if you never existed.'

'You know what you did. And now, you're questioning my character because I'm staying over with … I mean, how dare you?' I exclaimed.

'Sandy, please.' Nimmy begged. 'I had no idea they would toss you out like that. I've spoken to them and sorted things through. Please come back. Give me the address and I'll fetch you right now.'

'What do you mean "sorted things through"? You just said your family behaved as if I never existed.'

'Well, I've tried to make them understand. And ...'

'It doesn't matter anymore.'

'That's not fair!' Nimmy cried. 'Something came up at work yesterday. I couldn't leave soon enough.'

'What *you* did to me wasn't fair,' I said through gnashed teeth.

'Oh, Sandy!' The tone of Nimmy's voice simulated the whimper of an injured puppy. Something stirred in my being. Suddenly, I wanted to console him, see him, and fly into his arms. Then I reminded myself that this deadly charm of his was what I had fallen for. I wouldn't be in this situation if it weren't for him.

My eyes hardened. 'I think we're done here. It's over. You hear me? It's fucking over. I don't care anymore. Don't call me again. Ever.'

I hung up and stared at my palms for a wretched moment. The nerve of him! He had hit me and he hadn't stood by me but he couldn't bear the possibility that another man could. Or would.

I freshened up in the bathroom and shuffled outside to find Ritchie at the dining table with his PowerBook. He looked up at me and smiled benignly. 'You look more like yourself today, San. Please help yourself.' He made a sweeping arc with his arm. 'The coffee is there ... the cereal boxes are on top of the fridge. There's a loaf of bread and a couple eggs in the fridge. With butter and jam, if you'd like. There's the fruit basket there.' He pointed to a small teakwood dining table in the far corner of the sitting room near the kitchen. 'And some yoghurt in the fridge. I'm afraid I have only whole milk. It'll do you some good though ... you're fading away.'

He paused to take a sip from a cup of coffee that I guessed had grown cold.

I sank into a chair across him. 'Why did you call me last evening?'

'I was working on a public service broadcasting paper and I wanted to check something with you,' he admitted.

I helped myself to some coffee and a bowl of Cheerios in the kitchen.

'You have a way of somehow seeking me out whenever I'm in trouble,' I mentioned.

Ritchie shut down his PowerBook and eyed me intently. 'What exactly landed you in this mess?'

I briefly explained the unexpected turn of events last evening. Ritchie remained unfazed when I was finished. 'Sure, you were foolish, San, but don't beat yourself up over it,' he said. 'One day, you can write a book from these experiences. Or make a film, you know?'

I stared down at my lap.

Ritchie shoved his PowerBook into a bag. 'I need to bounce. Here's a spare set of keys for you.' He thrust a piece of cool metal into my palm and sprinted towards the coat-rack. 'Be careful, San,' he pleaded as he buttoned his coat. 'With this turn of events, your life truly could be in danger.'

I managed to arrange a number of room viewings once it became clear that student housing was beyond my reach. After seeing a single studio flat in Purley that afternoon, my third viewing for the day, I was on a train back to Central London when Sergeant Dennis Wheeler called me.

'Dario De Luca was turned in this morning,' he informed breathlessly.

'What happened?'

'De Luca was trying to flee to New York. He was found at Gatwick airport in the wee hours of dawn today,' Wheeler said tightly. 'He's in our custody now. We're testing fingerprints and collecting DNA to find out if he was behind the murder of Keisha Douglas and the attempted murder of Charlotte Hale. But right now, we're not sure if it's the same person.'

'Oh?'

'Well, we think there might be an alibi or an accomplice involved,' Wheeler admitted.

'Yes, Inspector Davenport cautioned me,' I remembered.

'And I'm cautioning you again. We think there are one or more unknown persons lurking around, looking for trouble.'

I swallowed uneasily. 'Thanks for the update, Sergeant. Any news on that flash drive? The one with that Bread Breakers' film I videotaped.'

'Not yet, I'm afraid,' Wheeler said. 'We've searched every corner of Ms Douglas' apartment and office, and poked into her gym locker at Fitness First. No one we've spoken to has it either. We're hoping that changes soon.'

~

I submitted my application for the Gregersen International Scholarships that night, grateful that Aiden McLeod and two LSE professors had stepped in to provide references.

Around 11.00 p.m., I exited the LSE library and strode towards Lincoln's Inn Fields through Portsmouth Street, a small alleyway near the library building. I was on Sardinia Street, leading to Kingsway, when I heard a scuffle of feet behind me. I turned around. No one was visible in my line of sight. I recalled Sergeant Wheeler's warning earlier that evening.

Panic seized me. My weak 'hello?' ricocheted back to me in the waves of a faint echo.

I considered ducking into The Old Curiousity Shop, a shoe-and-cloak depot en-route. But a glance over my shoulder found the shop closed for the day. The steady patter of footsteps behind me resumed. I picked up my pace. I contemplated screaming for attention, but realised I was the only soul on this side of the campus at this hour.

Instinctively, I moved closer to The Old Curiousity Shop. A tall shadow emerged from behind me. I froze in my tracks and gazed in unrestrained horror.

12

Unguarded

From the illumination of a lamppost overhead, I identified the contours of a rain hat and a long flowing robe with its cape billowing triumphantly in the air. I didn't dare turn around. I edged back into the campus towards Portugal Street and dialed Sergeant Wheeler from my mobile. My call went through to voicemail. 'Sergeant!' I yelped into the answering machine. 'I'm at LSE. S-someone's following me. Call me. I'm scared.'

As I clicked my phone shut, I saw a lone young man cycling towards Portsmouth Street.

'Hey! D'you have a minute?' I huffed, running to catch up.

But the lad was already pedaling away. I stared after him for a moment.

I started when I heard the click of footsteps again, this time somewhere from Portugal Street on my right. My skin crawled. I remembered there was a pub around St Clement Lane. I hastened towards it, desperate to escape from the clutches of the lonesome pathways.

Alas, the pub was closed. Holy cow, was this a dead-end too? Drawing closer, I found a narrow alleyway running around the back of the pub. The footsteps behind me grew louder. I darted blindly through the murky backside alleyway and found myself back in Portsmouth Street. I exhaled in relief and speed dialed Ritchie as I raced towards the steady whiz of traffic ahead on Kingsway. My call went unanswered.

'I'm just returning to your place …' I panted into his voicemail. 'S-someone is …'

A crushing blow to my shoulder knocked me down. The phone flew from my hand. A plaque that read 'Sardinia House' glowered down at me from a massive brick-red building. That caped figure towered over me and pressed a boot-clad foot on my neck. The sharp curve of a folding knife protruded from a gloved hand. I tried to scream, but the assailant clamped a hand on my mouth and shoved the knife against my quivering jaw. The smell of cold hard leather assaulted me. I kicked my legs, struggling to breathe. A police van began wailing behind me.

The figure suddenly leaped up and sprinted away into the darkness of Lincoln's Inn Fields. From the corner of my eye, I saw a blaze of angry blue lights swish by the main road on Kingsway, its rotating beacons alerting road users of impending police presence. Maybe there was a road emergency around here. Whatever it was, that siren – and my choice to move towards Kingsway – had saved my life. I lay there for a few moments, shivering and gasping.

Then the voice in my head shouted: *Run! He might come back and get you any minute.*

Wheeler returned my call as I squeezed out of the Kentish Town Underground half an hour later. 'Are you all right?' he asked anxiously.

Dropping my voice to a whisper, I recounted the details of the attack. Wheeler made notes from my vague descriptions of the assailant.

About five-foot ten or eleven. Large, brown sunglasses. A black, three-hole facemask. Black paint smeared on the face. Appeared to be a man, though it wasn't easy to tell.

Suddenly, I remembered Nimmy's insistence that he had been followed earlier this month.

'Sergeant, can the team get a copy of Corney and Barrow's CCTV footage for the evening of Eighth March?' I requested.

'Oh? What's *that* story about?'

'A friend's drinks were spiked in that pub,' I reported. 'Same day I went undercover at Bread Breakers'. I'd left Lambeth North at about four-thirty p.m. and …'

'… And met Keisha Douglas at the BBC, where she made copies of the video … yes, we know all that,' Wheeler recalled. 'What happened with this friend?'

I told him all of it, including Holborn police chief Gary Thompson's lackadaisical response.

A brief spell of silence followed. Then, Wheeler exhaled sharply. 'You think this could be related?'

'There are far too many coincidences for these to be random occurrences.'

'Very well, then. I'll follow up with that officer in Holborn. If he hasn't received a copy of that CCTV footage yet, I'll have one of our constables contact the pub,' Wheeler agreed. 'I'm sorry about the attack this evening. Stay safe, all right?'

'You look like a ghoul!' Ritchie remarked. 'Everything all right? Your voicemail was all mangled and I couldn't get through to you.'

I slipped out of my windcheater, flopped exhaustedly on to the couch and told him about my narrow escape at LSE.

'Why the fuck did you have to be out until midnight?' Ritchie blasted. 'If you have to stay out late, you should always call a cab!'

'If you're so insistent on a cab, why don't you foot those expenses yourself?' I snapped.

I regretted my words as soon as I uttered them.

Ritchie had welcomed me into his home and hearth, and I was yapping at him like a daft bloodhound.

'Let's figure that out later,' Ritchie said calmly. 'I've cooked us a delicious meal. C'mon.' He hauled me up and led me to the kitchen. I saw a small pan bubbling with yoghurt sauce.

'You haven't eaten yet?' I asked, surprised.

Ritchie shook his head. 'I was holed up with that horrid broadcasting paper.'

His eyes seemed to say otherwise. I dismissed that narcissistic thought at once. Of course, he had his nose in that paper. Why would he wait for *me* to have dinner?

'A traditional Nainital dish. My hometown special. Made with hemp seeds, coriander leaves and yoghurt,' he explained, setting the food on the table. He gestured towards two bowls of semolina and fruit salad on the countertop. 'And that's a kind of dessert.'

We piled the rice on our plates. I let the warm chutney slide down my throat, savouring the mellow tingle it left on my palate.

'You're a brilliant chef, Ritch, Thanks for having me here and …' I hesitated, '… it was extremely thoughtful to leave a spare set of nightclothes for me last night.'

A cloud of wistfulness settled on Ritchie's face. Beneath his punk, bad-boy façade was a buoyant, almost childlike peace. That thought strangely mollified me.

'I had no energy to unpack,' I went on. 'I was totally …'

'Oh, yes – that satin stuff,' Ritchie mumbled. 'Used to be Maya's. I found them among my things after I got to London. She had a habit of leaving her stuff behind whenever she came down from Boston to visit me in LA.'

'Maya?'

'My elder sister. She teaches English Lit at Boston University. She's the quirky, scatterbrained, type.'

Ah, it's NOT a girlfriend.

'She wanted to come down here around Easter,' Ritchie mentioned. 'But I won't be around.'

'Where are you off to?'

'Switzerland. Leaving on the Twenty-eighth. Back on the Fifth of April. Remember that contact I told you about at the ExCEL London career fair? He introduced me to Unilever. They liked my showreel. They've requested for a final face-to-face, and they're flying me in.'

'That's a great start for Flamingo Films, Ritch!' I exclaimed.

'Now, I have some good and bad news for you,' Ritchie said as we cleared the table a few minutes later.

'If it helps, the good news always seems sweeter after the bad news,' I replied.

Ritchie laughed. 'So be it. I spoke to a bunch of folks at Orange during my afternoon shift today, about a part-time job for you. No new openings right now, but I put out some feelers anyway.'

'Oh, that's very thoughtful, Ritch!' I said, surprised that he had gratuitously taken the pains to make such an inquiry with the telecommunications company where he worked as a part-time marketing associate. 'As for the good news,' he continued. 'My pal, Jayden's girlfriend, Kimberly has agreed to take you in for a while at her place in Cranford – near the Hounslow West station. She's originally from Denver. I think you'll feel quite at home there. You wouldn't mind that, would you?'

'Why, thank you, Ritch.' I cried. 'You didn't have to ...'

'Never mind all that. Give Kim a call right away,' Ritchie cut in. '079 81 696 799.'

I saved the number on my phone.

Suddenly, he broke into guffaws.

I looked up at him, startled. 'What happened?'

'Well,' he chuckled. 'Your pursuers won't have a clue where you'll be living!'

~

26 March

A throbbing headache festered in the crown of my skull when I awoke on Monday morning. It looked like the thin, hard pillows in my new room at Kimberly Ross' bedsit in Cranford's Chaucer Avenue didn't suit me. I rose unsteadily and flung open the heavy blackout window drapes. The view, steely and coruscating, was of a row of shingled, semi-attached houses across a yellowing road. I followed my nose to the kitchenette, where I found the remnants of a freshly made brew in a coffee pot. There was no sign of Kimberly. She was a cruise consultant with a tour operator. Or so she had said – she had been quite muzzy when she received me last night. Perhaps, she had already left for work. I poured some coffee into a cup and took a sip. Something that tasted like espresso but it wasn't too bad. Minutes later, I was on a bus to the Hounslow West station, thinking about how I could block the Sawants' attempts to sterilise Asha. As I hopped on the Piccadilly line for Holborn, a plan began to take shape in my head.

~

Later that morning, I found some time to call Craig Davenport between classes at LSE.

'Wheeler told me about the attack on Friday,' he said. 'I'm glad you're okay. We've requested Corney and Barrow for a copy of their CCTV footage for the evening of Eighth March. The pub is trying to be as cooperative as possible. I understand the person who spiked your friend's drinks could be involved in this case.'

'I believe so.'

'Well, any lead that can help us pin down Keisha's murderer will be a shot in the arm,' Davenport conceded.

'Isn't Dario in cust—' I began, but Davenport cut in.

'Dario De Luca isn't the perpetrator of Keisha's death or Charlotte's car crash – at least, not directly. There's no DNA match in either case.'

'No DNA match?' I spluttered.

'Nope,' the inspector reiterated. 'We have the doorman's testimony too. It's the same story Dario played out to Tim Herbert and Ben Reynolds. The doorman swears he saw Dario pop out at a quarter past eight.'

'What about fingerprints?'

Davenport snorted. 'Our perp is not that daft, right? He or she wore leather gloves. And the few random fingerprints we found weren't clear enough for our testers to make any assessment whatsoever.'

'Is Dario talking?'

'Oh, he is! Chap claims he had an emergency in Tunbridge Wells. A sibling fallen ill, he said. He was rushing to New York to pursue medical treatment for his brother. Why was he traveling alone then? Well, he just was. The brother was due to fly out later. A whole load of tosh, if you ask me.'

I didn't know what to say. After all, the investigation team didn't have much evidence against him yet.

'We think Charlotte's hit-and-run man is from somewhere around Europe,' Davenport added. 'Wheeler has reached out to Interpol with a request to access the INDIS.'

'INDIS?'

'The International DNA Index System,' he said. 'We're hoping to hit a jackpot with the DNA sample we have from that cigarette butt in the Wrangler. We haven't located a match in the UK. They're going through the Bosnian, Serbian and German databases now.'

'Oh, I didn't know there was an international DNA database like this,' I mused, surprised.

'There is, now. Launched just last year. Interpol connects individual databases across member countries. At the moment, all EU regions are in. Interpol is trying to rope in other countries, too. Comes in handy for Gordian knots like this one,' he grunted. 'It's no cakewalk though. A boatload of procedures involved in getting Interpol's rubberstamp to nose around another country's database.'

'If we have strong reason to believe this person is a foreign national …'

'That cigarette brand is our only trump card for now. You do sound like a stellar detective yourself, don't you?'

I took his blandishments as an opportunity to share my little plan for thwarting Asha's surgery.

'Investigating Ms Douglas' murder is our top priority right now. We don't have the bandwidth to take on a different case,' Davenport said exasperatedly.

'That *is* the point, Inspector,' I replied, equally irritated. 'Both cases are *related*. In this case, a young, mentally challenged woman is having a hysterectomy without a court approval in an abusive care home that has a surgery clinic run by a bunch of quacks.'

The chief detective inspector exhaled in deliberation. 'Ms Raman, there's no conclusive evidence to prove these events are related unless we get hold of that film.'

Dammit. We were just moving around in circles. But I desperately needed the backing of the squad to prevent Asha's surgery. 'If you can send someone from undercover to go along with me to Bread Breakers', we can tape what is going on at the operation theatre and deploy it as a source of evidence,' I explained categorically.

'All right, you win. We'll send a constable over,' Davenport relented with a sigh.

'Thanks.' I provided him the care home's address and rang off.

Then I called Alfred Maynard at the BBC. 'The show's on hold right now,' Alfred informed me gruffly, assuming that I desired to replace Charlotte on Streetsmart.

'Oh!' I said, a little surprised despite myself.

'Well, the investigation …' Alfred said, trailing off as if that premise were self-explanatory.

'I hope you've got room for a potential breaking-news commentary,' I announced before launching into a pithy of what I had in mind.

'Where the devil did you get that information from?' Alfred marveled.

'I have my sources,' I quipped. 'It's happening at three p.m. on Thursday. Twenty-ninth March.'

'Are you saying you want to be commissioned to do it right away?' Alfred asked incredulously.

'There's no time for that. We believe this event is linked to Keisha's murder. I'm just requesting you to download the material I send you. We can decide what to do with it later.'

'You want me to download a crock of bollocks when we aren't even certain we'll broadcast it?' Alfred retorted.

'For my friend's sake,' I beseeched. 'The squad is in on this, too.'

'Hey, she's my friend too!' Alfred protested. '*Was*,' he amended sadly. 'You said three o' clock, didn't you?'

~

27 March

I was on the train returning to LSE from an interpretation engagement I had undertaken for a translation agency that was paying me fifty pounds for the gig. Small money, but it was something.

Inspector Davenport's name flashed on my phone.

'We have a suspect down,' Daveport reported grimly when I answered. 'Jeffrey Stuart is dead.'

'*What?*'

'We found Jeff dead in his office last night. With, uh …' he hesitated briefly, '… a knife through his heart.'

Blood rushed to my ears. I glanced outside the train window. Patches of countryside flitted past me. With any luck, I'd be in Farringdon in half an hour. From there, I could get to Liverpool Street on the Met and hop on to the Central Line to Bethnal Green.

'I'll be there soon,' I said tightly.

~

'A doll lay next to Jeff Stuart with a pin in its torso. Set up to look like a black magic murder,' Davenport informed me in his office, an hour later.

I looked up at the inspector slowly.

'Are you all right?' he asked me gently.

I nodded weakly. 'I think the voodoo style is a ruse to mislead us.'

'Well, Jeff's post-mortem says he died of strangulation around half-past six yesterday. He was gone long before that knife was plunged into him. Looks like the killer is disabled in some way.'

I squirmed in my chair. 'How do you know that?'

'A wheel in the corner of his cabin. It belongs to a walker or a wheelchair.'

'Could it be an employee or a representative of a SIGNAL member firm?' I mused.

'We don't know yet. SIGNAL employees say Stuart was in meetings all afternoon with different groups of delegates,' Davenport replied.

'In his office?'

'In a conference room upstairs. He returned to his office around six. We're talking to everyone who signed in for a meeting with Stuart that afternoon.'

I remembered that Jeff had lied about a proposal to British Telecom, the night of Keisha's death. What was the name of the manager Jeff claimed had worked on that fictitious proposal? Greta? Gracelyn? Frieda? Gretchen?

Ah, that was it. *Gretchen Friedland.* Had Gretchen covered up for him? Maybe she knew something.

I jumped up hastily. 'Inspector. I have to go.'

Gretchen Friedland arrived at the lobby of SIGNAL's offices, looking like she hadn't slept in days.

'I understand you're here about Jeff,' she said curtly, ushering me into an elevator. As we rode up the carriage, I noticed a coffee stain on her silk blouse. Wisps of auburn hair clung to a disheveled bun at the nape of her neck. She led me into an empty conference room on the fifth floor and sank into a swivel chair.

'I'm on my way out. You'd better make it fast,' she warned.

I launched into a brief history of Lionheart, my relationship with Jeff Stuart, Keisha's death and Jeff's explanations when he was questioned. 'Since he mentioned you were in charge of a non-existent proposal, I need to know where he was on the Fourteenth of March,' I finished.

Gretchen scowled at me. 'My boss was murdered yesterday and you're digging for information to find out whether he killed someone?' she burst out angrily.

'It's not the way you put it,' I said gently. 'I think Jeff didn't tell the truth because someone was threatening him. We're trying to find out who murdered him.'

Gretchen's face crumpled. 'Jeff had a good heart,' she blurted, staring unseeingly at a video conferencing screen ahead of her. 'I don't know if anyone was threatening him.'

'Were you aware that Jeff told the police you worked on that proposal?' I inquired.

Gretchen nodded slowly and buried her face in her hands. I patted her shoulder as her muffled sobs spilled over the table. 'I'm sorry,' I consoled. 'I'm here to help. You have to believe me.'

'Jeff wasn't in the office that evening,' Gretchen said quietly. 'He was with *me*.'

I stared at her uncomprehendingly.

'J-Jeff and I were … in a relationship.' Gretchen sniffled. 'He spent that evening in my flat. He lied because he was afraid his wife would find out about us, you know.' Gretchen paused briefly, 'What with the police investigating and everything.'

As I gazed at her distraught face, I realised why she was so much more emotional than one would expect from a regular colleague or underling in a similar situation.

'Did his wife find out?' I asked softly.

Gretchen didn't answer for a long time. Then she grabbed a napkin from a tissue box, blew her nose against it and gave a light nod. I reached for her hand wordlessly.

'Jeff launched his own investigation into that care home,' Gretchen said suddenly. 'He was scared to approach the police because his wife would discover our affair. But he was troubled about the residents and children in that care home. I don't know what he found, but he thought at least three other care homes in the city are selling mentally disabled women to pimps dealing with clients of a large corporation.'

'So, Jeff was on to something?' I exclaimed incredulously.

Gretchen began peeling her nails. 'Yeah. I understand you're a journalist who's used to asking loads of questions, but I'm afraid that's all I know.'

'Thank you, Gretchen. Take care.'

I stooped out and walked by the waterfront. The colourful narrowboats along the leafy oasis ahead of me belied the guilt I felt within for misjudging Jeff.

When I looked up, I saw a woman on the sidewalk, hurrying towards the Paddington station in a bright red coat, her auburn hair glistening in the late afternoon sunshine.

Gretchen. She looked lost to the world.

A black sedan tore down the street, swerving dangerously towards the curbside.

'Gretchen, watch out!' I shrieked, sprinting across the road.

Car horns screeched all around me in a frenzy.

And then, it was over. The roar of a deadly collision. A torpedo of smoke and metal. Blood on my coat. Cries from a gathering crowd. I froze, then teetered dizzily on the pavement for a moment before collapsing to the ground.

28 March

A thunderous headache walloped against my ears when I awoke. A flush of dawn glazed the skies outside. Wednesday morning. I looked around disoriented. I was back at Cranford.

Bedmate Kimberly was fast asleep on the cot next to mine. I stumbled upstairs to the bathroom. How had I returned home last night? Perhaps, a kind passerby had decoded the garbled directions I must have churned out in my traumatised state. I snuck into the kitchenette, put the coffee maker on and collected today's newspapers at the door. Headlines from *The Daily Mail* caught my eye.

SIGNAL Employee, 29, Killed In Mysterious Road Accident, Investigations Underway.

I couldn't bear to read the rest of it. I dully sipped my coffee. My mobile phone bleeped. I glared at the reminder flashing on my phone screen: *Interview with Bradshaw. 10 a.m.*

Oh, God … not today.

Well, I had been rather persistent about it, hadn't I? I listlessly showered and washed my hair. Back in my room, I wound a shawl around myself, blotted my hair with a towel and crawled on all fours across the sea of clothes that lay in unsightly heaps on the floor, many of them Kimberly's. As I pawed through the mixed jumble in the semi-darkness, I stumbled over a stray drawer on the floor and stubbed my toe at the foot of the bed. Tears of exhaustion slid down my face as I cradled my big toe in my hands. Kimberly stirred. I vowed to find another place to live. A room I would have to myself. With a cupboard. I finally settled on a silk, coral pink wrap dress—a Zara ensemble that had become my staple outfit for tedious occasions like TV appearances and job interviews.

It was 8.45 a.m. when I yanked a camera bag and tripod from a storage closet outside LSE's offices. On my way to the EGG offices, I called Davenport and reported my meeting with Gretchen.

'We've rounded up some suspects but we don't have the license plate number of the sedan that knocked her over,' he sighed. 'However, a passerby saw something brown or yellow dangling from the rearview mirror. He said it looked like a bird.'

~

'Good morning, San,' Aiden McLeod greeted, approaching me in the lobby of the Pinwheel Interactive office. Why did his black fur-felt hat seem so familiar?

I rose from my seat and shook his hand. 'Morning, Sir.'

McLeod flounced on to an adjacent vinyl chair and placed a copy of the briefing document on the coffee table before us. 'There's a crisis involving another client. So, I won't be able to sit in on this interview like I'd originally thought,' he stated tersely. He thumbed through the sheets of the interview brief I had sent him. 'I need you to stick to this script like a Bible.'

I nodded tensely.

'EGG's main office is up on the tenth floor,' McLeod added. 'You will be escorted from there. Remember, the CEO doesn't answer personal or unexpected questions. Don't piss him off.'

~

Setting my equipment down, I drank in a triad of muted skylights and the graceful fall of silk, puce draperies hanging in goblet pleats from sleek wooden finials and panels. An aquatic garden beyond the French windows held my altering gaze as I unwound the tripod and fixed the camera.

The doorknob behind me turned. I swung around to see a tall, slim and clean-shaven man with an explosion of copper hair and amber eyes dancing behind crystal-framed eyeglasses. A silver flower-brooch glistered on the lapels of his bespoke grey-herringbone Saville Row suit, and an oval moonstone and diamond cluster ring on his index finger shone under the sway of a refracted sunbeam filtering in from the garden outside. Lord Melvin Bradshaw.

'Thank you so much for your time,' I blathered. 'Your secretary said I could start setting up my equipment in your office. I hope you don't mind.'

'Not at all.' He swept a gracious arm towards the camera. 'Shall we?'

He didn't sound as intimidating as he looked but his air of charisma commanded instant obeisance. Lord Bradshaw spoke passionately about his rise to the stallion of the corporate world. Twenty minutes later, I packed up my equipment, deciding it was by far the best interview I had ever done. But Lord Bradshaw didn't seem to think so. 'Was this your first?' he asked.

'Well, I've interviewed several leaders and celebrities back at ABP News.'

'Aha. I thought so. Aiden's account manager shared your profile with my executive assistant and I see that you do have a strong background. So, I concluded that you might be terribly distracted.' Lord Bradshaw adjusted one of his cufflinks. 'Please don't get me wrong. The lack of structure in our conversation gave it a rawness that made it a lot more authentic. And you clearly did your homework.'

I stared at him, confused. 'That's a good thing, isn't it?'

'I suppose so,' Lord Bradshaw chuckled. 'But you look like someone died and I coudn't help noticing that.'

I pondered over how close to home that figure of expression was. Many people *had* died. I didn't know how many more lives were in danger. Without any warning, a spell of tears billowed in my eyes.

'Jesus Christ! My sincerest apologies, Ms Raman.' Lord Bradshaw handed me a wad of tissues. 'I understand what it means to put on a strong face when all the bridges around you are falling. I've been there too, trust me. But, light always eclipses the darkness. Now, why don't you tell me what's troubling you? Perhaps, I can do something to help? Meanwhile, I'll get us some tea.'

Lord Bradshaw buzzed his assistant and requested for two Yorkshires. A placating sense of reassurance suffused me. Someone out there understood a fraction of what I was going through – without any questions or explanations. The article I had read about Bradshaw's scratchy foster home upbringing resurfaced on my mind. I gazed at the shadows of empathy in his eyes. 'I-I'm asthmatic. I lost my job. My landlord evicted me. I'm living in a dump. I haven't been able to land a full-time job or, at this time, even a part-time gig that can get me by …' I trailed off.

'Oh?' A frown wrinkled Bradshaw's forehead.

The tea arrived. I gingerly took a sip.

'Have you thought about applying for the Graduate Recruitment Scheme here?' Lord Bradshaw asked. 'We're accepting applications until May.'

A newsroom job was my first choice, but it was becoming clear that I would need to explore other avenues if my visa status stood in the way. 'I-I ... why, thank you but ...' I gabbled.

'If you're worried about a work permit, we process such visas all the time. Employee diversity is one of our strongest suits.' Bradshaw leaned forward. 'Are *you* all right though? You look like you're going to pass out.' He reached for the receiver. 'Would you like me to call a doc?'

'No, no!' I waved my hand frantically. 'I'm fine.' I sighed. 'It's just, y'know ... well, it's this investigation.'

I unveiled the entire story to Bradshaw, right from what I had seen at Bread Breakers', to the murders of Jeff and Gretchen.

'It sounds like an organised nexus,' Bradshaw avowed, mortified. 'Have they started making arrests?'

'I'm still trying to find out who's behind this racket. It's a hornet's nest.'

'I understand.' Bradshaw pulled out a leather folder from his desk and began scribbling into a small book.

'I'm glad I, uh, talked to you. I'm feeling loads better,' I admitted.

'Hopefully, this'll make you feel better still.' Bradshaw slid a cheque across the desk. A sum of ten thousand pounds stared up at me.

It had my name on it. 'What's this?' I mumbled, confused.

'Something I hope will see you through for a while,' Bradshaw replied. 'I know how expensive London can be for an international student and how much costlier an investigation of this sort might make that. I need to head to another meeting, now. Thank you for your time, Ms Raman.'

I gaped at him. 'I cannot possibly accept this, Sir!' I squeaked. 'I mean I ...'

Lord Bradshaw pushed his glasses up the bridge of his nose. 'The world needs youngsters like you, Ms Raman,' he said gently. 'There is a lot you can contribute one day. You mustn't let your pride come in the way of your safety—especially when your life could be in danger.'

'B-but …' I spluttered.

'Look, if it helps your reasoning, we've had thousands of applications for the Gregersen International Scholarships and our committee was considering you among others,' Lord Bradshaw revealed. 'We've been having some donor issues and we're working out the modalities. That's the only glitch, but it should be sorted in a few weeks. Please consider this as an advance disbursement. We'll make it official once the scholarship committee starts disbursing funds to all recipients. All right?'

'Thank you, Sir,' I gulped, picking up the cheque carefully.

'Do let me know if I can do anything more to help.' Lord Bradshaw offered me a lacquered business card and rose to leave.

A dazed trance dwarfed my senses. I couldn't believe my good fortune.

13

On A Roll

29 March

I hopped into Detective Constable Jesse Krantz's beat-up Ford Mondeo Hatchback on Westminster Bridge Road. In a double knit charcoal-grey coat over an Oxford blue Lacoste jumper and a pair of jeans, Krantz was dressed like a working class civilian to deflect any attention from his real job. We drove towards Royal Street.

'If they're really doing this without a court sanction, they'll get royally screwed,' Krantz muttered as he turned off the ignition in a car park near the Archbishop Park, a few minutes later. Then he turned to face me. 'Ms Raman, sending a cop out for a red herring of this sort hardly ever happens – Inspector Davenport made an exception for you because you've been one of the most cooperative witnesses Murder has possibly had. So, I hope you jolly well got all the facts right.'

'I believe I have,' I assured.

We strode swiftly down the winding alleyway that led to the Bread Breakers' surgery clinic.

Krantz knocked on the door. A young desk clerk in a plaid skirt opened the door a crack. 'Yes?'

'We-we have a problem,' Krantz stuttered. 'Our daughter is a resident here. We believe her hormones are interfering with her behaviour. She's becoming more aggressive. She was even given chloropromazine last week to keep her quiet. My wife and I want a surgical menopause for her.'

I didn't even flinch as he draped an arm around my shoulder with natural ease, as if it was obvious who his wife was. The clerk's gaze shifted to my hands.

She's searching for a wedding band.

I had long since removed Nimmy's ring from my finger. I inconspicuously slid my left hand into my coat pocket.

'Isn't your daughter with you now?' the clerk inquired.

'She has her period and is unwell today,' I explained.

'We want this done as quietly as possible,' Krantz whispered.

'D'you have an appointment?'

I wrung my hands. 'No, but it's urgent. Please.'

'We'll need to identify her on our records first.'

Jesse looked about him. 'Can we come in?' he asked uncertainly.

'Oh, of course.' The girl stepped back to let us in. 'What was her name, did you say?'

'Nila,' I replied promptly.

'I need the full name.'

I had no idea what Nila's last name was. Krantz cast me an unobtrusive glance.

'We registered her only as Nila,' I said finally.

'Okay-dokie. Let's see what we can do for ya.' She motioned for us to have a seat in the lobby, hurried to a ramshackle desk in the corner and grabbed the phone. For now, Krantz and I seemed to be the only souls in the reception area. We sat awkwardly and waited.

'Beth is the official record keeper. She isn't at her desk right now,' she informed after a few moments. I looked up at a wall clock ahead of me. 2.20 p.m. We didn't have much time. I bit into one of my knuckles to keep from hyperventilating.

'I can retrieve those records for you,' the clerk offered when she saw my expression.

'That's incredibly kind of you,' Krantz gushed.

The girl pressed a button near a side elevator. I heard her swear under her breath. 'That lazy sleazebag … smokin' on the porch all the time.' Her words faded away as the elevator doors swallowed her up.

I nodded at Krantz. 'Now!'

We made a mad dash for the stairs, hitting the first floor landing just as the elevator doors opened into another lobby on our left at the far end. The stairwell door opened up to a wall partition that concealed the view from the lobby. We scuttled behind it. A few doctors and members of staff strode up and down the corridor, but no one seemed to notice us as we raced towards the operating theatre. Krantz abruptly halted before a set of sliding doors leading to a small waiting room. As I caught up with him, I glimpsed a grubby board above me. It read 'Scrub Room'. 'Wh-what are you doing?' I hissed in a state of near-delirium.

'Do as I say!' Krantz ordered, shoving me inside.

'There. You look like a skilled young surgeon now,' Krantz teased, adjusting my scrub cap ten minutes later. We were in identical blue scrubs, caps and surgical masks.

I gingerly patted my bobtail through the perforations of my scrub cap. 'We need identification badges,' I mumbled. Most drawers I tried were locked.

'We're running out of time,' Krantz warned.

I spotted a badge next to a roll of linen in a shelf-corner. It bore the name of Hargreaves Remoe. 'Here.' I thrust the badge into Krantz's hands and rummaged around for another one with a woman's name. Krantz found a jumble of nameplates in an unlocked drawer. 'You're in luck, lady,' he reported, offering me one.

I blindly pinned it to the yoke of my billowy scrub shirt.

'The name on it is Claire Taylors …' Krantz froze mid-sentence.

The scrub room doors opened and two male nurses walked in, chattering loudly. I did a quick volte-face and pretended to wash my hands in a stainless steel sink. I sensed that Krantz was doing something similar.

'Yo, chocolate boy!' One of the nurses hollered in a different tone. 'Wanna join us for a beer this evening?'

My heartbeat quickened. Krantz's olive tan. They were calling out to him.

'Uh, I'll take a rain check on that, boys,' Krantz croaked out, moving towards the door. I lowered my head and quickly shuffled out after him. We slowed down our pace when we slipped in through the sliding doors to the waiting room.

Among the few people milling around were Shailaja and Jyoti, picking at their jacket sleeves. Nimmy paced back and forth, drumming his fingers against a white Formica desk every time he passed. Two nurses slouched behind old desktops. A third nurse stood in a corner, pacifying an inconsolable older man – presumably the parent of a patient.

Nimmy's anguished hazel eyes, now ringed with purple bags, met mine for the briefest splinter of a second. A faint sliver of mystification eclipsed his face. He raked a hand through his hair and sniffed the air.

Oh God … my eyes! They were light-brown all right, but they still looked South Asian. And the *Charlie* deodorant I always wore. He didn't recognise me, did he? The confused look on Nimmy's face receded nearly as soon as it materialised.

Everyone in the waiting room dissolved into the periphery of my vision as Krantz and I stormed into the operating room ahead of us.

Nurses and technicians were huddled around the operating table. Through the slit-like gaps that the space between their figures provided, I spotted the curly bobs of a heavily sedated Asha. Under the swarm of sheets and the hovering crew, she looked so wee and frail that my first impulse was to cry. But I couldn't break down just yet. I furiously began clicking photographs and sending them to Alfred, who was all keyed up at his workstation in the BBC offices, ready to download them.

Two nurses stiffened at the first jet of flashbulbs.

'What the devil are you two doing here?' one of them roared. A few shocked gasps followed suit. I continued clicking and forwarding them on WhatsApp.

A few shots of Asha, the operating team, a side profile of the anesthesiologist, which was the best I could get.

'Who let you in?' the anesthesiologist demanded.

'I'll alert the staff,' a nurse announced, rushing out of the room.

Krantz raised his palms, as if he was going to surrender – but I could hear him speaking sternly. 'Have you anesthetised that young woman yet?'

I continued my snapshot rampage. The wall suction, the operating table, the overhead surgical lights, the anesthesia cart …

I heard another irate voice at the door. 'What the fuck is going on here?'

I had no bandwidth to look behind me. I clicked another picture of Asha facing the viewing screens and monitors.

A bare hand reached out to grab the phone from me. 'Where'd that come from, Missy?'

I clicked photographs of the person coming at me and backed away simultaneously, knocking over a table on the way. Some bottles on a tray clattered to the ground.

When I looked up, I found myself staring into a pair of cold green eyes that I recognised, from my previous visit as Dr Tahseen's. Krantz darted forward and pinned the surgeon's arms behind his back. I zoomed in on Dr Tahseen and clicked more photographs.

'Confiscating this phone won't serve you any purpose,' I said, even as I sent the latest slab of pictures to Alfred. 'The pictures I've taken have already reached the BBC. They're probably broadcasting it live right now. We're also videotaping you on a hidden spy cam.' Sure enough, there was one clipped to Krantz's undershirt. It belonged to the Squad. There was a horrified silence. Then, many operating team members instinctively covered their faces with their hands and stooped out of the room. Krantz was flashing out his ID card.

'Detective Jesse Krantz,' he stated firmly. 'I want you to cease the procedure on Ms Sawant immediately.'

'Fuck!' Dr Tahseen bellowed. He turned to two nurses anxiously fluttering around the operating table. 'Take that kid back to the ward at once.'

'She hasn't been anesthetised yet,' a gangly young male nurse stammered to Krantz.

'Please don't let it go on television,' the other beseeched me, helping her colleague load an unconscious Asha on to the stretcher. 'This job feeds my family and …'

'Out!' Dr Tahseen snarled, pointing at the door. Then he held on to Krantz's sleeve. 'Listen …'

The constable jerked his arm away.

Dr Tahseen shifted his gaze to me. 'Look, this isn't what you think it is! Can we talk in my cabin downstairs? I can explain everything!'

'Talk right now,' I demanded.

Dr Tahseen fell into a chair. 'Are you still filming?'

'Yes.' I answered coldly.

'Well, I can't talk then.' Dr Tahseen rose to his feet and moved towards the door.

'No worries. You'll make a charming face on TV,' I hollered after him.

'No! Wait!' Dr Tahseen cried, wheeling around.

Krantz walked up to him. 'I have tonnes of questions for you, Doctor.'

A flurry of staff members barreled in, accompanied by three security guards.

Krantz flashed his ID card at the group. 'I'm from the CID. Dr Tahseen is going to answer some questions.'

Baffled, the group retreated. Krantz placed a hand between Dr Tahseen's shoulder blades and marched him out, motioning for me to follow.

In the waiting room outside, Shailaja and Jyoti ran towards the ward as medical staff members scurried back and forth agitatedly. Nimmy stood by the nurses' desk with a resigned expression.

'What's going on?' Shailaja was yelling.

A huge sigh stood out from the ballistic frenzy. It was Nimmy's.

In his parquet-floored consulting room downstairs, Dr Tahseen began hyperventilating again.

'Are you still videotaping?' he asked Krantz across the table.

Krantz shook his head.

He wasn't. But I was still audio-recording the scene, unknown to Dr Tahseen, who took a sip of water from a bottle on his table and flashed a beguiling smile.

'I understand that many current and former residents of Bread Breakers' are being treated or operated on illegally …' Krantz began tersely.

'There is a misunderstanding,' Dr Tahseen said. 'Bread Breakers' is a private charity started fifty-eight years ago by Valerie Rousseau, a legendary French businesswoman, genre artist and philanthropist. It was originally called Candela Centre for Assisted Living. It was renamed about ten years ago. Valerie founded Candela in memory of her mentally challenged daughter who died in her teens. Today, Bread Breakers' is seen as a warm, friendly and inviting home for mentally disabled, abused, and traumatised women and girls who need unconditional love, attention, rehabilitation and proper medical, psychiatric and general care too.'

'I don't see performing an illegal hysterectomy as providing proper medical care,' I pointed out. Krantz held up a hand, signaling at me to be quiet.

'The families or guardians involved are well aware of all the implications of any medical procedure they want for their children or relatives. We never perform surgeries without their consent or insistence,' Dr Tahseen said.

'All that is very well,' I said. 'What about the hysterectomy you were going to do today?'

'Ms Sawant's parents and caretaker wanted …'

'So, they insisted. What about Ms Sawant? Did she sign a consent form?' Krantz demanded.

Dr Tahseen looked at Krantz as if he had lost his mind. 'Ms Sawant is a mentally challenged woman who can't make informed decisions on her own. How can she provide her consent?'

'Why didn't you get a court approval then?'

'We're lobbying with the government to revise its health care policies and sterilisation laws,' Dr Tahseen explained. 'Right now, the courts won't sanction an approval for a hysterectomy in cases where patients can't provide their consent. But we're in the process of obtaining court approvals for a number of oncoming cases.'

'How could you think of operating on Ms Sawant without a court sanction?' Krantz probed.

'Any court would have vetoed our request,' Dr Tahseen said somberly. 'Have you considered what these women and their families face everyday? How bothersome it is to constantly keep cleaning up after someone else when she has her period or develops an infection? Or how traumatic it is for a mentally challenged girl who gets pregnant? She can't take care of her child. Her family has to bear the costs of raising that child, even if they're too poor to care for an extra family member. And what about the constant risk of sexual abuse these girls face?'

'Are you saying sterilisation will reduce the incidence of sexual abuse?' I burst out indignantly.

Dr Tahseen began to look uncomfortable.

'Now, let's start with the basics,' Krantz said. 'If Bread Breakers' is as established as you claim it is, why doesn't it have a proper web presence?'

Dr Tahseen took a deep breath. 'I told you. The care home was renamed ten years ago.'

I quickly did a Google search for Candela on my phone under the desk. The closest result I got was a Jessica Candela, who ran a retirement home in Arizona.

'Nothing with that name either,' I retorted.

'We're an old organisation,' Dr Tahseen began, as if he were launching into a mythological saga on Greek cultural evolution. 'We have a personal rapport with most of our residents and their families. It's really word-of-mouth that gets us fresh referrals and new residents. We already get more requests than we can handle. So, we thought we could do away with the unnecessary hassle of a web interface. But we realise we'll become archaic if we don't adapt to the twenty-first century, so we're working on it now.'

'Bread Breakers' isn't even on the Registry.' Krantz mentioned.

From my research, I remembered that the Registry is a forum for UK-based organisations to register as private charities. 'Would you know if Bread Breakers' is listed on the Registry under a different name?' I queried.

Dr Tahseen shrugged. 'You'll need to address such questions to the Board or Committee.'

Krantz perked up. 'What committee?'

'The CRCMD,' Dr Tahseen revealed. 'The Committee of Rehabilitative Care for the Mentally Disabled. It's a semi-autonomous committee, as far as I know.'

'Tell us more about it,' Krantz urged.

'It was formed by the Bread Breakers' board members. They're the key decision-makers. But the committee is now starting to support various initiatives ranging from disability rights to rehab.'

Under the table, I ran a quick search for CRCMD on my phone. The name popped up on at least eight different links among the results on the first page. I clicked on a link to the University College London hospital. CRCMD seemed to have a tie-up with the hospital. I spotted Secretary of State for Health Lord Howard Mount listed among the committee members.

'Is Lord Mount a member of this committee?' I asked incredulously.

Dr Tahseen reached inside his scrub to adjust his shirt collar. 'I believe so, yes.' He replied.

I glanced at a few other names on the repertoire.

Dr Andrew Whitaker, Kathleen Sanders, Dr Alexa Jones, Aiden … I blinked twice in surprise … Aiden McLeod. He seemed to be pretty much everywhere!

I scoured online and found that Dr Andrew Whitaker was a well-known British neurologist, Kathleen Sanders, an Oxford-educated parliamentary under the Secretary of State for Quality, and Dr Alexa Jones, a popular cosmetic surgeon based in Belfast.

Dr Tahseen was still talking. 'As you can see, we have parliamentarians and seasoned professionals on that committee. That should be enough to stand testimony to our credibility here.'

'What does Aiden McLeod have to do with a home for the mentally disabled?' I asked squeamishly. 'He's a full-fledged media honcho unlike the other members here!'

Krantz promptly made a note of my observation.

Dr Tahseen snorted. 'Can't a media guy support a private charity?'

'I'll need to speak to the Board members,' Krantz said firmly. 'But that's something we'll get to later. Now, I'd like you to tell me why children are kept in a garage on the Bread Breakers' premises especially when they're not mentally impaired in any way.'

'A garage full of children?' Dr Tahseen gabbled. 'Oh, you mean the playroom shed. It's a crèche. Not many workplaces have them, y'know. Even multinational org …'

'Get to the point, Doctor,' Krantz snapped.

'Well, uh, the crèche accommodates the children of many of our staff, security personnel, residents …' he trailed off.

Krantz cocked an eyebrow. 'Residents?'

'Er … kind of,' Dr Tahseen admitted.

'Dr Tahseen, it's either a yes or a no.'

'Well, a few of our residents are susceptible,' Dr Tahseen explained. 'We don't really know how it happens … you know how it is … they can't understand what's going on, but they get together with somebody and become pregnant. Occasionally, a couple of them are sexually exploited. But such cases are rare,' he finished after an uneasy pause.

'How can these women get sexually exploited or become pregnant when they lead such a sheltered life at Bread Breakers'?' I asked sarcastically.

'Many residents who've done well here have returned home to lead normal lives with their families or kith and kin,' Dr Tahseen pointed out. 'We aren't responsible for what happens to them once they leave these premises.'

'If they got pregnant outside these premises, why are their kids *here* rather than with their families or next of kin?' Krantz questioned. 'I mean those born to these former residents.'

'You've been grilling me non-stop!' Dr Tahseen retorted angrily. 'Bread Breakers' is going out of its way to support those children, financially and otherwise, because their families, in most cases, can't afford to care for them.'

'Ever heard of Social Services?' Krantz piped up sarcastically. 'Are you saying most other children in that crèche belong to medical staff, support workers and security personnel?'

'Y-yes,' Dr Tahseen mumbled.

Krantz jumped on the note of hesitation in his voice. 'Then why were some of those children abused on Eighth March?'

Dr Tahseen's eyes bulged in surprise. 'Abused? What are you talking about?'

I explained what I had seen and heard in the playroom that day.

Dr Tahseen furrowed his brow. 'Do you know what that support worker looked like?'

I offered a brief description.

'Oh, I think you're talking about Niah,' Dr Tahseen said finally. 'I didn't know she was *that* sort. Usually, our support workers place our residents' welfare before their own. I'll inform the Board and see that she's fired as soon as possible.'

'What about the young woman who was raped and killed in the bushes near the care home side door a few years ago?' Krantz pressed. 'The woman was a Bread Breakers' resident at the time.'

'I'm sorry … I wouldn't know of such a thing.'

'Besides the events in that garage on Eighth March, I hear that those children are being abused repeatedly,' Krantz said.

Dr Tahseen pushed a bunch of files back on the table and rose from his seat.

'I'm sorry, Detective. I wouldn't know. I've spent well over an hour answering your questions. I have work to attend to, now.' He moved towards the door.

Krantz sang a warning. 'We'll be back soon, Doctor. We aren't done here.'

~

'Bloody hell, these last few pictures look like war!' Alfred grunted at the BBC Broadcast House later that evening.

'It sure as hell was,' I assured. 'Thanks so much for downloading it all.'

Alfred shrugged. 'Anything for Kiki. Will you use these pictures as a form of evidence for the investigation?'

'That's the idea.'

Alfred tugged on his ear thoughtfully. 'I'm not sure we can run these as part of the exposé Kiki was talking about. But we could work an exclusive story around it.'

'You mean the exposé is off limits now?'

'Well, we wouldn't want to put out speculations and muddle the police investigation,' Alfred stated practically. 'That's why these photos aren't going on air right away. If the case is solved, we could do a documentary, perhaps. But I don't see that happening any time soon either.'

'I'll make a copy,' I said, hoping my disappointment wasn't obvious.

'Hey, Al! How's it going?' a bass voice called out as I transferred all the photos from Alfred's laptop on to a blank pen drive. I looked up to see a tall, young man with shell-framed glasses and spiked chestnut brown hair. I recognised him as a popular TV anchor.

'Hello!' Alfred greeted.

'I hope the dust has settled,' the man said, looking from Alfred to me. I knew he was referring to Keisha's death.

Alfred ignored his commiserations. 'Riz, meet Sanders, sorry, Sandy. She worked on Streetsmart and she was with Keisha on the Lionheart campaign. Sandy, this is Rizwan Elbaz, presenter of *The One Show*, if you've heard of it.'

'Oh, hasn't everyone?' I exclaimed. 'I love your spontaneity, Mr Elbaz.'

Elbaz grinned airily. 'It's mostly contextual. Those days of stale presenting are gone.'

'Perhaps, we ought to follow America's footsteps and get a guy like Bill O' Reilly to yell out our news updates with a pinch of dramedy,' Alfred joked.

'That'll be the day, Al, that'll be the day,' Elbaz said. 'You guys find a replacement for Streetsmart yet?' he added curiously.

'That show's on hold for a bit,' Alfred admitted. 'Ongoing investigation.'

Elbaz suddenly grew pale.

'What's the matter?' I asked.

Elbaz wrung his hands. 'Um—I just remembered something. I have no idea how this could've slipped my mind …' He seemed annoyed with himself.

'What the dickens are you getting at?' Alfred demanded, confused.

'Well … I have an envelope for you,' Elbaz told Alfred. 'Keisha handed it to me one evening – it was in fact the last time I saw her. I think it was a Friday – she wanted to leave it with you before rushing to a meeting.'

That discussion she had mentioned with Jeff, I remembered.

'But you weren't around. So, she handed it to me and said she'd pick it up on Monday,' Elbaz continued. 'She said it was important. I'm terribly sorry for not dropping it with you sooner. The truth is I completely forgot and it's been lying around in my drawer for weeks. I'll go get it.'

He retraced his steps and disappeared around a corner.

Alfred exchanged a perplexed glance with me. 'There's a bunch of scripts waiting for my review and I have to knock out a roadmap in an hour,' he grumbled.

Elbaz returned with a slim beige envelope. 'Here it is.'

'Thanks, Riz.' Alfred pocketed it and prepared to leave.

'Wait!' I cried. 'Can we see what's inside, please?'

'Can't it wait a day?' Alfred groaned.

'He says Kiki said it was important. It really won't take long.'

Elbaz looked on curiously. Alfred reluctantly walked back to me. We slit open the envelope and peered in. There it was. The little red keychain. The slim metallic case. The fading words 'high priority' stared up at us from the yellowing keychain label.

Impulsively, I threw myself into Elbaz's arms with a shriek. 'Oh, we've found it!'

Then I clutched Alfred's arm. 'It's *that* flash drive. The one with the care home videotape you saw earlier this month.'

I felt a sudden movement behind me as I stood on the platform at the Wood Lane Underground, twenty minutes later.

'Oh, I'm really sorry,' a little old lady said when I spun around. She adjusted the rim of her thick eyeglasses. 'My eyesight does me no favours when it gets dark.'

I nodded. 'No worries.'

The dame ruffled her skirts, walked ahead a few yards and squinted at the departure board. A few other commuters joined us on the platform. In the far distance, a red blob glistened on the pebbled tracks as it zoomed towards us. I turned sideways and glanced at the old lady.

'The train's pulling in,' I hollered, convinced that she hadn't been able to read the notice on the departure board. The lady turned to me. Her eyes grew as wide as saucers.

A split second later, I felt a palm slam against the small of my back. I teetered on the edge of the platform and fell headlong on to the tracks below. The last I saw was the greasy underside of the approaching train.

14

Horsepower

3 April

I re-adjusted the floppy cowboy hat over my blonde bob wig and ran a finger over the sleeve of my oversized red duffle coat, reconsidering my decision to commute on the trains like a travesty. But I couldn't shake off the smorgasbord of haunting snapshots from that night at Wood Lane: The scuffle of feet, the shrill cries of a young couple, the grip of hands pulling me to safety, the horrible squeak of wheels as the train screeched to a halt right before my face …

My phone buzzed.

'Yes, Detective Krantz?' I answered.

'We've made progress with a CRCMD committee member,' Krantz reported. 'Aiden McLeod from Pinwheel Interactive attributes his CRCMD membership to a recommendation from Paul Rubalcabo, a partner at EuroFirst, which is a client of his firm.'

EuroFirst. Carl. *That* was the missing link.

'Apparently, Rubalcabo actively supports disability rights,' Krantz rattled on. 'Meanwhile, McLeod says he has no clue about Bread Breakers'.'

'How can he not know about that care home when he's a committee member?' I spluttered.

'We're digging. McLeod put us on to Paul Rubalcabo's secretary and Verizon's communications director, Evelyn Weaver. She's another Pinwheel client. She introduced McLeod to Rubalcabo at EuroFirst.'

'Rubalcabo isn't a committee member, is he?'

'No. But he's in close contact with two private charities in Warsaw, three not-for-profits in New York, and many refugee shelters and care homes in London. He's also made donations to some special schools around here. Now, the Squad has seen the ninety-minute film Alfred sent us as well as the video footage from the surgery clinic. They've given a shout to the magistrates' court. We should be getting search and arrest warrants soon.'

'Thanks, Detective.' My hands shook as I rang off. Was Paul Rubalcabo Carl's boss? Were he and Carl behind four killings?

~

I re-read Aiden McLeod's LinkedIn profile. A boy scout, an alumnus of Goldsmiths, and a media relations consultant for the London office of a Hong Kong-based PR firm before joining Pinwheel Interactive ten years ago. As I continued digging on my laptop, I stumbled upon an image on Flickr. In the picture, McLeod and Rubalcabo had their arms around each other and smiled into the camera from a steel suspension bridge above the Thames against the backdrop of a massive building with taupe walls and steel girders. The Tate Modern Art Gallery.

A pair of birds perched atop the roof behind them. They looked like eagles. Curiously, I ran a Google search for Tate Modern eagles. I clicked on a link to an article in *The Evening Standard* and began reading: 'A pair of peregrine falcons have ruffled a few feathers in the art world with regular appearances at the Tate Modern ...'

A fusillade of memories descended on me. Nidhi embracing her date in a limousine, five months ago, as a falcon car-hanger swayed before them from the rearview mirror ... the glimmer of the gemstone on her date's finger in the limo ... Nidhi outside the Barbican with her companion, a fedora masking the man's face on both occasions. And then, there was the large garnet ring Aiden McLeod wore regularly.

Inspector Davenport's words, after the 'accident' with Gretchen, tumbled into my mind: *A passerby saw something brown or yellow dangling from the rearview mirror. He said it looked like a bird.*

I enlarged the Flickr image on my screen. One of Paul Rubalcabo's arms disappeared behind McLeod's back. His other hand was in his trouser pocket. I had no way of knowing whether he was wearing a gemstone ring. Aiden's garnet ring was clearly visible in the picture, though.

And the falcon ... McLeod and Rubalcabo ... Was one of them Nidhi's boyfriend? Did the boyfriend have a fetish for falcons?

'Ms Raman, we were discussing the principles enlisted in the Code,' the instructor's voice rang out. 'Didn't you get any sleep last night?'

A polite smatter of laughter followed from the media policy class I was sitting in.

'Um ... I was just thinking about the possibility of a public interest element in this piece,' I lied, waving a paper before me.

'Is that the Attard Vs Manchester Evening News case?' the instructor boomed.

I nodded meekly.

'We'll come to public interest soon enough. In this case, no information, under the Code, can be private if it has already emerged in the public domain.'

Relieved that I had saved my face, I slumped back into my seat.

Once class got over, I blazed out of the campus, realising that Nidhi could be in danger.

~

'My brother and his wife told you, you were never to contact any of us again.' Nidhi scowled as we sat in the Southall Black Sisters offices, an hour later. 'I agreed to see you because you sounded as if you were in trouble. But questioning me about my non-existent love life is an insult beyond my imagination!'

I wondered if I was naïve in expecting Nidhi to believe my thesis that the man she was dating could be involved in one or more deaths.

'Perhaps you just had business dealings with him,' I said finally. 'Anyhow, what you do is none of my business, all right? But the Squad behind Operation Douglas needs to know the identity of this man. And I'm cautioning you only because your life could be in danger!'

'I'm not obliged to disclose his identity,' Nidhi replied tartly. 'Look, I'm swamped with a campaign for a new homicide law. I have no time for your claptrap. I need you to leave.' She pointed at the door.

'Could you at least tell me if this man is Aiden McLeod or Paul Rubalcabo?' I urged.

'Shahana!' Nidhi yelled across the room. 'Escort Ms Raman to the door, will you? I'm running late for a meeting.'

A timid-looking girl appeared by my side as Nidhi rose from her seat and stuffed a stack of folders into a briefcase.

'I think he's taking you for a ride,' I whispered to Nidhi before Shahana led me away. 'Please watch out.'

~

4 April

I discovered that my Cranford roommate, Kimberly was infected with a contagious HIV-linked retro virus. Despite her refusal to let me leave, I managed to escape from that bedsit one night after securing the confidence of another landlord in Charlton, thanks to a letter from Alfred, stating I was a stringer with the BBC, and an electronic rental reference from Ritchie. I awoke in my new box room on Wednesday morning.

My phone rang as I made some tea and chatted with my new housemates in the kitchen downstairs. 'Hello?' I mumbled groggily.

'Sandy!' Megan cried breathlessly. 'Charlotte is coming out of her coma.'

I mouthed an apology to my housemates and hustled upstairs.

'When did she come to?' I shrieked.

'She spoke her first words yesterday. Around seven p.m.'

'Are they allowing visitors?'

'Check in with her Mum. Mrs Hale has hardly left her bedside.' Megan left a number with me.

I remembered her voicemail from last week, saying she was out of office. 'Everything okay with you?'

'There was a family emergency in Belgium so I was there for a few days. All good now,' Megan said.

'Take care, Meg.' A niggling thought chewed on me when I hung up. Charlotte was dating someone too, wasn't she? I wondered if he had ever visited her.

Charlotte was swaddled in blankets under a veil of contraptions in the Surgical Critical Care Unit in Kings College Hospital's Cheyne wing. An indomitable woman who was now no more than a pasty lump. Tears congealed in my eyes.

'She's sleeping now,' Charlotte's mother whispered.

I looked up at Mrs Hale. On a better day, her trim frame and carefully styled hair would have belied her age. But now, her face was taut with anxiety. I remembered that Keisha had once told me she was divorced. But Charlotte's father hadn't flown in to London to visit his ailing daughter. For that matter, it looked like the man Charlotte was seeing hadn't visited her either. Maybe things hadn't worked out between them.

'She'll be fine,' I assured Mrs Hale.

'She's been taken off the ventilator,' Mrs Hale mentioned optimistically.

'What do the docs say?'

'That it's a miracle she's made it this far after what she's been through. They were on the verge of giving up after the first few weeks. But an MRI scan last week showed some brain activity. She opened her eyes shortly after that.' Mrs Hale sounded eager and hopeful that her daughter would be back on her feet soon.

'What about the swelling in her brain?' I persisted.

'It's come down after the surgery,' Mrs Hale informed. 'But it may be a while before she can recover all of her functions.'

'Something beyond modern medicine is helping us here. And Charlotte's a fighter,' I said.

As if on cue, Charlotte's eyes fluttered a little.

Mrs Hale rushed to her daughter's bedside. 'Honey? Are you awake?'

Charlotte blinked once and squeezed her mother's hand weakly. I debated on whether I should speak to Charlotte, who might not remember me at all. But Mrs Hale took my hand and led me to her. 'Look who's here, baby!' she whispered, kissing her forehead. 'It's Sandy. You worked with her.'

Charlotte gazed wanly at me. A flicker of recognition misted her eyes. Her lips started moving, but no words came out. 'What is it, baby?' Mrs Hale prodded gently.

Charlotte stared at her mother, perplexed and disoriented. After a few moments, she looked right at me.

'H-horse,' she spluttered.

My heart skipped a beat.

'One,' she added, after some thought.

Mrs Hale looked confused. 'Horse one?'

I knew I was shooting in the dark, but I went for it. 'Who hurt you?'

'Horse,' Charlotte said decisively.

Mrs Hale turned to me. 'She got hit by a horse?'

'Do you want to write that down?' I asked softly.

Charlotte's eyes watered as she looked beseechingly at her mother and tried again. 'H-horsse … is … the one.'

That I was commuting in disguise after the Wood Lane incident did little to quell my fear of hopping into a train and becoming an easy target for the Mafioso who took the image of Sonny Corleone in my mind. Remembering that I could afford to be more lenient with my finances, courtesy of Lord Melvin Bradshaw, I flanked a cab outside Kings College Hospital.

As the taxi sped towards Westminster, a meliiflous string of chords and melodies resonated from the radio. A sense of déjà vu swamped me as I listened to the airy beats of the guitar. I jerked forward in my seat. 'Um, you wouldn't know this song, would you?' I asked the cabbie.

'Nope. It's on Radio 3 though. It's, uh …' the driver squinted into the display before him. 'Jazz on 3, I think. Jez Nelson's show. You a fan of jazz?'

'Um … yeah, thanks,' I mumbled.

A brief memory played out: my jovial razzing about Charlotte's 'fateful' tryst with the man she was dating … ah yes, *he* was the unsigned jazz guitarist she had interviewed on radio. I had even seen him – or rather, his frame – hidden behind a bright blue umbrella when he picked her up from the BBC studios weeks ago. Charlotte had mentioned his name too … what was it? It began with an H. Hemmings? Hawks? No, no. It was …

Horace.

That was it. My fingers grew cold and clammy.

I have to talk to the Squad.

The new comfort level I had developed with Jesse Krantz since our Bread Breakers' expedition, made him the first port of call. Krantz picked up on the fourth ring, sounding preoccupied.

'I'm in an apartment in Clapton. Our new briefing room,' he said sarcastically. 'A bloodied spray painting around this poor guy. Our team and two other boroughs are wrangling over which unit will take this on. We've got just three teams on call at any time too. Anything important?'

'Charlotte Hale is waking up from her coma,' I began before filling him in on my thoughts.

'Gordon Bennet! What a coincidence!' Krantz interjected.

'Gordon who?'

'Sorry – old British expression,' he chuckled.

'Did the Squad find anything?'

'Yesterday, our investigators found a driver's license under a floor liner in the Wrangler that was used to run Charlotte down. The license belongs to a British national, Horace Frederick Fitzgerald. It expired five years ago. One of us'd have called, but we got embroiled in this Clapton …'

'Is Horace the person who…?'

'Horace Fitzgerald is *dead*.'

'So, Horace isn't his real name,' I mumbled dizzily. 'How did you find out that he died?'

'Remember David Cooper from Moor Park? The guy whose Wrangler was stolen. We spoke to him and his wife, Justine, this morning. Justine is Horace's daughter. The Wrangler belonged to Horace, who later transferred its ownership to David. Horace died of a stroke twelve years ago.'

'David Cooper probably knows the guy who took his father-in-law's identity.' I surmised.

'Probably,' Krantz agreed. 'Wheeler is looking into whether someone applied for a passport in Horace Fitzgerald's name in the last three years. His death certificate isn't listed on any database yet, so the passport office wouldn't have suspected a thing. Try to find out if Ms Hale is referring to Horace Fitzgerald. Looks like we need more horsepower than we would for an entire caseload.'

---

5 April

'Is Horace Fitzgerald the man who hurt you?' I asked Charlotte gently at her hospital bed, the next afternoon.

Megan stood by, watching curiously.

Charlotte fumbled around at the bedside table. I rushed to her side. She looked up at me and closed her fist as if she were holding a pen.

She wants to write something down. I ferreted in my tote and produced a notepad and pen.

'Did they find fresh clues in that jeep?' Megan asked hopefully.

I nodded and peered over Charlotte's shoulder. When I saw what she had written, I turned back to Megan grimly. 'It's Horace all right. Charlotte thinks she saw his face as he drove up to her side and bumped her car over the median. Where's Mrs Hale?'

'She's at the pharmacy, getting meds for Charlotte. I'll let her know.'

I squeezed her hand lightly. 'I'll keep you posted, Meg.'

When I let myself into my new home in Charlton forty minutes later, the snowballing effects of exhaustion sank in. I steamed some soup in the kitchen and thought about Ritchie as I ate. Until now, I hadn't realised how sorely I missed him. Through the blitzkrieg that had besieged my life in England, Ritchie had remained a steady constant, right from the beginning. Lonely for him, I curled up in bed upstairs until my phone roused me from my siesta.

'Hello?' I rasped.

'We've got plenty of good news,' Davenport reported briskly. 'The INDIS approval from Interpol came through this morning.'

'INDIS?' I mumbled, struggling to reorient myself.

'The International DNA Index System I mentioned earlier. We found a DNA match for a Lorenzo Merdanovic. Bosnian origin. Chap was arrested in Sarajevo for cocaine possession in 1998, at the age of 18, while still in high school.'

'A DNA match for the guy who knocked down Charlotte?' I responded, surprised.

'Yes. And it's the same person who murdered Keisha Douglas.'

Blimey!

'Can we track him down?'

'We're getting closer,' Davenport rumbled. 'Wheeler got the details from the passport office yesterday. We think Lorenzo moved to the UK three years ago and applied for a new passport as Horace Fitzgerald. Our biometrics lab is examining Horace's passport photo and Lorenzo's picture from Bosnia's national police database to ensure that it's the same person.'

'Oh, when will we hear back from them?'

'In a couple hours. And, oh yes! We raided that care home this morning. Arrested a bunch of folks and moved the residents to other care homes.' Davenport cleared his throat hesitantly. 'But we found no trace of those kids, Ms Raman.'

My heart slammed in my throat. *Oh Lord!*

'Everyone our cozzers rounded up denied there had been any kids,' Davenport continued. 'I think those children have been moved elsewhere in a hurry … an attempt to shield them from police.'

'God knows if they're safe! We need to find them!' I hissed. 'How many were arrested?'

'The quack in the surgery clinic, a director and four support workers. We seized a box of bright violet and purple teddy bears from a storage facility. Those teddies were presented as gifts for residents to keep them quiet during …' Davenport gave an uncomfortable pause, '… their sexual abuse.'

Just like it must have been a tool to gain Asha's compliance when she was raped two years ago. No wonder Asha had run away on seeing the purple teddy Rosie brought during her visit to the Sawants', last November.

'A lady called Evie Mardling was supplying these teddies to the care home from Kent,' Davenport revealed.

'Right,' I said, remembering that Carl had once told me he ordered all those violet teddies I had seen in his pushcart from the same woman.

'One of the support workers we nabbed had a walker in her room. A wheel was missing. It's a match to the one we found in Jeff Stuart's office,' Davenport added. 'We also found a video surveillance technology in a car that she supposedly used. Her nifty little system was handy in gaining remote access to your conversation with Gretchen Friedland in that conference room at SIGNAL.'

'You mean that room was bugged?' I asked incredulously.

'Yes, unknown to SIGNAL authorities,' Davenport admitted sadly. 'This little perp got a nice video of what was going on up there, and she saw it all from her car down below. When she reported what she heard Gretchen tell you, she was ordered to get rid of Gretchen right away.'

'What's her name?'

'Rosie Flynn.'

'She murdered Jeff Stuart *and* Gretchen Friedland?'

'Sure did. We wrangled a confession out of her, but she was remorseless as hell. Classic sociopath. She staged Jeff's murder to make it seem like a disabled person was the perpetrator. Added a nice little voodoo twist of her own, too,' Davenport grunted. 'After Stuart, Friedland was next on her list of targets. She had been observing Friedland for a while. When the time came, she parked that sedan in an alley near the Paddington station and waited for her to come out before running her down.'

'Good heavens!' I moaned, wondering if Gretchen would have been spared if I hadn't elbowed my way in and pressed her for information.

'That's not all,' Davenport went on. 'Flynn admitted to bringing teddies as gifts to the homes of a few former residents who had become new mothers ... said she wanted to lure them back. My hunch is that these guys were collecting as many of those kids as possible so that they could be used for something else. We need to figure out the rest.'

My mind went back to Nimmy's description of his family's history with Rosie, the day after his drinks were spiked. Rosie had wanted the Sawants to give Asha's baby, Sunil, away to the care home. She had returned to the Sawants' in November because her earlier persuasions had failed. And she was familiar with the house because she'd been there once before, during Asha's time at the hospital.

Davenport's steady voice jolted me out of my reverie. 'We've got the CCTV footage from that pub, too. We could do with some help identifying the person who spiked your friend's drink. Can you and your friend be here at eleven tomorrow?'

I peeled off my clothes and sank into the foamy bathtub. I was nodding off to sleep again when my phone rang. My heart leapt when I glanced at the screen.

'Ritch!' I gushed into the phone.

'Sandy!' Ritchie gasped excitedly. 'The deal with Unilever's done! There's lots to tell!'

The film project he had landed was part of Unilever's integrated marketing campaign for an evolving European brand. I invited him to come over and rattled off the train routes to Charlton.

Ritchie enfolded me in a bear hug when we met at the station fifty minutes later. Closing my eyes, I drew in his fragrance from the napped fabric of his coat.

'When did you return?' I demanded when we disentangled ourselves.

'Just this afternoon. How've you been?'

'There've been two more murders,' I said quietly as we walked towards my place. 'But we're closer to cracking the case.'

Pausing outside, I turned my key in the lock.

Ritchie chuckled. 'You sound like an investigator yourself.'

'I've been talking to the Squad too much.' I laughed, ushering Ritchie in.

I felt his hand on my shoulder. I turned to face him.

'Are you safe, San?' he asked.

'Uh, I . . .' The intensity of his pupils thawed out the muddled mass in my mind. I broke my gaze.

'. . .I don't know,' I mumbled vaguely. Then I told him about the Wood Lane attack and the checque I had received from Lord Bradshaw. 'On the upside, I've landed a job interview with CNBC. I'm pinning my hopes on it,' I finished.

'That's bloody brilliant, San!' Ritchie exulted, following me into the dining area in the kitchen. 'But your life's in danger. We don't have much time left to crack this investigation.'

He wandered towards the large shingled windows and gazed out at the twilit gardens. 'This cottage is so beautiful. Hounslow didn't work out too well, did it?'

I shook my head.

Ritchie nodded pensively. 'Kim may have seemed like a good sort, but I guess everyone is crazy at some level or the other.'

I poured each of us a glass of wine. Ritchie lent me a hand as I set out to prepare rice and kidney bean stew.

'The CCTV footage arrived from that pub,' I mentioned halfway through dinner. 'I'm heading to the police station tomorrow to find out who spiked Nimmy's drinks.'

Ritchie scraped the last portion of gravy from the casserole. 'You think it might be Nimmy's friend, the one you spoke to in the hospital?'

'Carl.' I rolled my eyes. 'Let's hope Nimmy finds something on that video.' I wrapped a piece of cling film over the leftover rice and tossed it in the fridge. 'He, uh, is also coming tomorrow,' I added hesitantly when Ritchie raised a quizzical brow.

'Care for a walk outside?' he suggested.

'Sure,' I smiled.

'Will you be okay tomorrow?' Ritchie asked as we sauntered along the cobblestoned pathways. 'I mean, seeing Nimmy again and all that …'

I shrugged. 'I'll be fine.'

'I worry about you, San,' Ritchie went on. 'And I'm not sure what Nimmy is capable of. Possessive as a gnawing blister. He's hit you before, hasn't he?'

'It's all behind me now,' I whispered.

Ritchie squeezed my hand gently. A strong current rippled through my arms. A blend of indeterminable expressions flitted over his face as his eyes searched mine. Then he drew me close to him with a steady, feral passion. I shuddered as his mouth explored mine in raptures of euphoric warmth.

'Oh, Ritchie …' I gasped when we came up for air.

'Stay strong, San,' Ritchie murmured into my hair. 'You're a fucking genius and you're here to make a difference.'

I entwined my fingers in his and led him down a sleepy residential lane.

It wasn't long before an uneasy sensation wedged itself in my chest. Ritchie's animated ramble submerged into the rustle of leaves from a spray of bushes lining the sidewalk. I glanced over my shoulder discreetly. A lone car was parked near the sidewalk about a hundred yards behind us. It looked like a grey Cadillac under the canopy of fading neon lights.

'San?' Ritchie's voice was a distant echo. The car engine sputtered to life. Swallowing the mounting hysteria in my throat, I grabbed Ritchie's arm and began running. The engine roared over the din of screeching wheels.

I looked around wildly, but there was no adjoining lane we could turn into. A muffled bang reverberated in the air. I screamed. Ritchie shoved me down to the ground. A string of cold, hard pellets tore through the tranquil night. A bullet missed my ear by inches. The impact of Ritchie's blow sent us rolling down a hilly stretch of road, one on top of the other, until we slammed into a holly of fronds and berries. The car's façade loomed ahead through slits of air between the leaves that concealed us. The glossy muzzle of an assault rifle peered out from the car's passenger-side window. The finger on the trigger dithered a little, as if its owner was uncertain of our refuge behind the bushes. After a beat, more gunfire followed.

Ritchie lay flat next to me and pressed me to the ground. All but immobilised with fear, I dug into my coat pocket for my phone, hoping to dial triple nine. Another loud hiss ripped through the hedge. Shards of searing pain shot up my arm.

In the dancing shadows of a wall lantern from a neighbouring house, I saw streaks of blood spray Ritchie's shirt. I shifted my gaze to my arm. The fleece on the sleeve of my coat hung in tatters. Ritchie was already dialing triple nine. More lights turned on and a volley of voices emerged from surrounding houses. The car sped off into the distance.

'Hang in there, San,' Ritchie moaned weakly. 'We're getting you to a hospital!'

15

Steep Gradients

6 April

'Good grief! What happened to you?' Craig Davenport exclaimed, waving Nimmy and me into his cluttered office on Friday morning.

'Someone fired at me from a car last night, near my home in Charlton. The bullet grazed my arm a little.' I attempted a brave smile. 'The hospital folks said it would heal in a few days.'

Davenport frowned. 'You don't have a license plate number or a description of this person, do you?'

I shook my head. 'It was dark. The car looked like a grey Cadillac. And the firearm was some kind of an assault rifle. That's all I know.'

Davenport sighed. 'That doesn't help much. But it's evident that whoever is chasing you has figured out where you live. I think you should get the hell out of there. And stay safe until we get to the bottom of this racket. Meanwhile, I'll see if I can get the Bobbies out there to keep a look out for trouble.'

He turned to Nimmy, as though noticing him for the first time.

'Ah, our new witness.' He motioned for us to seat ourselves.

Nimmy nodded stiffly. In a raven black Peabody coat, he looked more like a Tom turkey than a target for offenders on the Operation Douglas radar. Other than a puzzled exclamation at the gauze on my arm, he had said little during our short walk to the police quarters from the underground station where we had met.

I turned back to Davenport. 'Any news on the photo IDs?'

'Same person it is,' Davenport affirmed. 'Rosie Flynn, Dario De Luca, David Cooper and this Bosnian chap, who is no doubt Cooper's friend, and goodness knows how many others are all in this together. Also, during the Bread Breakers' raid, care home director, Simon Webb, admitted that Aiden McLeod arranged for Pinwheel associates and clients as customers of care home residents that Simon handpicked as call girls.'

I stared at Davenport. 'Didn't Paul Rubalcabo at EuroFirst introduce McLeod to the CRCMD?'

'The National Crime Agency is looking into all homes and shelters that Rubalcabo made donations to,' Davenport said tersely. 'The FBI is investigating the three organisations under his patronage in New York, too. He's got a clean record so far. Now, are you ready to watch that video? Krantz spotted something odd on there. We're hoping either of you can explain it.'

I nodded.

Davenport reached for the phone. 'Ms Raman and her friend are here for the Corney and Barrow footage …' He paused for a moment. Then, 'Bloody hell! When will they get that server up and running?'

My heart was imploding like a sledgehammer.

'Well, get it to my office then,' the inspector barked into the receiver. 'And see that you log and barcode it properly.'

He rang off and turned to us. 'Looks like our storage area network has gone bust, so Krantz is fetching it from the evidence room.'

A few moments later, Krantz loaded the film from a hefty external hard drive onto Davenport's computer and played the portion he had marked from the hundred-minute footage.

Through the pixelated haze on the screen, skinny waitresses zigzagged through gregarious office-goers in the patio, juggling bottles, glasses, food plates and ashtrays. Nimmy and Carl were seated across Sal and Rick against a high rail in a corner. The crimson insignia of a UBS building glowered against the twilit skies behind Nimmy.

Sal leaned towards Nimmy, whispered into his ear and jumped up from his seat. Carl patted Nimmy's shoulder and rose at just the same time. Carl and Sal looked at each other in surprise and laughed before walking away together. They had headed to the washroom together, I remembered from my conversations with Carl. Nimmy continued chatting with Rick.

Moments later, Nimmy lowered his gaze, held up a finger and bent down.

'I think I was tying my shoe laces,' Nimmy explained, shuffling his feet beside me.

Rick held a menu against his chest and fiddled with his jacket. Then he slid the vinyl menu folder forward against the edge of the table, and tapped generous sprinkles of powder into Nimmy's drink. The rim of a small white container peeked out from between his fingers. Nimmy re-emerged from under the table and sipped his drink as he and Rick continued their conversation.

Davenport snorted. 'Blocking it with the menu, indeed! Hoping the CCTV wouldn't catch it, was he?'

I heard a loud wheeze next to me.

'R-R-Rick?' Nimmy stuttered.

Davenport and Krantz followed my stare. Nimmy looked like he was going to have a stroke. I placed a pacifying arm on his shoulder. Nimmy buried his face in his hands and moaned, 'How could *he* do this? If I hadn't helped him, he would've still b'in on the streets.'

'Didn't you know him from your days at the London Business School?' I asked, puzzled.

Nimmy shook his head. 'Carl and Sal, yes. Not Rick.'

Davenport and Krantz had a million questions in their eyes. But they held their horses for the moment. Krantz offered Nimmy a glass of water.

Davenport rewound the video to the scene where Rick rested the menu under his chin. Then he paused the film, enlarged the image and gawked at the screen.

'What's going on?' I demanded.

The inspector ignored my question. 'Krantz,' he bellowed.

The Detective Constable rushed to his side and peered over his shoulder.

Davenport turned to his underling. 'You weren't with Wheeler when he visited the passport office, were you?'

'No, I was viewing this footage, Sir.'

Davenport shifted his gaze to Nimmy. 'What did you say your friend's name was?'

'Rick Martinez,' Nimmy replied softly.

'Ahh!' Davenport frowned. 'Rick Martinez. Horace Frederick Fitzgerald. Lorenzo Merdanovic … they're all the same sodding person.'

~

As Nimmy and I ate lunch at a diner round the corner, my mind dredged up a memory of Rick's response to my mention of Saahil's death at that pub in Beaconsfield, where I had first met him last September. Hadn't he snorted then? Had he really just coughed like he said he had? Was Rick Martinez a sadist? Then, I recalled Rick's reference to a meeting with Aiden McLeod when I had run into him at the Gregersen Tower.

Perhaps, Davenport was right. Maybe Rick and McLeod were in on this together.

Nimmy picked on a hash brown. 'Does this mean Rick …?'

I looked up from the gooey puddle of baked beans on my plate and nodded.

'Yes. A DNA match is pretty strong evidence.' Without thinking, I placed my hand over Nimmy's. 'I'm sorry.'

A glassy look layered Nimmy's eyes. 'Rick was a poor, innocent kid when I first saw him. Carl introduced him to me at an LBS information session four and a half years ago.'

'London Business School?'

Nimmy nodded. 'Carl and I were invited as alumni speakers to address prospective students about career opportunities and such. Carl brought Rick to that event. He'd first seen Rick distributing newspapers in Piccadilly. When I saw Rick at the event, I thought he'd just arrived from a construction site, y'know, gaunt face, frayed shirt.' Nimmy toyed with the food on his plate. 'When I spoke to Rick, I learned he was a refugee who'd arrived from Bosnia a few months ago. He was living in a rubbish-filled hole under a supermarket stairwell, doing odd jobs and labouring for a decent career. Despite his situation, Rick nurtured a desire to study at LBS.'

He paused to take a bite.

'Why didn't Rick move in with Carl?'

'Rick was too proud to ask. Besides, Carl had some issues where he lived back then. A psycho roommate or something like that. Rick seemed so bright, ambitious and hopeful that I wanted to do something to get him off the streets. So, I arranged for him to stay with Sal until he found his feet.'

'I see,' I mumbled between munches. 'Was Rick granted asylum?'

'Not until much later.'

I couldn't help feeling sorry for Rick. Had his penury and status as an illegal immigrant driven him off-kilter?

'A couple months later, Sal introduced Rick to a wealthy couple in Northwood Hills. They didn't mind Rick's residency status, so he was their chauffeur until he joined Trychlen as a customer service agent about a year later. He worked his way up to the position of business development manager there. Last spring, he applied to LBS and got in. He was going to enroll this autumn.' Nimmy pinched the bridge of his nose. 'He was extremely grateful for my help. I have no idea why he ...'

'But I don't get it ... I *saw* Carl with all those teddy bears in the Tube that day. The same kind of teddy that Rosie had brought for Asha.'

Nimmy looked blank for a moment. Then he flashed a sad smile. 'I think I know what happened. Carl was looking for a special package of return gifts for all the kids who'd attended his boss' daughter's birthday party. So, Rick introduced him to Evie Mardling and Carl told me about her later. Evie specialises in rare, unusual stuff, usually handmade. I had no idea she supplied to Bread Breakers' though.'

'What happened to Rick's residency status?' I pressed gently.

'He was given asylum when he was a chauffeur for the Domwilles.'

'What was the lady's name?'

Nimmy gazed pensively at a spot on the table. 'I think Rick used to mention a Lettice Domwille. Rick said she still had a thing for her ex-husband.'

'Oh, had she divorced?'

'No. He passed away … I think it was a stroke.'

My stomach fluttered. 'How long ago was that?'

'About twelve years ago, I guess. Peter Domwille is her second husband. But she could never really get over her first. I think his name was Horace … or so Rick said.'

And that's how Rick became Horace Fitzgerald. It all added up.

'You'll be safer if you move back in with me,' Ritchie said as we sat in the Victoria Embankment Gardens two hours later.

I spooned the last dregs of my mango sorbet and stared absently at a posy of hyacinths iridescent in their reflection across a sun-kissed duck pond ahead of me. *Misleading charms.*

'I'm sorry, Ritch. I can't.' I shifted my gaze to him. 'If I stay with you now, you'll become a target too. If I'm going down, I don't want to pull you down with me.'

Ritchie reached across the table and slipped his fingers through mine. 'You know I won't let that happen, San,' he said fiercely.

My phone rang.

'Hello, Ms Raman!' Davenport greeted swiftly. 'Your guy, Rick Martinez, has been arrested.'

'Wow! Okay. What exactly happened the evening of Keisha's death?' I choked out.

'In the office, Ms Raman,' Davenport chuckled.

Ritchie and I were sat in his cabin half an hour later.

'Poor guy was forced into a life as a contract killer,' Davenport revealed as we sipped our coffee. 'Rick was receiving instructions from Aiden McLeod. Assisting Rick was Dario's job. Rick has no clue about Bread Breakers' or any part of the larger sex ring. His task, whenever he was contacted, was merely to dismiss or injure people.'

Ritchie was listening quietly, but I gasped in shock. It was one thing to accept that Rick had spiked Nimmy's drinks. But I couldn't imagine him in the garb of a killer.

'Rick was raised by his widowed grandmother in Sarajevo after he lost his parents as a child. Once his grandma died, he came to England, hoping for a better life. But the UK government didn't grant him asylum,' Davenport explained. 'In that situation, there wasn't much he could do around here. He had destroyed his passport and identification papers to avoid being deported. So, he couldn't return to Bosnia either. He was floundering for sustenance. When he found work as a chauffeur for the Domwilles, a large company offered him a regular day job, a legalised residency in the UK – and a new identity that Rick cleverly stole from Lettice's deceased ex-husband, Horace Fitzgerald.'

'Wh-what about … Rick is a jazz guitarist too, isn't he?' I spluttered. 'I mean … He appeared on The Charlotte Hale Show a year ago – as Horace, of course.'

Davenport nodded sadly. 'As a matter of fact, he is. And a darned good one too. I listened to that interview on a BBC archives section. But that talent didn't do more for him than get some extra gigs in a bunch of bars a few years ago. The circumstances of his first meeting with Charlotte Hale, more than a year ago, are indeed true. But, while he was at it, he recently reached out to Charlotte Hale under the pretext of wooing her into his life – once he knew she was involved in the campaign and that TV programme, of course.'

So, that's how Charlotte knew him as Horace. 'I guess the alias was a fine shot in the arm,' I said quietly.

'Well, Rick's relationship with Charlotte was carefully orchestrated after instructions from someone in the company that took him under its wing,' Davenport stated. 'This corporate bigwig has a carefully fabricated public veneer, which covers an underworld nexus of tie-ups with care homes and special schools that deliver young mentally challenged women as commercial sex workers to its clients. It employs illegal immigrants, gets them fake passports and gives them jobs in peer agencies like Trychlen. The don who runs it cashes in on the misfortunes of people like Rick, Dario and Rosie by hiring them as his lackeys in exchange for their loyalty. With all the witnesses we've spoken to, we have strong evidence that Aiden McLeod *is* the don. And his company, Pinwheel Interactive, fits as the perfect cover. We're going ahead with the arrest of Aiden McLeod once we find out where the Bread Breakers' children have been hidden. Rick's testimony against him will be used as evidence during court hearings.'

I sank back in my seat and exhaled slowly. So, Rick, unlike what Nimmy believed, hadn't been granted asylum after all. In his desperation for some deliverance from his hardships, he had sold his soul to a mafia setup.

'Why did Rick spike Nimmy's drink? Nimmy has nothing to do with this.'

'Ahh, the spiking business,' Davenport scratched his stubble reflectively. 'Rick wasn't threatened by Nimmy, Ms Raman. He was threatened by *you*. When you went undercover, the Bread Breakers' staff suspected it was *you* because you'd met Simon Webb just a few days before. The receptionist raised an alarm when she found you had vanished. Someone in the care home promptly informed McLeod. McLeod then sent word for Rick to give you a scare. So, he spiked Nimmy's drink. What's more, he followed Nimmy around and gave him a nice little nudge in that underpass at Holborn. The intent was to warn you to mind your own business by hurting someone close to you. McLeod and Rick both knew you were dating Nimmy.'

So, *that* was why Rick had left the pub early that day. 'How did they know I was dating N …?'

'Nimmy had told Rick,' Davenport said.

'How did Rick kill Keisha when it seemed that Dario was the one behind it?' I whispered.

'Rick arrived at Keisha's complex, Beacon's Bow, the previous night,' Davenport disclosed. 'A barbecue was going on by the community poolside, the evening of Thirteenth March. Keisha wasn't around, but Rick and Dario came in right on the heels of a large bunch of people signing in as guests of residents who had invited them. So, no one took much notice of Rick or Dario. They hung out by the poolside for a while. Dario had a set of spare keys to Keisha's apartment. He lent the keys to Rick and packed him off before Keisha returned from work and joined Dario at the barbecue. Rick got into Keisha's apartment block. All night, he skulked around in a lounge area in the basement. When Keisha left for work next morning, Rick rode up the elevator and slid into her apartment with the spare key. Meanwhile, Dario left late that night, after pretend-romancing his lady love at the barbecue.'

I remembered my frantic appeals for Keisha's safety with the man she was dating. Dario De Luca a.k.a. Kenneth Butler. Planted to help Rick kill her.

'So, Rick was lounging around at her apartment all day?' I yelped in disbelief.

Davenport nodded somberly. 'When Rick peeked from a window and saw Keisha walk in through the gates that evening, he hid in a broom closet. Dario dropped in shortly after Keisha returned home. He spent nearly an hour canoodling with

Keisha. During that time, he was setting the stage for Rick to execute his order.

'On his way out, Dario disabled the CCTV surveillance system near the fire escape route at the rear end of the building. After Dario left, Rick emerged from his hiding spot, did Keisha in and made his escape through the emergency exit stairwell to the rubbish yard in the back. Then he scaled the wall into the neighbouring compound and walked out from there.'

My eyes widened. Carefully planned. Premeditated. That was why Rick's entry and exit hadn't been recorded.

'What about Keisha's suicide note?' I mumbled.

Davenport snorted. 'All part of the ploy. Dario brought some food and champagne when he came in that evening. He made sure Keisha was sufficiently intoxicated before he began his little game. He suggested to Keisha that they write each other notes, spilling out the darkest thoughts that came to their minds …'

'And that day, Keisha was frustrated about many things,' I recalled.

'When Keisha passed out, Dario retained that little note and got rid of the other scraps of paper that went back and forth between them,' Ritchie surmised.

'And Dario didn't forget to remove every trace of alcohol on his way out,' I added.

Davenport nodded grimly. 'That's exactly what happened. By eight o'clock, Dario was already halfway through his shopping spree at Sainsbury. Meanwhile, Keisha prepared to go to bed early. When she turned off the lights, Rick crept up to her bedside, shoved a gun to her head and threatened to blow her brains out unless she took those sleeping pills.'

Tears rolled down my cheeks. Keisha must have consumed all of those sleeping pills, praying that he would spare her and hoping to call for help once he left.

'After Keisha gulped down those pills, Rick sat on her chest and suffocated her with a pillow, wearing gloves, of course,' Davenport said, sounding as if he were narrating a horror story to his grandchildren. 'Rick hung around long enough to ensure she was dead, all the while covering his tracks and scrubbing the house clean to remove his fingerprints. At nine-fifteen p.m., an hour after she died, he brought her mobile phone to the bed and pushed her finger against the button for Dario's number to make it appear as if she had called him then. That's why the fingerprints we tested on the phone and those bottles of sleeping pills turned out to be hers.'

I fought to keep my chin steady.

'Ricky boy didn't realise he had left footprints of his DNA on the nightdress Keisha changed into *after* Dario left. He was less mindful of his traces when he tossed a cigarette in the Wrangler he nicked from poor ol' David Cooper to get rid of Charlotte,' Davenport was saying.

An imperceptible swirl of blackness eclipsed me. I heard my name being called out. A murmur of voices followed. A cloud of soot ploughed into my chest. I doubled over and retched incessantly. The smell of plastic assaulted my senses. I felt my hair being held back gently as a polythene bag floated under my chain. Then, a pair of arms carried me away.

~

When I came to, I was lying against Ritchie in a moving cab.

'Where are we going?' I groaned.

'My place.' Ritchie brushed his fingers against my cheek.

I struggled to pull myself up. 'No …' I moaned, thinking about his own safety.

'Well, your place isn't safe, and you're not going back there,' Ritchie said sternly.

The taxi pulled into Gilden Crescent. In the distance, a string of freshly laundered clothes swung lazily over the balcony rails of a few apartment units in Ritchie's corner complex. A familiar semblance of comfort ensconced me.

Ritchie hustled over to my side and carried me in his arms with practiced ease. I laced my arms around his neck as the cab sped off behind us. Ritchie halted in his tracks when we approached the gate. The instant freeze in velocity sent me ramming into his chest.

'I'm sorry, San.'

Ritchie whirled around and stared at a large wallpapered truck parked beside a tree.

I peered out from the crook of his arm. 'What's wrong?'

'Shhh!' Ritchie whispered, scampering stealthily towards a thicket of hedge plants lining the curve of the road. At the corner, he turned to his left and crossed over swiftly. I slid off his arms and teetered on the sidewalk as Ritchie punched some numbers on his phone and murmured into it. A few moments later, he tugged me towards a watering hole ahead of us.

We sank into a lounge. 'What's going on?' I cried indignantly.

'I saw two figures lurking behind that truck in hoodies and ski masks. More lackeys, I'd reckon,' Ritchie sighed. 'So, we can't go inside or hang around there. A cab is picking us up from here.'

My blood ran cold. Neither of us could go back to our homes now.

~

'I'm sorry, sir. We've only got one double room at this time,' the concierge told Ritchie, casting an amused glance at the lone backpacks on our shoulders as we checked into a Travelodge Hotel in Covent Garden, half an hour later.

Ritchie looked at me apologetically. I shrugged and nodded. We obtained the keys and rode up the elevator. Once in the room, I sank into a pristine white bed and yanked off my boots.

Ritchie walked towards the balcony. 'Now that you're safe here, I'll return to my apartment to pick up some things and see if everything is intact.'

I ran over to Ritchie and hugged him tightly. 'Don't go, Ritch. I'm scared for you.'

Ritchie's eyes searched mine intensely. And then, before either of us could exercise any restraint, we were all over each other like wild hyenas, clinging and clawing as we plunged into a turbulent kiss and fell onto the bed. Every cell in my being torpedoed into an unmapped ball of flames as Ritchie nuzzled the hollow of my throat and caressed my breasts with febrile longing. I nibbled on his lower lip ravenously.

This is madness! I thought. The rugged contours of our friendship … our shared rollercoaster-journey … his untamed allure … the irrepressible craving … the sheer excitement of it … and somewhere in this melee, steady rivulets of an exquisitely agonising force that sang the song of love. I hesitated just for an instant before I unbuttoned his shirt.

A blend of hunger and concern glided across his aquamarine eyes.

'Is this something you want to do, San?' he whispered, cupping my face in his hands.

A strange spiritual coherence deepened my corporeal thirst with a vitality I had never imagined before.

'Yes,' I gasped, wrenching off my blouse and bra.

'I love you, San!' Ritchie murmured into my hair.

I was taken and terrified at the same time – taken, that our hearts were steadily blending into one life force; terrified, that I would lose him, just like I'd lost my Mum, Saahil, Keisha, and in some ways, even Nimmy.

My insecurity about Ritchie started with this investigation. What if his life was in danger too? I cradled him in my arms, worried that the sublimity of this moment would recede if I spoke.

The line of distinction between pain and pleasure faded away as Ritchie devoured my breasts with the intensity of a man possessed. He undid my jeans and lapped up the beads of succulence bubbling between my legs, stirring my soul with a visceral yearning, which was alternately delirious and enervating. Then, moaning my name over and over again, he slithered in and out of me, electrifying my tendons until we exploded into a surreal reality where desire and consciousness blurred into a plane of unbounded ecstasy.

'Oh, Ritch!' I wept when we lay spent in each other's arms.

Ritchie brushed my tears away and kissed me again. 'Oh God, San … I love you with all my heart,'

~

I sat in Alfred Maynard's office later that evening and filled him in on the identity of Keisha's killer and our theory that Aiden McLeod was the don behind the racket.

'Sweet Jesus!' Alfred exclaimed. 'Think it's a good time to release it as a breaking-news commentary?'

'I imagine the investigators will remain tight-lipped until everyone who's involved is convicted.'

'They're still investigating?' Alfred sounded confused.

A shrill hum began resonating into my eardrums. Were my ears ringing? I rubbed my ears blearily and tried to focus. 'Yes. Those kids, who vanished from the care home, are still missing. So …'

A disembodied voice boomed out over an intercom. 'What you just heard was a fire alarm. Please leave the building immediately. This is not a drill.'

A fire bell. Alfred jumped to his feet and began packing his things. Through his partially open cabin door, I saw people scamper towards the spiral balustrade leading to the lobby below. I rushed out to the corridor and peered over the railing. Alfred followed suit.

'Everyone's evacuating. Get out for God's sakes!' a middle-aged man hissed behind us as he scurried along.

'Anything serious?' Alfred asked the flustered man.

'A couple of edit suites on fire!' the man hollered over his shoulder.

A growing sense of dread enveloped me as I let Alfred grab my arm and pull me down the stairway to the lobby. We raced towards the closest exit. A small, but agitated, crowd swamped the gardens outside. I was ushered towards a row of people standing off to one side. A supervisor was counting the number of heads. Tufts of smoke wafted into the air from a corner of the building front.

Over the din of voices, I heard the hiss of fire engines and sprays. I coughed, grabbed my inhaler and moved to the farthest end to get away from the noxious fumes. Alfred was in tow, yelling to ask if I was okay. 'I-I'm asthmatic,' I rasped.

From the corner of my eye, I saw Alfred motion for someone behind him. A young man handed me a carafe and helped me on to a bench. I smiled weakly and took a few sips of water from his flask. A cluster of voices erupted around me.

'I'm jolly glad they're moving their offices to Salford ...' a young lady was saying vehemently.

An older woman whined, 'Hell, yeah ... this building stinks. They say the smoke detector near the HR suite wasn't working.'

A female announcement rang out from a portable public addressing system.

'This is a message from the fire safety administrator. I would like to assure everyone that the situation is now under control. No one has been injured so far and there are no missing persons. However, there could be some damage to three edit rooms and a portion of the human resources department. Measures will be undertaken to restore normalcy as soon as possible. Meanwhile, we recommend that all of you go home. Have a good weekend.'

The crowd began dispersing. I was half-certain that someone had followed me to the BBC, disabled some smoke alarms and set the building on fire in anticipation of my presence here.

I felt a hand on my shoulder. Alfred was peering at me anxiously. 'It would do you good to head home and unwind. Let me call a cab.'

I nodded gratefully. Alfred stayed with me until the cab arrived. I smiled wearily and hopped in.

Near a traffic light outside the White City Underground, the cabbie slammed on his breaks rather hard.

'Careful, mate!' I reproached, rubbing my side.

A reflection in the rearview mirror before me spewed out the side profile of a man lurking in the underground station behind a pillar, sharing a packet of crisps with a little girl who looked harrowingly familiar. The man's hat and dark glasses obscured most of his face. And the child ... I recognised her as Nancy, the feisty six-year-old from the garage-shed at Bread Breakers'. The man abruptly turned in my direction. It appeared as if he was looking right into my eyes, but his glasses hid his expression. The little girl's blonde hair caught the light of dusk as the traffic signal before us changed shades. Oh God ... it really was *her*.

'Could you stop just for a moment? My earring fell out of the window,' I lied.

The chauffeur halted outside the station with a grunt. I jumped out and scurried towards the station. By the time I approached the pillars before the turnstiles, the pair had vanished.

I smacked my forehead and groaned. This skulking-around business could be a ruse to trap me, I realised. I hurried back to the cab and slid in disconcertedly. Through the rear window glass, I noticed a pair of headlights flashing at me from a silver Vauxhall Astra several yards behind.

Fuck, someone is tailing me too.

I waved at the cabbie frantically. 'Go, go! As fast as you can!'

16

Aylesbury

9 April

'Your CNBC interview, San,' Ritchie reminded me on Monday morning, nudging me off the hotel bed. 'There's fresh coffee waiting for you.'

I stood up and stretched. Ritchie shrugged into a crisp blue button-down shirt. 'I'm leaving for a meeting with the manager of a post-production facility for the Unilever film,' he informed.

I drank my coffee, showered and put on a flattering beige linen dress suit I had bought at Debenhams on Saturday to replace the regular job-interview attire I had left behind in Charlton, along with everything else. Ritchie shuffled some papers into a briefcase. 'You look gorgeous, San. I'm leaving now. All the best. Be safe.' He kissed me and darted out.

I began applying makeup when my phone rang.

'Am I speaking to … uh, Sandy?' a hushed female voice inquired when I answered.

'That's me. Who's calling?'

'This is Eliza Rixon. I'm a security agent in Buckinghamshire,' the woman responded. 'Are you related to a Ms Asha Sawant?'

'Yes, I am. Is she all right?'

Rixon cleared her throat. 'I found Ms Sawant and about thirty other children locked up in a unit here this morning. Ms Sawant is, um, special, isn't she?'

'Yes. Uh, you say you also found thirty other children?'

'Those kids look like they haven't eaten for days. I found Ms Sawant crying in the loo. I coaxed her to give me a phone number of someone from her family. She's good with numbers, it seems. You're the only person I could reach. I hope you'll help me get them out of here.'

Asha … the kids … *Oh God!* The room spun around me.

'You can speak to Ms Sawant yourself,' Rixon said.

Before I could respond, I heard muffled howls and gasps at the other end of the line. There was no mistaking those high-pitched wails. They were Asha's.

'Asha? It's me, Sandy. Are you all right?'

There was more sobbing. A bout of coughs followed.

'Oh, God! Asha? Can you hear me?' I shrieked.

'They … they … they take me,' Asha sniveled in a broken voice. 'Wanna go back.'

'I'm coming, Asha!' I cried. 'I'll take you home. Do you hear me?'

'Uh-uh …' Asha mumbled softly.

'I love you, Asha. I'll be there soon.'

Rixon came back on the line. 'I'm sorry about that, Sandy. For now, Asha's in good hands.' She's just …'

'How can I get there?' I screeched.

'I can have my security agency send a vehicle to pick you up, ma'am. What's your location?'

I spewed out the address of the Travelodge hotel. 'I'll inform the police right away,' I added. 'Where exactly is this unit?'

'That's your call, but I wouldn't recommend it. If these kids have been abducted and their kidnapper gets wind of a tip-off to the police, they may all be killed.'

'Bloody hell!' I gasped. 'I'll wait in the lobby.'

'Thank you.' I heard a swift click.

My call to Nimmy went unanswered. I left a stricken message on his voicemail and made myself more coffee.

An automated text message reached me after a while.

'BMW 3-Series. Black sedan. License Plate number: M TF 3783.'

I grabbed my things and raced to the elevator. I debated against alerting the Squad until I rescued Asha and the children. Ritchie's phone was switched off. He must have been on the tube. I sank into a sofa in the lobby and shot Ritchie a text message. Just then, my phone rang.

'Eliza Rixon sent me to pick you up. I'm waiting outside,' the man informed.

I flew down the steps into a waiting limousine. As we took off, I noticed a car revving its engine several yards behind us. The same silver Astra I had seen outside the White City station last Friday. *I should tell Rixon I'm being followed.* I scrolled through the call register on my phone to ring her back, but I saw that she had contacted me from an undisclosed number.

~

'Where are we going?' I inquired.

'Aylesbury. Forty miles north-west of London,' the chauffeur replied.

Halfway through the journey, I remembered that I would miss my job interview with CNBC. *Dammit!* I reached for my phone to cite an emergency and reschedule it. A diminutive symbol crisscrossed the top right corner of my phone screen.

'I'm not getting any reception on my mobile!' I exclaimed.

The chauffeur shrugged. 'We're on the road, Miss. You could try again in a bit.'

Restless and anxious, I glanced behind me. We seemed to be in Watford, but there was no trace of the silver Astra anymore. When I turned back, I felt ill at ease. But I couldn't quite place a finger on it. 'Please hurry,' I begged, gazing in dismay at the snarl of traffic on the M25.

The driver looked flustered. 'I'm trying, Miss. I can't wish away this Monday morning traffic.'

After what seemed like ages, the limo entered a sprawling commercial estate near an unfinished construction site on a quiet road sandwiched between rows of parched brownfields and thatched-roof villas. A wooden placard by the gates read Bellwether Business Park. Below it was a chessboard of metallic nameplates, mostly empty – except for the logos of three companies, which looked like start-up consultancies.

'Here we go,' he announced as we pulled into a parking spot on the rear of a brick-wall building numbered 5. A stocky African-origin woman in a pinstriped suit nodded a cursory acknowledgment to the chauffeur and waved me in. A string of empty cubicles before me opened out to a small lounge and a set of revolving doors at the far end of a hallway.

Two security agents hovered in the lobby with walkie-talkies on their trouser-belts. A young, red-haired man manned the phones at a desk in the reception area.

The woman shot out a hand. 'Sandy? Thank you for coming. I'm Eliza Rixon.'

I offered a limp handshake. 'Where are Asha and the kids?'

'Everyone's fine for now,' Rixon replied, knocking on an antique brass grille door to my left.

'Let her in,' a thin male male voice called out from within.

'The gentlemen in there will give you a better picture of what's going on,' Rixon assured.

Hardly had I stumbled into the room when the door slammed shut behind me.

A balding middle-aged bloke in a crisp grey three-piece suit sat before a large mahogany desk. Another wavy-haired man stood by a modular, three-piece credenza behind the desk, desultorily sifting through the contents of a box file. A gnarled vein of sunshine snaked through a set of teal-coloured honeycomb shades by an awning window to my left.

The man rose from his desk and extended his hand. 'Thanks for coming here, Sandy,' he greeted in a thick Italian accent, gesturing at a leather chair before him. 'I'm Aldrigo Mexxo … you can call me Mex. Care for a cup of tea?'

I took off my coat and sat hesitantly. 'Mx Rixon said some children were trapped—'

Mez cut me off with a wave of his hand. 'Carlos, get the lady a cup of tea, please,' he ordered the man with the box-file. Carlos hustled to a small, wainscoted pantry in a corner of the office.

'We'll get to the children after you answer some questions,' Mez said smoothly.

When Mez's cold, arctic blue eyes bore into mine, the origin of my discomfort at the sedan struck me with the force of a groundswell. If I wasn't mistaken, I had seen a camel-coloured falcon swishing back and forth from a slender, curved hook attached to the rearview mirror. In my anxiety for Asha and the children I hadn't processed the image. Carlos placed a cup of piping hot tea on the desk before me. Aiden McLeod's men.

I have fallen into a deadly trap.

'Let's begin,' Mez purred. 'Were you the reason behind Horace Fitzgerald's arrest?'

'Horace Fitzgerald died twelve years ago,' I stated, fighting to sound calm.

Mez walked around the desk and squeezed my jaw. 'Don't mess with me, honey.'

He nodded swiftly towards Carlos, who retreated to the pantry.

I fumbled in my handbag for my mobile phone and tried to jam the speed dial for Ritchie.

'Go on, try it …' Mez crooned. 'We've insulated this building from mobile phone and Wi-Fi connectivity, just like we did for our entire fleet of cars.'

Sure enough, my phone had no reception. Carlos emerged with a wooden knife block and a skein of rope. A crippling wave of terror ran down my spine.

Mez tossed my handbag on to a Chintz couch. 'You haven't answered my question.'

'You mean Rick Martinez? Yes, I was responsible for his arrest.' I choked.

'Indeed,' Mez spat, holding me in place as Carlos wrenched my suit and dress away. I shivered in my sheer silk chemise and stockings as he bound my hands and legs to the chair.

'See how beautifully our plan worked?' Mez grinned. 'We knew you'd come running here like a mad hen if you thought that crazy chick was in danger.'

'Is Asha safe?' I pleaded.

'Oh, yes,' Mez smirked. 'Eliza posed as a domestic caretaker and got that kid out from her loony bin in Watford. She brought Asha to her car outside and called you from there, so you'd believe her if you spoke to the kid. Then Eliza sent Asha back in and returned to Aylesbury long before you arrived.'

'Why did Asha cry then?' I demanded.

Mez snorted. 'Silly wimp thought she was being kidnapped, didn't she, Carlos?'

Carlos guffawed. I shrank back when he grabbed a serrated bread knife from the block.

'If you'll just listen …' I began. My words dissolved into a strangled yelp as Carlos grabbed fistfuls of my hair and snapped my head back. 'Ours is a big business. Many care homes and refugee shelters send their residents to clients and research organisations that pay handsomely.'

'First, it was that lousy campaign and the fucking TV show,' Mez snarled. 'Then you started snooping around that care home, videotaping everything, asking questions. Before we realise what's happening, you plan a story on national television. We disposed of your friends. But you managed to elude us all the time … despite the fire at the BBC and numerous other attempts …'

I heard a defiant rip from the lacy fabric of my garment as Mez forced his hand under my chemise and plucked off my bra. Then he squashed my breasts until I could barely breathe.

'Because of *you*, our folks are counting bars in jail. And the funding for our stem cell research will be revoked. Big Bird ain't happy about all of this,' Carlos growled.

'Stem cell?' I gasped.

A cruel jab on the swell of my right breast sent a jolt of shock through my system. Carlos withdrew the knife and thrust it into my defenseless breast again. The scent of blood drifted over me. The knife sank into different areas of my right breast while Mez relentlessly pumped my left breast. I scrunched my eyes shut. Mez squished my nipples just as Carlos pierced a delicate spot near my cleavage. I gave in and screamed.

Carlos began working the knife on my left breast, infiltrating my tissue just deep enough to inflict unbearable pain each time. The luxury of passing out dissipated when Mez pushed my nipples inward with such force that I was left gasping for breath under the smouldering pressure of his fingers on my ribcage. Carlos was simultaneously digging the knife-edge into the bulging underside of my left breast. Then he swatted Mez's hands away and twisted my throbbing nipples in opposite directions.

An indefinable pressure descended on my lungs.

Now, I felt the bloodied knife-blade across one of my nipples. Tears of angst and imploration streaked my face. 'We'll chop off these little pink beauties, won't we?' Carlos taunted. Then he twirled my tortured nipple with the knife.

The pain was so excruciating that I thought my heart was starting to give out. When the knife fell to the floor with a clang, I realised I had pressed my feet to the floor and hurled myself against the chair to scrape it back. Carlos skidded along, grabbing the arm of the chair. I rammed into the surface of a casegood bookshelf behind me. Something landed on my lap from a shelf on the rack. A photo frame. Amidst a spray of key-chains, paper clips and figurines on the floor, a stray photo beckoned to the tangents of my intermittent consciousness.

A bespectacled lad at a sunny beachfront smiled at me from that picture with a small, squint-eyed girl staring vacantly into space. The sunlight accentuated the amber gradients of his pupils behind those glasses … A teenaged version of someone I must have met … Splinters of recognition grazed the fringes of my depleting cognizance.

Lord Melvin Bradshaw? What is his picture doing here?

The stench of a far-flung, yet numbing, possibility pervaded my senses.

Is Lord Bradshaw the Big Bird?

Mez grabbed the picture-frame, slid the photograph back into it and placed it back in the bookshelf. Carlos regained his balance.

Mez walked around to the front and issued a quick nod to Carlos.

This is it. I'm going to die.

'If you kill me, Lord Bradshaw will be disgraced. Publicly!' I proclaimed.

Mez looked a little off-guard, but Carlos rumbled with laughter. 'What's this, baby? What does Bradford whoever have to do with our dirty little secrets?' he sneered.

'I know that Lord Melvin Bradshaw, CEO of the Eric Gregersen Group, *is* your ring-leader,' I stated. Carlos jerked his hand off me – like he'd been bitten by a king cobra.

'I've got incriminating evidence to prove Bradshaw's involvement,' I lied, taking on a more imperious tone. 'The documents are with my solicitor, who is informed about my whereabouts at every stage. My solicitor will release them to the media if *anything* happens to me. And that's what he'll believe if he doesn't hear from me soon.'

'What sort of evidence do you have?' Mez inquired sharply.

'Circumstantial evidence and records directly implicating Bradshaw,' I rasped, coughing heavily. I pointed at my handbag on the couch. 'W-water. And my inhaler.'

The duo eyed me dubiously.

'If anything happens to me …' I began.

Mez fumbled around in my handbag. I alternately gulped the water he poured into my mouth and breathed into the inhaler he held out gingerly. 'The evidence is damning.' I wheezed. 'If it's ever released to the public …'

'Evidence, my foot. She has none. She's doin' it to save 'er bleedin' tits.' Carlos sniggered.

Mez motioned for Carlos to be quiet.

'I have nothing to lose,' I rasped. 'I'll just be another person you cross off your list. For you, it'll mean the collapse of a massive empire. The demise of Bradshaw. Is that what you …?' I coughed some more. '… overcame all your hardships for? To eventually give up your legacy because of a stupid mistake?'

'What's the deal, here?' Carlos questioned.

'You let me go and I keep silent. I'm also offering you a story on your success as an immigrant … on the BBC, ITV …' Steady ripples of lassitude stole my senses.

Mez's voice ricocheted through the periphery of my consciousness. 'Carlos, what are you waiting for? Get those pliers. This girl can't die yet.'

Sharp cool jets jerked me into wakefulness. I shrieked as cold wet globules of water seeped into the pores of my lacerations. It looked like Mez was washing off the congealing clumps of blood on my chest and stomach. I felt the ropes around my shoulders and wrists snap off. I found the armholes of my crumpled, stained chemise, which had slipped down to my waist. I slid my hands into them and haphazardly pulled the slip up to cover my battered torso. I tried to move, but my legs remained bound. The door rattled with the click of a keycard.

I heard Rixon holler, 'We've got another weasel to deal with!'

The door swung open and Ritchie staggered in. Varying degrees of shock, fear and anger flitted across his face as he attempted to rush to my side.

'Not so fast, dude,' Carlos crooned, grabbing Ritchie's shoulder.

'My lawyer has appointed this man to keep track of me,' I called out sternly. 'All evidence against Bradshaw is with my lawyer. If anything happens to either of us …'

Mez was already rolling my chair forward. A haze of turmoil and confusion clouded over Ritchie's face. I heard another chair being dragged behind me. Mez bound the hind legs of both chairs together. 'Blimey, what a load of guff!' Carlos spat, grabbing Ritchie's collar.

Ritchie landed a resounding blow on Carlos' jaw.

I watched in horror as Mez shoved Carlos aside and encircled Ritchie's throat.

'The news will go live tomorrow if you don't let us go!' I shouted desperately.

Carlos pinned Ritchie's arms behind him while Mez jammed his fingers into Ritchie's carotids.

'Just let go of him!' I begged.

Mez released his hold. Ritchie crumpled to the floor, coughing and gagging furiously.

'I have no idea what to do with them,' Mez admitted to Carlos.

'Let's get Big Bird here. He'll know what's best,' Carlos suggested.

'I s'ppose,' Mez sighed. 'What they're saying could be all fiddle-faddle, but we don't want to take any chances, right?'

Mez and Carlos dragged Ritchie to the chair behind me and swiftly bound his hands and feet.

'We'll be back soon,' Carlos hissed. 'Any dirty tricks, and you're both dead.'

'You're bleeding a lot, San,' Ritchie rasped, coughing painfully. Realising that my hands were free, I struggled to draw my chair closer to the desk, dragging Ritchie and his chair behind with me. Ritchie leaned back against his chair and pushed his feet against the floor to bolster my effort.

When I got within an arm's length of the pliers on the desk, I reached out and made a grab for it. With a fresh burst of resolve, I sawed away the ropes clutching at my thighs and ankles. I nearly fell as I scrambled out of the chair. It took me a while to steady myself as I fought for balance, after more than an hour of being tied up and tortured. Ritchie was trying to slacken the knots of rope around his wrists. I stumbled over to him. 'Hold on, Ritch. I've got it.'

Ritchie held his wrists up. The rope stretched taut between his knuckles.

Gritting my teeth, I squeezed the pliers with all my might, chipping away at the ropes until they fell off. Once Ritchie's hands were free, he quickly hacked off the ropes binding his ankles.

Gasping in unison, we collapsed briefly into each other's arms. Then Ritchie dashed over to the pantry, tripping over himself in haste and disorientation.

'What're you doing?' I called out weakly as he yanked open all the cupboard doors.

'You need first-aid at once! And it won't be long before they're back,' Ritchie informed.

I peered into my vest. My breasts were no more than shattered, bloody pulps now. And I was aching all over from the punishing position I had been forced into.

'This looks like Benzoin,' Ritchie muttered, hobbling back to me with a small bottle and a big wad of cottton. He knelt down before me, applied some of the antiseptic onto large swabs of cotton and gently cupped my breasts. All I wanted right now was for them to be left alone. I recoiled instinctively, but the effort triggered a string of coughing fits and painful wheezing.

'No, Sandy, you're bleeding badly,' Ritchie said firmly, dabbing at my welts and slashes. 'Keep pumping your inhaler.'

After a few moments, he stumbled over to the credenza and dug around swiftly in its alcoves. A box of teabags and a half-empty bottle of White Zinfandel crashed to the floor. Splinters of glass flew across the room and bubbling cataracts of blush wine splotched the zebra rug behind me.

'Careful, Ritch!' I shushed.

'I'll get us out of here,' Ritchie croaked, retracing his steps with a roll of gauze.

'They've disfigured me,' I sobbed as he worked the gauze steadily on me.

'At least the bleeding seems to have stopped,' Ritchie assured me, moments later. 'About what happened, it doesn't matter, San. I love you. Your real beauty is in there.' He pointed towards my heart and bent down to pick up my torn clothes from the floor. I gingerly slid my arms out of my slip. Ritchie clipped my bra on carefully. It would hurt too much to go without one.

Shrugging out of his suit and shirt, he pulled off his vest and slid it gently over my head. A curl of comfort glided across my skin from the hosiery of his vest. Ritchie wrapped his shirt around me and put his suit back on. I buried my face in his chest.

A jagged shard of glass flew past us from behind, followed by a piercing crash.

I shrieked and spun around, colliding into Ritchie. Ritchie nearly toppled over, but managed to hold on to the desk next to him. He steadied me and hustled over to the awning window. When he pulled back the shades, a stocky man in a peppercorn-black top hat and a navy trench coat shot an outstretched arm through the window he had just smashed. A scalloped axe swung from his other hand. The man at the window raised his axe and slammed it against the pane again. Larger fragments of glass cracked and fell through.

Gathering my wits, I pushed Ritchie behind me and stood protectively in front of him.

'San, he's here to help us!' Ritch cried, retrieving my duffle coat from the couch.

A growing cacophony of voices floated towards the door as Ritchie helped me into my coat.

'Get here … fast,' the man at the window snapped. 'The assholes are on their way in.'

Ritchie scooped me up. The man in the trench coat grabbed me through the craggy crests of broken glass that shot out from the window frames.

A barrage of footsteps descended on us, stippled with rabid yells. Mez's voice: 'They're making a run for it!'

Rixon was screaming, 'Get to the window and nab 'em, you idiot!'

Carlos darted across the room. Ritchie was halfway through the window. I heard a gun cocking. The man in the trench coat began running through a wizened lawn towards a neighbouring building at the far end of the complex, cradling me firmly in his arms.

'Ritch!' I screamed.

'I'm here, Sandy!' Ritchie panted, catching up with us from behind. 'Thanks, Aaron,' he added to the trench-coat man.

Bullets whizzed past us in all directions. The frenzy of voices behind us rose to a crescendo, as we careened around a corner of the building ahead. Then we dashed to a side facing a partitioning wall and flew back towards Building Number 5.

'What are you doing?' Ritchie cried breathlessly.

'Just follow me! I know this place better than either of you,' Aaron barked.

Aaron eventually lurched to a standstill and placed me on a dry patch of ground between the side of the building and the partitioning wall. 'Get in!' he ordered, stepping on a piston to his right. The ground moved to reveal a sliding trapdoor, which gave way to a retractable winding stairwell. Ritchie and I scrambled in.

'Thank God for the Redstone circuitry,' Aaron muttered, pushing another button on a wall once we were all inside. The door slid shut above us.

Holding onto the wall with one hand, Ritchie guided me down the block of stairs. The steps opened out to a compact stone-floored hall insulated with a gabled ceiling and redwood beadboards. French oakwood barrels lined the floor, and stanchions of wooden racks and slats were carved into the walnut-veneer walls.

'A wine cellar!' Aaron muttered. He unbuttoned his trench coat and wriggled out of a craggy brown pullover he wore over a faded sweatshirt.

He handed the pullover to Ritchie. 'Something to wear under that suit,' he commiserated.

'Thanks.' Ritchie slipped the turtleneck over his head.

I studied Aaron. Hooded grey eyes and upturned lips sandwiched a hawk-like nose in a fleshy pockmarked face. Surprising agility for a portly middle-aged oaf who resembled a retired Tube operator. Nudging Ritchie gently, I directed my eyes to Aaron as a silent question and returned my gaze to Ritchie with a raised brow.

'Aaron Curtis is a licensed private detective,' Ritchie said. 'I hired him to ensure your safety.'

I stared at the duo, baffled. 'When? How?'

'Aaron is a neighbour to one of my clients. I met him last Friday, the morning after you got shot,' Ritchie revealed.

'Good heavens! Why didn't you ever tell me?' I exclaimed.

'I didn't want you to freak out,' Ritchie admitted. 'I told Aaron everything he needed to know, I showed him your photos, which I downloaded from your Facebook profile. Since then, he's been trailing after you in an Astra.'

That explained the silver Vauxhall Astra I had seen outside the BBC last Friday and on the road when I was on my way here.

'I followed you more than half the way this morning until I lost you somewhere near Watford,' Aaron said as we strode down a winding pathway. 'Seemed like you were being driven towards Hillingdon or Amersham. The GPS guided me towards the M25, where I found your sedan again in all that traffic. I wouldn't be here now if I hadn't spotted you there. There's no phone reception here, whatsoever. So, I stepped out on to the streets and called Ritchie. Ritchie was dead worried that he couldn't reach you on the phone. So, I gave him directions to where I was headed, then guided him the rest of the way when I pulled into this complex.'

'So, you were here even before Ritchie arrived?' I asked Aaron incredulously.

'I was staking out the area. Studying entrances, exits, corners, escape routes ...' Aaron trailed off. 'The doors were locked and the windows heavily shaded. Of course, I had no idea what was happening to you inside. I wanted to be sure I knew the layout of this place before I barged in. I peered through a window and spotted those two charlatans on a speakerphone in a cabin. I'd figured out this place by then. I heard Ritchie's voice from another set of windows that I knew belonged to an adjacent cabin inside. So, I took a chance and crashed in.'

'Thanks, Aaron, we'd have been dead if not for you,' I conceded.

'This must have cost you a fortune!' I whispered, leaning towards Ritchie.

'You mean the world to me, San,' Ritchie murmured.

'We need to move faster,' Aaron said firmly. 'I'm guessing this corridor leads to an exit through a similar trapdoor opening out the other side. I spotted a piston near the bushes at the other end while landscaping the area. If my analysis is correct, that exit should lead directly to the main road where I've parked. C'mon. We don't have much time.'

Needles of fresh pain ravaged my breasts. I slouched against a wall and doubled over in anguish. I felt Ritchie's warm hands on my chest, kneading away the pain. 'Aaron, it's an ambush! Let's catch our breaths for a while here,' he called out.

'It really isn't much farther now,' Aaron coaxed.

'That looks like an entrance to a room or closet,' Ritchie said suddenly, pointing towards the contours of a slight projection from a slant in the wall ahead. 'Can you get us some help? We'll just hide in there and rest.'

Sure enough, the protrusion seemed to be a wooden storm door that camouflaged with the wall.

Aaron retraced his steps to Ritchie. 'I don't think it's safe …'

Ritchie laid an arm on Aaron's shoulder. 'My girlfriend is in no position to move any further, and neither am I, in fact. I think we'll be safe. We'll just stay put here until you fetch help.'

Ritchie clumped towards the door, stood on his toes and tugged at a rusted latch above.

Aaron frowned in consternation, but stepped forward to help Ritchie.

The latch rattled down with a screech. The door clanked inward, disgorging an intense half-circle of yellow light, which danced on the cold, stone floor like a hungry lioness evaluating the contents of her supper. 'Once outside, I'll call triple nine and drive to the nearest police precinct. Stay safe. I'll be back soon,' Aaron promised. Then he marched into a cloud of smoky nothingness.

'He's really good at this,' Ritchie told me. 'He'll be back with a battalion in a jiffy. C'mon now.' He tenderly brought his lips to mine. I wanted to kiss Ritchie back, but an acid reflux rode up my esophagus. 'I c-can't breathe,' I moaned. The last thing I felt before blacking out was Ritchie's laboured breathing and the tightening orbit of his arms around my waist.

~

I came to in a long shaft with Hickory-wood walls on all sides. The room was spartan, except for an in-built rack and two ivory club chairs. Random items nestled in the rack. Flashlight. Gas mask. Crescent wrench. A tatty old blanket. Ritchie pumped my inhaler for me and caressed my hair.

'Where are we?' I croaked into his sweater.

'Looks like a panic room or reading room. I don't see a phone or transceiver here though. Maybe there's a cordless phone in there,' Ritchie mused, walking towards the rack.

There was a sudden thud around the walls. 'Ritch, did you feel that?'

Ritchie pulled out of the rack and leaned against it with a worried expression.

A sharp upward pull followed the thud. I swayed on my feet. 'The room is moving,' Ritchie moaned, dazed.

A moving room?

I didn't rule out the possibility of an earthquake, but my instincts told me otherwise. I spotted a line of cushioned buttons on the wall by the door.

Oh fuck!

'This isn't a room,' I said quietly. 'I think it's an industrial elevator!' A luxury one at that. Most likely, eclipse-style – with a normal door that opened inward as if leading you into a room.

Ritchie jammed all the buttons, but to no avail. 'Gosh, San. It's my fault for getting you in here. Stay behind me. I'll handle this.'

'No,' I protested, trying to push him behind me. 'I can't have you …'

The elevator came to a halt. The room door doubled up as a sliding hatch as it swished open to one side. My gaze froze on the floor. A pair of shiny black Hawthorne leather boots glided into my line of vision. Raven black leather trim-will trouser cuffs swirled around the polished vamps of those boots. A familiar voice trilled into my ears. 'Lo and behold! What do we have here?'

I felt Ritchie's protective arms on my shoulders. I raised my face slowly. From the brim of a licorice-coloured wool-felt-Ferdora hat, a pair of gold-flecked amber eyes flashed at me through crystal-framed spectacle lenses. *Lord Melvin Bradshaw.*

17

The Betrayed One

A cloudburst of emotions exploded in my head. Withering anger. Homicidal embitterment. Vitriolic hate. A simmer of hope – and meandering through these variant excitabilities, an incandescent strand of awe. Whatever fucked-up state Bradshaw was in, the man never did leave behind his unflappable charisma. I found myself tongue-tied.

'Looks like you two are having a rough day,' Bradshaw commented. 'Hungry?'

Ritchie played along. 'We have reservations at the Savoy and we're getting late.'

'Hush, young man. I'm talking to Sandy,' Bradshaw responded, playing with the oval moonstone and diamond cluster ring on his index finger. 'It isn't what she thinks it is. A nice long chat is in order. Come along now. I'm not going to hurt you.'

We followed the magnate down the corridor and stopped outside a large glass door bordered by a cedar wood frame. Bradshaw pressed a button on a pocket remote. The door swung open to reveal an opulent office with a coffered ceiling and arched windows, framed by fluted pilasters. Bradshaw waved us towards a caramel-coloured leather sofa across a large fireplace on the left. Then he strode towards an antique wood and glass curio to the right and disappeared into an adjacent Plexiglass door. 'He's the mastermind behind this racket,' I whispered to Ritchie once I was sure Bradshaw was out of earshot.

Bradshaw reappeared with a rimmed melamine food tray. Three cups and saucers circled a steaming pot of tea on the base of a serving stand that held plates of baked rhubarb scones, treacle tarts, mini-sandwiches, and a caddy of fresh strawberries. Bradshaw placed the tray on a revolving Lazy Susan turntable in front of the sofa and seated himself.

'Nothing like a well-stocked larder,' he chuckled, pouring tea from the pot into each cup.

A faint dribble of pride ran through the turbulence of fury and resentment in my brain. The most powerful business tycoon in all of Europe was serving me personally – a small consolation for all that I had been through in the past year, and all those innocent lives this man had ruined.

'I wonder if you believe in spirit guides.' Bradshaw began as I squeezed out of my coat and nibbled on a scone.

I stared at him.

What in heaven's name is he getting at?

'Every soul arrives in this world with a purpose,' Bradshaw said. 'A purpose that determines the life lessons it will learn during the incarnation it has chosen … under the mentorship of its spirit guides from heaven. For instance, a soul that has opted to learn the values of love and compassion may choose those birth circumstances that aid its quest for fulfilling that life purpose. That's why we have orphans, people who are born into abusive or poor families, children who have birth defects.' He trailed off and sipped his tea.

I was too flabbergasted to respond. Ritchie remained poker-faced.

'Souls that choose to incarnate as individuals with mental disabilities are priceless to mankind,' Bradshaw went on. 'In their human frames, they may not be acquainted with their own existence. But they teach us to love unconditionally. They are souls that heal. They cure illness and disease with the beauty of their innocence and loyalty. We must offer our tribute by providing them a life that will give them all the happiness that would otherwise elude them.'

I couldn't hold my horses any longer. 'Why are you telling me this?'

'Because I had a mentally challenged sister. She gave me the inspiration to become who I am today,' Bradshaw replied in an even-keel tone. 'I've taken it upon myself to help women like her. The corporate backing of the Eric Gregersen Group has helped me reach out to many care centres more effectively than I might have been able to do individually. The organisations I'm mentoring have been extremely supportive of the stem cell research projects that EGG's pharma division in Warsaw is working on. We're on the verge of finding a cure for Ebola. We're keeping all this under wraps until we are a hundred percent sure of the results.'

I recalled Mez or Carlos saying something about stem cell research when they were torturing me – but hearing it from the horse's mouth made me more shocked and confused.

'Our scientists in Warsaw have been using cord blood stem cells to rectify neurological problems and find a cure for Ebola. When a woman gives birth, the blood in her umbilical cord contains hematopoietic stem cells. These cells are purified from blood or bone marrow. In the UK, we collect stem cells from care home residents who are new mothers. Since many of these women are mentally disabled, we financially support them, employ them in some of our facilities, whenever we can, and take care of their children. Thanks to these residents and support from their care homes, we're awaiting results from a final set of tests for our Ebola cure project.'

A sharp prickle of pain pulsated through my knuckles. When I looked down, I realised I had been sinking my nails in the leather couch all along – an involuntary reflex to the preposterous narrative I was hearing. 'If women from these care homes are being impregnated for such a noble cause, why are they being sterilised?' I demanded.

The twitch in Bradshaw's eyes was a dead giveaway that he had caught on to the note of sarcasm in my voice.

'We cannot have the same woman get pregnant more than once. In many cases, another pregnancy would be life-threatening,' he answered in a tone that reflected amusement at my lack of ability to understand what he thought was ridiculously obvious.

'You mean, these poor girls could get pregnant *again* because you use them in the flesh trade business?' I shot back.

'I ensure that their lives are as comfortable and normal as possible,' Bradshaw reasoned. 'That means experiencing every part of life that we do. Including sex. Why should they miss out on such divine pleasure?'

The breath of a muffled whisper from Ritchie tickled my ear. 'Don't provoke him. Just keep him talking till the cops get here.'

I ignored Ritchie. 'And make heaps of money on them through a prostitution ring?' I hissed. 'Isn't that the blood money you wrote me your cheque from?'

Bradshaw's face darkened. 'I've helped you financially and treated you with immense respect, from the beginning,' he snapped. 'I left an important meeting in Paris to come here and share my deepest thoughts with you.'

Only because you're afraid of me!

He must have believed Mez and Carlos when they frantically called him seeking his advice. Bradshaw slammed his cup of tea on the revolving table. A small jug on the tray tipped over and a thick jet of milk bled on to the plaid carpet.

What's taking Aaron so long?

Hoping to buy more time, I decided to switch tactics.

'It's just that … don't you see you're hurting other women like your sister, rather than helping them?' I mumbled, sniffing into my inhaler.

Bradshaw's eyes shone with a schizoid gleam. Yet, a chink of melancholy drifted from the depths of his callous stare like a weak scent of life in a comatose patient.

'My sister, Lillian was – and is – my life-force,' he insisted. 'Our parents were shot dead at home when I was nine. I guess it involved a drug cartel. Lillian was six at the time. We were in Ohio back then. Lil and I were shipped to an orphanage in Dayton. Lil was mentally challenged but she was persevering and enterprising – a spark of sunshine in this ill-defined go-nowhere world that I hated. I didn't want any part in this world, but I willed myself to go on for her. I cared for her, fed her, bathed her, sang her to sleep, spent time with her. She took care of me, too, in whatever way she could. Her golden curls, her innocent laughter, her blind faith in me …' His voice faded into a straggle of uneven breathing as he glowered into the distance with the expression of a man on his way to being exorcised. 'Then we got separated at the orphanage in Dayton. A couple from Pennsylvania adopted Lil. Shortly after, I was sent to a foster home in Raleigh. Not the best of places. North Carolina is a piece of shit and I detested the neo-Confederate culture of the South. The so-called caregivers were heartless devils.' He bent down to raise the trouser of his right leg. Then he rolled down a nylon sock to reveal a morbid black cast. He pushed a pin on it. A stunned gasp issued from my lips when the lower half of his leg came off. He waved the prosthetic in front of my face before clipping it back on. Ritchie looked equally mortified.

'Th-they broke your leg?' I stuttered.

Bradshaw disregarded my question. 'I missed Lillian sorely,' he went on. 'I stole money and hitchhiked all the way from Raleigh to Allentown, where Lil was. I lived on the streets for weeks until I found her. Her foster parents wouldn't keep me so I found a construction job, which landed me cheap board and room. I visited Lil everyday for six years. She was in a special school and she was happy. One day, her folks were out and the babysitter they hired ran out on Lil. When I dropped by, I found her crying at home all alone. So, I took her out to Cedar Creek Park, a couple miles away. We had a lovely picnic in the Rose Garden. On our way back home that evening, a gang of drunken guys teased and laughed at her. When I protested, they beat me up and tied me to a tree. Then they pounced on her and raped her one by one … right before me. They shoved broken beer bottles into her and pulled out her uterus. There were no cell phones back then. When they left, I managed to break free from the tree and ran to the street, begging for help.'

My heart lurched with a sliver of sympathy. When I glanced at Ritchie, I saw that he looked as discomfited.

'She died on the way to a hospital. She was twelve,' Bradshaw whispered. 'Since then, I have realised my life's purpose – to make women like her shoulder the burden of all the agony my sister suffered so that they rise to be martyrs, just like Jesus.' He let out a grunt, something between a satirical snort and a sardonic laugh. The disturbing magnetism of his snigger drew my gaze to his face. Behind the irises of his dilated pupils, there was not an iota of soul, just a blanket of stilted emptiness, which glazed his features with the insouciance of a zombie.

I broke out in a cold sweat. This man was a permanently traumatised waif who had lost his mind to tragedy. If I had to put it less euphemistically, he was genuinely deranged – a sociopath with delusions of grandeur.

'Jesus Christ bore the collective burden of all wrongdoings in the world,' Bradshaw declared. 'That's what I'm encouraging these young women to do, so that they attain salvation in the afterlife. I see them as incarnations of my sister. My inspiration from Christ's selflessness led me to rechristen Candela as Bread Breakers', when I funded them 10 years ago.

'After Lillian died, I was carted off to the Fannings, to a new set of foster parents in Bloomington. It's a small, sleepy town in Indiana. I spent a few months there. Aiden McLeod, a fellow foster kid from Raleigh persuaded me to join him in England after the Gregersens adopted him. I had once saved that fucking moron in Raleigh – when he was on the verge of committing suicide. Since then, I've been the closest thing to a brother for him.'

No wonder McLeod had kept mum about Bradshaw when the Squad was hot on his heels. Bradshaw had clearly won his loyalty for life.

A grating recollection scavenged on my mind – Aiden McLeod's sudden email of consent to an interview with Bradshaw, right after my undercover expedition at Bread Breakers'. Now, I realised why Bradshaw had agreed to see me: *to find out how much I knew … of what I knew.* He and McLeod were in on this together.

Aiden McLeod, for his part, had mediated between Bradshaw and his lackeys so carefully that none of their minions, except a handful like Mez and Carlos, had an inkling of who the real don was.

'Wasn't he Aiden Gregersen then?' I asked.

'Aiden kept his biological father's name … just like I did,' Bradshaw replied smoothly. 'The Gregersens were extremely wealthy. They ran a thriving pharmacy in Wapping. In Bloomington, the Fannings did their best to keep me comfortable but I'd made up my mind. It was 1980. I burned their house down on Christmas Eve. I hid behind the trees in the Fannings' garden and watched it all go up in flames. Then I jumped on the Amtrak to New York. From there, I was just a boat ride away to England. I was sixteen.'

I recalled *The Herald-Tribune* article I had read last year, referencing the Fannings' fight for insurance money in a mysterious Christmas Eve housefire. I stared down at my feet, dazed. It wasn't the Fannings' greed – it was Melvin Bradshaw's remorseless evilness.

'Aiden's adoptive dad, Eric, processed all my papers and offered me a job as a cashier in his shop,' Bradshaw revealed. 'I lived with the Gregersens and earned my stripes in the business. I'd already missed middle and high school in the US. So, Eric charted out a plan of action to help me complete my education. Because of my background and gap years, it was difficult to gain entry into an inner-city school. A counselor we met had me take an IQ test. It turned out that I fell in the 'genius' category – probably like you. Eric pulled some strings and flaunted my IQ certificate everywhere until it got me a chance to complete my GCSEs and A-levels at home in two years.'

If Eric had taken the trouble to approach a counselor for an IQ test, hadn't he obtained regular psychiatric services for his troubled son? Maybe young Melvin had charmed him so much that he had never sensed anything amiss. I was too chicken to ask.

Bradshaw rose from his seat. 'Soon, I earned a Bachelor's in Economics from Oxford. Later did an Executive MBA from the London Business School.' He began pacing back and forth in front of the fireplace. 'By then, Eric had retired and handed over his business to me. I renamed it as the Eric Gregersen Group and got a backing from venture capitalists to expand it. Aiden went on to launch his media agency, Pinwheel Interactive.'

'When did this ...?' The term 'sex racket' was floating in my mind. I groped for a better word. 'When did this, uh, care home charity work start?'

'I met an elderly lady at a London art gallery – Valerie Rousseau – a genre artist who founded Candela as a tribute to her dead daughter. The daughter was mentally challenged,' Bradshaw explained. 'Val's husband deserted her ages ago and she had just handed the care home's operations over to her nephew, Simon Webb.'

Simon Webb whom I had first met ... Dr Tahseen's reference to Valerie Rousseau the day Jesse Krantz and I prevented that surgery on Asha – it all came racing back now.

'Val was poorly and Simon needed money. So, I pitched in as a secret investor and recommended that the board establish a committee of sorts. It started out as a small team, but eventually spiralled into a national committee for the disabled. No one knew of my involvement or contribution. A group of lousy jackasses from the government renamed it as the Committee of Rehabilitative Care for the Mentally Disabled. Eventually, I struck similar arrangements with three other care homes in the city.'

So, that's what Jeff Stuart found out, I recalled from my discussion with Gretchen Friedland.

'We made money through clients. These residents could keep them company whenever they wanted entertainment,' Bradshaw cackled. 'The care homes received commissions. Virgin women brought us the highest rates. Those who got pregnant were the best sources of cord blood, which we supplied to EGG's pharma division in Warsaw for stem cell research projects. We also sterilised many of these women because we wanted to keep them around for other things. The extra money from their clients was re-invested back into the stem cell research.'

Bradshaw strode towards a U-shaped Demilune desk across the couch and seated himself on a porter's chair. 'EGG was buying out a bunch of smaller companies. So, I hired large teams to support this underground operation—mainly refugees and immigrant students who weren't getting jobs anywhere. I arranged for resident permits and placed them in various companies I owned and controlled, so that they would do my bidding. As I grew more powerful, I began to develop my own brand. My personal trademark is the falcon. That comes from a souvenir my birth parents once left me. It's all I have of them.'

He retrieved a small gilded treasure chest box from his desk drawer, walked back to us and flipped it open. An antique white bird lay inside, its scaled broadwings majestically poised to fly and its aureolin yellow beak parted, as if it was preparing to strike an unassuming prey.

'I brought this with me to England,' Bradshaw was saying, waving the box at us. 'It has always been my good luck charm. Today, every vehicle in my fleet has a falcon car-hanger. When my reputation began preceding me, I realised it was critical to preserve it.' He slipped the box into his suit pocket and returned to his desk.

'And then, two years ago, I met a widowed lawyer at a charity event in London. Nidhi Sawant was a defense solicitor at the Snaresbrook Crown Court at the time. She's got a lot of legal, political and media clout from her years at Snaresbrook. I charmed Nidhi into my life. I've been leveraging all her contacts ever since. Got tonnes of free PR, too. She thinks I'm going to marry her now, that foolish cow!' Bradshaw scoffed, flashing a cocky grin.

As an afterthought, he added, 'Well, Nidhi wanted the high life too, you know: the glamour and power that come with all the wealth. So, that was a fair trade-off.' He shot a finger out at me. 'Once I learned about *your* investigation and realised *you* were living with her, I decided I'd have to get rid of her, too. For now, she'll be handy to do some damage control for the mess you've created for me, but then ...'

'Where have you kept the children?' I squeaked, uncrossing my legs. As I shifted my position, a stabbing jet of pain engulfed me. Under the pretext of folding my arms, I cupped one of my breasts as inconspicuously as possible and closed my eyes in endurance. I felt Ritchie's palm on my back.

'Your questions never stop, do they?' Bradshaw intoned coldly.

He dug back into the drawer. A swishing sound followed. My eyes flew wide open. An anguished howl skewered my eardrums from behind me. I swung around. Ritchie was slumped on the floor beside me. A growing puddle of blood tinted the carpet before him. I screamed and fell to the floor beside him. Reams of blood flooded my hands as I tried to apply pressure on both his legs – I didn't know where Bradshaw had shot him. Ritchie's sea-green pupils constricted with insufferable agony but a sliver of clarity layered his disorientation.

'Try to get outta here, San!' he groaned.

I scooted behind Ritchie and tried to drag him towards the door – a pathetic attempt to scarper from an unhinged ogre when my efforts to buy time had disastrously backfired.

'San, watch out!' Ritchie called out weakly. The next instant, I slammed into the wall behind me. The impact of that blow to my head sent a bronze sculpture of galloping horses from a vintage Parson table in a corner crashing onto the floor. I slid down the wall until I landed on the floor. The sidelines of my vision caught an image of Bradshaw looming before us, the barrel of an automatic thrust against Ritchie's temple. Holding his bleeding right calf with one hand, Ritchie flailed his other arm and tried to kick at Bradshaw with his left leg. Bradshaw placed one of his boots on Ritchie's left foot to keep it still. He let out another injured howl.

A metallic taste crept into the roof of my mouth.

Oh God! Am I going to lose Ritch too?

I would never forgive myself if he died. I crawled over to Bradshaw and clutched at one of his ankles. 'Let him go!' I shrieked. 'Kill me instead. Please!'

Bradshaw tried to kick me away from him. Grabbing his other ankle, I slithered between him and Ritchie, and yelled, 'Kill me! *Please!* It's all *my* fault. He has nothing to do with this.'

'Don't, San!' Ritchie protested weakly, reaching out for me with one hand.

'Tell me what damning evidence you have against me and I'll spare him!' Bradshaw snarled. 'If not, the next shot's blowing his head away.' He pressed the barrel harder against Ritchie's head with one hand, and squeezed his jaw with the other. 'This baby has a silencer and the room is soundproof. No one'll hear a peep.'

'The c-care home!' I spluttered. 'It's all my doing!'

'Do you have any document that directly implicates me or EGG?' Bradshaw boomed.

'No! I have nothing against anyone! Please … please, please spare him.'

Bradshaw looked down at me pitifully.

'Is that good enough for you?' I screeched.

Bradshaw flashed a triumphant smile. 'Aha! I thought as much!'

A growing cauldron of anger and despair razed my solar plexus. An animalistic growl erupted from the pit of my stomach as I pulled one of Bradshaw's legs towards me. Bradshaw teetered to a side and fell flat on his stomach. His prosthetic had come off. For a moment, there was a deafening silence as he clipped it back on. I dragged myself closer to Ritchie. The nose of the barrel had gorged on his skin, leaving a rankling wound on his temple. I stroked his face and kissed him clumsily. 'He's going to kill us, San!' he moaned.

I wondered about Aaron. It must have been half an hour or longer since he had left to get help and I was beginning to lose hope that anyone would come to our rescue now.

I felt my head snap back. Bradshaw was dragging me back by my hair. I squealed in pain. He jostled me towards a wall and issued a tight slap across my face. I keeled over to one side. I saw tufts of silky brown on the floor – clumps of my hair. Bradshaw pulled again at the roots of my hair until I was forced to face him, his nose just inches away from mine. A pair of daggers shot out in vivid streaks of saffron gold, alternatively dilating and contracting with psychotic rage. But his voice held steady as he murmured, 'The betrayed one pays the ultimate price of the betrayer.'

My joints and muscles pulsated with every permutation and combination of pain that must exist in eternity. I fought to keep my eyes open. Bradshaw tweaked one of my ravaged breasts. I couldn't do more than mewl in numb distress. 'You think I'll have a common immigrant girl undo everything I've built over my sister's blood?' He shook his head. 'You *won't* ruin it for me. You will *not* bring down any more of my men. You and your lunkhead will *not* get in the way of my stem cell mission!' A morbid grin blazed across his lips. 'I'm putting an end to this rumpus once and for all.' His voice assumed a singsong tone as he added with finality: *'Ta-da!'*

I heard the barrel retract before me. I curled into a tight ball and braced myself for the inevitable.

And then, three shots rang off in the air, one after the other.

Epilogue

10 days later

I sipped my Earl Grey and groggily skimmed through a pile of newspapers.

An article in *The Independent*: 'Girl, 19, busts sex racket. Lord Melvin Bradshaw arrested'.

A more even-handed feature in *The Telegraph*: 'Bradshaw meets his waterloo, 30 children rescued from Strattonshire'.

A dramatic story in the *Mirror*: 'Teen triumphs over US-born British Lord'.

'Happy birthday, San!' Ritchie greeted, rolling over to my bedside in a wheelchair. 'You aren't a teen anymore now, are you?' He gingerly set a box of Lindor Truffles White Chocolates down on the bed. I leaned forward and kissed him tenderly, careful not to disturb the cast on his leg.

'Charlotte's up and about,' I mentioned.

'We'll visit her once we get outta here,' Ritchie said, stroking my hair.

'How are the kids?'

'Social Services have them. That scuzzball would've burned them alive if he hadn't been caught.'

As part of a raid on Bradshaw's establishments, the police had found the children stashed away in an abandoned EGG bottling plant in a northeastern island off the coast of Great Yarmouth on the brink of the North Sea. Your only mode of transport to get there was the ferry – unless you had a chopper. Someone had come in and fed the children once in a while.

If Bradshaw had followed through with his planned arson rampage, those children's bones and skeletons would have been lying around forever until they were either engulfed by the sea, from global warming, or discovered by someone who would have traced the barn to an unidentifiable name Bradshaw had originally bought it in. A clever beast, through and through.

Ritchie handed me a chocolate from the box. When I unwrapped it, a sleek platinum solitaire ring sparkled at me. I gasped in disbelief.

'Will you be with me, Sandy?' Ritchie whispered, taking my IV-free hand in his.

'You still need a 'yes' from Appa and Sri,' I warned, but I was already grinning through the mist in my eyes. 'They're on a plane to London right now.'

'That day, your lungs collapsed and the medics had a tough time reviving you. On Ninth April. I actually lost you for a few minutes, San. Then you were in a coma for four days,' Ritchie said gruffly. 'Don't ever do that to me again.'

'We wouldn't be here if the bobbies hadn't arrived just then and fired at him,' I said quietly.

'A stonking shit show!' Ritchie muttered. 'If that old bleeder's bodyguards hadn't been strutting around outside that trap door, Aaron would've fetched the cops much sooner than he did.'

We weren't doing too badly. Ritchie had undergone an operation in his leg and received treatment for some internal bleeding in his neck. My lungs were getting better. I was on medication for my dislocated shoulder, and a bacterial infection and some cysts I had developed from the ruptured blood vessels in my breasts. I was also doing physical therapy to get my arm working.

The head nurse poked in. 'You've got visitors, Ms Raman.'

'Send them in.'

Nimmy walked in, followed by the rest of the Sawants.

'Happy twentieth, San! I'm glad you're getting better,' Nimmy gushed, offering me a big gift-wrapped box. 'In case you don't know, you're a national hero now. The papers say multiple job offers are pouring in. You have a book deal and I read you've been invited to produce and host your own talk show on the BBC. Have you decided what you'll do?'

'I have to figure it out.'

'A little gift from the rest of us. Happy birthday, child,' Ashok interjected, pushing another parceled present into my lap.

'We didn't realise what that surgery could have done to Asha. She's doing quite well now,' Shailaja said.

Nidhi was sobbing into a handkerchief. 'I hadn't the foggiest I was dating the devil,' she hiccupped. 'To be honest, I began to have doubts about Melvin after you met me in the office. I dug around a bit and later found a post-it note from Aiden among some car insurance papers in Mel's glove compartment. That's when I went to the police – around the Ninth of April, I think.'

'Yes, Davenport mentioned that the police were on a high alert, but they couldn't do much at the time without evidence for a warrant. You deserve the real thing, Nidhi. I'm sure true love will find you if you believe in yourself.' I took Ritchie's hand in mine instinctively. From the corner of my eye, I saw a look of defeat on Nimmy's face.

The head nurse peeped in again. 'Ms Hoffman and her crew are here for your scheduled interview.'

'We'll let you get on with that,' Ashok said, motioning for his family to follow him out.

A tall chestnut-haired woman walked in with a make-up artist and a cameraman in tow.

Sky News crime correspondent Beryl Hoffman.

'Hello, Sandy. Thanks for your time, especially when you're still recovering,' Beryl smiled.

'Not at all. Meet Ritchie. He's a producer from Los Angeles – now a filmmaker in London. Also from LSE.'

'Oh, we'll be speaking to you, too,' Beryl told him.

The make-up artist started dabbing foundation on my face.

'She's the one who exposed the perp behind a massive sex racket – risking her life all along,' Ritchie said. 'I was just the muscle at the end.'

'Let's start from the beginning.' Beryl dredged up a copy of *The Guardian* from her briefcase and opened the broadsheet to the third page. The topsy-turvy letters of a familiar headline jumped out at me: '*The Rants of a Sociopath*.' The commentary I had filed just two days ago, from the hospital recovery room.

'It's too bad she can't change into a nice outfit, but I've styled her hair and added some colour to her face,' the make-up artist announced. I looked down ruefully at my pale-pink hosiery slipdress.

'She's looking lovely,' Beryl said, handing me a lavalier mic as the cameraman fussed over the tripod. Then he adjusted the lights and gave a thumbs-up.

'That was a brilliant article you wrote in *The Guardian*,' Beryl began. 'Let me first read a few lines to our viewers.

'The betrayed one pays the ultimate price of the betrayer. That was the lesson Eric Gregersen Group's chief Lord Melvin

Bradshaw learned as an orphan after losing his mentally challenged sister to a violent gangrape in Allentown, Pa., thirty-seven years ago. Life had betrayed Melvin, who went on to lead a parallel life as the kingpin of an underworld sex racket, exploiting special needs female care home residents across the UK and impregnating some of them to use their cord blood for stem cell research at his company's pharmaceutical division in Warsaw. When the business mogul's crimes caught up with him, he would ultimately pay the price of that betrayal.'

She looked up. 'The betrayed one pays the ultimate price of the betrayer. What does that mean to *you*?'

I felt an odd sense of closeness to Lord Bradshaw as I spoke. 'That's only one-half of life's story. In time, one finds that the betrayer pays the ultimate price of the betrayed one, too. I've realised that this philosophy and its converse are really two polar opposites blending to form one unified force. Like yin and yang. For me, it's that unified force, which completes the circle of life.'

Beryl looked mystified for a moment. 'I s'ppose that does make cosmic sense,' she said at last. 'On to my next question …'

Acknowledgements

The concept of 'self-made' is narcissistic at best; every endeavour is a team effort, where several individuals are working for us and with us, behind the scenes and otherwise, because they believe in our cause. I will start with giving gratitude to God for making this happen.

Countless professionals have played a role in the fruition of this novel over several years, even as I wrote it amidst studying for two post-graduate degrees, multiple country-to-country relocations or secondments, and hectic, full-time newsroom jobs on Wall Street. I can never thank them enough, but I will try.

Anuj Bahri, my literary agent at Red Ink, reposed his faith in me as a writer with potential and never wavered in his commitment to this novel. My wholehearted indebtedness to **Subhojit Sanyal**, my primary editor at Red Ink, who spent hours with me across continents, often at the expense of his sleep, going so far as reviewing street views and satellite maps on Google as we scoped out a crucial site.

All my love to my family and friends for being my rock and my anchor – my mother, **Swati**, and my father, **Amar**, who urged me never to give up, my partner, **Swami Ganesan**, who encouraged me to think big, invested in my research for this book and helped me stay focused and grounded, and my sister, **Namrata** and my friends **Mike Saraswat**, **Ishan Jalan, Gaia Ines Fasso** and **Rachel Curtis**, who have each reviewed various materials, including chapters of this book, ahead of its publication. I am truly blessed to have all of you in my life. I must point out that Mike, my old friend and former classmate at the London School of Economics, inspired the character, Ritchie. As a London-based film producer and director, Mike served as a guiding post in terms of mapping out Ritchie's own career aspirations in the film world.

Manasi Subramaniam, who originally acquired this novel at HarperCollins, gave it an opportunity to be where it is now. My HarperCollins editors, **Prerna Gill** and **Swati Daftuar** have put weeks and months into making this novel as compelling as it can be. I am in awe of their meticulous attention to detail and their discerning approach to fiction, astute observations, and their intelligence, kindness and wit. Thanks are in order to HarperCollins's **Shantanu Ray Chaudhuri** and **Diya Kar Hazra**. Thanks to **Sharvani Pandit** at Red Ink, for her Midas touch to the novel, and to **Aanchal Malhotra** and **Sanya Sagar** at Red Ink for their active outreach and enthusiasm.

The research for this novel would not have been feasible without UK television script consultant and former Metropolitan Police Forces official, **Jackie Malton** and former Scotland Yard officer **David Imrie-Cook**. Jackie and Dave sketched out various possibilities integral to my plot, and contributed significantly to my development of every murder squad and police procedural scene in this book. I sincerely appreciate Doughty Street Chambers barrister **Ben Silverstone**'s inputs on the development of cases for the Crown Prosecution Service in the event of a murder trial. Thanks to officials at the **Old Bailey** in London for allowing me to physically attend a murder trial in court on extremely short notice. I am indebted to former BBC World Service executive **Matilda Andersson** and **Barrie Kelly**, who was a TV Series Producer at BBC Worldwide at the time of my research. Matilda and Barrie took great pains to go through every detail of programme commissioning at the BBC and the process of developing an exposé, investigative story and documentary in the context of various scenes in this novel. I must mention that Matilda, whom I have known since 2006, inspired my creation of the feisty Keisha Douglas.

I cannot fail to mention **Morgan Radford** of NBC News in New York for assisting me with all my follow-up questions related to an investigative story of the magnitude that Sandy takes on. I must acknowledge that **Pavithra Selvam**, previously a London-based digital planner for pharmaceutical companies around the world, assisted me with crucial scenes directly relevant to the plot of this novel.

Many thanks to **Evi Boukli**, a senior lecturer at the London School of Economics at the time of my research, and to **Peter Dunn**, formerly at the UK Victim Support Office, for their inputs on human rights, victims and witnesses, as well as to **Gerhard Payrhuber** of Maytree Foundation for his insights, which helped me realistically conceptualise various developments concerning Bread Breakers' and the disability charity, SIGNAL. I sincerely commend National Health Services obstetrician and gynaecologist **Dr Arasee Renganathan** who took me through the implications of hysterectomy and the legalities involving the concept of informed consent.

My sincerest thanks to **James Mendelssohn**, **Vinod Surana**, **Beatrice Berglund** and **Khadijah Carter** for assisting me with outreach for my preliminary investigations. I am beholden to Sage Publications' Managing Director and CEO **Vivek Mehra**, without whom this novel may not been possible, and to agent and author **Paula Munier** of Talcott Notch in Boston. My respects and gratitude to my business editor, **Jessica Davies**, and my former boss, **Tim Lawson**. I drew upon their fine technique and acumen for news and narrative development to add the finishing touches to this novel.

It is likely that several others contributed to the culmination of this exercise. For all those whom I may have failed to mention, I plead your forgiveness. But, rest assured, your love and grace dwell within me and always will.

With all my heart,
Nish

Author's Note

If I were to draw analogies, I would liken journalism to a photograph and fiction writing to a photo-realistic painting – perhaps, in the style of Picasso's earlier masterpieces.

This novel grew out of some of my own, rather extraordinary, adventures as a journalist. And those experiences have culminated into a belief in my combination of distinctly ordinary and real settings with elements that are figments of my own imagination.

A majority of scenes in this novel, including those ranging from aspects of a police procedural to the dynamics of programme commissioning at the BBC, are based on extensive and full-fledged research on the field.

References to activities on every site and location, within the BBC's White City complex, are also based on exhaustive enquiry even as the public service broadcaster was, in reality, intending to shift a majority of its London operations to Salford, a metropolitan borough of Greater Manchester.

The scenes unravelling against the backdrop of that landscape are purely fictional albeit within starkly realistic settings. I have also exercised some leeway in terms of allowing my imagination to run wild in certain instances – within the contours of what is realistically feasible, of course.

A classic example of that flight of fancy on my part is the introduction of an international DNA database, which had not existed in reality at the time of my research. Likewise, certain organisations such as EuroFirst, SIGNAL, Topaz, Pinwheel Interactive and the Eric Gregersen Group are entirely fictitious.

Finally, I cannot fail to alert you to the possibility that not every detail may be entirely accurate, regardless of how remote the probability of such an occurrence may be. This includes the granularities of a hysterectomy, which span different types of procedures – right from surgeries that solely involve tying up one's fallopian tubes (known as tubal ligation) to those targeting a removal of the ovaries, uterus and/or even the cervix.

But … as the old adage goes, 'all is fair in love and war' – and I shall lend a little twist of my own to rephrase that: 'All is fair in love, war and fiction.' Aloha.